"I think you'r...

Gwen frowned. T... her face but her b... part of her was tel... she realised. It was... see it out of the corner of his eye.

"Big talk," she said aloud, consciously trying to relax.

Tonight Del wore black jeans and a white shirt, the sleeves rolled up to his elbows. Little things impinged on her consciousness: the clean scent of him, the way his jaw was just a bit dark with a day's growth of beard.

She remembered how he'd looked with nothing on.

"It looks like you're pretty good," he observed, nodding at her pile of poker chips and tossing down the table's ten-dollar minimum. "I didn't expect to see you here tonight."

Gwen immediately raised him twenty. "I figured I needed to get warmed up for the tournament," she explained.

"And here I thought you were pretty hot already..."

"If I said I'd be your lover, no strings, the entire time we were in Stockholm, you'd do it?" asked Joss.

The situation was rapidly slipping out of Bax's control. "Look," he said, backpedalling, "it's not that simple to retrieve stolen property from a serious criminal – even if it is your property."

Something predatory entered Joss's eyes. "Sure it is."

Before he could react, she'd risen, pushing his shoulders back against the office chair.

"What are you doing?"

"A feasibility study," she told him, and placed one knee on either side of his thighs, straddling him. And when her mouth touched his, all he could feel was the hot, slicing arousal.

He had no business doing this, Bax told himself even as he closed his eyes. She was a client, or a potential client, they were in his office, at his desk and oh hell, she was all he could feel with only her lips on his and the warmth of her thighs bracketing his own.

"What kind of game are you playing?" he asked hoarsely.

"Just making sure we have chemistry." She sat back. "After all, the best detectives and their sidekicks always have it."

HER HIGH-STAKES PLAYBOY

&

SEALED WITH A KISS

BY
KRISTIN HARDY

MILLS & BOON

Pure reading pleasure™

*First published in Great Britain 2009
by Harlequin Mills & Boon Limited,
Eton House, 18-24 Paradise Road, Richmond, Surrey TW9 1SR*

Her High-Stakes Playboy was first published by
Harlequin Enterprises Limited under the title *Certified Male*
in 2005. This edition published January 2009.
Sealed with a Kiss was first published by
Harlequin Enterprises Limited under the title *U.S. Male* in 2005.
This edition published January 2009.

Her High-Stakes Playboy © Kristin Lewotsky 2005
Sealed with a Kiss © Kristin Lewotsky 2005

ISBN: 978 0 263 87218 7

14-0109

*Printed and bound in Spain
by Litografia Rosés S.A., Barcelona*

HER HIGH-STAKES PLAYBOY

BY
KRISTIN HARDY

This book would not have been possible without the generous help of Tyra Bell-Bloom of the Venetian Resort, David Brandon of Brandon Galleries, Gini Horn of the American Philatelic Society, Chris Johns of the Las Vegas Police Department, Bill Welch, retired editor of the *American Philatelist* magazine, and, of course, Stephen, the Hardy part of Kristin Hardy. All errors are mine.

Dear Reader,

I'm a firm believer that you've got to try new things in order to stay fresh, both as a person and (for me) as a writer. Gwen's book marks my first dip into romantic mystery/suspense. I've watched other people do it for a long time and was itching to try my hand at the genre. I'm an avid mystery reader, so building a suspenseful story of my own was a fun challenge – layering in the mystery and suspense while keeping the focus on the emotional development and the trademark Blaze® heat took some doing, but in the end I think it worked.

I hope you'll write to me at Kristin@ kristinhardy.com and tell me how I did, and whether you'd like to see more books of this type from me in future. Sign up for my newsletter at www.kristinhardy.com for contests, recipes and updates on my recent and upcoming releases.

Have fun,

Kristin Hardy

Prologue

GWEN CHASTAIN CHEWED HER LIP and studied her cards. "D'you have any jacks?" she asked, one leg curled up under her on the kitchen chair.

The man across the table from her scratched at his salt-and-pepper hair and frowned. "Well, now, I can't say for sure, here. Is that the one wearing a crown?"

"No, the one wearing a crown is a king."

"Ah." He nodded thoughtfully. "Is it the lady?"

She giggled and swung her free foot back and forth at the knee. "You know a jack's not a lady, Grampa. No fair trying to fool me."

"Well, then, I'd better just say go fish."

Gwen reached for the cards just as the kitchen door opened and her mother swept in wearing a swirl of bright color, her hair covered with a red-and-orange patterned turban. "Gwennie, why aren't you ready? We have to leave for the library now."

Gwen swung her foot harder. "Can I stay here with Grampa instead?" She didn't want to go stand in front of a room full of kids and tell what it was like to live in Africa. She knew she ought to feel lucky to be able to do it, her mother told her all the time. She didn't feel lucky, though. She just felt weird. They always looked at her like a zoo exhibit.

Her big sister Joss bounded into the room. Joss was

nine, a whole year older than Gwen, and never felt weird about anything. Joss loved being the center of attention. She could make even Gwen think living in Africa was a cool thing. But then Gwen would remember that Africa was more than zebras and elephants.

Africa was heat and flies. Africa was longing for the cool blue San Francisco Bay that glittered now outside the window. Africa was driving into a dusty village with her physician parents to be surrounded and stared at, unfamiliar hands plucking at her sun-bleached hair, touching her white skin.

Africa was always being different.

"Let the girl stay with me, Glynnis," her grandfather said. "You're going back too soon as it is. We'll play cards until Mark gets home and then we'll all come meet you at the library."

"Well…"

Gwen knew she ought to change and go with her mother and Joss, but she didn't want to. Sometimes when she and Grampa were alone they'd play poker and drink cola from frosty mugs and he'd let her win all his pocket change. She crossed her fingers.

"Come on, Mom," Joss said, bouncing impatiently.

"All right, she can stay." Glynnis ran a fond hand over Gwen's hair and Gwen felt a surge of warmth swamped by guilt. Then she turned to give her mother a kiss and wished, as she always did, that she could put the bad feelings away. She knew what her parents did in Africa was important. She just wished, oh, she wished as the door closed behind Joss and her mother, that it could be someone else's parents doing it.

The tablecloth was a cheerful blue patterned in dancing teapots. Gwen rubbed one of the spouts. In Mozambique they didn't have kitchen chairs, just stools, and the oiled wood of their low, round table was only covered with a brightly dyed tablecloth on special occasions. Some of the Physicians Without Frontiers workers lived in a special compound, but Gwen's parents liked living out among the people they were there to help. It was a priceless education that they were getting, her mother insisted. It would make them like nobody else.

But Gwen didn't want to be like nobody else. All Gwen had ever wanted was to be ordinary.

_1_

"YOU HAD SEX *WHERE?*" GWEN CHASTAIN stared at her sister, Joss, who leaned nonchalantly against the counter of the stamp shop's kitchenette.

Joss adjusted the strap of her splashy red sundress. It was too provocative for the business of selling rarities, but Gwen knew better than to tell her. "In the elevator of the Hyatt Regency. Loosen up a little bit, Gwen, it's not like we got caught."

"Normal people don't have sex in glass elevators."

Joss rolled her eyes. "If you'd ever stop dating boring men, maybe you'd find out. You need to date a guy who's not afraid to mess you up a little. You need to have sex on elevators, let your hair down a little while you're still able. You act like you're sixty already."

"And you act like you're sixteen. It's a good thing Mom and Dad are in Africa," Gwen muttered, pouring herself a mug of coffee, careful not to splash any on her tidy taupe suit. A faint hint of makeup accentuated her blue eyes, framed by stylishly discreet glasses that made her look older than her twenty-four years.

Joss snorted. "Are you kidding? Honey bunch, your mother's done wilder things than that."

"Way more information than I needed to know," Gwen told her, doctoring her coffee with soy milk.

"Haven't you ever talked with her about when she was young?"

Gwen gave her a queasy look. "This is not a conversation I want to have. I haven't even had breakfast yet."

"Shoot, when Mom and Dad were dating, they—"

Gwen stuck her fingers in her ears. "La-la-la, I can't hear you," she sang out.

"Oh, c'mon, you can't say you've never been curious."

"Not about the sleeping together parts, no. I suppose you asked her all about them."

"Of course." Joss grinned at her and turned to open the little refrigerator. "So how can we be sisters when you get so freaked out about everything that Mom and I do?" she asked as she fished out a can of Coke.

"Are you kidding? Sometimes I wonder if I'm even from the same family." How else could a person who prized normalcy as much as Gwen explain her free-spirit mother happily taking her doctor husband, her young daughters and her six years of medical training into a life in the African bush? Gwen looked at Joss, vivid and curvy, her dark hair tumbling down her back in a gypsy mane, so unlike Gwen's quiet not-quite-brown, not-quite-blond French twist. Joss had turned positively wild after Gwen had moved back to the States at fourteen. Joss had stayed in Africa while Gwen had settled into her grandparents' San Francisco home and a college prep course with a sigh of relief.

And wished her mother's wild streak good riddance. Gwen was all about discreet, down to her understated loveliness that was only apparent to those who looked. Her straight nose tipped just a bit at the end. Her chin was just strong enough to hint at a stubborn streak. Only her mouth spoiled the picture, a little too generous, a little too promising. Dusky pink lipstick accented it only faintly. Anything more, she knew, would only attract attention. It was hardly what she wanted during work hours.

"You just got the Chastain conservative gene," Joss said, cracking open her Coke. "It skips a generation. God knows Daddy didn't get it."

"And you have no idea how that pains Grampa." Gwen turned to leave the kitchen, passing through the door to the main showroom.

"Not nearly as much as it pains him that Daddy married a woman who was raised in a commune." Joss grinned, trailing after her.

"I'm serious, Joss," Gwen protested.

"I know, I know, he wants to leave him the stamp empire." She snorted. "Giving up sunrise on the veld for little squares of colored paper."

"Some of those squares of colored paper are worth half that veld." Gwen punched in the multipart code that deactivated the sophisticated alarm system on the front door; as always, she left the back door armed unless they were using it.

"Okay, so Grampa plays in the big leagues. Dad would still be miserable doing it. Grampa should leave it to you. He's practically handed it over to you already as it is."

"He's not leaving it to anyone." Gwen set her coffee on the top of a crimson-lined display case containing stamp tongs and mounts. "He'll take it apart as soon as he and Grandma get back from their trip. It just takes time." She pulled out her keys and walked to the front door, stooping to undo the floor lock. "He's had some of these clients for decades. You don't break that up overnight." Opening the door, she stepped outside to unlock the sliding steel gates that protected the little storefront. Beyond her, traffic whizzed back and forth on Clement Street in San Francisco's Richmond district.

"Sure you do." Joss took one side of the gates, pushing it back to the wall. "Tell 'em you're going out of business and to find a new advisor. I'm sure Grampa could recommend a bunch of people."

"That's not the point. Some of these guys might just want to get out of investment stamps period if Grampa's retiring. They trust him. He's got a couple of accounts he's liquidating already." Gwen finished tucking her side of the gate back into its hidey-hole and turned to the shop door. Glancing at her slim gold watch, she frowned. "I see Jerry's late again. Nice that he's dependable."

"Oh, lay off Jerry. He's okay," Joss countered, following her back inside.

"Jerry's hot for you. Of course you think he's okay."

Joss rolled her eyes. "Please. Don't tell me you're jealous."

"Of Jerry? Hardly." The truth was, Jerry gave Gwen a faint case of the creeps for no good reason she could name. On the surface he seemed fine, and if he was maybe a little too slick, a little too accommodating, that was her own problem. His references had checked out over the phone. Coins, granted, not stamps, but at least he had experience with fine collectibles. She had a few too many degrees of separation from the dealer in Reno to get a personal verification, but there had been nothing to confirm the small stirring of uneasiness she felt about Jerry. And the truth was, if he hadn't been on board and trained, Gwen couldn't have gone to the estate sale in Chicago two days earlier.

She didn't know where the restlessness had come from. Maybe from watching her grandparents leave for a three-month tour of the South Pacific. Maybe it was just the time of year. She'd had an undeniable urge to get out, stretch her wings. Vying with some of the top dealers in the world to come away with best properties did nicely. "Jerry's just not my type."

"Well, you don't have to love everyone who works for you," Joss threw back.

The original plan had been for Gwen to hire someone to help run the store during her grandparents' long-planned trip. Then Joss had shown up broke and in need of a job. Gwen ought to have been impressed that it had taken almost two weeks before Joss was so bored she'd suggested hiring another clerk. Too bad Gwen had let herself be talked into Jerry.

"I've got no reason to think Jerry isn't fine. I'm just a little uncomfortable around him," she said irritably, punching her code into the cash register to start it booting.

"He's noticed. I think it hurts his feelings the way you hang out in the back room and never talk with him."

"You talk with him just fine. That was the deal, remember? You work the store, I work the investment accounts." And avoid Jerry.

"The front of the store's important, too," Joss reminded her. "We made some money while you were gone. Jerry's good at selling."

"I don't doubt it." Gwen picked up her coffee mug. "Call me if you get a sudden run and need help. I've got to log in the new acquisitions and get them into the safe."

GWEN STUDIED THE TEAL-BLUE stamp through the magnifying glass. Across it a stylized steam train chugged—left to right instead of the right to left as it was supposed to. She checked the perforations and used tongs to turn the stamp so she could study the back. Inspect, confirm, log. This was the part of an acquisition she relished—poking through to get a firsthand look at all the new treasures, finding the hidden surprises.

And in this collection there had been more than a few.

She rolled her shoulders to loosen the muscles, then adjusted the headset she wore to keep her hands free during phone calls. For a minute she allowed herself to just sit in the blessed quiet of the back office. She'd always loved the store, from the time she'd begun helping out her grandfather at fourteen. After college it just hadn't seemed right to move on—working the business had engaged her mind fully, and her econ and accounting degrees had made her more valuable to her grandfather than ever.

The place didn't feel the same without him, even though he was only on an extended vacation. "Practice retirement," Hugh Chastain had laughingly labeled his wife's cherished four-month trip to New Zealand, Australia and Polynesia. So what if the process of shutting down the business hadn't proceeded on schedule? There would be time to close things down properly when they returned.

Gwen tried not to mourn it.

Even though she had a nagging sense that she ought to be out fighting her way up the corporate ladder, she didn't regret a minute of the three years she'd spent since graduation learning the investment ropes, polishing her expertise. Stamps fascinated her—the colors, the sometimes crude art, the shocking jumps in value of some of the rarities. The clients who chose investment philately over, or in addition to, the more traditional stock market were driven by a certain streak of romanticism, she suspected. There was no beauty or history to an online stock account. You couldn't pick up a mutual fund with tongs.

Not that they kept any of the investment accounts in the store, of course. A safe-deposit box was the place for holdings whose values could reach into the hundreds of thousands or even millions.

Or it ought to be, she thought, glancing at the wall safe with her usual twinge of discomfort.

She put her grandfather's stubbornness out of her mind

and resumed the process of inspecting and logging the new collection. The auction catalog had focused on the plums, the Columbian Exposition issues and the 1915 Pan Pacifics. She'd never expected to find a mint block of four early Cayman Islands stamps, and the profit from their sale would more than pay for the trip. She already had plans for the Argentinian and Brazilian issues.

Thoughtfully she set down her stamp tongs and reached for the Scott catalog just as the phone rang. She punched a button and a man's voice greeted her.

"Gwen, how've you been? It's Ray Halliday."

"Hi, Ray." It was amazing how quickly word got around about who was and wasn't at an auction, she reflected. Suddenly people you hardly knew became your best friend.

"Did you go to the Cavanaugh sale?"

He knew the answer to that already or he wouldn't be on the phone to her. "It seemed worth the trip."

"How'd you make out?"

He undoubtedly knew the answer to that, too. "I'm looking it over right now."

"Anything interesting?"

"Maybe." She turned back a page or two and lifted a quartet of stamps from their mount to inspect them. "Don't you have a client who specializes in Caribbean issues?"

"Yeah, why?"

"I've got a nice little block of four early Cayman Islands. Very fine, by the looks of it."

"I didn't see that listed in the catalog."

Gwen grinned. "Pays to actually get out and do some legwork, Ray."

"I suppose this is going to cost me," he grumbled.

"I've got to get something for my time and travel," she said reasonably. "The question is, what's it worth to you?"

The dickering over price didn't take as long as she'd expected. After eleven years in the business, they'd finally realized she was no pushover. Her grandfather had taught her well.

"Anything else I might care about?"

"Just some South American issues that already have a home."

"Stewart Oakes, no doubt," he said sourly.

"Now, Ray, what kind of businesswoman would I be if I told you all my secrets?"

"A wealthier one. I'll pay you more than he will."

"If I need the money, you'll be the first to know."

She was still chuckling as she depressed the button on the phone. Might as well call Stewart while she was thinking of it. She hit a speed-dial number.

"Stewart Oakes."

"You missed out at the Cavanaugh sale."

"Gwennie." The pleasure was warm in his voice. Only her family were allowed to call her by that nickname—her family and the man who'd helped her understand life in the U.S. back in the early days when she'd first arrived from Africa. Stewart Oakes had been her grandfather's employee and protégé, but at thirty-five, he'd also been young enough and hip enough to introduce a shy fourteen-year-old to grunge music, Thai food and a culture she'd been separated from since she'd been a toddler.

"Got some goodies for you, Stewie."

"Always nice to know you're thinking of me."

"Well, you're going to love these."

"I bet."

"Careful, now, I thought you were giving that up."

"Hey, I moved to L.A. and left behind my home poker game, didn't I?"

"And we miss you every week."

"Nice to know I'm appreciated."

"And we miss the money we used to win from you."

"Cheap shot, Chastain."

She laughed and reached for another catalog even as the intercom buzzed. "Hold on a second, Stewart." She pushed the button for the intercom. "What do you need, Joss?"

"I've got too many people out here. Can you come out?"

"Where's Jerry?"

"He still hasn't shown up."

Gwen gave herself a moment to steam. "Okay, I'll be right out." She took Oakes off hold. "Stewart? I've got to run help Joss at the front of the store. Can I call you back?"

"I'll be here."

Gwen gathered the stamp albums together and slipped them into one of her desk drawers, locking it carefully. Even so, it nagged at her a bit that some one hundred thousand dollars in stamps was protected only by a desk lock that any self-respecting toddler could pick. A hundred grand of the most liquid, easily portable wealth known.

In countries with unstable stock markets—or none at all—stamps provided a relatively safe investment. Gold coins were heavy, they took up space. Mounted properly, a stamp worth thousands or tens of thousands of dollars could be slipped into a square of cardboard, tucked into a wallet or the inside pocket of a suit, walked over international borders and converted into cold, hard cash in virtually any major city in the world.

SHE WAS BACK IN HER OFFICE when four o'clock hit. A muted "hallelujah" from the front, followed by the rattle of the steel security gates, told her that Joss was closing up. It had been a good day, all in all, Gwen thought in satisfaction as she stacked up the stamp albums. She'd logged three quarters of the collection, had set aside the cream for important clients and found stamp dealers only too happy to take on the rest. They'd make money out of the deal. It was a small triumph for her.

Joss stuck her head into the room. "The front is all locked up, nice and tight."

Gwen swung back the white board that concealed the wall safe. She inserted her key and spun the dial of the combination lock. "First thing tomorrow I'm firing Jerry," she told Joss. "Then I'm going to put an ad in the help-wanted section." The dial moved smoothly under her fingers.

"You can't just fire someone out of the blue, can you?" Joss asked. As the day had gone on, her defense of Jerry had ebbed. "Can't he take it to the employment board? What if something came up?"

"And what, he couldn't even call? Joss, he's been late to one degree or another for seventeen of the twenty days he's worked for us."

Joss raised her eyebrows. "You kept track?"

"Of course I kept track. I'm an employer, that's what you have to do. If he wants to protest, I can show cause." Gwen spun the dial to its final position and opened the door.

And stared in alarm.

2

"DID YOU OPEN THE SAFE WHILE I was gone?" Gwen's voice sounded unnaturally loud in her ears.

"No." Joss crowded up behind her to look at the stack of stamp albums in the safe. "What are you talking about?"

"The books have been moved. I always put them in the same way every time. Joss, you swear you haven't touched anything?"

"Cross my heart."

Stay calm, Gwen ordered herself. Maybe she'd been careless the last time she'd unlocked the safe door. Maybe she hadn't put things back the usual way. In her gut, though, she knew.

Someone had been in the safe.

She spilled the albums onto the desk, opened them with shaking fingers. There was no point in bothering with the blue books that held the store inventory or the green book that held some of her own acquisitions. They didn't matter. Not now. She focused solely on the burgundy albums that held her grandfather's collection—the books that held his treasures, his pride and joy, bits of his childhood.

The books that held his retirement.

Holding her breath, she opened one and flipped through to the back, made herself look.

And her mouth went dry as dust. "They're gone."

"What's gone?"

Gwen battled the wave of nausea that threatened to swamp her. "Grampa's best stamps. The Blue Mauritius. The one-penny Mauritius. The British Guiana one-cent. And maybe more." *Definitely more,* the voice of certainty whispered to her. She'd seen at least two other blank spots as she'd flipped through.

Gwen squeezed her eyes tight shut and then opened them to stare at the empty squares. Why had her grandfather insisted on keeping his collection close at hand instead of safely in a bank vault? She knew his reasons, knew the joy he got from regularly looking at his holdings, but they didn't outweigh the risk.

And now her worst fears had come to pass.

Joss stared at her. "Those were his big stamps, right? My god, what are we talking about—forty, fifty thousand?"

"Not even close." Gwen's lips felt stiff and cold. "The last Blue Mauritius auctioned went for nearly a million dollars."

HALF AN HOUR LATER, GWEN stretched to ease the iron pincers of tension. She'd gone through every one of the books meticulously, recording what was missing.

It was worse than she'd imagined.

The four most important issues of her grandfather's collection were gone: four nearly unique single stamps and one block of twenty, in aggregate worth some four and a half million dollars. The inventory books were missing another thirty to forty thousand dollars in more common, lower-value issues.

"Grampa has other investments, right? This is just a part of what he's got." Joss didn't ask but stated it a little desperately, as though saying it would make it so.

Gwen shook her head. "He says he trusts his judgment when it comes to stamps, that he doesn't know anything else as well."

"This is it? This is all he has for retirement?"

"Had," Gwen said aridly. "There's maybe a million left at this point."

Joss spun and reached for the phone. "I'm calling the cops."

"No!" Gwen's tone of command was so absolute, it stopped her dead. "That's the one thing we absolutely can't do right now."

"What are you talking about? There's millions of dollars in property missing. We've got to do something."

"But not that," Gwen emphasized.

"Why not?" Joss glared at her, inches away.

"All an investment dealer like Grampa has is his reputation. He's still got about twenty-five live accounts right now waiting to be closed out, some of them with millions in holdings. And every one of them has a clause in their contract that if he sells their stamps below current catalog price, he'll have to make up the difference."

"So?"

"So, if they hear about the theft and decide they don't trust him anymore, they may want out immediately. If he has to sell in a rush instead of at the right time, and if buyers know he's hurting, he'll definitely have to sell below catalog." Gwen swallowed. "And there goes the other million."

Gone. All gone. It made her shiver. They were his pride and joy, part of what made the philately business vibrant to him. The loss was unimaginable.

She leafed through one of the store inventory albums, staring at the empty squares. A fifteen-cent stamp showing Columbus's landing, worth maybe three thousand dollars. An 1847 Benjamin Franklin stamp worth six. Why bother, she wondered suddenly. The store inventory stamps were chump change compared to the major issues. Gwen chewed on the inside of her lip. Then again, the important stamps would be difficult to unload immediately; there would be questions. The inventory stamps would provide a thief with money in the meantime.

A thief who knew how the world of fine collectibles worked.

"Jerry," Gwen said aloud.

"Jerry?"

"It couldn't have been anybody else. The alarms weren't tampered with, the security company doesn't have any record of the slightest glitch. It had to be him." Gwen rose to inspect the safe. "Nobody appears to have messed with this, but then I doubt he was an expert safecracker. Somehow I see Jerry as taking an easier route." She turned to lean against the bookshelf full of reference catalogs. "Tell me he didn't cook up some reason to get you to give him the key and combination."

Joss's eyes flashed. "Give me a break. I left them right here, safe and sound."

"Here?" She resisted the urge to rant at Joss's carelessness. "I told you to keep them safe. Where did you put them?"

"In the desk drawer." Joss raised her chin. "I locked it."

A lock any self-respecting toddler could break.

"I didn't want to lose them. I figured this would be the only place I'd need them so I might as well leave them close by." She stared at Gwen. "You don't know it was Jerry."

It wasn't Jerry Joss was defending, Gwen knew. Joss didn't want to think it was Jerry because she didn't want to think she was at fault for the theft. But she wasn't at fault. Gwen, in the final analysis, had made the decision to hire him. Gwen had been the one in such a hurry to get out of town that she'd left Joss in charge of the store and the safe.

If anyone was at fault, it was she.

The key and combination lay in the paper-clip compartment of the drawer, Gwen saw, but it didn't mean a thing if Jerry were as quick as she thought. "Was he ever alone in the shop?"

"Of course not," Joss snapped. "I was here to open every morning and here to close down and set the alarm at night. Things were always locked up. I checked."

"Was he ever alone here at all?"

"Never." Joss paused, then stiffened slightly. "Except…"

"Except when?"

Joss closed her eyes briefly. "Yesterday. Lunch. He offered to buy, but the deli was shorthanded and not delivering. He said he'd pay if I went to get them." She hesitated. "I was broke."

"How long were you gone?" It wouldn't have taken much time, Gwen thought, not if he'd been prepared.

Not if he'd known what he was looking for.

"Fifteen minutes, maybe twenty," Joss told her. "There was a line and they'd missed our order."

"Convenient."

"How was I supposed to know?" Joss flared. "We'd hired him. I thought that meant we were supposed to trust him. There's an explanation," she muttered, grabbing the phone and punching in a number. She waited and an odd look came over her face.

"What?" Gwen asked.

"Jerry's cell phone. It's shut off." She set down the receiver.

Gwen swallowed. "Why change the number on a cell phone unless you don't want to be found." On impulse she turned to her keyboard. It took only a minute to send a quick e-mail out to a stamp dealers' loop she belonged to, asking if they'd recently acquired the five-cent Ben Franklin or the Columbian landing stamp. If they popped up somewhere, it might give her an indication of where Jerry was fencing them. It might give her a place to start from.

Mostly it was a way to keep busy. Activity kept her from screaming. She had to get them back, pure and simple.

"That son of a bitch," Joss muttered suddenly. Taking two steps to a cabinet on the wall, she yanked out her purse. "Give me your car keys."

"Where are you going?" Gwen demanded, rising.

"To find Jerry."

"I DON'T THINK THIS IS A GOOD idea."

"It's your chance to live on the edge," Joss snapped, driving so quickly that Gwen's silver Camry bottomed out at the base of the hill.

Gwen winced. "So how do you know where he lives?"

"We went out to see a band while you were gone. He invited me back for a drink."

Gwen looked at her in horror. "You didn't…"

"Of course not," Joss told her impatiently, following the streets into the Mission district. "I saw his building and thought I could probably live without seeing the inside."

Gwen nodded. "I thought you were sure he didn't do it. So why are you flying off the handle?"

"I want to find out." Joss scanned the street for an opening and started to whip into a space to park.

"Why don't you get out and let me do it?" Gwen couldn't bear Joss's Braille-style approach to parallel parking. Still, even with her experience, it took several tries to get the car in place. "Okay, it's probably smart to see if he's around," she said aloud as she got out of the car. "If there's a reasonable explanation, maybe we'll find it out and then we'll know to look somewhere else." Where else, she had no idea, but she knew in her gut that it came down to tracking the stamps stolen from the store inventory.

They stood on cracked sidewalk looking up at a sagging Victorian that had seen better days. "He might have been a snappy dresser, but he sure lived in a pit," Gwen commented, studying the peeling gray paint on the shingled building.

"Now you know why I decided not to go in."

It was a residence hotel, the kind of place that catered to the transient trade. Gwen's stomach began to gnaw on itself. She'd never bothered to check to see how long he'd been living at the address he'd given. Then again, at a place like this, twenty dollars to the front desk clerk would pretty much get the person to say whatever he wanted.

And, with luck, twenty dollars would get them into his room.

It took forty. "Why do you want him?" An unsmiling dark-eyed woman, her hair skinned back from her face, stared at them from behind the desk.

"He's got something of ours," Gwen told her.

"Yeah, well, he's got something of ours, too," the woman said sourly. "He skipped on the rent." She studied the folded twenties Gwen had slipped her and the line between her brows lessened. Abruptly she jerked a thumb at the hall. "I'm cleaning out his room right now. Wait for me at the top of the stairs."

The dim stairwell held the musty smell of a building that had seen too many anonymous people pass through. The paper on the walls might have been flocked forty or fifty years before. Now it was dingy and scarred. At the end of the hall a parallelogram of light from an open door slanted across a cleaning cart sitting on the bare pine floorboards.

Gwen glanced at Joss. Footsteps sounded on the stairs behind them. "Over here," the woman said briskly, walking past them toward the open door.

It was less grim than the hallway only because of the weak late-afternoon sunlight that streamed in through the single window onto the dirty beige carpet. What little of it that wasn't covered by the bed and bureau and uncomfortable-looking chair that constituted the main furnishings, anyway.

"I ask him for his rent and he says tomorrow." The woman stood nearby. "Always 'tomorrow' with him."

Empty drawers gaped open in the scarred bureau. No clothes hung on the open steel rack in the corner that served as a closet. Gwen drifted to the window. She itched to pull out the drawers, look underneath them and on the ends for hidden envelopes, to check under the mattress, but she didn't think the forty dollars would get her that far. Instead she poked her head into the tiny bathroom.

"You have a lot of business?" Joss asked, squinting into the cloudy square of mirror fastened to the wall.

The woman shrugged. "Hey, I'm just the desk clerk. Trust me, if I owned this dump, it would look a lot nicer."

"No idea where he went?" Gwen asked, walking over to stare out the window across to the neighboring building.

"Nope. We don't exactly get a lot of forwarding addresses around here." The woman dragged a vacuum cleaner in from the cleaning cart.

"Mind if I look in this?" Gwen asked, gesturing at the trash can.

"As long as you've had your shots." She jerked her head toward it. "A real pig, this guy. Nothing in the trash can if it could go on the floor."

Gwen poked gingerly through the refuse. Cigarette cartons, an empty toothbrush wrapper, a screwed-up McDonald's bag that still held the scent of stale grease. Then her eyes widened. In the bottom of the bin were scraps of cardboard, the thin type that came on the back of a pad of paper.

The type that could be used to make a stiff pocket for a stamp.

She pulled some out of the waste bin, staring at Joss. In her eyes Gwen saw knowledge and acceptance.

And a bright flare of anger.

The woman picked up the bin. "Okay, you guys had your chance to look around. I got to get back to work."

Gwen nodded slowly. "So do we," she said and turned toward the door. Her foot scuffed against something. An open matchbook. Clement Street Liquors, it said—the business next door to the stamp shop. She leaned down to pick it up.

And glimpsed writing on the inside. Excitement pumped through her. Maybe it was nothing but maybe, just maybe…

"What's that?" the woman asked.

"Matches." Gwen held them up. "I could use some. All right with you?"

"Sure, whatever."

"Thanks for letting us look around," Gwen told her, already walking out. She didn't say a word to Joss about it until they were outside, waited in fact until they were in the car. Hope formed a lump in her throat.

"Jerry buys his cigarettes at Clement Street Liquors," Joss told her.

"Bought. Jerry's long gone."

"The question is where?"

Gwen opened up the matchbook and showed Joss the writing. "Maybe Rennie will know." It was just a name and a phone number, but maybe it would lead them to a guy who'd know where to find Jerry. She dialed the number on her cell phone, her heart thudding.

"Thank you for calling the Versailles Resort and Casino, can I help you?"

Gwen blinked. "I'm looking for a guest named Rennie," she said and spelled it out.

"Last name?"

Gwen hesitated. "I'm not sure. Try it as the last name."

Keys clicked in the background. "We have no guest under that name."

"Can you search under first names?"

The operator's voice turned cool. "No, ma'am."

"Okay, thank you." Disappointment spread through Gwen, thick and heavy, as she hung up.

Joss looked at her questioningly.

"A hotel. They don't have him listed."

"So much for our lead. What do we do now?"

Gwen started the car. "We go home and call Stewart."

"YOU'RE MISSING *WHAT?*"

Saying the words aloud made them more real. "The Blue Mauritius. The red-orange one-penny Mauritius. More." Her stomach muscles clenched.

"Does Hugh know?"

"Not yet. They're on their trip for another twelve weeks. I don't know what to do, Stewart." The words spilled out, and for the first time since she'd opened the safe, tears threatened. "He could wind up losing everything, *everything,* and it's all my fault." It was a relief to let the panic out. Stewart would know what to do. Stewart would help her. If anyone could.

"It's okay, Gwennie. It's going to be okay," he soothed. "Hugh has them insured, so even if we can't get them back, he'll get replacement value."

"But he doesn't," she blurted.

"What?" His cool disappeared.

"The premiums went too high. He let the insurance lapse last year except the basic policy on the store. He put all the money into the business." And his granddaughters were the weak link.

Stewart cursed pungently. "Dammit, what was he thinking? Why the hell didn't he have them in a safe-deposit box?"

"You worked with him for ten years, Stewart. You know how stubborn he is."

"That's no excuse for not having them protected, though. That was the first thing he taught me—protect the clients' holdings and protect your own."

"It wasn't just financial with him. He was a collector at heart."

Stewart let out a sigh. "I know. Come on, it's still going to be okay. We're talking about world-famous issues. They're not going to be easy to unload, especially if your thief is someone who doesn't know the stamp world."

"Oh, I have a good idea who the thief is," she said grimly. "We hired on a new clerk, Jerry Messner, about a month ago. As near as I can tell, he's bolted."

"Coincidence?"

Gwen laughed without humor. "He had motive, he had opportunity. Security wasn't compromised from the outside. You tell me."

"You called the police?"

"Not yet."

"Good. Keep it that way for now. The last thing you need on this is publicity."

Gwen nodded. "That was my thinking. I'm hoping we can get them back before we have to tell anyone."

"Any ideas?"

"Maybe. The prize issues aren't the only stamps missing. There's another twenty or thirty thousand in value gone from the store inventory. Common issues he can unload pretty easily, get himself some money to tide him over."

"Well, isn't he a greedy little bastard," Stewart said, an edge of helpless anger in his voice.

"I put out a few feelers on the loop, asking if there's any

action out there with the low-cost issues. I'm keeping quiet on the high-value ones for now."

"Smart thinking."

"If it is, it's the first smart thing I've done since Grampa left."

He sighed. "Don't beat yourself up, Gwen. There's no point. The thing to focus on is getting them back. I'll tell you what, e-mail me a list of everything that's gone. I'll make a couple of quiet phone calls to a few people I trust, just to see if they've heard any word of some of the issues coming on the market."

"As soon as we hang up," she promised, reaching over to switch on her computer. "And Stewart?"

"Yeah?"

"Thanks. I feel a lot better knowing we've got some help."

"It's going to be okay, Gwen. Trust me on this."

And for a moment, as Gwen hung up the phone, she felt as if it actually would be.

Joss stared at her as Gwen logged on to the Internet. "So, what did he say?"

"He's going to ask around, see if anything's surfacing." Gwen sent Stewart the file she and Joss had compiled earlier.

"Is he going to tell people why he's asking?"

"Stewart understands the situation. He'll keep the theft quiet."

Joss rose to pace around the office. "You know, I'm surprised. I would have picked you for the first one to run to the cops."

"Normally I would have been," Gwen told her, clicking on her e-mail in-box. "These are different circumstances." She scanned the contents of the messages that popped up in her preview pane. "I just don't want to blow—" The thought evaporated from her brain as she stared at the words on-screen.

Joss crowded up behind her. "Did you get something?"

It took her a couple of tries to speak. "It's a dealer. He just bought a Ben Franklin, same perf, very good condition. It sounds like one of ours."

"Well, call him."

"I am." Gwen scrolled down, searching for the contact signature at the bottom of the e-mail. And then suddenly she was yanking open the desk drawer and pulling out her purse.

"What? Where is he?"

"Las Vegas." The blood roared in Gwen's ears as she pulled out the matchbook and compared it to the numbers on-screen. "It's the same area code as where Rennie is."

Joss's gaze took on a particular stillness. "Call it," she ordered, her voice barely audible.

Hands shaking, Gwen dialed the number and listened to the tones of a phone ringing hundreds of miles away.

"Versailles Resort and Casino," an operator answered crisply.

Gwen resisted the urge to cross her fingers. It couldn't just be coincidence the stamp had surfaced there, it couldn't. "Jerry Messner, please." She crossed her fingers. All she needed was a chance.

There was a clicking noise in the background. "How was that spelled, please?"

Gwen told her.

The keys clicked some more. "One moment, I'll connect you."

And the line began to ring. Gwen banged down the handset hastily and stared at Joss. "He's there."

3

LIGHT, COLOR, NOISE. SLOT machines chattered and jingled in the background as Gwen walked through the extravagance that was the Versailles Resort and Casino.

"You want to tell me what I'm doing here again?" she asked Joss over her cell phone as she walked across the plush carpet patterned with mauve, teal and golden medallions. Ornate marble pillars soared to the ceiling overhead, where enormous crystal chandeliers glittered. Waitresses dressed in low-cut bodices and not much else hustled by carrying drinks trays. The casino had the sense of opulence, a decadent playground for the wealthy, though it was open to all comers.

Under the luxury, though, was the reality of gambling. The air freshener pumped into the cavernous main room of the casino didn't quite dispel the lingering staleness of cigarette smoke. The faces of the gamblers held a fixed intensity as they hoped for the big score. Or hoped just to break even. She couldn't have found anyplace more unlike herself if she'd tried.

Then again, she couldn't have looked more unlike herself if she'd tried.

"You know why you're there," Joss said. "You've got to find Jerry."

A balding man in his thirties glanced up from his computer poker machine as Gwen walked by. "Hey, baby," he said, toasting her with a plastic glass that held one of the free drinks handed out by casino waitresses. After a life-time of wanting to be unremarkable, Gwen had gone the other way completely. Exit Gwen and enter Nina, the bombshell.

"I look like a tart," she hissed, tugging at her tight, low slung jeans and her scrap of a red top.

"You don't look like a tart. You just look like a woman who's not afraid to flaunt what she's got."

"Yeah, well, the flaunting part's working." A bellhop walking by tripped over his own feet and stumbled up with a grin. "Joss, this is not my style. This should be your job."

"It had to be you," Joss told her. "Jerry knows me too well. He'd recognize me in a second."

"Like he's not going to recognize me?"

"All Jerry's going to register is blond, tight and built. I doubt he's going to think much beyond his gonads. Any-way, you were always in the back room. He hardly saw you. And no way would he expect you to look like this. You're different head to toe."

"Tell me about it," Gwen muttered, resisting the urge to pull up her neckline. "And don't think I didn't notice you took my regular clothes out of my suitcase."

"I didn't want you to be tempted to backslide," Joss said smoothly. "You've got to be Nina through and through."

Joss had effected quite a transformation, Gwen thought, catching sight of herself in one of the enormous gold-framed mirrors that hung on the wall. Gwen—tidy, under-stated Gwen—was gone. In her place was Nina, whose Wonderbra-induced cleavage alone was likely to distract Jerry from recognizing the person underneath. How Joss had managed to get her into a good salon without notice, Gwen had no idea, but her brownish hair was a thing of the past. Now it had the same streaky, sun-bleached blond look it had had in Africa, only better. The makeup artist had made her eyes more vivid, her smile more bright, somehow without making her look as if she'd troweled on the makeup. She was undercover and, she had to grudgingly admit, she looked good.

Just not like herself. Still, the sooner she got the job done, the sooner she could turn back into Gwen. "All right, well, I'm in the casino, so it's time to get to work," she said briskly.

"What's the plan?"

"Haven't a clue. Wander around and get the lay of the land. Watch for our friend. I'll figure something out and call you tomorrow."

"Have fun," Joss said a little enviously. "Put a five spot on red for me. I've always liked red."

"Right."

Gwen switched off the phone and tucked it into her pocket. She was here. She was incognito. Now she just had to find Jerry, cozy up to him, figure out where the stamps were and spirit them away from him, all without being recognized.

Piece of cake.

Gwen drifted steadily through the ranks of slot machines and computer poker games, scanning the players. No Jerry in sight, but then he didn't strike her as the type for a sucker's game. He'd want cards, where he could influence the outcome.

She resisted the urge to yawn. Between the shopping, the styling, the packing and the flight to Vegas, it was nearly eleven—about the time she usually clocked out for the night. Since it was a weeknight, the ranks of the players had thinned out some. Maybe Jerry had gone to bed, too.

Yeah, right. She snorted at herself as she passed the croupiers at the craps tables. Jerry was more likely to stay up all night, sure in the knowledge he was going to hit it big, throwing away her grandfather's money all the while.

As she crossed the broad carpeted avenue that separated the slots floor from the green tables of the real games, the suffocating crowd and noise lessened, replaced by a steadily rising sense of purpose. The people playing at these tables still relied on chance, but they knew their games, and the knowledge gave them a sense of confidence.

Gwen ambled casually down the aisles between tables, as though she couldn't quite decide where to stop. No point in telegraphing to everyone that she was on the hunt. A tall, ebony-skinned dealer smiled at her. "Baccarat, lovely lady?"

Gwen shook her head, a faint flush tinting her cheekbones.

A burst of giggles rose from the blackjack tables behind her. "Oh, come on, Rennie, you know you're a winner," said a woman's voice.

Gwen whipped her head around to see two female dealers laughing with the player sitting at their table. A single male player.

Rennie.

What were the chances that two guys named Rennie would be at the same hotel as Jerry? Coincidence? Maybe, but Gwen didn't much like coincidence. She was a bigger fan of probabilities. Odds were that Rennie might very well know Jerry, and if he did, he could just lead her to him. And that was enough to make him her new best friend, she decided as the dealer going off shift walked away.

Gwen sat down next to Rennie and slid some twenties across to the dealer.

"Change a hundred," announced the current dealer, an ample redhead with laugh lines liberally marking her middle-aged face. She slid a stack of chips across the table and used the paddle to push Gwen's money into the bill slot.

Gwen studied Rennie out of the corner of her eye. His brown hair was a bit long on top, disordered, she imagined, by a long night at the tables. Even as she watched him, he ran a hand through it again, pushing it out of his eyes. He didn't hunch tensely like the gamblers she'd seen at other tables or sprawl with exaggerated confidence. He just sat loose and relaxed, a glass of what looked like whiskey at his elbow, next to the stacks of chips that attested to a combination of luck and skill. He wore jeans and a pine-green shirt patterned in faded burgundy and gold. Clearly he'd chosen more for comfort than style.

Then he turned toward her, and she understood why the dealers had been giggling with him.

He looked as though his habitual expression was one of wry amusement. A startling green, his eyes held a glint of devilry that invited her to join in. His sideburns were just a bit long, making him look a bit like some nineteenth-century rake. A day's worth of beard darkened his jaw.

And his mouth…

Adrenaline skittered through her veins.

"Welcome to the fun house," he said.

The dealer shuffled the decks and refilled the shoe.

Flirt, Gwen thought feverishly. *Keep him talking.* Nina wouldn't be struck dumb by his looks. Nina would be enjoying herself. "You looked like you could use a little company."

"What I could use is luck. Did you bring any with you?" He looked her over.

Gwen glanced at his stacks of chips. "You don't look like you're having any problems with Lady Luck to me." Lady Luck probably fell for that killer grin just like every other woman he met. She couldn't be thinking about that now, though. She had to strike up a relationship with Rennie—and fast. If she let him walk away, she gave up her link to Jerry.

"Can I get you something to drink?" A waitress stood at Gwen's elbow, tray in hand.

What to choose, Gwen wondered. She'd prefer white wine, but that didn't really fit with her profile. A martini, maybe? Or… "A cosmopolitan, please." At the expectant look of the dealer, Gwen pushed out two five-dollar chips. Her natural leaning was to bet a dollar at a time. Nina, though, wouldn't do anything by halves. Nina would take chances.

With brisk efficiency the dealer laid the cards out. Gwen worked to concentrate. It wouldn't do her any good to have found Rennie if she wound up broke and leaving the table in fifteen minutes. And she wasn't about to put up another hundred. She'd already dipped into her savings account to finance the trip; she was going to make it last.

Her hand held an ace and a two, for a soft thirteen. The dealer had a seven showing and Rennie had a four. He took a sip of his whiskey and tapped his cards to indicate a hit. Gwen couldn't tell if the three he got satisfied him or not, but he didn't bust. He took a sip of whiskey and glanced over at her with interest. "Waitin' on you, darlin'."

Gwen tapped her cards, embarrassed to have been caught watching him. The seven she drew made her forget all about it, though. The dealer drew a nine and flipped over her hole card to show eighteen. Gwen's surge of triumph was probably completely out of proportion to the fifteen dollars she'd won, but it was a good way to start.

Rennie turned over his cards to show a four and a nine and gave her that devilish smile again. This time it sent a pulse of adrenaline through her system that had nothing to do with nerves. "Looks like you brought me that luck."

"Maybe I'll stick around," she said carelessly, picking up the chips the dealer slid her way.

"Maybe you should." He had a way of looking at her as

though she were the only thing in his field of view that interested him, as though the game were irrelevant now that she'd arrived.

Her cosmopolitan appeared at her elbow.

He raised an eyebrow. "Girlie drinks?"

"A woman's got to do what a woman's got to do."

"And I'm sure you do it well." He lifted his whiskey and touched it to her glass.

Cool and sweet, the drink slid down her throat easily.

The dealer coughed. "Bets, please."

Gwen studied her bet circle. Aggressive but not foolish. She slid six five-dollar chips into the circle.

Rennie gave her that look again, the one that said he knew exactly what she was thinking and it amused him. "Living large?"

"Feeling lucky."

And her feeling was borne out when the dealer busted, leaving them both ahead.

"So, you out here for business or pleasure?" she asked casually.

"Business, but no reason it has to be all work. How about you?"

"Pleasure. I was supposed to meet a friend named Jerry, but he had to bail." This, of course, was his lead-in to talk about his own friend named Jerry, but he didn't bite.

Instead he just raised an eyebrow and pushed out a couple of chips. "A friend friend or just a friend?"

Gwen flushed. "Just a buddy."

"His loss is my gain." Rennie shifted in the chair. He had broad shoulders on what looked like a rangy build. That was all right—she liked leanly built men. He gave her a slow smile that had her stomach turning cartwheels.

Gwen blinked. Wait a minute. Back up. This was not part of the program. It was one thing to flirt and convince him she was interested. It was another thing to do it so well she convinced herself. He was the enemy. She needed to remember that. Get close, sure, but keep her distance.

The dealer flipped them a new hand with quick, economical motions. Gwen checked her hole card and tapped for another. Rennie did, too, but he took it too far and busted.

"Bummer," Gwen said, stacking her chips.

"I thought I had enough breathing room."

"You know what Penn and Teller say—Las Vegas is powered by the Hoover Dam and bad mathematics."

He studied her and took a swallow of whiskey. "That's a pretty cynical opinion for a player."

"I look at it as a challenge." She tipped her glass to take a drink and found to her surprise that it was nearly empty.

"And you like challenges?"

"I think they make life a little more interesting."

"You don't look much like the type who likes to be bored." He pushed a short stack of chips into his betting circle.

"How about you?"

He gave her that smile again and her pulse bumped a bit. "I'm all for excitement." He considered. "Then again, there's something to be said for just hanging."

Gwen checked her cards. "Just you and your buddies. You know, whoever you're here with?"

"Not necessarily," he answered, tapping the table for another hit. "My buddies can fend for themselves."

"Are they around?"

He gave her an amused look as she moved to hold. "You seem awfully interested in my friends. A guy could take it kind of personally."

"I don't think you should do that," she said quickly, pleased to see she'd won another round. "I was just curious."

"I'm much more interesting than my friends."

The look he gave her this time sent a shiver right down to her toes. The cocktail waitress set another cosmopolitan by her elbow, and Gwen fell on it as though it were salvation.

CHIPS SAT STACKED IN COLORED towers in front of her. She had no idea what the hour was—in a Vegas casino there were no clocks, no windows. High noon looked like midnight when you were at the tables. Time was irrelevant. The only thing that mattered was the flip of the cards, the spin of the wheel, the roll of the dice.

She felt no fatigue—far from it. She was wired, playing on house money. Her luck had been solid so far, but it was beginning to flag. Gwen drew a queen to a hand that was already twelve and busted.

Rennie looked at her. "We got a bad trend going here," he observed, gesturing at his own busted hand. "I'm thinking it's time to knock off while I'm ahead." He pushed his chips to the dealer, asking for a consolidation.

Panic seized Gwen. He couldn't leave—how would she find him again? She knew almost nothing about him, aside from the fact that he had a sexy smile and a weakness for banter.

And maybe a weakness for her.

Nina, of course, wouldn't be shy about putting her looks to work for her. No way would she just let the guy walk away. If Nina were trying to follow the trail of millions of dollars, she'd do whatever was necessary to persuade him to stick around. Gwen sent him a look from under her lashes as she collected her consolidated chips from the dealer. "So, how about a drink?"

4

WAS IT HER IMAGINATION OR was there more devilry in his smile? "Sure." He slid his handful of hundred-dollar chips into the pocket of his jeans.

Cosmopolitans, Gwen discovered as she rose from the table, had more of a kick than white wine. Her heel caught in the carpet as she slid off the stool.

"Whoa." Rennie caught her as she stumbled. "Here, why don't you grab my arm?"

"That's very gallant of you." His bicep was a solid swell under her fingers. The contact shivered through her. He wasn't built lightly at all, she realized as he tucked her hand against his body. The guy had some very real muscle. Her imagination instantly conjured up images of washboard abs and cannonball shoulders.

"Just call me Sir Galahad," he said. "So, where do you want to go?"

"Let's find a nightcap."

"You sure? We've been drinking for the last two hours. Have you had dinner?"

Gwen thought back but couldn't remember. "Something on the plane, maybe." He was an inch or two taller than she was, even in her spike heels, she realized. There was something alarmingly cozy about him standing there holding her hand against him protectively.

He looked down at her a moment and considered. "How

about if we go to the Reef Bar. Maybe we can get some food there. Trust me, you'll be happier tomorrow."

The bar was dark and yet lit with an aqua luminescence from the aquarium that took up one wall. Tropical fish made bright flashes of color amid rocks and waving green fronds. Music played in the background, but there was no crowd and no dance floor.

Quiet and dark was perfect for her purposes, Gwen thought as they took seats off in a corner. Or maybe not. The tabletop was about the size of a dinner plate, she realized. By the time she'd scooted onto her high stool, she found herself much, much closer to him than she'd anticipated. Close enough to find herself staring at that enticing mouth. Close enough to find herself noticing the way the aqua light reflected off his cheekbones. He really was gorgeous, she realized, not to mention sexy as hell.

Okay, reality check. Getting distracted was not good. She was here only to try to track down Jerry. Recreation with Rennie—one of the bad guys—was out of the question.

On the other hand, she'd do what was necessary to accomplish her purpose.

A waitress appeared, dressed in the bikini top and sarong uniform of the bar. "What'll it be, folks?"

Rennie studied the drinks card that sat on the table. "An Anchor Steam for me," he said. "And an order of potato skins."

"Sorry, guys, kitchen's closed. If you want food, you'll have to go to the coffee shop."

"Let's stick here," Gwen said quickly. No way did she want to go to a bright and noisy coffee shop. Anyway, Nina would probably sniff at coffee. She'd want a real drink. "How about a Courvoisier?" She wasn't exactly sure what Courvoisier tasted like, but she liked the idea of swirling a brandy glass.

His eyes were very dark in the dim light as he studied her. "My name is Del, by the way."

Gwen leaned closer to him. "What?"

"My name. It's not Galahad, it's Del."

"Del?" All the fun evaporated in an instant. She stared at him. "Wait a minute. You're joking, right? I thought your name was Rennie."

He shook his head. "'Fraid not."

Disaster, Gwen thought. *It was a disaster.* This was supposed to be Rennie, her conduit, the one who was going to lead her to Jerry. If he wasn't, then she was back to square one, no better off than she'd been when she'd walked into the casino. Worse, because Rennie had been around there somewhere. Now where was she? No lead, no closer to finding the stamps. Instead she was stuck here with him while the true Rennie was still out in the casino somewhere. She struggled to master her disappointment.

And ignore the small, sneaky sense of relief that lurked underneath.

"So, where'd you get the idea I was—who was it—Ronnie?"

"Rennie. That's what the dealer called you."

He looked at her, mystified.

"Before I sat down," Gwen clarified. "I thought the dealer said something like 'You always win, Rennie.'"

She watched the answer dawn. "Ah. She was joking around with the other dealer."

"Which other dealer?"

"The one who left when you came up."

"Was that her name?"

He shrugged. "I don't know. It sounded like a nickname."

"What did she look like?" Gwen asked sharply, thinking back. But she'd fastened so quickly and completely on him that everyone else was a cipher. She cursed under her breath. "I can't picture her at all."

"Does it matter?"

He was looking at her attentively—way too attentively. Relax, she told herself. "No, it's no big deal. I was just surprised." So how willing would the staffers be to help her find Rennie? And would she be back on shift the next evening? Maybe a quick conversation with the other dealer would help. Then again, Gwen didn't want to make Rennie suspicious.

"Boy, you've got some serious wheels turning in that head of yours," Del commented. "Not that it's not an entirely gorgeous head, but if I were Rennie, I'd be a little scared."

He'd leaned back to watch her, the frank curiosity on his face more than a little alarming. She needed to defray that, pronto. *Flirt, Nina, flirt.*

Gwen traced a pattern on the tabletop with one fingertip and sent him a look of promise. "Who cares about Rennie or whoever? You're here and I'm here, that's all that matters."

The amusement was back in his smile as he leaned forward and propped his elbows on the table, putting him disconcertingly near. "I suppose. You're holding out on me, though," he added conversationally.

Alarm surged through her. "What—what do you mean?"

A beat went by. "Your name. You know mine, I don't know yours."

"Oh." She almost sighed with relief. "Nina."

"Nice name. So what brings you to Vegas, Nina?"

"A couple days off. I wanted to get out of town."

He watched her for a moment, his mouth curving in a way that suggested he could see more than she wanted. "Searching for people named Rennie?"

Gwen flushed. "No. I just wanted a break."

"From what?"

"Oh, life." That much was true. She thought of the restlessness that had plagued her of late. "You know, you get tired of being stuck at home."

"Where's home?"

"San Francisco."

Genuine pleasure slid over his features. "No kidding? That's my stomping grounds."

"Really? Small world. What are you here for?"

"I'm doing a series on poker. I'm a sportswriter for the *Globe.*"

"You're a journalist?" Gwen asked faintly. That was all she needed—a curious reporter around.

Again he gave her that look. "I don't think I'd dignify it with that word necessarily. Let's just say I can bang out twenty column inches on the Giants versus the Dodgers by deadline."

"You don't sound thrilled with it." The waitress set their drinks down in front of them.

Del shrugged. "It's a living. What about you?"

Gwen swirled her brandy glass to buy time. Lying wasn't in her nature. Then again, the last thing she wanted to do was give any personal details to a reporter, especially to a reporter who was entirely too interested in her earlier gaffes already. Even if he was a sportswriter. "I'm an accountant," she told him. It wasn't really a lie. She did the books at Chastain Philatelic Investments. She just did a whole lot more.

"Seriously?" He grinned, sending a little flutter through her midsection. He was so close, she realized suddenly. Close enough to whisper. Close enough to kiss.

Gwen blinked. "Yes, seriously. Why, what did you think I did?"

"I don't know. But I could have guessed a couple dozen possible occupations for you and none of them would have included accounting."

She could just imagine. "So, what occupations were in your couple dozen?"

"Oh, I don't know," he said offhandedly, "neurosurgeon, astrophysicist, president of the World Bank…"

"You know, if you'd have said lingerie model, I'd have had to belt you." She reached out a hand to mime slapping him. He caught it in his and held it to his face.

Heat bloomed through her. Sensation piled on sensation, the rough stubble of his day's growth of beard, the strength of his fingers on hers, the slight calluses on his palm.

It lasted only a second or two and drove every thought out of her head except the desire for more.

Del released her hand, changing his hold to bring her fingers to his lips. Warm and soft enough to make her melt. "Whatever you do, I'm sure you're very, very good," he murmured.

Eyes wide, Gwen sat stock-still, forcing herself to breathe. "I…excuse me for a minute," she managed to say and stood up on knees that trembled only a little.

DEL SAT WATCHING HER WALK away and waiting for the drumming in his head to stop. He hadn't been able to resist the impulse to touch her. The sudden urge to have her had surprised him, though. He considered himself a civilized man, but there was nothing civilized about this overwhelming need to drive himself into her deep and hard.

Colorful fish circled lazily in the aquarium beyond. He'd sat down at the blackjack table for a change of pace, to kill a couple of hours, not to hook up with a woman. Then Nina had sat down, fragrant, silky and looking hot enough to melt wax.

It wasn't completely outside his experience to have a woman hit on him, but it certainly wasn't his normal style to bite. He'd learned from personal experience—in his relationships and in his professional life—that the easy pickings were generally not the way to satisfaction, they were just…easy.

There was something about her, though, more than the looks. The combination of the promise in that wide mouth and the sharp intelligence in those eyes had captured his attention utterly. But something else was going on, something more than blackjack, more than sexual jousting. What about the consternation over his name? And why had she pumped him so hard about his friends?

And how was it that he didn't really give a damn about any of it, so long as he could have her?

He watched her cross the room toward him again, in her low-cut jeans and skimpy, fire-engine-red T-shirt. The confidence was back in her swagger, in the toss of her head. For a moment earlier she'd seemed like a high school girl, completely undone by his move. It seemed incongruous for a woman who looked the way Nina did, a woman who'd probably been romanced every way possible.

"Welcome back," he said as she sat.

"Thanks. I'm happy to be here."

He grinned and raised his beer. "Well, here's to being here." Her eyes watched him over the rim of her glass, the deep aqua of the Caribbean. Her scent drifted across to him, something that whispered of dark nights and forbidden passion. "So, how'd you get so good at blackjack?" he asked.

"My grandfather's got a weekly game. Blackjack, poker, whatever. I usually sit in with them."

"Win much?"

She shrugged. "I walk away with my share of pots."

"That's because you've got a genetic advantage." He propped his chin in his hand. "They probably can't concentrate a lick with someone who looks like you at the table, and on top of that you're smart."

He couldn't be sure in the dim bar, but he'd swear she flushed. "I've known most of them since I was about ten. I'm sure they can ignore it."

"You underestimate yourself. I don't think any man who sees you can ignore it."

She gave him a smoky look and propped her arms on the table herself. "Really?"

"Really."

"And would that include you?"

He felt the stirring in his belly. "What do you think?"

HIS MOUTH. SHE COULDN'T STOP staring at his mouth. She couldn't stop wondering how he tasted. The table had shrunk, or maybe she'd inadvertently moved her stool closer to him when she'd returned, because when he reached out to tangle his fingers in hers, it was only a small movement.

This time there was no shock, just the hot and sexy snap of connection. All the way to the bathroom and back— merely an excuse to get away and think for a minute— she'd thought about what it might be like with him. It wasn't the sort of thing Gwen would do, but she wasn't Gwen, was she? She was Nina. Nina wouldn't just sit and wonder what it would be like to kiss this man. She wouldn't wait for him to make the move. Nina would satisfy herself. Nina would just do it.

His eyes seemed darker, deeper as she leaned closer. She flicked a glance at his mouth and her tongue darted out to lick her own lips. She wanted this, she thought, tipping her head slightly. For tonight Jerry and the stamps could take a backseat. For tonight she just wanted.

And then their mouths came together and she didn't have to want anymore.

Her fingers were still curled in his but she didn't feel it.

All her awareness was concentrated in the feel of his mouth on hers. He didn't just kiss, he savored, feasting on her as though she were some rare delicacy. A shift, a nip, a quick slick of tongue. There was a sumptuousness in the slide of lip against lip, temptation in the taste. Her system began to buzz.

When his hand slid to cup her neck and pull her closer, Gwen went willingly. When his mouth opened against hers, she made a little sound of pleasure in her throat. It didn't matter that she hardly knew him, that he was just a pair of teasing eyes and a devilish smile. Something about him tempted her to take a risk. Something about him sent desire surging through her with an intensity she couldn't recall feeling before.

In the casino a cacophony indicated that someone had won a big jackpot, but neither of them even registered the noise. All that mattered was this moment, this place, this feeling.

If he'd felt the need to take before, now Del fought the urge to plunder. Up close, her scent wove around his senses, making him imagine her naked, hot and urgent against him. Her mouth was warm and alive. She tasted of Courvoisier and arousal, he thought hazily. Driven by the slide of her tongue over his, the nip of her teeth, he only wanted more.

And so he took the kiss deeper.

The teasing swirl of her tongue around his had desire coiling in his belly. She might have been an enigma, but her trembling response didn't lie. Throughout the night she'd been an odd mix of uncertainty and confidence. There was nothing tentative here now, though, only a heated certainty that sent urgency thudding through his system.

Finally Del broke away. He sat for a moment, waiting

for his system to level. It was going to take a while, he realized. "You pack quite a punch," he told her.

"So do you." It took her two tries to get the words out. Gwen stared back at him, breathing hard. She wanted, oh, she wanted. If he could take her this far with just a kiss, how much more was waiting for her? Her lips still felt as though they were vibrating, she realized. And she wanted more. She leaned toward him again, but he stopped her.

"Maybe we should go somewhere else," he said, staring at her. "Someplace less…public."

She nodded, not in answer to the words he'd said but to the question in his eyes. "I think you're right."

"Oh, yeah?"

Gwen leaned forward to press a kiss on him. "Oh, yeah," she breathed. Del tossed a twenty on the table and rose, catching her hand.

And a bubble of exhilaration began to swell in her chest.

It wasn't her usual style. Gwen dated clean-cut, serious men who took her to a few weeks of movies, concerts and dinners before they segued into decorous sex. That part usually lasted until she was bored mindless with them. She certainly didn't pick up the kind of men who hung out in casinos. She definitely didn't kiss them in bars the first night she'd met them, even if they did have perfectly delicious mouths.

And she absolutely didn't wind up in bed with them.

Maybe it was being in Vegas, maybe it was the cosmopolitans, but suddenly it didn't matter. Suddenly what she wanted was this moment with this man. She could go back to being careful and deliberate Gwen tomorrow.

Nina was taking over.

5

THE ELEVATOR WAS A BLUR, THE walk down the hall a desperate trek broken up by pauses to just stand fused together, desperate to get their hands on one another. Finally they stood at a door, Del fumbling for his passkey.

Gwen had never known anything like this before. Certainly sex had involved some excitement, but all to a manageable level. Getting swept up in passion was what Joss did, not Gwen. Gwen kept things tidy and controlled.

But now she was Nina, and Nina wanted no truck with tidy and controlled. Nina wanted hot. Nina wanted the rough feel of a man's hands, the pumping urgency of his body.

Nina wanted it all.

Gwen leaned against him, up on tiptoe. "I want you naked," she whispered over his shoulder. "Now."

And the door latch clicked open.

Inside the room Del groped for a light switch, and a recessed light in the entryway came on. It was as though Gwen had a fever in her blood. She was hot, light-headed with wanting. Del turned to her and she flowed into his arms.

She'd never been kissed like this. She'd never had a hot mouth and a pair of hands fling her into arousal so quickly. As he pressed her against the wall and took the kiss deeper, she could taste a faint hint of the bourbon he'd been drinking. The stroke of tongue against tongue sent desire arrowing through her. He was hard, she could feel it, and she shivered a little with anticipation as she shifted her hips in response.

He groaned. With an exultant laugh Gwen broke the kiss and let herself nuzzle his throat, the skin taut under her lips. She could feel his hard-muscled body under the shirt and made a noise of impatience.

"More," she breathed. "I want more." Her mouth still on his, she stepped back enough to push his shirt away from his shoulders, and he shrugged it off.

And she caught a breath of delight. His was a body made for movement, the arms hard and sculpted, the belly corrugated with muscle. She traced her fingers down over the ripples of his abs. When he sucked in a breath, she dipped lower to trace over the swell of his hard-on under his jeans.

She wanted the feel of his skin against hers. Gwen reached for the hem of her own top, but Del caught at her hands. "Oh, no, that's for me to do," he murmured. He slipped his hands around her waist, sliding over the bare skin and up under the stretchy crop top she wore. His fingers trailed up her back, and the immediacy of the contact made her shiver, and shiver again when he slid them around to the front to fill his hands with the curves of her breasts. The fabric diminished the sensation, and she strained against him with a noise of frustration. She wanted his touch on her naked breasts. Instead he slid his hands up her sides and along her arms, until the rolled-up shirt was just a memory tossed across the room.

"God, you're gorgeous," Del said hoarsely as he stepped back and just looked at her in her sheer black bra. She flushed and glanced down, pulling her arms in toward her in what seemed like a reflex action. Catching her wrists, he pulled them gently aside. "Let me look at you. You're such a turn-on."

She was delicious, all soft and curvy. He wanted more, though. One minute she was all confidence, the next minute self-conscious. There was something about the way she met his eyes, suddenly hesitant. He wanted it gone. He wanted her wet and abandoned, twisting against him. He wanted to hear her cry out. He wanted to taste her. Reaching down, he unzipped her jeans. "These come off. Now."

Slipping the denim down, he savored the feel of her silky skin against his palms, then pressed her back onto the ridiculously high sleigh bed that mirrored the decadence of the rest of the hotel. One at a time he pulled off her spike-heeled shoes. Her jeans followed and he tossed them aside.

She sat up. "I want to…"

"No." He pressed her down. "Let me." He started at her instep, kissing the tender skin, then tracing the inside of her calves with his tongue. Working his way up her thighs, he pleased himself by teasing her, licking close to the silky lace at the vee between her legs, going just under the edge before moving away. Because he had plans and he was nothing if not a patient man.

Rising, he stripped off his own jeans and leaned over the bed. Her breathing became more ragged and she shuddered a little as he moved up over her flat belly, along the sides of her waist. With a snap he unfastened the front clasp of her bra and peeled back the cups.

Dry-mouthed with anticipation, Gwen stared up at him. The touch, when it came, wasn't the cupping of a hand or the brush of fingers but the stroke of a tongue, wet and warm against her. She licked her lips and waited for more. When he bent to her breasts again, he took his time, until the suction and rub of his tongue over her swollen nipples started an answering resonance down where she was wet and fevered.

Tension tightened her and she twined her fingers in his

hair, drawing him up to her so that she could press a hard, openmouthed kiss on him. She curved her arms around him, mad for him to lie alongside her, but he kept away. "Later," he promised and moved back down her body.

This time he focused on her breasts, kneading them, rolling the nipples with light pressure as he kissed his way down her body. The brush of the hair on his forearms against her body made her shudder, the warmth of his lips made her toss and turn. When she felt him slip off her lacy underwear, she slid her fingers into his hair. "Oh, god," she breathed.

The mattress gave just a bit as he settled himself between her legs. She felt the brush of his hair against her inner thigh, felt the warmth of his breath. Every atom of her being was tensed in anticipation. Her hips moved just a bit, involuntarily. He gave a chuckle deep in his throat and settled himself between her legs. "Not until you're begging."

Lightly, maddeningly lightly, his tongue brushed the lips that enfolded her clitoris. When he separated them, she gave a hum of satisfaction and expectation, but he ignored the hard bud where she ached to be touched. Instead he licked at her folds, dipped inside her, touched her everywhere but the point that would give her release.

She clawed at his shoulders, pulled him toward her. "Please," she managed. "Oh, please."

And then his mouth was on her, sending her gasping and flinging her head back into the pillow. Hard and relentless, he drove her, tongue tracing maddening patterns that sent her flailing upward toward some crest, some climax, some pinnacle of ultimate release.

Yet just as she was trembling at the edge, he backed off again, leaving her achingly unfulfilled while he teased her with other touches, his hands on her breasts, his mouth against her thigh. She dragged at him, hands on his head as she urged him to take her over.

And he did, his mouth driving her up, sending her gasping, hips jolting against him, seeking that final touch. But just when he had her shuddering, crying out mindlessly, just when she could feel the climax looming, he moved away.

"Don't stop," she cried raggedly, the pressure of the unrealized orgasm pounding through her.

"I'm not. I'm just changing gears." Breathing hard, Del slid off to stand beside the high bed. She felt a little thrill as he pulled her to the edge, stepping close enough to stretch her legs up the length of his torso, her ankles hooked over his shoulders. Stiff and hard, his cock jerked just a little with arousal as he sheathed it. Then he took the head of it and slid it into the slick cleft between her legs, running it up and down a few times, each brush of the smooth skin against her engorged clitoris making her gasp.

"Oh, like that," she rasped, but he shook his head.

"I think you're resourceful enough to do it for yourself," he murmured and in that instant pumped his hips to slide into her up to the root.

Thick, hard, solid, it dragged a cry from her. Moving against him, she savored every bit of friction as his cock slid in and out, in and out. She trembled on the edge of orgasm.

But she didn't quite go over. It was taunting to feel so much, to have his hands sliding up and down her legs and still have her desire remain unslaked.

She had to do something or she'd go mad. She needed hands on her breasts, needed something to ease the throb. One hand crept closer to the vee between her legs. When her finger slid into the warm wetness, when she felt the slide of it over the hard knob of her clitoris, she gasped.

"Oh, yeah, touch yourself," Del said softly, and Gwen swore he got harder. "Show me what you like." He caught her ankles and moved them apart a little, watching her avidly, watching himself move in and out of her.

Any vestige of self-consciousness was gone. Gwen circled her finger over her clit, each touch tightening the tension that strung her taut, each touch in time with the hard, swift strokes of his cock. She was almost delirious with the sensation that battered her from all directions. Close to the edge, she was so close she didn't think but raised her free hand to her breast, brushing the tender skin, squeezing the nipple.

"Oh, man," Del cried out raggedly, even as the bolt of sensation flung her over the edge to orgasm. It was hard, jolting, tearing staccato cries from her as the pleasure battered her over and over again. And even as she was still shuddering with pleasure, he groaned and spilled himself.

SOFTNESS. WARMTH. DEL REDMOND woke to find his face pressed against a fragrant spill of hair, his arms full of silky, curvy woman. It wasn't an experience he'd had very much of since his divorce two years before. Or very much the year or so before his divorce, come to think of it. He liked it, the way Nina fit in his arms, spooned against him. He liked it a lot.

As to the night before, well, it had been mind-blowing, pure and simple. The way she'd touched him, the way she'd moved, had brought him astonishing release. The two of them might not know each other from Adam outside of bed, but in it they were incredibly compatible.

Of course, he was in Vegas to work, not to have a fling with a woman. Then again, so long as he got the job done, who was to care? And this wasn't just any woman. This was a woman who attracted him, who aroused him.

Who intrigued him.

A low whine had him glancing at the nightstand to see

his muted cell phone flashing. Recognizing the number, he gave a quiet curse and slipped his arm out from under Nina. She rolled over with a sleepy murmur, dragging the covers with her.

Del rose and headed to the bathroom. "Redmond here," he said, closing the door and sitting down on the edge of the tub.

"It's ten-thirty in the morning. Where's your copy, Redmond?"

"Morning, Perry, how are you?" Del could picture Ed Perry, the *Globe*'s comfortably paunchy sports editor, his balding head counterbalanced by a neat Vandyke.

"How am I? Not nearly as good as you, I'm sure. So where's my column on the poker life, champ? What are you doing—drinking, chasing after women?"

Del glanced uneasily at the door. "I wrote a story yesterday. I'll get it filed this morning."

"You know, I send you to Vegas, plum assignment. This is not what I expect in thanks."

"Hey, this was your bright idea, not mine." Walking to the counter, Del pulled his electric shaver out of his leather toilet kit.

"Who was the one bitching about another year covering the All-Star game?"

"Me," Del admitted.

"Is that a razor I hear? Are you shaving?" Perry demanded. "You really *have* spent the day in bed."

"You're the one who's always telling me to multitask," Del reminded him. "I'm not a gambler, Perry. The last time I was in Vegas was when I played here in college."

"Not a gambler, huh?" the editor grunted. "So how was it again you fleeced me for forty bucks in last week's poker game?"

Del moved the razor in circles over one cheek, then the

other. "Look, a friendly poker game with the guys to drink beer and shoot the shit is one thing. Out here you're talking hard core. These people are up all night. Everything I own reeks of cigarette smoke." He ran the razor along his jaw.

"Switch that thing the hell off, will you? It's buzzing in my ear like a mosquito."

"Bitch, bitch, bitch."

"Me? What about you? Anyway, you were getting stale. I figured something different would shake you up."

Del snorted. "Hardly. You just wanted to distract me from the newsroom job."

"Newsroom job?" Perry repeated innocently.

"Don't give me that. You know I want to apply for that opening in the metro section."

Perry sighed. "Del, you've got a good gig here in sports. Why do you want to gum up the works going after an entry-level reporter's job?"

"You just don't want to have to break in a new writer."

"I just don't want to see you get shot down."

"Why would I be?" Del scowled. "I've worked on the sports section for nearly eight years, since I washed out of the pros."

"Yeah, and the whole time there's been a crew of bright-eyed kids over in the newsroom busy building their contacts so they can get half a dozen city hall staffers on the phone for a story. You can get Felipe Alou. You can't compete, Del."

"Let them tell me that," he snapped. "I want stories that take work. I want to dig, not just interview a bunch of genetically gifted millionaires."

"You've got a gift for interviewing genetically gifted millionaires."

Del sat back down and leaned his elbows on his knees. "I've got a little bit of one for investigation, too. What about that series I did on the BALCO scandal?"

"Some good work there," Perry admitted reluctantly.

"I want to do more."

"Fine. The doping scandal's still going. Follow it up."

"It's not enough, Perry."

"What is this, an early midlife crisis? Is this about the divorce?"

"No. Maybe. I don't know." Del rose and scrubbed a hand through his hair. "I just know I took the easy way out for way too long and it didn't get me anywhere I wanted to be. I want to make something happen, not just take what comes my way."

"Sports not good enough for you?" A hard note entered Perry's voice.

"You know better. I just want to do something that didn't fall in my lap, you know?"

"Life's so tough when you're a golden boy." The sarcasm was rich in Perry's voice.

"It's not that," Del said simply. "I feel like I let myself down by not trying. And I let everybody else down, too."

There was a silence and then a long sigh. "Okay, fine. You really want me to forward your application to the news desk, I'll do it. But I'm making no guarantees."

"I'll make my own."

AT THE SOUND OF THE CLOSING bathroom door, Gwen's eyes opened and she breathed a silent sigh of relief. He was out of the room. She might have had a momentary brain lapse the night before, but now she could get up, get dressed and get on with it. Time was a-wasting and Jerry was out on the loose with four and a half million in stamps. She didn't have time to lie around. She moved to the edge of the bed, wincing at the slight soreness between her legs.

And winced again at the thought of the night before.

From the day she'd started having sex—at a respectable

nineteen—she'd vowed no one-night stands. None of those cheap, tawdry scenes of waking up the morning after with a total stranger. And now, fueled by too many cosmos and too much Nina, she'd popped her one-night-stand cherry. It was just the sort of fiasco Joss would get involved in, coming to town for a serious purpose and getting distracted by sexy eyes and clever hands.

Gwen paused and a slow smile stretched unbidden across her face. And what clever hands they were, not to mention the rest of the machinery that went with them. She wasn't a novice when it came to having sex, but her interludes tended to be moderate, dignified. Not for her, wild monkey sex where the positions changed by the minute and the lovers clawed and gasped.

At least, not until now.

Yawning, she rose and began to sort her clothes out of the tangle on the floor. Then again, sex—however amazing—was her last priority right now. One night? Okay, she'd been restless lately. She could give herself one night. It was over, though. Today was for Jerry-hunting and she couldn't lose focus. The stamps were the only things that mattered.

Gwen slipped into her black lace underwear and hunted around for her bra. The ideal thing to do would be dress and beat a hot retreat—if only she weren't dying to use the bathroom. How would Nina play it? At ease and in control, of course. Say good morning, go in and powder her nose and be on her way with a swagger. Not self-conscious, not in a million years. Nina ran the show.

At the sound of the bathroom door opening behind her, Gwen clutched her clothing to herself in reflex action. *Relax,* she told herself, willing her arms to loosen up. Nina was totally comfortable being naked and would act that way.

"Good morning," she said and gave him a bold look.

Del stared. "Um…"

Gwen's confident smile wavered. "What?" She touched her nose.

"Your eye, it's a little…"

She whirled to inspect herself in the mirror over the bar. Everything was fine around her nose, but the white of one eye had a brilliant turquoise circle on it. One of the damned colored contacts that Joss had insisted she wear had moved while she'd slept. "Oh, for god's sake," Gwen muttered and went into the bathroom without a word.

It was just as well, she figured as she pulled out the contacts and dressed. Forget about awkward segues, now she'd just be ready to roll. Hand on the doorknob, she took a deep breath and walked out into the room.

Del had pulled on his jeans but hadn't bothered to fasten the top button. His waistband hung tantalizingly open below the rock-hard ripples of his belly. She remembered the way the muscles had felt under her hand, with their light dusting of springy hair.

Before she could speak, he walked over and pressed a kiss on her. "Good morning. Sorry for getting distracted before."

It didn't matter that they'd spent the night together, it didn't matter that they'd done much, much more, the kiss had her lips buzzing. Taken off balance, she faltered. "They were probably a bad idea. Something new." *Stupid,* she thought immediately. And certainly never should have admitted to doing anything goofy.

"If it matters, I like the real color better," he remarked and slid the fingers of one hand along her jaw, curling them around her neck. She read his intentions in the darkening of his eyes and stepped back hastily even as she felt the first fizz of desire begin to bubble in her system.

"Well, got to get the day started," she said briskly. "I should get rolling."

"Why?" He moved toward her again. "You're here for pleasure. I can help you with that."

"I've got business that can't wait." Although if she didn't get away from him soon, it would have to.

"Business?" He lowered his hands, interest flickering in his eyes. "I thought this was a vacation for you."

Gwen coughed. "Oh, yeah, well, you know, business and pleasure, better together."

"Is this about Rennie?"

That stopped her for a moment. "Where'd you get that?"

"That's who you were looking for when you sat down last night, wasn't it? Rennie?" Del backed up to lean a hip against the bureau.

She flushed. "I don't think that's any of your business."

"You're right," he agreed, "but it's kind of an odd thing. Makes me wonder."

The last thing she needed was a curious reporter on her hands. "There's nothing to wonder about," Gwen snapped, checking her jeans pocket for her room key. "Last night was last night and this is today. And I've got things to get done."

"So I see. Doesn't mean we still can't spend some time together."

Had she thought he had devilish eyes? Now they were just way too perceptive and persistent for her own comfort. She needed to cut this off—now. "You seemed like a nice guy last night. Don't turn into one of those jerks who can't take no for an answer. It was a one-nighter. Deal with it."

The look in his eyes hardened. "I don't have any problems with the word no. I just don't take bullshit very well."

"What's that supposed to mean?"

"You tell me. You're kind of a moving target."

"And you're kind of an asshole." She shook her head like a dog shaking off water. "Why are we even having this conversation? I am out of here. Have a nice life."

"Give my love to Rennie."

She answered with a rude word. Unfortunately the pneumatic closer prevented the door from slamming, so she had to listen to his laughter all the way down the hall.

6

GWEN STOOD ON THE SIDEWALK near the corner of Sahara and Decatur, squinting in the late morning sunlight. Away from the Strip, Las Vegas was anonymous and pedestrian—computer stores nestled up against muffler shops, fast-food joints and video stores filling up the minimalls. It was like any city in America.

Except for the temperature.

Not even dark glasses blocked the merciless desert sun. Baking heat shimmered up in waves from the sidewalk. It was a good thing she'd worn something skimpy when she'd left the air-conditioned comfort of the hotel, not that Nina's wardrobe held anything else. Of course, Gwen would have chosen a sleeveless top and shorts rather than Nina's clingy lime tank dress. It was right for Nina, though. She'd wear an attention-getter.

And get attention it had, from the elevator, through the casino, to the front door. It had certainly brought the door-man on the run, and the cabbie had been ready to throw aside his day job to show her around. Instead she'd had him take her out to the boulevard of strip malls and drop her at LV Rarities.

A low chime sounded as she pushed open the door. Inside the shop provided a cool, dark contrast to the sun-baked outdoors. In the quiet confines of the store, it felt as if the air never moved; spotlights just shone down endlessly and timelessly on the glimmering coins and stamps and antique jewelry in the display cases.

"Can I help you?" A man with salt-and-pepper hair combed discreetly over a thinning patch appeared from the back.

"Hello," Gwen said coolly. He was about her height. From the way he held himself, she was pretty sure he was sucking in a paunch.

"Hot enough for you today?"

"Oh, a little warm, maybe. Nice and cold in here, though."

"Only the temperature. Our merchandise is hot."

Gwen raised an eyebrow. "You sell stolen goods?"

"No, no," he said hastily. "I meant top-of-the-line."

"I'm sure." Never hurt to have him on the defensive if what she suspected was true, Gwen thought and walked slowly around the U of display cases, bending over occasionally for a closer look at the precious goods inside. "So, what are your specialties?"

"Whatever you're looking for, we've got." He smoothed his hair. "What's your name?"

"Vera." Another character was called for, she'd decided on the way over. She was trying to hunt down Jerry as Nina. The last thing she wanted was for him to find out that someone named Nina was asking questions about him. "My—" she paused "—friend has just won big at the casino and he wants me to pick out something nice."

"We've got some gemstones or some gold wafer jewelry that would look fine on you."

Gwen waved a dismissive hand. "I've already been jewelry shopping. I'm interested in owning something with a little more distinction. You carry rare stamps, right?"

"Oh, I could set you up with some interesting pieces for a few hundred each."

She flicked him a glance. "I want valuable stuff. Don't you have anything really rare? What do they cost?" She wandered back and stopped in front of him.

"How much money are you looking to invest?" he countered, unable to entirely disguise the hint of eagerness in his voice.

Gwen traced a pattern on the glass of the display case. "Oh, we don't need to get specific just yet. What could I do with, say, three to five thousand?"

"Looks like someone brought luck to the table."

"I do my best." She didn't flirt, but she gave him a smile of vague promise. "So, what's your best?"

His eyes brightened. "I might do better showing than telling."

In another lifetime, bub. "Bring them out, then. If I like what I see, I might be back later this week."

She watched his nostrils flare as he took a breath. "Give me just a minute." He stepped in the back and came out with a plush catalog. "We have the German 1864 one-schilling or the Great Britain 1882 one-pound." He opened the pages to show her each.

Gwen nibbled her lip, watching him watch her. "Do you have anything more colorful? You know, Pony Express stamps or something with airplanes?"

He laughed indulgently. "It'd take a little more than five thousand to get you a Pony Express stamp, but I've just picked up a nice 1847 Benjamin Franklin stamp that might suit you."

"Yeah, I bet in a town like Vegas you pick up nice pieces all the time."

He shrugged. "It's a business. They need money, I need stock."

She looked at the stamp in its clear holder and felt a thrill of excitement. She recognized the perforation pattern, the width of the border around the stamp—characteristics that were as sure identifiers as fingerprints to a person. The stamp was from her grandfather's inventory. "So, how do you know it's for real? You have a certificate or something?"

He cleared his throat. "This is a recent acquisition. I don't have paperwork for it yet, but I hope to."

"Then how do you know it's authentic?" she asked casually, flipping the pages of the catalog to spy another stamp from the store collection. And another. "Do you know where they got it?"

"I don't ask those questions."

I'm sure you don't, Gwen thought. "How much?" she said aloud.

He looked at her and looked at the stamp, considering. "Oh, normally I'd ask six thousand, but since you look like you might be interested in long-term collecting, I'll take five to get you started."

Outrage flooded through her. Five? The catalog value of the stamp was thirty-five hundred.

"Of course," he said silkily, brushing his fingers over the back of her hand, "that price includes personal advice on the investment value of rare stamps, perhaps in a more… conducive setting. Who knows, you might even get me to drop the price even further."

It made her skin crawl but she took care not to show it. "Well, you can start by telling me more about this stamp. I guess every one of them has a story. Tell me—" she looked at him speculatively "—did the guy who sold it to you say where he got it?"

"I make my business buying and selling, not asking."

"How do you know it was his to sell?"

The dealer moved his hand away. "The appraisal takes care of all of that," he said briskly, seeming to realize that he'd already said too much. "Are you interested?"

"Let me think it over." She gave him an intimate smile, but she'd let her moment slip away, she understood. He wasn't going to tell her any more. "Can you set the stamp aside? I need to talk with my friend. I'm sure he'll want an appraisal."

"For you, anything." His hand drifted south of his belt. "And think about what I said. I can teach you a lot about stamps and maybe throw in a tour of the city. I've lived in Vegas for twenty years. I can show you all the sights."

"I'll bet you can," Gwen told him. "I'll just bet you can."

BACK IN HER ROOM, SHE DIALED Stewart's cell phone. "I've found him," she said without preamble.

"Huh? What?" She could practically see him trying to catch up. "Where?"

"Vegas, of all places."

"Vegas! How'd you find him?"

"I tracked the 1847 Benjamin Franklin. A guy from out here answered that posting I put on the loop."

"What do you mean, out here? You didn't go carting off to Vegas to find him, did you? For god sakes, Gwennie, use some sense. Your thief could be dangerous."

"Stewart, I've got to get those stamps back."

"So, what, you're going to grab him and pound him until he tells you where they are? Point a gun at him and make him sweat? This isn't a movie."

"I know," she said, her excitement dissipating. No, it wasn't a movie, but the whole thing certainly felt unreal. "And I don't know where he is exactly, anyway. I just know he's been here. The dealer's got three of our stamps."

"You sure he bought them from your guy?"

"They're ours, that much I know. Where he bought them, I can't be sure. He's giving me the runaround." Gwen rose and began pacing, the cordless phone in her hand. "He had to get it from Jerry, though. It's too soon for them to have changed hands more than once."

"I'm surprised he'd bother messing with you."

His confidence warmed her. "I didn't tell him who I was or why I was asking. I couldn't take the chance of it getting back to Jerry."

"Even if you didn't tell the dealer your name, I can't imagine anyone trying to get around someone like you. You mean business and it shows."

Outside on the Strip, a giant video screen showed a phalanx of dancers gyrating through a dance from the latest hit show. "I'm kind of in disguise."

"What does that mean?"

"Well, I didn't want Jerry recognizing me before I figured out what was going on. Joss fixed me up...." She stopped helplessly as Stewart began laughing, a deep belly laugh that went on and on. "Well, it's not that funny," she said frostily.

"Little Gwennie undercover." Amusement was rich in his tone. "Sorry, I'm sure you look great."

"Actually I'm a total babe," she informed him, flopping down in one of the dark red upholstered chairs by the window. "The cab driver volunteered to take the day off and give me a personal tour of Vegas."

"I'm sure he did," he said more soberly.

"So did the stamp dealer, but what he didn't give me was anything on Jerry I could use."

"Assuming it's this Jerry in the first place."

"It's Jerry, all right. Anyway, I wonder if you know the guy here. Tom Horton of LV Rarities?"

Stewart considered. "I've met him once or twice."

"You think you could give him a call, see what you can find out?" For now, Horton was her only link to Jerry and Jerry was her only link to the stamps.

"I'll do better. I'll come out and do it in person."

Half of her was relieved, half of her felt like a kid whose parents were taking over. "You don't have to do that, Stewart. I've got it under control for now."

"You're only three hours away, Gwennie. I can be there tonight."

"You've got a business to run," she protested.

"So what? This is Hugh's future we're talking about."

"I want to do it myself," she burst out, knowing as she said it that it was true. There was silence on the line. "I'm sorry, I didn't mean it to come out that way. Look," she tried, "it was my fault the stamps got taken. I need to do this, to at least try to make it right. Can you understand that?"

"I suppose." His tone was guarded.

"I need your advice and I need your connections. I just don't need you here right now. You're still helping me, though."

"Not enough."

"More than enough," she countered. "If you can get anything out of Horton, that would be huge. I'll call if I need you out here."

"Promise?"

"I swear. You're always first on my list, you know that."

"Oh, I bet you say that to all the middle-aged guys you know." The tone was a little too hearty, but he sounded mollified.

"Only you." Relieved to have the difficult moment past, Gwen smiled. "Were you able to find out anything on the other stamps?"

"Big goose egg, which is good news for you. As near as I can tell, no one out there is putting out feelers on the Post Office Mauritius stamps or the inverted Jennys. I'm still waiting to hear on the two-penny."

There wasn't a name for the level of relief she felt. "Maybe he's lying low."

"Probably," Stewart agreed. "You don't have a lot of time to waste, though. Swear you'll call me if you need help?"

"I do. I'll keep hunting and let you know what I find out."

"Same goes. And Gwennie?"

"Yeah, Stewie?"

"Be careful."

DEL CAME OUT OF THE CASINO office and stopped, surveying the room with the same amazement he always did. Noise, motion and color as far as the eye could see. Day or night, it was all the same, with the same nameless faces and bodies lined up at the slot machines and the craps tables in a sort of numb gambling daze, mechanically placing the next bet, the one that was going to win them big.

To one side of him lay the hotel registration counter. In an ordinary hotel it would be immediately inside the front door. In a Vegas hotel getting to the registration desk required a Sherpa guide and provisions. The hotel designers knew where the cash money part of the business came from and they put it right up front. Del remembered a reporter in town to cover a UNLV football game losing three hundred dollars at blackjack before he ever even got checked into his hotel.

A curvy blonde walked by and gave him a smile of promise. And all he could think was that she didn't hold a candle to Nina. Not the sleekly sexy Nina of the night before, but the Nina of this morning, with her hair tousled and her eyes shining their natural blue-gray. Underneath the glossy packaging was an unstudied, intriguing woman who stayed on a man's mind—at least, on his.

Get over it, he told himself, remembering her words. The strange thing was, he didn't seem to be able to. Del shook his head, wondering about himself. He'd been involved with plenty of women in his life and he'd been interested in plenty of others who didn't return the favor. It wasn't a problem. If a woman didn't want him, there were bound to be others who did. He wasn't hung up on challenges or afraid of rejection. He was a pragmatist.

Certainly he'd had more than his share of experience with golden girls, genus California, species beach babe. He'd even gone so far as to marry one—and discovered that underneath the polish and packaging there wasn't a whole lot else.

Maybe that was why Nina stuck with him, because the more of her package and polish he got under, the more levels to her there were—clever, funny, smart, subtle, stubborn. That and the fact that there was something going on with her that wasn't quite kosher. There was probably an easy explanation for it, but if so, why didn't she just say something? Maybe it was simple, maybe it was innocent.

And maybe she was out of her depth.

Not his problem, he reminded himself. *Get over it.*

But it was hard to get over it when he looked up to see her walking by, leggy and curvy in all the right places, with a loose-limbed stride that made his mouth go dry. Her bright hair swished around her shoulders. Those legs, those legs were nothing short of stupendous. But it was her eyes that got to him, those eyes that couldn't disguise the hardheaded intelligence within.

And then she saw him and stopped. Her gaze flicked in his direction, then out at the casino, then back at him, as if she were debating something. Then like a kid sent to do an unpleasant errand, her feet all but dragging, she approached.

"Hello," she said, not sounding at all happy about it.

"Hey, there." He admired her. "So, were your errands a success?"

She blinked and flapped her hand vaguely. "Sort of."

"Sort of," he repeated and crossed his arms, watching her with interest. He wasn't about to push. If she had something to say, the play was all hers.

Gwen squared her shoulders with a hint of defiance. "Don't get any ideas because I stopped."

"I wouldn't dream of it."

"I came over here…" She hesitated and suddenly looked very young. "I came over here to apologize for this morning. I shouldn't have called you an—"

"Asshole?" he supplied helpfully. "I believe that's what you said."

Her face flamed. "Yes. I'm sorry. I'm not usually a name caller. I'm just a little stressed out right now."

"Those must be some errands."

Something flickered in her eyes. Caution? Fear? Whatever it was, it shut her down. "It'll be fine."

"And how's Rennie?" He couldn't resist poking a little.

"Get off the whole Rennie thing, already, will you?" she snapped. "It's nothing."

"I guess you are kind of stressed."

Her eyes flashed with temper.

"Look," she began. And stopped abruptly, staring at something or someone behind him. He turned to see. The door to the casino offices had just closed behind a guy with dark blond hair and a casino staffer. Del couldn't hear much of what they were saying above the chatter of the slot machines, but the blond guy was sounding persuasive.

Then again, he looked like the kind of guy who spent most of his time trying to talk someone into something. The whole package was just a little too slick, a little too pretty. His hair was disarranged and gleamed just a bit with gel, his shirt and jacket were tailored just a little too sharply.

He put his hand on the staffer's shoulder as if he was his best buddy.

Operator was the word that sprang to mind.

Nina was riveted.

7

SHE COULDN'T SEE WHERE HE'D come from. One moment she'd been standing there, fumbling her way through an apology and avoiding Del's eyes. The next Jerry had been there talking with someone who wore the dark blue jacket of the casino management.

Her heart jumped into her throat. This was the telling moment. Would her disguise hold? Jerry glanced across at her, looked away and glanced more deliberately this time, even as he continued his conversation. Had he recognized her? No, the look wasn't one of identification, she realized. It was the same look a glutton might give to a plate of gooey cream puffs set in front of him.

Only she wasn't a cream puff, and Jerry was going to find that out the hard way.

The shock of locating him was fading as her mind started racing through the possibilities. She'd found him, sure, but at this point keeping contact with him was like trying to grasp water. He could walk any minute, and she'd be in the same spot she'd been in five minutes before.

Establishing some kind of connection with him, even for a moment, was imperative. Right now she didn't even know his room number, and the hotel desk clerks resolutely refused to budge on that matter. Cultivating a staffer might help, but who knew how quickly that would pay off? She needed to get to Jerry now.

The two men moved toward the archway that led to the bank of elevators. Gwen's decision was instantaneous.

"I have to run for a minute," she said to Del without taking her eyes off Jerry.

"But we were having such a good time." He followed her gaze. "Ah. I see. Find your man?"

She glanced back at Del quickly. His look told her she wasn't fooling him even a little. It was something she couldn't afford to think about, though. She hurried toward the bank of elevators, turning the corner just as Jerry disappeared inside a car.

"Hold the elevator," she called out desperately.

She saw him move toward the control panel of the empty car, but the door was already closing. Gwen could only stand and watch in helpless defeat as it went. And then she looked at the sign above the car. Express elevator to concierge level. Penthouse suites. Either he was visiting someone or that was where he was staying.

Seething with suppressed fury, she walked back into the casino. The little creep had cashed in her grandfather's stamps so that he could roll around in a five-hundred-dollar-a-night suite. She gritted her teeth. She'd get the rest of the stamps back somehow, some way.

And she'd get Jerry while she was at it.

"You run well in heels," someone said. She turned to see Del.

She flushed—she could feel it. A more accommodating guy would have taken the hint, but no, he just hung around. Until she could convince him that nothing was going on, she'd have him keeping an eye on her—surveillance she could ill afford. "I thought I left my phone in my room," she lied.

He gave her a skeptical look. Embarrassed, Gwen moved her gaze to the wall behind him. And then she saw it, the sign that stood by the door to the casino office. Circle of Champions Poker Tournament, it read. Enter Now. "There's a poker tournament?" she asked blankly.

"Yeah." Del watched her. "Texas Hold 'em. It starts Saturday. What do you think I'm doing here?"

"You told me you were writing a story on poker," she said, resisting the urge to shout. The casino suddenly felt stifling, as though there wasn't enough air.

"Exactly. I'm playing in the tournament and writing a first-person series on what it's like."

Gwen stared at the sign. Oh, it fit. It was exactly the way a slick little operator like Jerry would think—use the stolen money as a stake to win even more. Or lose it, but guys like Jerry never thought of that. They always looked for the easy way. And if she wanted to keep an eye on him… "Are they still taking entries? Do you think I could get into it?"

"Got ambitions of winning a bundle?"

"You have no idea," she said grimly and opened the glass door.

GWEN STOOD IN LINE BEHIND half a dozen people, waiting her turn at the registration counter. A slender auburn-haired woman in low-cut white pants and a lace-up leather vest walked into the office and stared at the tableau. "You have got to be kidding," she said in disgust as the men all stared at her. "I so do not have time for this." She got in line behind Gwen and tapped her foot impatiently.

"You could come back later," Gwen pointed out.

The woman shook her head, what looked like real diamonds glittering in her ears. "Too close to the limit as it is."

"There's a limit?"

"Uh-huh. Seven hundred and twenty players, period. World Series of Poker lets in anyone who can pay the fee.

Unlike some casinos that don't want to let us make any money." She raised her voice.

"You talk foul, Roxy, you're not gonna get in," called the gray-haired clerk at the counter.

"Do my registration for me, Tommy, and I'll make it worth your while when I win," she tossed back.

Tommy just snorted.

Roxy jiggled on the balls of her feet, then turned her attention to Gwen. "So, I haven't seen you at one of these before." She looked at her assessingly.

Gwen shook her head. "I just happened to be in town and figured I'd give it a try."

"Gotta get your kicks while you can, right? You play a lot?"

"I've got a weekly home game."

"Watch out, honey bunch, 'cause this is a whole different ballgame. You might think twice about that ten K you're about to cough up."

Gwen glanced at her with pursed lips. "This wouldn't by any chance be a move to get me to drop out of line, would it?"

"Shoot, that obvious?" Roxy asked in disgust. "I'd better brush up before the playing starts." She grinned, sticking out her hand. "Roxanne Steele, last year's champion."

"Nina Chatham." Gwen shook. "So, you won last year, huh?"

Roxy nodded. "Finished just out of the money in the World Series main event, too. That's right, boys," she said more loudly, "the chicks are moving in."

"I got a place you can move into, Roxy," said the man at the front of the line as he walked away from the counter.

"In your dreams, Buchanan." She slapped hands with him as he walked by and turned back to Gwen. "So, a weekly home game, that's it?"

"Well, one of the players who used to be in the game was a high-stakes regular in Reno, so we got it second-hand." Roxy's pitying look got Gwen's back up. "Another guy competed in last year's World Series. He pushed us all into studying up so we'd be better to practice against."

"How'd he do?"

"Not great. Fifty-fourth."

Roxy whistled. "Fifty-fourth out of twenty-seven hundred some-odd players is pretty damned good. You ever beat him?"

"Took a couple of pots from him in our last game," Gwen said with enjoyment. "One of them was a bluff on a pair of treys."

"Nice," Roxy said admiringly. "You might just have the chops for it. Maybe I'll see you around. After all, we chicks got to stick together."

"Don't we just," Gwen murmured.

DEL STOOD, MIND BUZZING. HE knew what she'd be doing inside—filling out paperwork, handing over the ten-thousand-dollar stake money, getting her number. What he couldn't figure out was why. Nina didn't strike him as the tournament type. Then again, he didn't know quite how to categorize her. One minute she was giving him an awkward apology, all but scraping her toe on the pavement. The next she was practically vibrating with excitement at the sight of the little hustler. Not like a woman who was intrigued or turned on, though. She'd had more of the quivering intensity of a hunting dog pointing at its quarry.

Maybe she was right. Maybe he was so hung up on investigating stories that he *was* imagining things. Maybe it was all in his head.

Then again, maybe it wasn't.

He waited for her to come out and fell in alongside her

as she walked, her hands full of rule sheets and tournament information.

"So, I guess you made it in." He gestured at her paperwork.

"I don't have time to talk with you right now."

"Do you know anything about how the tournament works? You don't have a lot of time to find out." She stopped impatiently and turned to face him, mouth open to say something. Del held up his hands. "I'm not trying to bug you," he promised. "Have lunch with me, I can help you out."

She gave him an indecisive glance.

"I'll keep it to poker, I swear."

"All right," she said reluctantly.

He steered her into a café and held up two fingers to the hostess. "You're in the second half?"

Gwen nodded. "It starts Sunday night."

"Saving the best for last."

The hostess led them to a table and seated them. Del opened his menu. "So, you know what you're doing?"

"Why does everybody keep asking me?" she snapped. "I'm going to do just fine in this tournament. I might just surprise you."

"She said with steely determination in her eyes."

Gwen glowered at him. "Don't mock me."

"Sorry. Bad habit. I've seen you play blackjack. Granted, it's not Texas Hold 'em, but you look like you can handle yourself okay."

The waitress stopped for their drink order.

"Thanks for the vote of confidence," Gwen said when they were done. "I'm just glad I got in."

"I'm impressed. You make a decision and you go for it. Gotta love a woman who walks around with a spare ten grand in her purse for emergencies."

"That's what cash advances are for," Gwen said breezily, though the reminder of the stake money required for tournament play made her stomach clench. She dearly hoped all those years of playing poker with her grandfather were going to pay off, because otherwise she'd just tossed away a huge chunk of her future. "Sign and smile."

"And think about the bills later?"

"I'm too busy worrying about how I'm going to spend the other nine hundred and ninety thousand of the prize money."

"An optimist, I see."

"Remind me to gloat at you when I accept my check."

A mural of the Strip covered one wall, showing casino after casino, from the Venetian down to the glossy black pyramid of the Luxor. "God, what a weird town this is," Gwen said, shaking her head.

"How so?" Del took his beer from the waitress.

"Well, look at it." Gwen gestured, waving at the Eiffel Tower of Paris, the pyramid of the Luxor, the pumped-up Manhattan skyline of New York, New York. "It's like Disneyland on steroids. You've got all this kid-friendly stuff, you've got the roller coasters and the wave pool at Mandalay Bay and Circus Circus and then you've got taxicabs advertising strip clubs, complete with photos and call girls in the hotel lobbies."

"Call girls? Here?" He looked around hopefully. "No one told me."

She fought a grin. "I just think it's a strange mix."

"So if you feel that way, why are you here?" The look, she saw, was back. "I mean, you came for a getaway, not the tournament. Why here? Why not San Diego or Mexico?"

Gwen busied herself taking the wrapper off her straw. Her and her big mouth. That had been Gwen talking, not Nina, who probably loved the luxe decadence of Vegas. Then again, Nina never apologized or explained about anything. *Brazen it out,* she reminded herself. "Anyplace that's going to let me turn fifty bucks into two hundred is okay with me. Anyway, the tournament's worth it all."

"That's right, you're planning on winning the million."

"Just watch me."

8

PRACTICE, GWEN THOUGHT AS SHE walked through the casino. If she was going to be even remotely competitive against a field of more than seven hundred in the Texas Hold 'em tournament, she needed practice. As much as she cringed at the idea of sacrificing another few hundred dollars to the Las Vegas gods, Gwen knew it was a necessary evil.

As were the tight, low-rise turquoise pants she wore. The fact that her devotion to aerobics and Pilates meant she could fit into them and still breathe did little to make her comfortable with the admiring stares she earned as she walked into the poker room. She'd find a table with both men and women and play a few hands just to get limbered up, she figured.

She walked up to the entrance to check out the rules posted and then stopped. "Oh, yes," she whispered, staring at the table across the way where Jerry was sitting. What better way to strike up an acquaintance than over a friendly game of poker? She fluffed her hair and licked her lips. Who knew, maybe they'd hit it off.

She'd make sure of it.

A squadron of butterflies skittered around in her stomach as she neared the table. What if Joss were wrong and he recognized her? Stewart had laughed at the idea of her undercover. Maybe it was ludicrous. What if all she accomplished was to tip him off that he was known? What if he wouldn't talk to her at all?

And what if he did?

Okay, so what if he did? She squared her shoulders and took a deep breath. Nina could handle him. Nina knew how to have guys eating out of her palm and she'd have Jerry, too. Gwen remembered the way he'd looked at her that afternoon. *Like taking candy from a baby,* she told herself.

And tried to believe it.

Besides, she had experience now striking up an acquaintance with someone she thought could give her information. She'd done it the night before and it hadn't been a disaster.

Outside of finding herself the next morning with one very inquisitive man, of course.

That didn't count, though, she told herself hastily. She had zero intention of winding up anywhere near a bed with Jerry. The very idea of his hands on her raised the hackles on the back of her neck.

Jerry turned to look at her as she stopped. "Well, hello, there."

"Hello, there, yourself." Gwen pulled out a chair. The sign said the limit on bets was ten dollars minimum and twenty dollars maximum. It would fit in her budget so long as the cards went her way. "Room for another player here?"

"This seat here is the lucky one," he said, patting the chair to his right.

"I'm sure it is, but I'll take my chances," Gwen said, sitting on his left, where she'd generally bet after him. The later, the better was her motto. It wouldn't hurt her a bit to take some of Jerry's money.

"I see you know the game."

She gave him a provocative smile. "Sugar, I know every game there is."

To her left sat a couple of guys she figured for conventioneers out for the night. They were like Mutt and Jeff— one tall and narrow, one short and plump.

To Jerry's right sat a middle-aged couple wearing wedding rings. A horseshoe dangled from a silver chain around the woman's neck. From their accents, Gwen pegged them as from Arkansas, maybe, or Oklahoma. From the fumbling way they finished out the hand, she pegged them as beginners. The conventioneers, she'd reserve judgment on. Jerry, she figured, was a player—or at least fancied himself as one.

Gwen passed a handful of twenties to the dealer.

"New player, change a hundred," the dealer said briskly and pushed a stack of five-dollar chips toward Gwen.

"Sorry I couldn't hold the elevator for you this afternoon," Jerry said to her as the dealer swabbed the deck around on the table in front of him, then gathered it together for the more conventional shuffle.

"I'm flattered you remembered me."

"Oh, I'm good at the important stuff—cards and women. Shoot, I almost stopped and came back down for you."

"What a prince."

"Yeah, that's me."

The dealer gathered the deck together and tamped it a few times on the table. "Blinds?" he called.

"That's you, Fred." The woman nudged her husband. She sat in front of the white plastic disk, or button. Fred was to her left, which meant that he bet first throughout the hand, starting with the small blind, a required bet of half the minimum—in this case, five dollars.

"I guess that makes me the big blind," Jerry, next to Fred, said with a leer that Gwen ignored. Carelessly he flicked out the table's minimum bet required for the big blind; the two five-dollar chips clicked as they hit Fred's.

With a flick of the wrist the dealer dealt them their pairs of facedown pocket cards. Gwen pulled up the corner of her cards to discover a pair of queens. She allowed herself the luxury of a small frown. "I thought you promised me luck," she complained to Jerry.

"I can't guarantee the cards, doll, I can only guarantee me."

"Big talk," she scoffed.

"I'll show you how big, if you want."

Gwen resisted the urge to groan and instead ordered a martini from the waitress who stopped by. Maybe it would help her ignore the fact that he was a cretin. Judging by the sound of Jerry's voice, he'd already knocked back a few himself.

Fred folded without laying a bet down, frowning at the five-dollar chip he'd sacrificed to the small blind. Jerry seemed to like what he had, tossing out a ten-dollar chip. Gwen nibbled her lip. He might have something, but then again, her pair of queens made her competitive right off the bat. With a made hand, she could afford a little risk. More importantly, she needed to drive players away from the table and get Jerry to herself. Quickly she doubled Jerry's bet.

The conventioneers matched her with confidence perhaps fueled by the beers at their elbows. Fred's wife turned a chip over and over again in her hand before nervously tossing it out.

The dealer turned over the flop—the first three of the community cards—to reveal an ace and two nines. Two pair for Gwen, though given that everybody at the table could count a pair of nines from the flop, it didn't really mean much. The queens, though, they gave her a nice, warm feeling.

The betting came around to Jerry. "You going to bring luck to me?"

"Probably as much luck as you bring me," Gwen returned.

"You sit here long enough, I can guarantee you'll get lucky."

Gwen didn't cringe. She congratulated herself for that. Nina wouldn't. Nina wouldn't care how classless his innuendoes were, so long as she achieved her goal. Gwen raised and watched the betting continue. Fred's wife folded before the next community card—the turn card—which was a queen. Gwen gave a mental hallelujah. If all went well, she'd make a little money on the deal.

When the betting came back to her, she raised—and substantially. It was time to see just what the convention-eers were made of.

Mutt didn't hold on to see what the dealer would turn over for the river card, the last of the five community cards. Instead he folded. *Conservative,* Gwen diagnosed. He'd be hard to break but might be easy to push away from the table with a series of high bets, assuming her luck held. Jeff checked, playing wait and see and also giving the scent of blood in the water. Jerry raised.

"You gonna keep up with me?" he asked with a wink.

Gwen smiled and called, matching his twenty dollars in chips and adding twenty of her own. "I'll leave you in the dust." She flicked her gaze to the side as she said it, though, adding a bit of false bravado to her voice. He had something, she figured, maybe two pair, maybe the start of a straight, but probably not enough to beat a full house.

She nodded to the dealer for the river card. He turned it over to show a two. Jeff folded, leaving only Jerry and Gwen. The betting went around again, with each of them raising. Finally Jerry checked.

Gwen gave him a smile like a cat at a dish of cream. "Full house," she said, flipping over her pocket pair.

Jerry blinked. "Well, hell," he said feelingly, not bothering to turn up his cards.

Gwen raked in the chips. "Looks like I brought that luck, sugar, just not for you."

DEL WALKED UP TO THE POKER room, tuning out the familiar hubbub of the casino. With the tournament due to start in just a couple of days, he was itching to log some time at the tables. Granted, he was writing about an average guy's experience at the tournament, but he had a couple of ten spots riding with various hecklers at the paper who were betting he wouldn't last the first day of play.

Practice made perfect—so said his mother and every coach he'd ever had. A couple of hours at the tables, he figured, couldn't hurt.

He looked over the room, searching out a table that seemed favorable. And saw Nina curled up at the table with the hustler, giving every appearance of being charmed. Del watched for a moment, felt the clutch in his gut that was becoming familiar.

Okay, so why did he care? Maybe she was the type who liked variety. With looks like hers, he couldn't blame her. And yet for every minute she was the man crusher, there was an instant when she looked like an uncertain teenager playing dress-up. Like the contact lens that morning, he thought with a smile.

Only idiots got hung up on women who didn't want them, he reminded himself. Then his eyes narrowed as the little hustler brushed a hand over her shoulders. She tensed for a moment, almost flinched. It was small, but Del saw it, just as he saw her take a breath and then, he swore consciously, lean closer to click her glass with the hustler's. Like a woman who was pretending to have a good time.

And suspicion rolled back over him.

It was none of his business—hadn't she told him that just that morning? He'd do well to listen to advice and leave well enough alone. Del Do-Right, his sisters had always called him in amusement. Always ready to help the maiden in distress. She wasn't his to save, though she might just need saving.

He watched her flinch again at the hustler's touch and consciously loosened his jaw. It wasn't his problem. Then again, he'd come downstairs for some poker practice. Why not be congenial, play at a table where he knew someone?

And he walked over.

FRED AND HIS WIFE were long gone. Mutt had taken a look at his dwindling supply of chips and decided to call it a night. Jeff had followed, leaving the table to Jerry and Gwen.

"Want to move to another table?" the dealer asked.

"No, this is perfect," Gwen told him, admiring her own stack of chips.

"Looks like it's down to you and me," Jerry said, leaning toward her.

Just what she'd been hoping for.

"Not exactly," said a voice over Gwen's shoulder, and Del Redmond sat down beside her. "Evening." He handed a pair of hundred-dollar bills to the dealer.

"You want a bigger game, pal." Jerry threw him a look of sulky dislike.

"This one suits me fine," he said pleasantly and reached out for his chips.

The waitress came by to take a drink order from Jerry. Gwen took a swallow of her martini and leaned toward Del. "What are you doing here?" she hissed.

He gave her a bland smile. "Just getting in a practice game before the tournament starts." He leaned forward to look across her. "You playing in the tournament?" he asked Jerry.

"Yeah."

"Me, too. Del Redmond." He reached out to shake hands.

"Jerry Messner."

"I'm doing a story for the *San Francisco Globe* on the experience. Maybe I can interview you later."

The dealer cleared his throat. "The game, gentlemen?"

This time the chemistry was totally different. There were no amateurs at the table, and Hold 'em was a game designed to encourage big bets. Del took a stack of chips between the fingers of one hand, splitting it into two stacks and riffling them together like cards. She remembered how those hands had felt on her body, the way they'd made her feel.

And wasn't that just the last thing she needed to be thinking about? *Pay attention to the game,* she scolded herself. Nina wouldn't let it get to her. Nina would put it in a box and set it aside. Nina wouldn't be so blown away by chemistry because Nina would be used to it. Nina would be in control.

Gwen only hoped she could be.

This hand, Jerry was the small blind. Gwen tossed out her bet for the big blind and turned to see Del watching her with that look that said he knew a joke and she and Jerry were the punch line.

She wondered if he was as good at Hold 'em as he was at everything else.

Her pocket held a ten and a king, both clubs. Potential for a straight or a flush, but not one she was going to bank on unless the flop turned up something. Then again, attacking might throw both men off balance. Jerry bet twenty dollars in chips. She raised him twenty. Del merely lifted an eyebrow and kept up.

Then the dealer turned over the flop to reveal a three of clubs and a ten and a five of spades. The pair of tens gave her something, but she was going to put her faith in the turn card and the river card. *In the meantime bluff,* she figured and did what she usually did when she had a good hand.

"Now, don't you go doing that again, babe," Jerry told

her at her frown, tossing down a pair of ten-dollar chips. "Last time you did that, you were sitting on a pair of ladies."

She raised him. "You figure I got something sweet?"

"I don't," Del said. "I think you're bluffing."

Now she did frown for real. Trust him to read not only her face but her body language, whatever part of her that was telling the truth. Her leg, she realized. It was bobbing, and he could see it out of the corner of his eye. "Big talk," she said aloud, consciously trying to relax.

Tonight Del wore black jeans and a white shirt, the sleeves rolled up to his elbows. The little things impinged on her consciousness: the clean scent of him, the way his jaw was just a bit dark with the day's growth of beard, the look of his lean wrists as he reached down and tilted up the corner of his pocket pair for a look.

She remembered how he'd looked with nothing on.

"Your bet."

Gwen jumped and glanced to see Del grinning at her. Jerry had put down twenty on the flop. She doubled it. When Del raised on that, she nibbled the inside of her lip. The turn was a jack of clubs.

When she had her chance, she raised, then raised again.

The dealer turned over the river card to reveal a club. She could have kissed him. With a disgusted noise Jerry folded. It was down to Gwen and Del.

"It looks like you're pretty good at Hold 'em," he observed, nodding to her pile of chips and tossing down the ten-dollar minimum. "I didn't expect to see you down here tonight."

Gwen immediately raised him twenty. "I figured I needed to get warmed up," she told him.

"I thought you were pretty hot already." He called and looked at her.

She paused for effect, checking her pocket cards and tapping her finger against them. It was worth seeing if she could draw him into another raise. She began bobbing her leg again.

Del raised her. Gwen smiled and checked. She flipped her cards over. "Wall-to-wall clubs." She gave him a challenging stare. "Don't know me as well as you thought you did."

"Oh, yeah, I do." He turned up his pocket cards to show a full house.

She uttered a sharp, pithy curse.

He raised his eyebrows. "Pretty spicy language there."

"I don't like being played."

"You'd better go home now, then," he told her.

It reminded her of why she was there in the first place and she turned her attention back to Jerry as the dealer shuffled. "So, when's your first round in the tournament?"

"Tomorrow." He sounded petulant, out of sorts at being ignored.

"Well, here's to luck, then." She raised her glass to his and licked her lips.

"Maybe I'll get lucky."

"Maybe you will."

Gwen played the next hand more conservatively. Her pile of chips was down after the big loss to Del and she needed to recharge. The flop turned the single king in her pocket into a pair, and the river made it a trio. Del, to her disgust, folded early, but she was able to lure Jerry into betting enough that she had a solid take when they finished the hand.

"You better leave me with some of my money, babydoll," he complained, "or I won't have any of it to spend on you."

"You got plans to spend money on me?" She turned away from Del, deliberately ignoring him. It made her more conscious of him than ever. When Jerry reached out to brush his fingers through her hair, he caught her unawares and she jerked back just a bit.

"Take you out for a drink after. They got that fancy revolving bar at the top of the hotel. How about if we play a few more hands, then go on up, have a nice time?"

She gave him a warm smile of promise. "I can't think of anything else I'd rather do."

"That sounds good," Del said from behind her. "Why don't you let me buy you two a drink? I can interview you both about the tournament."

She could have spit. He was nothing but trouble. He'd already figured out she wanted to get Jerry to herself and seemed hell-bent on sabotaging her. "Oh, I think three's a crowd. He and I have plans to—"

"Can I have a fake name?" Jerry cut in suddenly, as though not tracking the conversation too well. The tequila sunrises he'd been sucking down all night seemed to finally have begun blurring his words. "I mean, I don't want to show up as me."

Del's expression was harmlessly affable. "Sure, we can give you a pseudonym. People just want the story." He signaled to the dealer to consolidate his chips. "Why don't we call it a night here and go chase down some liquor?"

Anger vibrated through her as they walked from the poker room to the bank of elevators. She didn't know what he thought he was up to, but as soon as she got a chance, she was going to find out. Better yet, she'd jump down his throat first, ask questions later. The casual brush of his fingertips in the small of her back as they passed through a crowd of people had her tensing. She could feel his touch through her shirt like four small coins of heat. "Hands off," she snapped.

"You say something, babe?" Jerry asked, knocking obliviously into a woman passing on his other side.

"Not at all. I'm looking forward to the view."

A large party of conventioneers milled about at the express elevator that led to the revolving bar. When the doors opened, Jerry crowded in with them. Del gripped Gwen's arm and held her back. "We'll catch the next one," he explained, waving at Jerry as the doors closed.

As soon as the car was gone, Gwen whirled to him. "What in the hell do you think you're doing?" she snapped. "You are *not* invited to this little jamboree."

"It's been a long night. I figure I could use a drink."

"I need to talk with him."

He shrugged. "So talk with him."

"In *private*. Is it that hard for you to believe that I'm interested in someone else?"

His stare was direct. "It's hard for me to believe that you want him."

"Everything was going perfectly until you came along," she muttered, stomping onto the express elevator as soon as the doors opened. "I was having a good time."

The door closed, leaving just her and Del inside. "Really?" He punched the button for the restaurant. "You didn't look like you were having much fun at all."

Suddenly the space felt very small. Gwen leaned against the brass railing that encircled the glass arc of the elevator and swallowed. "What's it your business?"

Del stepped closer to her. "That's what I keep asking myself. There's no real reason I should care, but I watched you flinch every time he touched you and I didn't like it."

"I didn't flinch."

"Sure you did—just a hint, before you caught yourself." He ran his thumb across her cheek and sent heat singing through her. "You might have convinced him because he's too drunk to see it, but it didn't fool me."

Suddenly she felt a little dizzy. "And who made you the expert?"

"I know how you act when you want to be touched," he said, leaning in toward her. "Remember?"

"You're jealous," she managed, feeling his lips a hair's breadth away from hers.

And then his mouth came down on her. All day she'd been pushing him back, setting up defenses, trying for distance. In one swift move he stripped them all away. In one swift move he showed her how desire could slice through it all. She thought of herself as strong; he made her weak. She thought of herself as calm; he made her wild. She thought of herself as controlled; he brought out the frenzy.

And, oh, it felt right. She knew she should be worrying about Jerry, she knew she should be worrying about the stamps, but all she could think about was the soft, driving heat of Del's mouth, his body against hers. It felt so right, washing away the creeping unease Jerry's frequent touches had built. She felt clean and right and ready. She wanted more. With a soft sound Gwen pulled herself closer.

He didn't know what drove him. It wasn't her challenges, though she'd thrown them out with abandon. It wasn't the way she looked, drenched with sexuality. It was the bright spark of her, the riddle, the complexity, that drew him in. Knowing that she wanted him, knowing that she didn't want to, knowing that she would yield to him in spite of herself.

Knowing that they weren't finished with each other yet, not by a long shot.

The elevator slowed and Gwen jerked away, breathing hard. "This is my time with Jerry and I don't want you here," she said intensely, turning away as the car shuddered to a stop.

"Maybe you can ask him about Rennie."

Quick as a flash she rounded on him. "Don't you dare mention that name," she said urgently, gripping his forearm with surprising strength. "This is not a game, Del. I don't know what you think you're doing, but you have no idea what's at stake."

Del shook his head. "What's going on, Gwen?"

"It's none of your affair."

"It's pretty hard to walk away from. You're pretty hard to walk away from. Show me what you're holding."

She shook her head, eyes turbulent, mistrustful. "They're my pocket cards, Del, and they'll stay down." And as the doors opened, she turned away.

9

"HELLO?" THE VOICE WAS FROGGY with sleep.

"Joss." Gwen held her cell phone, her hands-free cord connecting it to her ear as she walked down Flamingo Road, away from the Strip.

"What time is it?" Joss croaked. Something thudded to the floor in the background.

Gwen gave a half smile. "Seven." The morning air was cool, the casinos out of sight and out of mind behind her. The constant atmosphere of the gambling had begun to stifle her. Out here she could almost breathe.

"Great. You have all day and night yesterday to call me and you pick the crack of dawn today instead." Gwen heard the sound of a jaw-creaking yawn. "Your timing is perfect."

"I wanted to catch you before you got busy."

"I was busy. Sleeping."

"Sorry."

"Well, I'm up now, so talk. Why didn't you call me yesterday? What's going on?"

"I found Jerry."

Joss choked.

"Are you okay?" Gwen asked in concern.

"Yeah. Just took me by surprise there. You do get a kick out of springing things on a person, don't you?" She coughed again. "So, what happened? Did he recognize you?"

Gwen studied her reflection in the window of a video

store. "Hadn't a clue. Although he was pretty well oiled at the time, so that might have had something to do with it. He's quite a drinker, our Jerry."

"What about Rennie? Did you find out anything there?"

"Not exactly. I found a guy I thought was Rennie," she said, her mind drifting to Del. Absently she found herself touching her mouth with the fingers of one hand.

"And?"

"And nothing." She dropped her hand. "It was a mistake." Exaggeration of the year. She frowned. "I don't want to talk about it."

"Why'd you bring it up?"

"No reason."

Joss made a sound halfway between a snort and a laugh. "I've known you pretty much since the first day you could talk and you've never said anything for no reason. Who's the guy? What's his story?"

A palm tree planted during some long-ago urban-renewal project curved up from a niche in the sidewalk, its fronds making a basket-weave pattern of shadows on the pavement. Looking down the street, Gwen could see reddish-purple mountains rising in the distance. "I'm not sure."

"You're dying to tell me, I can hear it in your voice."

"I'm not—"

"Never argue with your older sister."

Joss was right, she was dying to tell someone. And before she knew it, the whole story came tumbling out.

When she'd finished, she could hear Joss clapping. "Honey bunch, your first one-night stand. You've grown up."

"Don't be smart. I could have screwed up everything."

"Oh, don't be such a drama queen," Joss said impatiently. "Did you have fun?"

Fun didn't quite describe it. "It was pretty amazing."

"Amazing enough for a rematch?"

"Joss, let me just worry about Jerry."

"I don't see how the two have anything to do with one another."

"Because Del's a reporter, remember? He's decided something's up and he won't let it go."

"Well, something *is* up."

"And he's the last person who needs to know that. We've got enough to worry about right now without winding up on the front page."

"Do you really think he'd do that?"

Why not? Gwen wondered. He didn't know her and she certainly didn't know anything about him. "I don't know. I just know I'm trying to work Jerry and he keeps getting in the way and I can't get rid of him."

"Do you really want to?"

"What I want to do is get back the stamps and I can't do it if he shows up every time I try to get Jerry to give me something I can use," she said impatiently.

"What's your plan?"

"I've got to find out if Jerry's got the stamps with him and the only way I'm going to do that is to get into his room." Simple enough, as plans went. Only the execution was tricky.

"So bribe a maid."

Gwen turned so that she was cruising along Paradise Road, parallel to the Strip. "Oh, yeah, I'm sure they help with break-ins all the time. Besides, I think he's on concierge level."

"So?"

"So that means getting into a special elevator that requires a passkey and past the host up there and then getting into the room. It's not going to be easy."

"It's four and a half million, Gwen. Easy is too much to expect."

"Yeah. There's an upside, too, though."

"Yeah?"

"Jerry's fenced three of the store inventory stamps that I can tell, but according to Stewart's sources, no one's making noises on the market about the really valuable ones. That gives us some time." Gwen only hoped it would be enough.

"Want me to come out? I could stay out of sight."

"No. You've got to watch the store. Besides, someone's got to be around in case Grampa calls."

"Yeah, I know." Joss blew out a breath. "So, back to this Del. What do you want to do about him?"

What did she want? Gwen sighed.

"Hey," Joss laughed. "You sound like your dog just died. Has this guy actually gotten under your skin?"

"I don't know. Every time I get within ten feet of him I get this incredible urge to either strangle him or to rip his clothes off and boff his brains out."

"Well, at least you're clear about things."

Gwen rolled her shoulders. "I can't think about him right now. I just can't. I've got more important things to worry about." Four-point-five million, she couldn't forget.

Not even for Del Redmond.

IN THE ENORMOUS BALLROOM the mass of people at the tournament reception ebbed and flowed like some giant amoeba. Chandeliers glimmered overhead. In the corner a band played a Jimmy Buffett tune, the music only slightly louder than the hubbub of several hundred voices talking all at once. It was the sort of scene Gwen avoided like the plague.

These weren't normal times, though, and if there was even a chance of running into Jerry, she had to take it. So she'd forced herself to put on the magenta slip dress, pin on her competitor's ribbon and make an appearance. She'd scout around, she told herself, see if she could find Jerry and lure him to dinner. Liquored up a bit and bathed in the warmth of wide-eyed female fascination, who knew what he'd say? It should have been a piece of cake.

She'd never expected to walk into party central.

Standing just inside the doorway, she gave herself a silent pep talk. Taking a deep breath, Gwen prepared to dive in.

"Coming to meet the players?" asked a voice behind her.

She turned to see Del. He wore a pewter silk shirt and black jeans. His eyes were very green. No matter what words had passed between them the night before, he was a familiar face, and Gwen found herself smiling at him in relief. "Where did this mob come from?"

He shrugged. "Well, they've been telling everyone who walked into the casino for the past week to come tonight and meet the players. Appears everyone took them up on it."

"Came for the food and open bar, more like it," Gwen said.

"Same difference. The point is to get 'em here, get 'em all loose and excited about playing. When they're ready to leave, the only way out is that nifty little escalator outside that goes down to the casino."

"Convenient."

"And no accident. I'm sure the cost of this is a drop in the bucket compared to what they'll haul in from all the little stops their guests make on the way out."

"Cynical."

He shook his head and gestured for her to walk ahead of him. "Realistic."

They wove their way farther into the room, past the various gambling tables that had been set up around the perimeter, from roulette to blackjack. They stopped in a little clearing where the craps table was located.

"I guess they're trying to give us a little variety." Gwen nodded at the croupiers.

"Maybe the craps tournament is next week."

"Now there's an id—"

"Hey, poker chick," a voice called from behind her. "How ya doing?"

Gwen turned to find Roxy, resplendent in a pair of black leather pants and a silver halter top. Laughing, she carried two bottles of beer in each hand.

Gwen nodded at the bottles. "Planning ahead?"

"Nah. I'm here with a couple of the guys and I lost a bet. Loser had to go to the bar." Adroitly she managed to drink from one of the bottles without spilling. "So, who's your good-looking friend?"

Gwen turned. "Roxy, this is Del Redmond. Del, this is Roxy Steele. Roxy won the tournament last year."

"Congratulations. You planning to do an encore?"

"Maybe." Roxy winked at him. "Are you a player or just her rooting section?"

Del's lips twitched. "A player, but I'm pretty good at rooting, too."

"Tall one, aren't you?" Roxy stared up at him.

"Guilty as charged."

"So, when are you up, stretch?"

"First wave," he told her.

"Great. I'll give Nina here a list of the guys I want you to bust out of the tournament for me, okay?"

"Consider it done."

Someone shouted Roxy's name from down the way. "Okay, I'm being paged. Hey, nice to meet you. I'll see you at the final table." She raised one hand with bottles in jaunty salute and walked off.

"So that's Roxy," Gwen told him with a laugh.

"And the world of poker will never be the same."

Gwen gave Del a thoughtful look. "She's right, you are a tall one."

"One of my many fine qualities. It's particularly helpful in getting the attention of the bartender. Can I get you a drink?"

"Sure. How about a cosmopolitan?" Gwen told him.

"More girlie drinks?"

"I am a girl, in case you hadn't noticed."

He looked her up and down. "Oh, I've definitely noticed."

He was as close to her as he'd been in the elevator. He'd kissed her, she remembered, pressing her back against the glass, his mouth hot on hers. System suddenly humming, she stared at him.

And a drunken partygoer pushed them apart, en route to the craps table.

It was enough to break the spell.

"I'll go get those drinks," Del told her, backing away.

Gwen nodded and watched him walk off, lean and rangy in his black jeans. She didn't want to think about the moment that had just passed. She didn't want to think about the night before. She didn't want to think about him. Instead she cast about for a distraction.

A shout from the craps table behind her caught her attention and she took a few steps over to watch. At her end of the table a bearded man in a polo shirt blew on the dice in his hand and tossed them to the far end. When he frowned disgustedly, she figured he hadn't gotten the results he'd hoped for. The croupier hooked the dice with his stick and handed them back.

Taking the dice, the bearded guy glanced around and stopped when he saw Gwen behind him. He tossed the dice a bit in his palm and held them out. "A kiss for luck?"

Gwen grinned and pressed her lips to the red cubes. He threw them out and a cheer erupted.

"So, can I get you to give me a kiss for luck before the tournament starts tomorrow?"

She turned to see Jerry at her elbow. Involuntarily she tensed, then consciously forced herself to relax and give him a slow smile. "Well, I don't know. If I give you luck, then I won't have any for myself."

"Just stick around me." He smirked. "I guarantee you'll get lucky."

"So you've told me." Gwen surveyed the reception crowd. "You ever been in a tournament before?"

"First time," he admitted, taking a swig of the beer he held. "I figure I'm a natural, though. I've been doing pretty well in the poker room all week."

"Except last night," she pointed out.

"You had an unfair advantage."

"What was that?"

His eyes shifted, his gaze skating somewhere below her clavicles. "I was being a gentleman."

"Careful. Real winners focus," she reminded him.

"Oh, I'm focused all right," he said with a lascivious smile, "and I'm already a winner."

"Really?"

"A big winner. I don't even need to win this tournament. This is just for fun."

"Really?" Ignoring the rush of excitement, she moistened her lips and leaned closer. "Tell me more."

Jerry puffed up like a peacock in his bright blue shirt. "Well, I—" He stopped, frowning, and reached in his pocket for his cell phone. With a glance at the display, he flipped it open. "What do you want?"

The cockiness became, if anything, more pronounced, but his eyes narrowed with purpose. This wasn't a social call, she thought, this was business.

"Look," Jerry said, "you get what you pay for. And if

you don't pay, there's a penalty. Deal with it." He glanced over at Gwen. "Just a second," he said into the phone. "Hey, babe," he said to Gwen, "I've got to take this. Give me five minutes, I'll be right back and we can pick up where we left off." He sauntered back toward the door.

Gwen watched him go. Just what kind of deals did a guy like Jerry have in play, she wondered? A deal that involved the Post Office Mauritius, possibly? Could she afford not to find out? She drifted after him, trying to ignore the twinge of guilt she felt at abandoning Del. It had just been a funny little moment. It still didn't make any sense to be involved with him. She was here to get a job done.

Glancing out in the hall, Gwen spied Jerry behind a seven-foot-tall ficus in a waist-high terra-cotta planter. He leaned against the wall, his back to her as he spoke into his phone. She crept nearer.

"Hey, I agreed to do a job for a reasonable price. Then you sit there telling me you can't come up with it. That's a problem." He paused. "Price jump? Think of it as a late fee, my man. You increased my cost of doing business. It's the law of supply and demand in action. I've still got what you'd call a supply, and you've got the demand."

Gwen could hear the squawk of protest from the phone. "Oh, give me a break. We went over this already," Jerry said impatiently. "You're lucky I'm still talking to you. Come up with the rest of the money and we'll do business. Otherwise, leave me alone, I'm busy."

He was silent again, then laughed a bit. "Sure, sure, you wanna go with the installment plan, fine. You give me your installments and I'll give you mine. That's more like it. I knew you had it in you." Suddenly he straightened. "Here? What are you doing here?" He began to pace back and forth a few steps, tension vibrating in his voice. "I told you I'd come to you. Where the hell do you get off…okay, okay,

I'll come meet you. But don't get any ideas about getting cute. The merchandise is safe and I've got a couple of guys watching my back who know what's going on. You want to see your goodies, you'll play it clean." He hunched over the phone, now totally absorbed. "All right, all right, fifteen minutes."

Gwen stepped hastily back toward the door as he hung up the phone. Then she stepped outside as though looking for him. Flipping his handset closed and tucking it away, he walked back toward her.

"Hey, baby."

"You ready to party now?"

"I'm ready to do everything," he told her with a wink as he stopped beside her. "But I gotta go meet a guy right now. I'll be back soon, though."

"The party'll be over by then," she said with a pout.

He slid his fingertips up and down her arm. "Maybe we can have ourselves a little party of our own, then."

It made her skin crawl, but she didn't react. She was Nina, and Nina used the power at her disposal to get what she wanted. "Don't be gone too long."

"Half hour," he promised and leaned in. For a kiss, she realized, turning at the last minute enough to deflect it to her cheek.

"Hurry back," she said, standing in the doorway and watching him walk away.

"I got to hand it to you, you don't waste time," Del commented from behind her. There was a little edge to his voice and he stood holding their drinks and watching her steadily. "Strike out?" He stepped out into the hall to stand with Gwen.

"Not exactly," she said without looking at him. She was a little embarrassed, but it was outweighed by equal parts of hope and anticipation. This was her first real chance to find something out and she couldn't afford to let it pass, even if that meant looking like a get-around gal. She flicked him a distracted smile. "Thanks for the drink but I've got to go."

Jerry was just stepping onto the escalator to the ground floor. If she hurried, she could keep him in sight.

10

IT WASN'T HIS BUSINESS, DEL thought as he watched her hurry away, the skirt of her pink dress swishing. Then again, sticking his neck into what wasn't his business was starting to become habit, at least where Nina was concerned. He watched her walk off, bright and leggy and gorgeous. He had to be out of his mind to keeping worrying about her. For a couple of minutes there, it had actually felt as if they'd reconnected. Then, the minute he'd turned his back, she was running after Jerry again.

Why couldn't he let it go? Why couldn't he let *her* go?

The problem, of course, was that he had a pretty good idea it wasn't chemistry that had her chasing Jerry, any more than it had been chemistry the night before. Something was going on.

And wherever a little hustler like Jerry was running off to at a minute's notice, it couldn't be anywhere good.

Del set the drinks on a nearby bussing tray and brushed off his hands. It really couldn't hurt for him to follow along.

JERRY GOT OFF THE ESCALATOR on the ground floor and sauntered through the broad concourse that surrounded the casino for all the world, as if he had nothing on his mind. Maybe he didn't, Gwen thought, trailing him from as far back as she dared, focusing only on keeping his blue shirt in view. The phone call she'd overheard had sure sounded like an assignation between uneasy allies. More to the point, it seemed to involve some sort of property that Jerry was holding. Now, maybe it was perfectly innocent and aboveboard, in which case she had no business being nearby. But maybe, just maybe, it had to do with stamps.

And if so, she couldn't run the risk of missing it.

The horizon was dark and the air was cooling off when she stepped out onto the Strip. Even on the crowded pavement she could see the royal blue of Jerry's shirt bobbing with his stride, moving away from her in the direction of the Venetian. In her magenta dress she'd have been conspicuous anywhere else, but the crowd of tourists and hawkers and working girls on the sidewalk masked her quite effectively.

The gondolas floated serenely through the fake lagoon of the Venetian as Gwen walked by, not hurrying, not dawdling, always watching the back of Jerry's neck. Keep him in sight, that was all she needed to do. Keep him in sight, see where he went and who he met. Hopefully she would learn something.

Hopefully she could figure out what it meant.

A passing pedestrian bumped into Gwen, turning her half-around. She brushed off his apologies and started forward again, then stopped.

Jerry was nowhere in sight.

Panic washed over her. She couldn't lose him now. He could have gone anywhere—into a casino, into the liquor store on the corner, into a passing cab. She hurried the last few steps to the liquor store and peeked around the corner. A block down the street he sauntered along.

Now she faced a problem. On the boulevard she was inconspicuous. On a deserted side street all it would take was one glance back from him and she'd be busted. She wasn't sure he'd buy sexual jealousy as her reason for being there, or if she wanted to deal with the fallout of that particular excuse. Still, he didn't seem to have the least concern about being followed. It was worth taking a chance, she thought as she turned the corner herself, walking past the posters advertising specials on rum and vodka. The Dumpsters in the alley behind the store were overflowing, redolent with the stench of ripe trash.

Suddenly an arm swept around her from behind. Fear sprinted through her. A hand clamped over her mouth before she could scream. "Where do you think you're going?" someone whispered harshly.

She struggled uselessly. He was bulky but strong and dragged her effortlessly back into the alley. The hand on her mouth made it hard to breathe. She struggled against panic. Who was he? A mugger? A rapist?

"You keep being nosy, you're gonna get hurt."

She twisted against him. Then the words he'd whispered penetrated her brain and a new fear arose.

And a new need to escape.

Galvanized, Gwen raked her heel down her attacker's shin, digging in viciously, and stomped the spike into his foot. Her reward was a bellow of pain. She twisted away from the hands that held her, stumbling toward the mouth of the alley, and opened her mouth to scream.

"You bitch, you're going to pay for that. You—"

A form hurtled toward the attacker.

It was Del.

The assailant ducked back so that his reach missed its mark. Del backed up, balanced and surged in with a pair of quick punches, balletic in their form, ferocious in their violence. "Nina, get out of here," he yelled, ducking a right hook from the attacker.

She could only stand frozen, watching their struggle. Del struck again and a fountain of blood erupted from the assailant's nose and mouth. Groaning, he sagged over onto the ground.

Del ran to her. "Come on, let's go."

It was only when they were back among the lights of the Strip that the reaction hit her and she began to tremble. Del stopped once they were in front of the Doge's Palace at the Venetian and safely among the crowd.

"Are you hurt?" he demanded brusquely, his hands on her shoulders.

"No," she said, her voice more unsteady than she'd like. "No," she said again more strongly. "I'm fine."

"Who was he, Nina? What did he want?"

"I don't…a mugger, I guess. I've never seen him before."

Del paced away from her and then turned back.

Her hands began to shake. With an effort she fought it back. She was not going to fall apart.

Del studied her. "Come on, let's get you back to the hotel," he said abruptly.

"I'm fine. I don't need your help."

"I'm doing it for my benefit. I'm not going to be able to relax until I know you're inside and safe."

"I don't need you to take care of me."

"Goddammit, Nina, don't argue. He's long gone. Just admit that you missed it this time out and call yourself lucky. Now come on."

She should have fought. She would have fought, but she was suddenly exhausted. "All right."

DEL SHUT THE DOOR BEHIND THEM and slapped on the dead bolt. He watched Nina make her way to the sofa. The trembling that had worried him became more pronounced until she was shaking hard.

It made him feel helpless. He wished for the Nina who spit and snapped, the Nina who'd toss him out on his ass.

Anything would be better than the terrifying paleness and air of fragility that hung around her. He prayed that she wouldn't cry. That would do him in.

Turning to the armoire, he opened up the door that hid the minibar refrigerator and pulled out a small bottle of vodka. He dumped it unceremoniously into a glass and handed it to her.

"Drink it."

She didn't question, just took an obedient swig. Instantly she broke into a coughing fit. When she'd finished wiping away the tears from choking, she seemed steadier. Though she still held the glass, knuckles showing white, she looked a little more like the Nina he knew, the one who gave as good as she got.

He drew up a chair to face her and sat down. "What's going on, Nina?" he asked flatly.

"What do you mean?"

"No more stories. The door's locked, it's just you and me. Time to stop pretending. I think that guy wanted something and it wasn't your money." He didn't want to think about the sick, cold fear that had clutched his throat when he'd looked into the alley and seen that animal with his hands on her. Instead he concentrated on his frustration.

"I don't know what he wanted."

"Okay, let's do this another way. How about you just tell me why you were out there to begin with?"

"What were you doing there?" she flared.

She was recovering, he noted with relief. "To keep an eye on you."

"I don't need taking care of."

"No?" he asked grimly. "You sure looked like it tonight."

"I didn't need your help," she snapped. "I'd broken free of him."

"Yeah, you could run a long way in those shoes."

"I've taken self-defense courses. I know how to handle myself."

Del rose and began to pace. "Something's up. You're in some kind of a mess—it doesn't take a genius to see it."

"I can take care of my own business."

"Like you did back there? Goddammit, Nina, tell me what's going on."

"Why?"

"I don't know. Maybe because I care what happens to you, although the reasons for that might be escaping me right now." He stopped. "I can help you if you let me."

She stared at him, eyes huge, face pale. It was as though she were trying to see inside of him. As though she were trying to decide whether to trust, even as he was trying to figure out whether she was scamming him. Finally she sighed.

"For starters, my name's not Nina."

AS THE VODKA SNAKED ITS WAY into her system, the trembling eased. In the bright lights and comfort of her room, she could forget the way it had felt to be gripped in the darkness, the fear that had choked her. Del crossed back to sit in his chair and she moistened her lips.

How much to tell him was the question. She could trust him, but how far? She took a breath.

"I worked with Jerry in San Francisco. He managed to steal some merchandise, some very valuable merchandise, and I'm trying to get it back." She took another belt of the vodka. It slid down more easily this time.

"Are you an investigator?"

She shook her head. "Just a person."

"What was the merchandise?"

Gwen straightened her spine. "Stamps."

"Stamps," he repeated.

"Rare stamps. Some of the issues he took are one of only a handful that exist in the world."

"Did you call the police?"

"No police," she said quickly.

Suspicion flickered in his eyes. "Why not?"

"I've got my reasons."

"That's not good enough."

"It'll have to be," she flared.

He nodded. "I'll hold on to that for now. Okay, what are they worth?"

She hesitated. "In the low seven figures."

"What!" he said explosively. "I don't care what your reasons are, call the cops."

"No."

He frowned. "You're not being straight with me."

"I am," she protested.

"You're not. Were they stolen property to begin with?"

"No, of course not." His eyes said he didn't entirely believe her. Should she tell him more? Could she trust him with all of it? Caution, innate to her, took over and she remained silent.

"So Jerry worked with you?"

She nodded.

"Then why doesn't he know who you are?" Again the skepticism.

"Well, he was new. I didn't have a whole lot of contact with him. I mostly worked in the investment part of the business. Jerry worked up front, in the store." She glanced down uncomfortably. "Also, I don't usually look like this."

"Like what?"

"You know…" She gave an embarrassed shrug. "Nina. Blond. Tight. My personal style is a little more toned down."

"No wonder you've been so hard to figure out. I thought maybe you just had a split personality. So who's Rennie?"

She closed her eyes. "I'm not sure. It was a name written in a matchbook I found at Jerry's. It had the number of the casino here, so I figured Rennie might know where to find him."

"Which is why you were all over me when you thought I was Rennie."

"It's less important now that I've got an in with Jerry."

Del nodded. "So, what happens now?"

"Get close to Jerry, find out if he's got the stamps with him. Search his room if I can. I think he's too dumb and disorganized to have done anything with most of them. He's sold a few of the more common stamps he boosted, probably for living expenses. A friend of mine confirmed it with the dealer." She set down the vodka now, absorbed. "I think he's working with someone, someone he was going to meet tonight."

"Which was why you were following him."

"Bingo."

"What about the guy who jumped you?"

"I don't know," she said quickly.

"He looked a little too nicely dressed for a mugger."

"Maybe. I'd think it was random except for something he said when he first grabbed me."

"What?"

"I don't remember exactly. Something about where did I think I was going." *You keep being nosy, you're gonna get hurt.*

"A warning, maybe?"

"From who, though?"

"Maybe he's working with someone?"

"I don't know." She tilted her head consideringly. "I thought at first that Jerry had lifted the stamps on his own. Now I wonder. When he was talking on the phone, it was almost like he was ransoming them."

"A commission job, maybe."

"Maybe. Then again, that conversation may have been about something totally different."

Del nodded. "Jerry's still the key, though."

"Absolutely. I keep thinking if I can flatter him enough and get him drinking, maybe he'll talk."

"And maybe he'll expect a little something from you after the talking's done," Del said with an edge to his voice.

"Nina can take care of herself."

"I'm sure she can, but how about Gwen?" He gave her a searching look and took her hands.

"Gwen's doing okay."

"Yeah? Well, maybe you don't have to go peddling your virtue to Jerry to get information. He and I are well on our way to becoming buds."

"You are?"

"Yeah. I'm supposed to interview him tomorrow. Once he gets talking, who knows what he'll say, particularly after a few beers."

"Great minds think alike. I figured I'd drag him out for a drink after play is over. If he's won, he'll be cocky. If he's lost, he'll want to drown his sorrows."

"I don't like the idea of you being alone with him."

"We'll be in public," she reassured him.

"What if I come along?"

"Del, you can't. He won't talk if you're there, not like he will if we're alone."

"I still don't like it," he muttered. "Not after tonight."

Gwen looked up at him. "Why are you doing this?"

He hesitated, staring back at her as if trying to figure it out himself. "Maybe I just can't resist a puzzle. Besides—" he reached out and tucked her hair back behind her ear "—I have a soft spot for Nina."

The sweet, simple gesture rocked her and, illogically,

tears threatened for the first time since the incident. She looked down.

"I'm sorry, you're probably wiped out." Del stood. "I should lay off and leave you alone now."

Mechanically Gwen rose and walked with him to the door.

"I don't know how to thank you for what you did tonight."

He stopped and faced her at the door. "Shucks, ma'am, it warn't nothin'."

"I mean it. That guy could have really hurt me." And the thought of it had marched through her head ever since.

"But he didn't and you're okay. You're tough. You would have had him anyway. Now get some sleep." He leaned in to kiss her on the forehead and turned to open the door.

"Wait." The word hung in the silence. She hadn't known she was going to say it.

Del turned back to look at her inquiringly.

"Stay with me, please," she said in a rusty voice.

"You sure?"

She nodded. "Not to, you know…I just really don't want to be alone right now." Just then the idea was impossible to face.

Del turned and folded her into his arms. "I'll stay with you as long as you want," he murmured, kissing her hair. And he swung her up in his arms and carried her back to the bed, lying down next to her to hold her—just hold her—as the tears and shudders finally came.

11

So now he had a pretty puzzle on his hands, Del thought the next morning as he sat at his desk and checked voice mail. Gwen needed help, he'd offered it. But she wasn't telling him everything, and for all he knew, she could be conning him. He didn't want to believe it, thinking of how it had felt to hold the warm, fragrant bundle of her against him. The problem was, he just didn't know and he didn't know what to do about it.

He did know what to do about the call from Greg Jessup at the *Globe* city desk, though. It was probably only to set up a phone interview, Del told himself as he dialed Jessup's number. Still, it meant he had an opening, a chance.

The tones rang in his ear, then with a click the line connected.

"Jessup."

"Del Redmond, Greg. You called?"

"Hi, Del. Yeah, Perry over in sports handed along your application for our opening in metro. I wanted to talk with you about it a little if you've got the time."

If he had time? He'd make time. "Sure."

"You've got a track record with the paper and Perry gave you a thumbs-up, so I don't really need to go into the usual who, what, where. I guess what I'm really wondering is why. You've got a solid long-term career on the sports desk. Perry tells me you've got the second highest reader-response rate of all his columnists. Why are you coming after what's practically an entry-level job in metro?"

Jessup was a newsman to the core, Del reflected. No time wasted getting to the point. "I had a chance to do a series last year on the whole doping scandal. Investigative. I dug up sources, wormed my way in where I didn't belong and I came away with information solid enough that the folks running the litigation wanted to talk with me."

"I hope you cited the fifth."

Del grinned. "I told them to do their own jobs. The thing is, it gave me a taste for investigative work. I want to do more of it. Work on real stories, you know?"

"Well, that's just the problem. You understand you wouldn't get to at first, right? And you'd have to take a pay cut."

"Yep."

Jessup was silent for a moment. "I don't know, Redmond. I hear where you're coming from, but I'm just not sure you know what you're in for."

"Who've you been interviewing for this job? What kind of background do they have?"

"They're young," Jessup admitted.

"Doesn't experience count for something?"

"Not when it's all sports columns."

"It's not. Take a look at the BALCO series."

"I did. It was good work," Jessup acknowledged, "but it was still sports. I want to see how you handle something that's not a game."

"Give me an assignment."

"That's just it. If you're a reporter, no one's going to give you an assignment. There's nothing so easy as the nightly game to write up. You've got to be out there digging, fighting for the stories and getting them before the competition does. You've got to constantly be alert."

"I am digging up stories. Hell, I've stumbled into something out here in Vegas that's about as juicy as they come."

"Mob corruption?" Jessup snapped to attention.

"What would you say to a heist, a poker tournament and a couple of the rarest stamps in the world?"

"Sunday-supplement stuff."

"You think? If four and a half million's at stake?"

"That makes it sexier. What do you know about it?"

He'd blurted it out without thinking. Now he backpedaled. "Not a whole lot yet. I'm just giving you an example. The point is, I know how to dig."

"The point is, you're onto a story that we could use. You want me to take a second look at you, you'll hunt down that story."

"I don't know if this particular one—"

"This was a real story, right, Redmond? I mean, you weren't just spinning something out of your ass to impress me, were you?"

Del controlled the surge of irritation. "It's real."

"Good. Then get it on my desk."

And he disconnected with a click.

"NOW SEE, THIS IS THE WAY TO start out a tournament," Roxy told Gwen. The first wave of round one had opened up earlier that afternoon. They watched now from a few rows up on the temporary aluminum bleachers that lined the perimeter of the playing area. From there they could get a good view of the forty tables that crowded the room, supplemented by the view from the wide-screen televisions that hung overhead. "No stress, just a chance to sit back and keep an eye on the ones who are taking the big pots, see who you need to worry about in the next round."

The ballroom had changed from the night before. It was perhaps crowded with as many people, but gone was the social atmosphere. Now a sort of hyperintense circus giddiness had taken hold. Some wore outlandish costumes. Others carried lucky tokens ranging from rabbits' feet and coins to photographs. The players were a mixed bag, from guys barely out of high school who'd probably soaked up their strategy from computer simulators to craggy-looking graybeards with a lifetime of poker experience etched into their features.

"Hey, what about that hunka hunka burnin' love?" Roxy gestured to a sideburned player in a sequined Elvis-style jumpsuit. "I think I want his baby."

"I can see it now. You'll have him in an Elvis pompadour and teething on poker chips."

"Who said anything about having a he?"

Only a bit over ten percent of the three hundred and sixty people who'd opened the first wave would advance to round two, breaking the losers hand by hand. In the end only five percent of the tournament entrants would finish in the money. For now, though, everything was possible.

"I can't believe they're going to cut down all these players to forty in only two days."

"And then do it again for our half of round one," Roxy reminded her.

"I wish they'd let us just start all at once."

"Maybe they don't have enough tables. Last year they had the whole opening round start at the same time. Smaller, I guess. We just played every day until we hit their target."

"How late?"

"Eleven one night, two in the morning the next. The deeper you get, the slower they go. Minimum bets start at a hundred dollars and go up every two hours for the rest of the tournament. This group will winnow down pretty quickly. I'm guessing they'll take it until ten or eleven tonight."

"Makes my behind hurt to think about it."

"They give you breaks and dinner, so it's not so bad." Roxy propped her feet up on the bench below them. "The tough part is the way they're constantly consolidating the tables as people go out. Just about the time you get used to how one group plays, either you're getting tossed to another table with an opening or someone with a whole mess of chips drops into yours."

It made Gwen just a bit queasy to contemplate. "Why don't they just play each table down to one winner."

Roxy shook her head. "Changes the dynamics of the game too much when you drop down below six players. You lose the advantage of being the late bettor."

"On the other hand, lower pocket cards are stronger with a shorthanded table," Gwen reminded her. "You might try using a suited queen eight to beat five players where you wouldn't trust it to beat nine. I think they like to keep the pressure on."

"Keeps things exciting. That's why they let the play go on so long if they need to—when you've been at it for ten or twelve hours and you're brain-dead, that's when you find out what you're made of. Watch and learn, grasshopper. Watch and learn." Roxy stared across the room. "Hey, there's your boy. Now that is what we call in Montana a fine-looking specimen of a man."

Gwen followed her pointing finger and felt the jump of adrenaline in her system. Under the pitiless lighting over the tables, a five-o'clock shadow darkened Del's jaw. A dark gray Alcatraz T-shirt stretched over his shoulders. His hair was a little disordered, as though he'd had his hands in it. From the grandstand she could look her fill at his hollow cheeks, the firm line of his mouth. Only his eyes were hidden, behind mirrored sunglasses. The eyes were the single biggest tell in poker. Expression could be controlled, but the expansion of the pupil at a good hand or contraction at a bad hand was involuntary. Del, apparently, was taking no chances.

"I could turn into a poker groupie for a guy like that. I'm sure I could give him a few Hold 'em lessons."

"Down, girl."

Roxy gave her a sidelong glance. "Didn't you tell me before that you didn't want to get involved with him?"

"I don't," Gwen said firmly.

Roxy studied her and looked out at the tables. "Yeah, maybe I'll hold off. Never been a poacher and I'm not gonna start now."

"There's nothing going on between us."

"Oh, really?" Roxy's eyes were amused. "You've got to bluff a whole lot better than that if you want to make it out of round one, honey."

Gwen glowered at her and turned to watch the games.

Del and Jerry were playing at different tables, though as she'd already seen, that could change at a moment's notice. Still, competition at this point wasn't head-to-head so much as a matter of holding enough chips to stay alive.

"Who's that asshole?" Roxy asked, pointing.

Pointing at Jerry. He wore a baseball cap turned backward and a shiny silver Oakland Raiders warm-up jacket. Compared to his tournament persona, he'd been positively low-key when they'd played a few nights before. He was, in short, a punk. Cocky and hyper, he stood and paced, he talked to himself, he gloated when he won and sulked when he lost. "If he were at my table, I'd have to kill him," Roxy observed.

He was already earning decidedly hostile glances from some of the players at his table. Unfortunately for them, he was more than holding his own. He had that edge of instability that made him impossible to predict and could tip him into either riotous success or disaster at a moment's notice. For now, the cards were with him. His increasing hoard of chips stood haphazardly in uneven, tilted towers that he fiddled with constantly.

Del, by contrast, was a study in calm. Whether he held a made hand with a pair of aces or a hand begging to be folded, he maintained the same focused expression, watching everything, reacting to nothing.

If he was composed, he was also a predator, ruthlessly competitive, able to sniff out the weaknesses of his opponents. Traditionally the player who was the big blind was in a position of vulnerability compared to the rest of the table. Del seemed not to know that. He fearlessly attacked from the blind, throwing his competitors off balance so that at the end of the hand they discovered they'd been expertly fleeced as Del raked in their chips. He relentlessly sought out his competitors' vulnerabilities while presenting a smooth, inscrutable wall to them. His neat stacks of chips rose steadily.

Gwen had seen him play, so she hadn't expected him to be dead money in the first round, but she hadn't been prepared for his lightning attacks and parries. Jerry appeared to carelessly throw out chips on a hunch. Del wagered with an inexorable authority that made it clear he was pushing to do just what he wanted. He'd clearly mastered the other players and was picking off their chips at his leisure.

The hand at Del's table ended, and a skinny, jumpy-looking guy who looked as if he was on break from college raked in the pot. He'd knocked out one player on the hand and taken a surprising amount of chips from the others, including Del. Now the table was down to Del, the young kid and five others.

And raw nerve.

"This should start getting interesting now," Roxy murmured into Gwen's ear. "Looks like your boy's the big blind."

Gwen watched Del push out a stack of thousand-dollar chips as though they were Necco wafers. If he had no visible nerves, though, she was awash with them, her mouth dry as dust. The kid pushed out the small blind and the dealer dealt the pocket cards. With the lazy elegance of a master fencer toying with his opponent Del casually raised without even looking at his cards.

"So, does he have steel ones or are they actual flesh and blood?" Roxy whispered to her.

"They felt like flesh and blood, but they might have changed since I saw them last," Gwen whispered back.

The tension ratcheted up.

The rest of the players at the table folded after a glance at their pocket cards. Del took a quick glance at his and raised, putting pressure on his foe.

The kid rose from his chair, bouncing a little on his toes and muttering to himself. He curved his fingers around his stacks of chips. For a moment he held on, licking his lips. Then he pushed them all forward. A little mutter rippled through the crowd around the table. All in, Gwen thought tensely. It would be up to Del whether to match him or to check, refusing to bet.

The kid stared at his chips with a certain fascinated horror, paced around a little, swinging his hands.

Del sat in his chair, taut and coiled, studying the kid as much as his hand. Seconds ticked by. Nerves twisted in Gwen's stomach. Finally in a smooth, decisive move Del pushed his chips forward to match the kid.

It was like that moment on a roller-coaster ride after the first descent, when the car was racing up the next hill. The tension had eased a fraction, but everyone in the room knew that the stomach-dropping stuff was yet to come.

Both players turned up their pocket cards. It was pointless to hide anything, since no more betting was possible. The kid had a pair of kings. Del had a suited jack and ace. The rest of the hand would play out quickly.

The flop held a jack and a king. Gwen clenched her hands together. Three kings versus two jacks—the kid had him. This was it. There was no possibility of retreat. Folding was meaningless. Everything was at stake.

Two cards still remained in the hand, though, and anything could happen. The dealer flipped over the turn card to reveal another jack. It gave Del three of a kind, but the kid's three kings still outranked Del's hand.

It all came down to the river card.

The dealer laid the card facedown on the green baize. He paused a moment, with innate theatricality. Gwen wanted to scream with the tension. The kid scrubbed his hands through his hair. Del sat, as relaxed as though he were back in his room watching television.

The dealer put his hand on the river card and flipped it over.

And the ace of spades lay on the baize.

Gwen whooped and clapped before she even realized she was doing it. Del had taken the hand with a full house. He'd nearly doubled his chip count in a single hand.

Victory.

He looked up and winked at her.

"Looks like your boy knows how to play Hold 'em," Roxy observed.

"That he does," Gwen said, "that he does."

12

PLOTTING TO PLY JERRY WITH drinks and get him drunk enough to tell her something was a good idea in theory but not nearly so entertaining in practice. So far she'd been regaled with a replay of every hand of his round, though the details had been glossed over somewhat in Jerry's favor. He dragged out the description of his final winning hand that bumped him to the next round until she wanted to scream.

"An' then the flop gives me my other ace. I know these other two guys at the table and they're acting like they've got something good but the guy on the end is blinking too much and the guy next to me is beginning to sweat. I figure they're bluffing, so I go all in. Balls to the walls, you know? I figure I'll either win big or I head on up to 5111 and call it a night."

A little leap of excitement went through her. At least she had his room number now. It was a start, anyway. "What would you have done if you hadn't gotten the full house on the flop?" she asked him. "You just coughed up ten thousand to enter the tournament. That's a lot of money."

He snorted. "Chump change. I could go out tomorrow and come back with fifteen, twenty grand, easy."

"Really," she said, with a pretty good idea of just how.

"Oh, I'm set, all right. This time next week I'm gonna

be rollin' in dough. Yo bartender!" He thumped the bar. "'Nother round here. My ladyfren's fallen behin'."

The bartender gave him a glance. "I think you might have had enough, friend."

Jerry straightened up. "I think I know when I've had enough," he said, clearly taking pains to speak distinctly.

The bartender gave a long look at Jerry and a longer one at Gwen. "Buddy, everybody's got a job."

"An' yours is to pour drinks."

"It's also to take care of you. That includes not letting you get drunk and rolled by some pretty lady." He paused. "No offense," he added with a look at Gwen.

"None taken, I'm sure," she said coolly.

"I wanna drink," Jerry said obstinately.

"You go out of here and hurt yourself or somebody else, the law says it's my responsibility," the bartender told him. "You look like you've got a pretty good buzz as it is. Why don't you ride it?"

Jerry fumbled in his pocket and slapped his card key down on the bar. "I'm staying at the hotel, pal, so I ain't gonna get in any car. Now bring me a drink."

The bartender flicked a look at the security camera at the end of the bar, then back at Jerry impassively.

Jerry gave him back a stubborn stare. "Dammit, everybody thinks they know what's good for me." He stood unsteadily and leaned toward Gwen. "Gotta go…you know. Be right back, okay. Make him give us a drink." And he weaved off to the bathrooms.

Gwen sat at the bar, staring at the blue-and-gold plastic wafer of Jerry's passkey out of the corner of her eye. It practically vibrated, sitting there out in plain sight. And yet there was no way to just pick it up, not with the bartender watching her.

"Your friend's had a little too much tonight. I'd hate to

see something bad happen to him." The bartender leaned his hands on the inside of the bar and stood staring down at the key.

Gwen swallowed and pulled her shoulder bag up into her lap. "I know." She pulled out her lipstick and a small mirror and proceeded to outline her mouth.

"The safety of our patrons is our first concern." He lifted her glass and replaced the bar napkin underneath it.

Gwen finished and gave him a brilliant smile, capping her tube of lip color and sliding it back into her purse. And stealthily removing her own passkey.

"You enjoying yourself at the casino?" the bartender persisted.

"Very much." She slung her bag back over the chair back, keeping the key in her other hand and safely out of sight. *Go away,* she telegraphed to the bartender, but he was obviously in no hurry to leave and just as obviously hanging around to keep an eye on Jerry's key.

The seconds slid by and she sipped her martini. The bathrooms might have been out in the lobby, but it wouldn't take forever for Jerry to get there and back. Fighting the urge to lick her lips, Gwen palmed her passkey and rested the elbow of the other arm on the bar. And prayed. On the television monitors overhead, Paul LoDuca hit a homer over the wall in Dodger Stadium.

"Yo, service," called a guy sitting with some friends down the bar.

"Just a minute." The bartender looked at the passkey and then at Gwen, who blinked at him innocently. She casually folded her arms on the bar, resting the hand with her card key closest to Jerry's.

"Hey, buddy, can we get a coupla beers down here already?" The guy slapped the polished surface of the bar.

With obvious reluctance the bartender stepped a few

feet away to the taps and began drawing the beers. Any minute, she thought, any minute she'd get her chance. She took a quick glance at the security camera, which was panning away from her. Her pulse thudded in her temples.

The bartender gave Gwen a long stare before he turned to walk down the bar and deliver them.

As soon as his back was turned, she used her fingertips to slip her room key over Jerry's and slide his into her hand.

Score! Heart pounding, eye on the bartender, she dropped her hands back into her lap and put the key into her purse.

"Hey, babe."

Her vertical leap would have qualified her for the Olympic high jump.

"Edgy, huh?" Jerry made a clumsy attempt at pinching her butt, but she shifted out of his way.

Gwen gave a faltering laugh. "You were quick."

"Not quick at everythin'." He leered at her.

Gwen took a big swallow of her martini.

The bartender reappeared. "You get your key all right, sir?"

"Right here." Jerry held it up and squinted at him. "Do I get another drink?"

"Not here, sir. Perhaps up in your room."

"Depends if I get company," he said archly.

Gwen shook her head. "You might have made it to round two, I'm still waiting for my heat. I've got to finish this and call it a night." She tipped up the last of her martini and rose. "Congratulations on moving up." She gave him a light thump on the shoulder and walked out.

SHE WALKED INTO THE ELEVATOR, a bubble of excitement swelling in her solar plexus. By the time she hit Del's floor, it was practically floating her off her feet. She hurried down the hall.

Del opened the door almost before she'd finished knocking and swept her inside. "'Bout time. I've been going nuts here. Are you all right? Did he touch you? What happened?"

"He was a little too hammered to paw anyone, let alone Nina." Because it felt too good not to, Gwen stepped closer and pressed a quick kiss on him. "You might ask me if I found out anything," she mentioned, twirling into the room.

Del's mouth was still ajar from the shock of the kiss. His gaze flicked over her from head to toe. "Did you find out anything?"

"I did, funny you should ask. Now ask me what I came away with."

"What did you come away with?"

She held up the passkey. "Ta da!"

"Your key?"

"Oh, no. This is not my key. This would be Jerry's key." She did a little dance step and turned in a circle.

Del whistled admiringly. "Nice. How'd you manage that?"

"Oh, alertness, timing and manual dexterity."

"If you tell me you picked his pocket, I'm going to be a little scared."

"Not that much manual dexterity. He put it down on the counter and went to the men's. I managed to swap it for mine under the eagle eye of the bartender, who seemed to think I was a woman of questionable virtue looking to take advantage of Jerry's condition."

He raised his eyebrows. "Well, you have to admit you did take advantage of Jerry's condition."

"But my virtue is hardly questionable."

"I can vouch for that. So, what do you plan to do with the key?"

"Wait for the right time and search his room, of course." She sat on the high bed and bounced a few times. "He's got no address that I can find. I figure he's got to have the stamps with him."

"What if he's got them locked up in the safe?"

She grinned, eyes merry. "Oh, no. I just happened to mention what a challenging time I was having with my safe, and he told me he never uses them since the time he locked his wallet up in one and forgot the combination."

"Well, isn't that convenient," he said admiringly.

"Isn't it just," Gwen agreed.

"So, when do you think the right time's going to crop up?"

She considered. "That part's going to be a bit tricky. Any ideas?"

"Yes, but it would mean sacrifice on my part."

"Sacrifice?"

"Vast sacrifice."

She leaned back on one elbow. "Do tell."

"Well, as you know, I had an interview with Jerry today for my series of articles. You know, to get the gritty reality of life in a poker tournament."

"I'm sure that was a fascinating experience."

"Oh, it was, it was. We shot some pool, drank some beer, talked about tournaments, making the big score, you name it."

"How's his pool playing?"

"He'd better not plan on making his score that way. To hear him tell it, though, he's already got two feet on easy street. Winning the tournament will just cement it."

"Did he tell you any more about his big score?"

"Just that smart guys figure out how to get ahead."

She snorted. "I'm sure."

Del stuck his tongue in his cheek. "Also that if he didn't get laid soon, he was going to find a pro."

"'Gritty reality,' I think you said?"

"He invited me to come out with him tomorrow night

after the tournament play ends to visit a gentlemen's club and enjoy some fine exotic dancing."

"Is that how he put it?"

"No, I believe he said he wanted to go hit a titty bar and get a load of some pussy."

"That's our Jerry, charming to the last."

His eyes glimmered with humor. "I told you it was a guy-bonding experience."

"And did you take him up on his invitation?"

"I told him that to my everlasting regret I'd have to say no."

"I see. Not a big fan of gentlemen's clubs, are you?"

"I prefer private sessions with amateurs, thanks. But I'm willing to sacrifice for the cause." He leaned against the armoire opposite the bed. "It occurs to me that if I go to the gentlemen's club with Jerry, I'll be in a perfect position to keep tabs on his whereabouts and call when he heads home to warn anyone who might be taking part in a little breaking and entering."

"It's not breaking and entering if you've got a key," she informed him smugly.

"Tell that to the hotel security."

"Or not."

"Anyway, I'll look him up before the tournament starts tomorrow afternoon and take him up on his offer."

"Assuming your group reaches the magic number by a decent hour."

"We're already down below one-fifty. I think we'll do it by nine or ten."

"Leaving plenty of time for the gentlemen's club."

"Do I know how to have a good time?" He crossed over to sit on the edge of the bed. "Anyway, I'll keep an eye on him, you do your search and I'll call you when we head home. Piece of cake."

"Very nice."

"We do make a good team." He kicked his shoes off. "So, if you swapped your key for his, I guess you can't get back into your room. What are you going to do?"

"Well, I figure Jerry's going to blunder downstairs, bitching about his key not working. They'll think it got demagnetized and recode it. It happened to me one time on a trip. They don't reset the door code unless you actually lose a key. It would probably look a little funny if I go down there tonight saying the same thing."

"Agreed."

"So I figured I'd wait until tomorrow morning and tell them I locked my keys in my room. I show ID, they give me new keys, no one is the wiser."

He stretched out facing her. "Of course, that does leave you with one problem." His eyes had become very dark.

"Which is?"

"Finding a place to sleep tonight." He ran a thumb along the line of her collarbone.

It shouldn't have made her pulse jump. After all, they'd already had sex. They'd slept together just holding each other the night before. There shouldn't have been any mystery to it. But when he leaned closer, her lungs took a breath of their own accord.

"Do you have any ideas about that?" It took her two tries to get the words out.

"Depends." He stroked his hand over her cheek and up into her hair.

"On what?"

"Whether you care about sleep." And his mouth was on hers.

13

DEL SAT AT A TABLE IN THE conservatory café at the casino, waiting for Gwen to finish swimming laps and come meet him for breakfast. In the meantime he sucked down orange juice and reviewed his notes. Between hands the previous night he'd been scribbling madly and interviewing players. Now he pondered and framed his actual article.

Movement flickered in his peripheral vision and someone sat across the booth from him. It wasn't Gwen, though, but a dark-haired guy with a narrow face.

"Can I help you?"

"You're Del Redmond, right?"

Del blinked. Five hundred miles from his home, it was the last thing he'd have expected to hear. "And you are?"

"Pete Kellar, stringer for the *Globe*." The guy's speech was staccato. His chin punched the air assertively. "Greg Jessup asked me to look in on you." He squinted. "I gotta say, your head shot in the paper doesn't do you justice."

"So, what are you looking in on me for?" The kid didn't look old enough to be a stringer. He barely looked old enough to have graduated college. It didn't stop him from settling in as if he'd been invited, though. He'd apparently read all the books on getting ahead in journalism.

"I talked with Jessup yesterday about assignments. He said you were running down some kind of theft or conspiracy story. I've got contacts with local law enforcement you might be able to use."

"Law enforcement's not involved."

"You don't know that," Kellar countered. His eyes were close-set and aggressive. Del imagined he practiced the look in the mirror. "They could be undercover. What's the deal with this anyway? Jessup couldn't tell me a whole lot."

And Kellar wasn't about to find out anything further from him, that was for sure. It was pretty obvious that the kid was a scrapper, Del thought, taking a drink of his juice. Kellar wanted to make points with the story, prove himself. "It's still too early to say what's going on. I'm just looking into things."

"Pass me a list of your sources, let me help."

Fat chance, kid. "I'm all set for now. Give me your card and I'll call you if I need anything," Del said pleasantly.

He held the card between his fingertips and looked at it. Stringer was an exaggeration. The card said freelancer, which explained Kellar's eagerness. He was probably looking for a means to shoehorn his way into the *Globe* organization. Jessup no doubt figured it couldn't hurt to have two people working on the same story. Or fighting over it— some editors believed in editorial Darwinism, and Jessup just might be one of them. Well, the story wasn't going to give Kellar a way in, that was for sure. If anyone was going to get mileage out of this story it was going to be Del.

He glanced across the room and saw Gwen walking in under a tree fern. "My breakfast date is here," Del said, "and you're in her seat."

"An interview?" Kellar's eyes lit avidly.

"No, just a date."

"Oh." Kellar rose. "Okay, I'm out of here. You'll call me?"

"I'll let you know if I need anything."

Kellar took a long look at Gwen and gave an appreciative nod. "You do that." He walked away.

Gwen arrived at the table and gave Del a kiss. "Who was that?"

"Just a guy I know."

She glanced at the business card on the table. "A freelance newswriter? Just a guy you know?" She stared at him a long moment, but he didn't say anything.

"Well, let's order some breakfast."

VEGAS WAS ALL ABOUT transporting reality: the Manhattan skyline of New York, New York, the gondolas of the Venetian, the scale-model Eiffel Tower of Paris. Restaurants like Nobu of Manhattan and Olives of Boston had established branches in the desert to cater to the more discerning palates of the visitors accustomed to luxury. She wasn't so surprised to see them, but she'd never in a million years have expected to discover an outpost of the Guggenheim there. The themes were still typically Vegas—the pursuit of pleasure—but the quality was surprising. Not only that, it was right off the gaming floor, so gamblers could take in art in between hands of cards.

"So, how do you want to do this?" Del asked her.

The polished wood underfoot rang as they walked through the open gallery. The blond maple ceiling soared overhead, above the copper-colored walls.

"You mean tonight?"

"Well, we could talk about your gallery strategy, but yeah, I think talking about tonight would be more practical."

Around them the space was mostly empty. Gwen guessed that the slots and gaming tables held more appeal for the guests than fine art. Most would duck in to see the exhibit just so they could say they had, so they could feel a little less dissolute after a week spent eating, drinking and gambling.

"What time are you meeting Jerry?" She stopped in

front of a painting of a group of peasants drinking in a tavern, a red-faced man playing a guitar and singing a no doubt ribald song, judging by the expressions on the faces of his audience.

"When play is done. Ten or so, I'm guessing. We'll grab bar food at the strip club."

"Lucky you. Is he planning on making a night of it?"

Del circled around a Rodin marble of Romeo and Juliet clasped together in a frozen desperation, passion in the touch of their hands, the lines of their bodies. "I'm guessing Jerry will get there, knock back some drinks, get a few lap dances. After that, who knows? He strikes me as the kind of guy who wouldn't blink at going looking for a pro."

"Class act all the way," she said with distaste.

He grinned. "Teach you to interview a little more thoroughly in future."

"Hey, he's a con man," Gwen protested. "Everything checked out on him initially. I got the impression from my sister, Joss, that he partied, but nothing too far out of control."

"So maybe he's making up for a month of clean living."

They walked onward to a tableau of lords lying about in a forest clearing. Above their heads a woman was swinging, skirts afroth, breasts nearly exposed in her low-cut gown.

"How long do you see him staying at the bar?"

Del considered. "I don't know, a couple of hours, maybe?"

"So I should watch for you to leave, add a half hour for safety and clock an hour for the search," she calculated. "That gives me slush time at both ends."

Del considered. "I don't like it. Too risky."

"What would you suggest?"

"You've got a cell phone, right?"

She pulled it out of her purse and held up the flat silver handset. "Don't leave home without it."

"Okay, so we exchange numbers. I call you when we get there, let you know we're in. That gives you the thumbs-up to go on up to Jerry's room and search. Try not to get too messy with any of it, though, nothing you can't straighten up in a hurry. We don't want him to know you've been there."

"Aye, aye, Captain."

He gave a faint smile. "Keep an eye on your watch. Call it ninety minutes from the time I call you, no more. When we leave the club, I'll call you again, give you plenty of warning."

"And Jerry's not going to notice you wandering away to make all these phone calls?"

"At the club? Trust me, he'll be preoccupied. I figure I'll just head up to the bar or something."

"How about after? It'll look suspicious if you wander away at both the beginning and the end."

"True." He thought a moment. "Okay—I'll check my messages when we leave the club, make like I've got to call someone back for work. Instead I'll call you. That'll be your signal to beat it."

"That could work. What would the code be?"

"Elvis has left the building?"

"Funny."

"The series on search engines is over?"

"You're a regular laugh riot."

"Okay, how about this?—I'll say 'I've filed my interview.' Jerry will like that because he's the interview."

Gwen studied the painting before her, an unholy excitement buzzing through her veins. Tonight could end it all. Tonight she could find the stamps and finish this business. "I like it."

"Good. You know how to search a place?"

"I've read my share of police novels," she told him. "I

know the procedure. Besides, it'll be easier because it's not his home, it's only a hotel room."

"True."

"And stamps aren't like gems or coins. There are only so many places you can hide them."

"Well, if you want to be sure, we can go upstairs and you can practice your searching techniques on me." He pulled her against him for a kiss.

Gwen laughed up at him, her hands on his shoulders. Then she sobered. "Thank you for doing this. I'm really not sure how I would have done it on my own."

"I think you would have figured it out. Nina's a pretty tough cookie."

And Gwen wasn't. She needed to remember that. Whatever chemistry was between them existed between Del and Nina, not Gwen and Del. She gave him a quick peck and made a move to separate.

"Hey." He scooped her closer. "I don't think we're finished yet."

Nina wouldn't be, Gwen reminded herself. Nina would take all she could get. And so should she—before it ended.

FLASHING LIGHTS AND ROCK music filled the club, the bass throbbing until it vibrated Del's bones. Chrome glittered on the rack above the bar, outlining the edge of the stage, on the vertical poles that the dancers swung and twirled around.

In this environment the naked bodies of the women dancing were just another part of the glossy show, the relentless spotlights above the stage picking out one pair of pneumatic breasts after another.

Del took a swallow of his overpriced bourbon and squinted down into the glass. Maybe he should just start downing them like Kool-Aid. It would be one way to make the evening less painful.

He worshipped the female body as much as the next guy. Especially certain female bodies, he thought, remembering Gwen's curves. But sitting in a club with a roomful of horny guys staring at a cavalcade of cartoonishly well-endowed, untouchable women twisting onstage was hardly his idea of a good time. He preferred a little quality one-on-one time with a woman he could connect with mentally as well as physically.

Still, he'd promised Gwen two hours, minimum, and that was what he was going to deliver.

Jerry nudged him. "How about that redhead, she hot or what?" The redhead grabbed the pole and did something Del would have sworn was anatomically impossible. "She comes offstage, she's going to be dancing right here, partner," Jerry boasted, slapping his thighs and signaling the waitress for another beer.

"Knock yourself out," Del said and took another swallow of bourbon. "Just don't expect to get your rocks off."

"Hey, man, it's all about the fantasy," Jerry said.

Sure it was about the fantasy—guys like Jerry had the fantasy that they were going to get off with the women dancing and the women had the fantasy that they were going to empty out the guys' wallets. He had a pretty good idea whose fantasy had the higher likelihood of coming true.

He thought of Gwen, hot and silky against him, and his cock stirred. Now that was his idea of a turn-on. Consoling himself with the knowledge that he'd end his night with Gwen, he checked his watch and eased back in his seat.

THE ELEVATOR STOPPED AT THE concierge level. Gwen wiped her damp palms on her denim miniskirt and waited for the doors to open. It would be okay, she told herself. Sure, the concierge level had an attendant at the lobby bar, but that person's job was to take care of the guests, not to police them. She had a key, after all, so who was going to stop her as long as she acted as if she belonged? It was just like playing Texas Hold 'em, she reminded herself—bluff, bluff, bluff.

When the doors opened, she squared her shoulders and walked out onto the floor.

A young, blond attendant stood behind the bar in a vest and bow tie. "Good evening."

Gwen gave him a brilliant smile. "Hi."

He smiled back at her, dazzled.

She walked by without stopping, trying to read the numbers on the doors without appearing to look too much. *Act like you belong here.*

She saw it on the right, just a couple of doors in from the lobby. Holding her breath, she slid the card key into the lock and pulled it out. With a little electronic peep and a smooth metallic snick the door unlocked. Relief made her weak. Telling herself the front-desk clerks hadn't recoded Jerry's lock the night before was one thing, being sure was another. She slipped inside and stood in the dark, waiting for her heart rate to level.

The light switches were by the door, just like every other hotel room. When the lights came on, though, it was clear that this room wasn't like any old hotel room. It wasn't a suite, it was a sybaritic palace. What seemed like half an acre of plush carpet covered the living room area, running from where she stood, past a built-in bar to a wall of windows. A glance into the bedroom showed her that it was just as large. How she was ever going to search it all in an hour, she had no idea.

Methodical. The thing to do was be methodical. She knew what she was looking for, knew that it couldn't be tucked into the bottom of a toothpaste tube. It had to be in an envelope or fold of cardboard and it had to be somewhere clean and dry. No matter how big the rooms were, there were only so many hiding places in them. It would be easier because she wouldn't have the kitchen area to go through. Or much of one, she amended, glancing at the built-in bar, with its glossy black marble counter and back-lit bottles of liquor.

She started in the living room, moving around the perimeter from the door, checking the back sides of the art, the mirrors, the undersides of the lamps and side tables, the back of the armoire that held the television. She pulled out every drawer she could find, checking the backs and undersides. The area behind the bar had a surprising number of them, not to mention bottles of liquor and boxes of snacks. None of them were opened up, though, so she figured she was okay.

She turned the couches and chairs on their sides, checking to see that the bottom fabric hadn't been cut or disturbed. She checked under cushions, along piping, between the springs in the back of the couch. Puffing a bit, she checked under and behind the television. She checked the corners of the carpet to see if it had been pulled loose.

No envelopes were to be found.

NIGHTS COOLED OFF QUICKLY IN the desert, Del thought, taking a deep breath of the chill air.

"Fucking dipshit bouncers," Jerry groused, brushing sidewalk grit from his hands. He picked up his cell phone from where it had fallen from his pocket onto the ground.

"Rules say no touching the lap dancers," Del said mildly.

"I didn't touch her."

"Jerry, you had your hands on her tits."

"She liked it."

"You figure that was when she was smacking you or when she was calling for the bouncer?"

"Assholes," Jerry mumbled. "Throw me out on the street. I was spending good money in there."

"And I'm sure they loved you for it."

"You coulda backed my play, y'know."

"Sorry, buddy." Del gave him a friendly pat on the shoulder. "I make it a habit to avoid fighting bouncers with scar tissue around their eyes. It's not a real healthy pursuit."

"Yeah." Jerry stumbled a bit on the sidewalk, though it was perfectly even.

"So, what now? Want to stop somewhere else?"

"Nah. We go into another bar and they'll just pull the same bullshit. Let's go back to the hotel."

Del pulled out his cell phone. "Gotta check my messages," he said briefly and dialed his voice mail. He listened a moment, then cursed for form. "Frigging editors think they own you," he muttered, skirting a man handing out handbills in front of an arcade. Dialing Gwen's cell phone number, he prepared to give her the code to flee.

And his phone beeped and flashed No Signal.

A shiver of alarm whisked down his spine.

14

GWEN STEPPED INTO THE BEDROOM and checked her watch. The bathroom hadn't taken long. She'd used a little over forty-five of her allotted ninety minutes. A half hour or less for the bedroom and she'd be out. Systematically she began checking under the mattress, under the box springs, on the back of the headboard, searching for an envelope taped in place. It wasn't underneath or behind the armoire, though she wasted precious minutes wrestling the piece away from the wall.

Did the fact that it was empty mean that he didn't have the stamps with him or that he'd hidden them somewhere else? It didn't pay to think the latter. She needed to search everywhere she could to be sure.

So she opened up the doors of the armoire, pulling out the first drawer with a sigh.

"WHY DON'T WE DUCK IN HERE and get a couple of bourbons?" Del nodded at a cocktail lounge as they walked through the casino.

Jerry shook his head. "Hell, forget that. I got a suite with a bar. We go up there, put some triple-X on the tube and have our drinks there."

"Wouldn't you rather go see some live bodies?"

"Not if they're gonna toss me. Besides, I'm out of fives."

He pulled his key out of his billfold. "I'm gonna go on up. You coming?"

Del pressed redial on his phone, but he couldn't get a line out. He glanced at his watch. An hour and a half, they'd agreed. An hour and a half after the start, she'd be out. It hadn't been quite that long, though. Now, it was always possible that she'd been hyperquick. She could have finished already, be riding the elevator down or even safely back in her room with the stamps. She could be safely out of harm's way.

Or she could be knee-deep in Jerry's things.

They were coming back without warning, earlier than he'd promised. If she were in the room, there'd be no good excuse and no telling what might happen. At best, security and arrest. At worst?

With a sense of increasing desperation, he followed Jerry onto the elevator.

GWEN SLID THE LAST DRAWER back into the armoire. Carefully setting the swinging upper doors back where they'd been, she backed away and gave a final check to the room. She'd taken care to put everything back in its initial position. Not that Jerry would even know, given his obvious tendency to throw things around and generally make a mess.

She wouldn't give in to dejection. Just because she hadn't found it didn't mean it wasn't there to be found. She just hadn't looked in the right spot.

Gwen walked back into the living room, mentally ticking off all of the places she'd checked. She glanced at her watch. An hour and twenty minutes. She could afford five more and still have a margin for error. Time for a tour of the room to see if she'd forgotten anything.

She walked slowly and carefully, stopping occasionally to double-check a possible hiding place. Then she passed by the bar, with its glossy marble counter. She glanced behind it and stopped. The refrigerator. She'd checked behind the televisions and behind the safe, but she hadn't checked behind the refrigerator in the bar.

And time was rushing by.

She hurried back behind the polished peninsula. Quickly she crouched in front of the refrigerator, sliding her hands into the nook that held it. It was a close fit, impossible to fit both hands.

Swearing, she struggled to grip it in the narrow cabinet and shift it enough to check one side at a time. She moved it half an inch, then an inch, easing her hand back. She felt smooth metal and polished wood. She inched her fingers back a bit more—

And touched paper.

Adrenaline sprinted through her. It might be just a piece of paper that had wound up there. It probably was. But maybe, just maybe, it was an envelope.

She licked her lips and bent to push the refrigerator again.

And something knocked against the outer door.

Her heart leaped into her throat. Wildly she looked around for a hiding place, then realized the lights were still on. She could hear it now, the rustling of someone working to get a key into the slot. Her heart slammed into her ribs as she careened across to slap down the light switches, cringing at the sound of Jerry's loud and drunken voice outside. She ran back to the center of the living room and stood like a hunted creature at bay. Not the bathroom, not the closet.

Outside the card key snicked into the lock.

And she dived behind the counter of the bar.

"HERE WE GO," JERRY SAID drunkenly. "Is this a room or what? Just need a coupla chicks up here and we're in business."

Jerry'd become more hammered as his last drink from the club had hit, Del observed. Unfortunately he appeared to be one of those drunks who hit a certain level of inebriation and just stayed there, soused but alert to a point.

And focused on a goal.

Jerry stumbled to the couch and fumbled for the TV remote, staring at it blearily. "Hey, we need a coupla beers over here. I'll take care of the ennertainmen'." He managed to get the television on and squinted at the on-screen menu, trying to focus.

"I'll get the drinks." Del walked past the couch toward the bar, every atom of his being on alert. He couldn't see a sign that she'd been there, but he knew she had. He wondered if she was still in the room—there was a better-than-average chance that she was. He scanned the room, looking for likely spots.

And froze at the sight of a silver cell phone sitting on an end table.

"Scopin' out m'digs, huh?" Jerry said from behind him.

Del looked over his shoulder at Jerry on the couch as he walked toward the bar. "I thought you were working on the entertainment."

"Friggin' remote don' work." Jerry's voice was petulant and slurred.

Jerry's alcohol saturated vision didn't work, more like it. "Let me grab a couple of beers, I'll see what I can do," Del said over his shoulder. He deviated off course just enough to scoop up the phone, the back of his neck tingling as he waited to hear Jerry say something. Jerry was quiet, however, preoccupied with the remote.

She was still here, Del thought wildly, ticking off a list of possible hiding places—the shower, the closet, under the bed. He walked behind the bar.

And stumbled to a stop.

"Trouble walkin', thass it, y'cut off," Jerry mumbled.

"You better hope I can walk well enough to get your beer to you," Del threw back distractedly, staring at Gwen curled up in the furthest corner of the little U behind the bar. He pulled open the door to the little refrigerator mechanically, yanking out a couple of beers and setting them on the bar as his mind raced through his options.

One thing wasn't an option—getting Gwen out the door undetected.

"You growin' the hops back there?" Jerry looked blearily back from the couch.

Del turned to pick a bottle of Wild Turkey off the shelf behind him. The harder the liquor, the quicker he could put Jerry under, he calculated, mixing himself a weak bourbon and water and doubling Jerry's. "Beer's for wimps. How about some good old Kentucky bourbon?" He crossed to the couch and handed Jerry his drink. Grabbing the remote, he sat himself. "So, let's see, we want to check out some movies here?" He punched some buttons.

"Hey, turn on Beach Babes Gone Wild," Jerry directed him. "It's got that Misty Mancos in it. She's hot."

Del had an idea, but to carry it out he'd have to keep Jerry occupied. Porn and alcohol sounded like the ticket, and if Jerry passed out, so much the better. Del waited until the film was in full swing and half of Jerry's bourbon was gone before making his move. He rose. "Gotta hit the head."

He crossed to the guest bathroom, off a small hallway just before the door to the bedroom. Focus, he thought as he flipped on the light and fan. Every second counted. As soon as he closed the door, he began unspooling toilet paper, bunching it into a wad bigger than his fist. When he judged he had enough, he shoved it down into the toilet, packing it in the drain. It would work, he hoped, and pushed the flush handle.

"Shit." He didn't entirely have to fake his outburst as the water flowed up over the edge of the bowl and onto the floor. "Goddamn it," he complained, bursting out into the living room.

"What are you bitchin' about?" Jerry looked over from the television, where two stupefyingly endowed women were wrapped around one another.

"Your plumbing. The damned thing is pouring all over the floor. Get in here and look at this."

Jerry levered himself off the couch and stumbled over to the bathroom. "Ah, shit, what a mess."

"Hey, not my fault." Del stood at the door and glanced back to see Gwen peeking over the counter. He jerked his thumb toward the door and stepped back into the bathroom and closed the door. "Maybe if we flush it again."

"No, don't—" but Jerry didn't get a chance to finish the sentence as the water overflowed again. The noise effectively masked the faint click of the door, which Del was pretty sure he heard only because every fiber of his being was attentive for the sound.

The sound of Gwen getting to safety.

GWEN PACED AROUND HER ROOM, too amped on adrenaline to even sit down. Nearly an hour had passed since she'd stumbled through the door. Still, her system stubbornly refused to level. She'd tried to pour herself a drink but her hands had shaken too badly. Had Jerry heard anything? Was Del all right? It had all turned out to be a nightmare, especially since she'd walked away with nothing.

During the nerve-wracking walk from Jerry's room to the elevators, she'd fought to remain relaxed, taking her time even as every fiber of her screamed to run to the exit. A smile and nod to the concierge, as though she had all the time in the world. When the car came, she'd stepped on board, heart thudding, giving in enough to press the 'close door' button.

It had only been when she'd shut the door of her own room, safely inside, that she'd taken a full breath. And another, and another, until she still felt in danger of hyperventilating.

The sudden knock on the door made her jump. It was probably nothing, she told herself, but her imagination painted security standing outside the door instead, ready to lock her up for breaking into a guest room. She looked through the peephole.

It was Del.

He burst through the door when she opened it and pulled her to him, his arms coming around her hard. "God." He held her. "That scared the hell out of me." He pressed his face into her hair and inhaled.

Held close to him, Gwen finally began to shake, really shake, as though she could let loose because he was there. "It did a number on me, too, when—"

His mouth was on hers before she finished, hard and demanding. And that quickly the adrenaline residue of fear flashed over into passion. All she could register was need. She wanted his skin against hers, his body on hers. She wanted him inside her. And most of all she wanted it now.

It wasn't about romance. There wasn't a vestige of anything soft or tender about it. It was pure passion, hard and rough and uncontrolled. All the anxiety, all the tension, all the frustration of the past several hours poured into the heat of their fused mouths. Magnified by fear, desire became manifest.

Gwen gloried in the feel of Del's hands moving roughly over her body. She wanted it fast, she wanted it urgent. Every atom of her body seemed supernaturally sensitive. His teeth scraped against her lower lip and she moaned. His hands slid down to squeeze her breasts and she caught her breath. His fingers slid up under her skirt and she cried out. In that instant she felt supremely alive.

She tore blindly at his shirt, wanting it only off, not caring how. When he stripped her tank top off over her arms, she caught herself to him, nipping greedily at his shoulder, his throat. "I want you inside me," she murmured feverishly, leaning over to the bedside table for the condoms they'd left there. "I want your cock. Now."

With a noise of frustration Del turned her around and bent her over the couch, pushing her skirt up over her hips. When he saw and felt the warm curves of her framed by the red silk of a thong, it almost undid him. Gritting his teeth, he held on long enough to free his aching cock and roll the condom on even as Gwen reached back to touch him, stroking the lightly furred skin of his balls, the tops of his thighs.

And he thrust himself inside her.

Gwen cried out, her head arching back as she clutched at pillows, pushing herself back against him.

It was too fast, too hard, too rough, he thought in some sane part of his mind. But he'd stood by while she'd been in danger and now some primitive instinct drove him to mark her as his. Her tight, wet heat around him dragged him closer to the edge of control with every stroke. Her breasts filled his hands. She surrounded him, inflamed him. As he drove himself home, as he felt her shudder and contract around him, he pulled her hard against him and spilled his soul into her.

The silence was broken only by their breathing. When he thought he could stand without falling over, Del pushed himself upright. "Oh, man," he muttered. "Oh, man."

"You can say that again." Gwen stood shakily, one hand on the couch.

"Are you okay?"

"I'm not okay." His heart clutched as she turned to him. "I'm fabulous."

It took him a moment to catch up. "Yeah, that was…you were okay with that?"

"It was incredible." She sat on the arm of the couch and let herself fall back onto the cushions, stretching her arms out languorously. "Of course, if you wanted to give me some basis of comparison, I could give you a more accurate assessment."

He grinned. "Coming up, ma'am."

"WANT SOMETHING TO DRINK?" Wrapped in a terry cloth hotel bathrobe, Gwen stood at the minibar.

"Beer, please."

She handed Del one, grabbed a bottle of water for herself. He studied her. "So, you're okay?"

"Oh, yeah." She flopped on the couch beside him. "So, what happened with Jerry?"

"Everything's fine. He's passed out." Del twisted the top off the beer and took a long drink. "I don't think he figured out a thing. You got out at just the right time. Five seconds later he was in the living room calling housekeeping. God, I about flipped when I saw your cell phone lying there."

"I know. I realized I'd left it out when I was already behind the bar. Why didn't you call me?"

"I tried to. Couldn't get a signal." As though the tension had come back, he rose to pace across the room. "So, did you find them?" His eyes glowed green with excitement.

"I think so. I'd just found an envelope when you guys came in. It's wedged behind the refrigerator, I'm pretty sure, but I couldn't get it out."

"You're kidding."

"It's okay. Now I know where it is. Next time I'll get it."

"Next time." He turned to stare at her. "There isn't going to be a next time."

"Sure there will. We'll work out a better plan." Gwen opened her water and took a long pull.

"Oh, yeah? How do you figure?" He set the beer roughly aside. "We thought this plan was foolproof and it almost blew up in our faces."

"So? We'll figure out something else," she said impatiently. "Maybe I get a new phone, or you do."

"It's too dangerous. What do you think Jerry would do if he knew you were in his room sniffing around, particularly given what's at stake?"

"Probably try to get me into bed."

"Are you even listening?"

She'd underestimated the level of his agitation, Gwen realized. She'd underestimated the level of her own. She took a deep breath. "We're both tense over this. I think we should talk about this later once we've both calmed down."

"I don't want to calm down."

"Just because you volunteered to help doesn't mean that you're suddenly running the show," she exclaimed. "This is my hunt, Del. You're not going to stand there and tell me what I can and can't do."

"You're not going to do something that's going to put you at risk," he retorted.

Gwen took a deep breath. "Okay, we both need to take it easy. I'm not stupid, Del, I'm not going to take a ridiculous chance. But I do still have the key and I know where the stamps are."

"You think you know where the stamps are," he corrected.

"I'm going to get back in there and find out for sure. Not now, though," she placated. "For now we play wait and see. If the right opportunity presents itself, then we make a move. Agreed?"

"Maybe," he said reluctantly.

"Well, it's not like we can do anything else tonight." She reached for her sash. "Do you have any other ideas for ways to keep busy?"

15

EVERYTHING LOOKED DIFFERENT when you were the one at the tables, Gwen discovered. If she'd felt mild tension in the room the previous nights she'd been in the bleachers, now she felt an anxiety and strain so thick that it seemed to weigh her down.

Why had she thought entering the tournament was the way to go? She could monitor Jerry without the crushing pressure of knowing she could lose her place at the table and her ten-thousand-dollar stake in one night. She was in it now, though, obligated to play through to either win or lose. Cashing in her chips to get her money back wasn't an option. Chips now only meant points in the game.

"You okay?" Del asked as he stood beside her.

Gwen nodded. "Yeah, sure, no problem." She grimaced. "Except I feel a little sick."

"Don't worry, you're going to do fine. Just remember, you're only playing eight people at a time. Focus on them, not the big picture."

Gwen nodded. It helped to think of it that way. "I've been playing with the same people for years. Doing this feels a lot like jumping out of the plane without a parachute."

"You've learned from those guys, though. They might have their tells, but it's harder to bluff people who know you. Take what you've learned from them and go to the next level." He squeezed her hand.

"You do a nice line in pep talks."

He gave her a crooked smile. "I like to think of myself as multitalented."

"Oh, I can definitely verify that."

The MC began to call for players to go to their assigned seats.

Gwen looked at Del. "I guess that's me."

"Okay, relax and have fun." Del leaned over to press a kiss on her. "It's a little freaky at first. Don't do anything sudden, just take a couple of hands and let yourself get used to the feel of things. You're going to do great."

Fighting panic, Gwen took a deep breath. "Swear?"

"Damn," he said obediently and she grinned.

DEL SAT AT HIS HOTEL ROOM desk the next day, punching the keys of his laptop in a rapid tattoo. He knew plenty of guys on the paper who stuck with the two-finger hunt and peck. As far as he was concerned, you did the work and learned the drill. He'd done it when he'd been playing sports and he'd done it when he'd started on the paper and taught himself real typing.

His cell phone rang and he picked it up and flipped it open. "Redmond."

"At least you're answering on the first try today."

"Hello, Perry."

"What are you up to?"

"What does it sound like I'm up to?" Del rapidly finished typing his current sentence and hit the keyboard command to save the file. "Writing a story about how two women cleaned up in their first night of play yesterday."

"Ah, the sound of a column being finished. Warms an old editor's heart."

"Save the shtick, Perry. We both know you're not even fifty yet. What's up? The series okay?"

"Better than okay. I was reading the article today on the little hustler. Got any photos of this poseur?"

"He doesn't want any photos taken."

"Interesting."

"Kinda makes you wonder where he got his stake."

"Kinda does," Perry agreed. "I don't suppose it's got anything to do with a certain theft?"

Del closed his eyes briefly. "Jessup's been talking."

"He came and asked me if you were for real or if I thought you were putting him on about this story. I told him you were many things, including an occasional horse's ass—"

"Not often," Del put in.

"Not often," Perry agreed, "but that you were not the type to put anyone on."

"He believe you?"

"He seemed to take it okay. So, what's going on? What have you bumbled into out there, anyway?"

He'd opened Pandora's box, Del thought sinkingly, and putting the story back into it was going to be a job. He'd regretted his discussion with Jessup almost immediately. Now the more he discovered about Gwen, the more he was certain that doing a story on the stamp theft was the wrong move.

The question was, what would it do to his chances on the paper if he came back now and told Jessup to forget about it? Bye-bye, news job. Bye-bye, future. "It's not as big as I thought. I'm going to check it out a few more days and report in. I thought it would be a chance to show Jessup my stuff. Now I don't know."

"You know he's waiting for you to come up looking bad on this," Perry said impatiently.

"Yeah, I know."

"If you want this news job, I'd find a way to dig up a story."

"There's a complication."

"There always is with you. Let me guess, the hustler is actually a redhead with big blue eyes and enormous—"

"No, the hustler is a nervy little guy."

"But the redhead is somewhere in the picture."

"Well, actually she's a blonde," Del admitted.

"Del Do-Right."

He'd told Perry about it in a weak moment, after a few too many beers. "A classy guy wouldn't have brought that up."

"She throw her arms around your neck and beg you to save the family farm from the villains?"

"Actually no. She yelled at me and told me to mind my own business and that she could take care of herself."

"She should know."

"Maybe. The more I find out, the more I think maybe this story is a bad idea. I've been trying to think how to handle it with Jessup."

"Oh, just telling him that you're pulling your application will probably work," Perry said lightly. "Redmond, you *putz,* reporters aren't supposed to get involved. Rule number one. You know that. He finds out you've been suckered on your first story, you won't get near his precious news desk."

"I haven't been suckered."

"Well, I hope you haven't been suck—never mind," Perry said hastily. "Anyway, it might put him off you, but it won't put him off the story. If he likes it—and he does—he'll give it to someone else. Your best bet is to file something lukewarm but well written and tell him the story didn't pan out."

"Thus pulling my application."

"Yeah, but maybe keeping him off the story."

Del drummed his fingers on the desktop. He knew Perry was right, but that didn't mean he had to like it.

And he didn't. Not one bit.

Perry cleared his throat. "It's not my place to say, but you don't know this woman. She's probably not worth throwing this all away over. Can you even trust whatever it is she's telling you?"

"Yeah." He thought, anyway.

"You don't sound too sure."

"Don't push it, Perry."

Perry was silent for a little while. "This is the first one you've really gotten involved with since your divorce, isn't it?"

"Yeah."

"Hey, I've been there, too. Divorce sucks. It's hard to swallow failure and it's easy to go looking for something to erase that. But you've been in Vegas, what, a week?" He blew out a breath. "You just met her, Del. She's not going to be the one—they never are. Trust me on this."

Del pushed back from the desk and swung his chair around so he could look out into the pitiless sun of the Las Vegas day. "Don't worry, I'm not going off the deep end."

"I hope not. You've got the chance for a new career here. Something it sounds like you want. Don't throw it away on a Vegas squeeze."

Del hung up the phone and stared out the window at nothing for long minutes. Finally he came thoughtfully back to his computer and logged on to the Internet. *You don't know this woman.* Maybe it was time he started to. He brought up a search engine and plugged in her name.

THEY SAT IN ALIZÉ, ON TOP OF the Palms casino, staring out over the lights of Las Vegas. The gargantuan hotels along the Strip looked oddly graceful by night, reduced to streaks of color—the green of the MGM Grand, the red and purple of Rio, the lighted arc of the Wynn. The twinkling lights of the rest of the town looked diamond sharp in the dry desert air.

Despite the lateness of the hour, she was still buzzed from playing. She felt alert, energized and just a little bit wild. The lighting was dim, the heavy linen draped over the tables crisp. It gave her a decidedly Nina-like urge to do something just a bit outrageous.

Del raised his wineglass. "To making it to round three and to seeing us both at the final table."

"The final table? I'd just be happy to get through tomorrow night and make it into the money rounds."

"And I'm sure you will. You ran some pretty fearsome bluffs tonight."

It was probably the relief of surviving a second night and moving forward that was making her so giddy. "Speaking of bluffs, how did you get a table here tonight, anyway? Tell them you were Phil Hellmuth?"

"You don't get reservations at Alizé the night of," he told her. "I had confidence in you."

"Really?"

He nodded. "Just like I have confidence in you in other ways. You'll get those stamps back, I know it."

"I wish I were as sure," she sighed.

"I can see why the work fascinates you," Del said casually. "I was doing some research on stamps on the Internet today."

Her head came up like that of a doe scenting a predator. "Why were you doing that?"

"I figured I ought to know more about it. Anyway, I'm a journalist. Research is what I do. And the more I know, the better I can help. So Chastain Philatelic Investments is your family business, right? Is Hugh Chastain your uncle or your brother or something?"

"Grandfather," she said. "You've been busy."

"Not busy, just curious."

"Ah, you know what they say about curiosity and cats," she scolded and he felt something brush his leg.

He looked down. "What the...?"

"Maybe it's that cat," she said smoothly, and he felt it again, this time a satiny toe stroking up against his leg, under his pants.

It brought all of his nerves to awareness. "I think you're trying to distract me."

"Oh, no, if I were trying to distract you, I wouldn't do something like this," she said, stroking his leg with the side of her bare foot. "I'd do something like this." The stroke over his crotch was quick and soft and had his cock twitching under his napkin.

"Oh, goody, here comes the chocolate fondant cake," she said smoothly as the waiter walked up. Del just sat watching them go through the ritual pouring of the crème anglaise, grateful of the drape of linen in his lap.

And Gwen savored a bite of her cake, her tongue licking over the fork even as her toes stroked his balls.

"You're enjoying this, aren't you?" he asked tightly.

She took another nibble. "Yes, you want a bite? It's wonderful."

"I'm sure." He ground his teeth.

His jacket covered up his erection as they left the restaurant and made their way to the taxi line downstairs.

Gwen stretched against him in a movement that did nothing to ease the aching hard-on. "I can't believe it's after one in the morning and we're just leaving dinner," she murmured.

"Vegas is an all-night town."

"I guess."

There was something abandoned about her tonight, something loose and open. "I hope you were happy with yourself in there," he murmured.

"You liked it?" She gave him a naughty smile. "It's a little something I've been thinking about."

"It's not a little something now."

She wiggled against him. "I feel that. I've got a few more fantasies."

"And what would those be?"

"Well, I'm living one right now," she told him impishly and took his hand to rest it on her lower back. For a moment he just savored the smooth curve of her back into her haunches until he registered the fact that…

"You're not wearing any—"

The doorman turned to him. "Where to, sir?"

With a slow grin Del handed him a tip. "Versailles, please."

The doorman leaned down to tell the cab driver as Gwen slid across the seat. Carefully, he noticed, grinning broadly.

"Hey, kids," the cab driver said, "we having fun tonight?"

"Nothing but," Del said blandly.

The vinyl seat of the cab felt cooler to Gwen without her thong. Just her imagination, she told herself as the cab driver stopped at the light that led to the street. Del's hand stroked her leg. "You should be careful provoking people like that," he murmured in her ear. "They might retaliate."

And then his hand went higher. She jolted as his fingers slid up between her thighs to find her, nothing but her. To find where she was wet, already hot from teasing him during dinner, from imagining what came next.

Gwen stared at him but he looked steadfastly ahead. The first touch came when she didn't expect it, as the cabbie was checking for traffic to turn onto Flamingo Road. One minute a tease only, then the next those clever, clever fingers had plunged into her slick wetness to find her clitoris.

Gwen fought not to gasp.

"So, where you folks from?"

"San Francisco," Del said, stroking that hard nub, sliding against it in an irresistible tease that she couldn't react to. She wanted, oh, she wanted to pump her hips and moan. Instead she stayed stock-still, staring at the back of the cabbie's head while he chattered, oblivious.

"No kidding. I'm from the city, too. I moved here about a year and a half ago."

"You like it?" Del asked. He didn't flirt around with ways to tease her, just a slow, measured touch that was driving her insane, dragging her closer and closer to orgasm even as they waited at the light to turn onto the Strip.

"It's okay. I really miss the city, though, the arts community, you know. I hung out with a lot of creative types when I was there."

"Good arts scene," Del nodded, making conversation even as he was making her insensible with pleasure. He was relentless, driving her up with warm, wet strokes, each brush, each touch taking her closer to that zone where she just didn't care.

"I'm forgetting stuff already, though. I was trying to tell someone the other day about that café at the foot of Russian Hill—I can't remember the name of it."

The orgasm broke through her as Versailles came into view. Gwen made a strangled sound and tensed against the seat, trying not to shudder.

"What'd you say, ma'am?"

"I believe she said it's called Aah's," Del said helpfully as they pulled into the massive portico with its crenellated marble overhang.

"Aah's? Nope, that's not the one I'm thinking of."

Gwen took a minute to gather herself enough to get out of the cab, sliding carefully across the seat.

"That was evil," she told him as they walked into the hotel. The hour was late, and even in Vegas, there were few people around.

Del stopped and pulled her to him to press a hot, hard kiss on her. "That was hot is what it was. You have no idea what it does to me to feel you come like that, to get you that wet."

She slid her arms down his body. "You have no idea what it does to me." She moved her hips lightly against him.

"Upstairs," he said raggedly. "Now." They began to walk again. "So, tell me some more about these fantasies."

"I've been having these ideas about elevators," she whispered to him. "I keep finding myself in the car, waiting all that time to get to the top. I don't know, there's something about it that gets me thinking about the possibilities."

They stopped in front of the banks of elevators and Del unbuttoned his jacket. "Fast ride," he commented.

"But a hot one." She leaned in to take his earlobe between her teeth. "For a couple who's prepared."

"Did I ever tell you I used to be a Boy Scout when I was a kid?" he asked, pulling her close so that she could feel him hard against her. "You know their motto."

"Always prepared." His cock felt like granite to her.

"Always. Where's the damned elevator?"

Gwen rummaged in her purse to find a condom and tear open the package. "My question exactly. You're a rise-to-the-occasion kind of guy, aren't you?" she asked, kissing him with lips and teeth and tongue and pressing the condom into his palm.

"You kiss like that, you're going to get more than you bargained for sooner than you expect."

A chime rang and an elevator door opened up behind them. She stepped on and pressed the door-close button. "Oh, I hope so." She propped herself against the brass rail that ran around the car. "Top floor, cowboy."

The doors closed, the lights dimmed and control disappeared. In what seemed like a fraction of a second, Del had himself out and sheathed. When he slid into her, she cried out. It was crazy, insane to take the chance, and yet she laughed exultantly as she felt him slide gloriously home inside her.

Her legs were wrapped around him, her arms clawing his shoulders as she savored each savage stroke of his body into hers. He poured in the long temptation of the evening, making no attempt to slow his pace, no attempt to hold back. He was all surging, stroking and rock-hard deep inside her, where she craved him. Around them lights glittered on the Strip, but nothing like the show of seeing Del lose control, lose himself in her as she lost herself. And when he burst into groaning orgasm, she cried out at the sheer glory of being alive.

16

DAY OR NIGHT, THE CASINO looked the same, save only the number of people hunched at the slot machines. Now, for example, the fact that it was just shy of noon was revealed only in the ranks of empty gambling tables. Gwen shook her head to dispel the thought just as someone swooped down on her from behind.

She yelped even as she recognized the persuasive mouth and hands. "You scared me to death," she accused.

"Oh, I don't know, you feel pretty lively to me," Del countered, giving her a final squeeze before releasing her. "So, where do you want to go?"

She shrugged. "I don't care. Anywhere they've got lunch."

"I was thinking we could get outside the casino for a change. Celebrate both of us making it into the second round."

She gave him a bawdy wink. "I thought we did that last night."

"And memorably. But it's a big enough deal it deserves some extra treatment. Let's go. I'm stir crazy."

"Me, too," she confessed. "Getting out would be fabulous."

He kissed her. "Good." They walked out the front door, but instead of leading her onto the Strip he walked to the valet parking attendant and picked up a key.

"You've got a car?"

"I thought we both could use a break from the Strip. Unless you'd like to go back inside?"

She gave a giddy laugh and got into the spiffy red coupe that pulled up. "God, no."

It was easy to forget that there was life outside of the casinos. Las Vegas seemed to float in its own dislocated pocket of existence. It seemed that she'd always lived in the shadow world of recycled air and cigarette smoke, surrounded by people with the worn look of too many hours of gambling, too little sleep. The long hours spent in the casinos, the marching rows of the resorts banished all thought of the desert, except for the stupefying heat that slammed the senses the moment a person stepped outside.

Now it was all behind her, in another world, and her only reality was the open road.

As they drove along the freeway that paralleled the Strip, the line of casinos only looked more incongruous without the benefit of their elaborate facades. On the Strip it seemed as if the casinos dominated the known world. Now, from the outside, they seemed as absurd as moss flourishing in the desert.

Gwen stretched and let her right arm dangle out the window, surfing the slipstream of air as the last of the casinos gave way to the suburbs. "This is great. I forgot what this was like, the out-of-doors."

"It's a nice reminder, isn't it."

"Of course, you know we should be at Versailles watching Jerry."

"Knowing Jerry, he's probably still in bed with a hangover. We'll be back by afternoon, when he gets up. You can't watch him every minute, you know."

"I just keep thinking I'm going to miss something and so much for my chance to get the stamps back."

"Let it go. He told you he was expecting his big score

next week. We've got time. Give yourself a break." Del headed toward the hills that formed an arc on the horizon.

It was an artificial world out here, vivid green lawns shockingly incongruous against the sere desert landscape. The housing tracts seemed to stretch for miles.

"So, where are we going?"

"Hoover Dam."

Gwen blinked. "You big on public-works projects?"

"Seemed worth seeing. Besides, one of the guys I met at the tournament told me about a barbecue joint in Boulder City. I thought it would be a nice break from resort food."

"I'll buy that."

The subdivisions finally gave way to the open desert and Gwen caught a breath of pleasure. "Now this is more like it."

Away from the artificial constructs of suburbia, the desert emerged in all its subtle beauty. Pink terrain, gray-green sage, golden-brown mesquite and pale blue sky all blended together in a pastel fantasy. The serried ranks of ruddy hills rose sharply in the distance, stark and clear in the dry desert air.

Gwen took an exultant breath, savoring the spicy scent of the air. "This is wonderful," she said, buoyed by the sense of light and openness and space.

Del gave her a sidelong glance. "I thought you might like it, Gwendolyn."

"It's not Gwendolyn." She flushed.

"Really?" he asked with interest. "What is it short for? Gwendy? Gwenda?"

"Stop it."

"Come on, fess up. It can't be that weird."

She sighed. "Guinevere."

"So, what's wrong with that?"

"Oh, don't be nice. It's ridiculous, I know it. It was my mother's idea."

"A romantic."

Gwen watched the landscape roll by a few moments before answering. "My mother's something of a free spirit, you might say. She and my dad are doctors working in Africa."

"Takes more than a free spirit to be an M.D."

"Oh, I know that. She's brilliant. She works unimaginably hard and she's very passionate about making a difference. I guess what I was trying to say is that she marches to her own drummer." Gwen could admire it, be often puzzled by it, but never really understand. "I was five when she convinced my dad to join Physicians Without Frontiers. My sister Joss was six. They scooped us off to Zimbabwe."

"You went to Zimbabwe?"

"And Botswana and Tanzania. I got out when I was fourteen. Joss stayed until she was grown. My mom thought it was a good cultural experience for us."

"She was probably right."

"I suppose." Gwen turned to study him. "Where did you grow up?"

"Huntington Beach."

"Surf's up?" she asked dryly.

"Some of the time. We didn't live in luxury or anything. I was just a normal kid."

"That was all I ever wanted to be. Just a normal kid."

Del reached over and took her hand, lacing his fingers with hers. "And you weren't?"

"It's hard to be normal when you're a blond white kid in Zaire," she said simply. "We'd come back to the U.S. for a month every year, stay with my grandparents. I just wanted to eat hamburgers and watch TV like everybody else. My mom had other ideas."

"Which were?"

Gwen stared out at the deep red rocks surrounding them. "Making us the poster children for a global society."

"Heavy load for a kid," Del commented, slowing down a bit to take a curve. The freeways had given way to a narrow highway that dived between ranges of hills.

"We'd go give talks at schools and stuff. The way they'd look at us…" She sighed. "Joss loved it, but she always liked being the center of attention. I've always been more comfortable on the sidelines."

"Must be harder now."

She could feel herself tense, she thought in annoyance, wishing she'd never started this line of discussion. He didn't want to hear about Gwen. He was a guy. Nina would be his thing. *I have a soft spot for Nina.* Ordinary Gwen wouldn't even register on him.

"Does it feel awkward, being dressed up?"

"Not as much as you'd think. It's Nina they're looking at, not me. It's not so bad." Now that she thought about it, she'd stopped feeling awkward and conspicuous as the days had passed. It had become kind of fun. Maybe there was more Nina in her than she'd realized.

"So, you said you stayed in Zimbabwe or wherever until you were fourteen. Why did you leave?"

"We'd come back to visit my grandparents like we did every year. It was so great I just hated going back. I was evil for a good two months after that, the way only an adolescent can be. My parents finally broke and let me move in with my grandparents. I said it was so I could get into a good college, but I think they knew."

"And loved you enough to let you go."

"Yes. And my grandparents loved me enough to give me a home."

"The grandfather who taught you to play poker."

She laughed. "You remembered."

"He must be loving the fact that you're here playing."

"Well, he doesn't know," she said, suddenly uneasy.

"He and my grandmother are off on a long trip to the South Pacific."

"My grandparents did that when they retired."

"Well, he's not quite there yet. They call this their practice retirement. I was supposed to be minding the store until they came back."

"The stamps?"

"Yes, I—oh," she broke off as they rounded a curve and the deep blue of Lake Mead swung into view. Framed by the serrated lines of the pastel hills, it stretched away from them, cool and sapphire-dark. There were houses here, but they blended pueblo-style into the desert, colored in warm ochers and rose tones, topped with ruddy terra-cotta roofs.

The road curved around through the hills now, first rising steadily, then dropping in great loops toward the dam. When the tangle of high-voltage towers materialized, it was a shock after the open landscape. Then the dam itself appeared, its smooth, warm curve blending seamlessly with the hills around it.

"Do you want to drive across?" Del asked. "We can."

Gwen shook her head. "Can't we ditch the car and walk?"

"Whatever you'd like."

The heat was there, ever present, but she was too preoccupied with the sight ahead of her to really notice. They passed a monument to the workers, a pair of almost unearthly winged figures seated with arms pointing to the heavens. Beyond them the dam stretched around.

"Do you ever get the urge to step up on a railing like this and just jump out into space?" Gwen asked idly as they stopped to lean over the waist-high concrete wall and stare down at the dam. It was like looking into a giant funnel, the broad curve tapering down to the narrow bottom, where the Colorado River flowed away in a gleaming ribbon.

He cocked an eyebrow at her. "This isn't the part where you start talking about your suicidal thoughts, is it?"

"Good god, no. It just always seems like you could just jump out and soar away like a bird, you know? Part of my mind whispers 'Go ahead and do it, you could fly.'" She wrinkled her nose at him. "See if I ever share my innermost thoughts with you again." They stepped back from the rail and began ambling slowly along the dam. "So, tell me more about life as a surfer boy."

"Life as a surfer boy? Not exactly. We lived inland, not on the water." When he slipped his arm around her, it was the most natural thing in the world.

"Did you surf?"

"Some. Skied, went rock climbing in the desert."

"You've got that look." She stopped in front of the bronze dedication plaque.

"You think so? Mostly I played sports."

"Yikes. A jock? You weren't one of those football guys who dated the cheerleaders, were you?"

"Not football, baseball."

"And the cheerleaders?"

He grimaced and the fun faded briefly from his eyes. "Married one."

"Married?"

"Divorced," he elaborated, holding up his ringless left hand. "You can't always trust everything you see with the golden girls."

Something about the way he said it discouraged her from asking more. She turned to a safer topic instead. "So, you played in high school?"

"College, too. It covered my tuition."

"You didn't go pro, did you?"

He shook his head. "I was good in high school and okay

in college, but I was nowhere near good enough for the pros. I found that out pretty quickly."

She stopped and leaned against the concrete wall to look at him. "That must have been tough to give up your dream."

Del shrugged. "It wasn't my dream so much as what was easy. Just like marrying Krista. Just like sportswriting. I was good in English and it seemed like a good way to take what I knew and parlay it into something."

"You don't seem thrilled."

"I don't know." Seeming suddenly uncomfortable, he began walking. "I've just always taken the easy way out. I'd like to do something because I made it happen for a change, not because I was good at it and it fell into my lap."

"So, what do you want to do?"

"I don't know, something meatier than sports, I guess. Tell stories that really matter. I think I'm ready to make a change."

They'd reached the other side of the dam, Gwen realized in surprise. Del leaned on the railings to look out at Lake Mead, cradled between the walls of the canyon bridged by the dam. He looked back at her. "You getting the urge to climb up on the rail and jump off here?"

She shook her head. "Here it'd just be like jumping into a pool."

"That's the difference between us, I guess. I want to dive in and you want to fly."

THE SUN WAS SETTING BY THE time they got back to the hotel. Del turned the car back over to the valet and they trailed into the hotel, sunburned and spent.

"What are you doing tonight?"

"I thought I'd take a nice cool bath to wash off all the dust." Gwen gave him a thoroughly naughty look as she got off the elevator. "Care to join me?"

"I'm your man." He followed her to her door, where she fumbled her key out of her purse. She opened the door, took two steps and stopped abruptly.

"Oh, my god."

17

THE ROOM HAD BEEN TOSSED thoroughly and by someone who didn't much care how much of a mess they made. Del followed Gwen through the haphazardly thrown-around clothing and personal items. "Careful," he said, catching her before she walked over broken glass. "See if anything's missing."

Gwen walked through the room in a daze, picking things up and setting them down, her breath hitching unsteadily. Del swept some papers off the sofa and pulled her down to sit on it. "It's okay," he said softly, catching her hands between his, but they were ice-cold.

"Someone's been in here," she whispered, shivering. "They've been through everything."

It was a violation, at least as much as her attack. That they'd searched Jerry's room just days before didn't make it easier. This didn't have the look of a purposeful search, Del realized. It had the look of maliciousness. "Make any enemies at the tournament?"

Gwen turned to him and it was as though they arrived at the same point at the same time. "The stamps."

"But why would someone break in here looking for the stamps?" she asked.

"Maybe they knew you were at Jerry's. Maybe they've noticed all the time you've spent with him and they figure he handed off something to you. Maybe it's a warning."

For the first time she registered the torn drapes, the split pillows. "We're going to have to report this, aren't we?"

"Don't see how we can avoid it."

Her face paled. "I don't want the police in on it."

"Why the big hush job?"

"I don't want them in on it," she repeated.

"That'll be up to hotel security."

"They can't know about the stamps. They can't report it." She rose and began to walk agitatedly through the mess.

"Is anything missing?" He had to ask her three times before she could answer.

"I can't tell. Everything is such a mess. There wasn't much of anything to take. My computer and jewelry are in the safe. Nothing else…" she spread out her hands.

"You should open it just in case, but the safe doesn't look touched."

It hadn't been, near as he could tell. Perhaps whoever had tossed the room had been disturbed.

Or perhaps they just wanted to send a message. *We're watching you.*

ONE THING WAS CERTAIN—THE head of hotel security was watching her. Tall and gaunt-cheeked, Howard Ahmanson had disillusioned-cop eyes that surveyed the world with a cynical stare. Currently he'd turned the cynical stare on her. "Know any reason someone would have broken in here? Anyone got a grudge against you? Old boyfriend? Someone you beat at the tables?"

Gwen shook her head. "Nothing like that. Anyway, I'd hope it wouldn't be that easy to break the locks."

"You trying to say it was an inside job?"

"Not at all. I have no idea what kind of job it is. I just know I haven't made any enemies and I don't have any jilted lovers running around."

"And nothing's missing, you say."

"The only valuables I had were in the safe, and that held."

"Whoever got into your room was a pro. We could call the cops and get them to look for prints, but the perp probably used gloves. Anyway, if nothing's missing, the only thing you could charge them with would be destruction of property."

Gwen sat on the couch and massaged her temples. "Do I have to file a report to get the property damage waived?"

"Eventually. Not tonight, though. You can change rooms when you're ready. Just go down to the front desk."

She nodded.

"You know," he said casually, "seems funny that someone would go to that much trouble to make a mess in the place of someone who doesn't have an enemy in the world. Looks to me like someone's maybe trying to tell you something." He gave her a long look, then walked to the door. Just before he reached it, he turned. "You think of anyone or change your mind, you let me know, okay?"

"Okay."

"And put on the dead bolt when you're in here."

The door closed behind Ahmanson. Del walked back toward Gwen. "He's right, you know, you should file a police report. You should call the cops, period, blow the whistle on things."

"No," she said abruptly. She huddled on the couch, the shakes just starting. "I can't."

"Gwen, we don't know what's going on here. Someone tried to hurt you four days ago—"

"You don't know that that was connected," she said hotly.

"And you don't know that it wasn't. And now we come back and find your room torn apart. Nothing's gone but everything's a mess and it looks a whole lot like it might be connected to Jerry and to the guy that grabbed you the other night."

The shakes got stronger. "I can't get the police involved."

"You've got hundreds of dollars in damage to the furnishings here. Unless you win the poker tournament, you're going to damned well have to."

"It's my problem, Del." Nina wouldn't be shaking. Nina wouldn't be on the edge of tears. She'd take it in the gut, hold up her head and go on. Gwen took a breath.

"God, you're doing it again," he said disgustedly.

"What?"

"Channeling."

"What do you mean?"

"You think I don't see it? You think I don't know when it's going on? One minute you're you and then the screens go down and someone else is looking out of your eyes. All of a sudden you're being Nina."

He saw a whole lot more than she'd given him credit for. A whole lot more than she wanted him to. "What's wrong with Nina?"

"She's not real. She's not a person, she's just a construct, someone you use to give yourself guts. Well you've got guts already, so why don't you have the guts to be yourself?"

"Maybe I don't want to be just Gwen. Maybe I like being Nina."

"Well, being Nina has you taking stupid chances, thinking you're some sort of superwoman who can go up against the bad guys. Maybe you can't, and being Nina is just going to get you into a dangerous situation you can't get out of. You've got this thing about being Nina and it's going to get you into some very bad trouble if you don't watch out."

"What about you? Who were you talking with that first night at the blackjack table, anyway? If I'd been Gwen, I'd never have come up to you and you'd never have given me the time of day. You probably still wouldn't. I might be

Gwen inside, but I'm Nina on the outside and Nina's your golden-girl fantasy. So don't go lecturing me, Del," she snapped and turned to the windows. She pressed her forehead to the glass, feeling the warmth left over from the Las Vegas day.

Outside the sun had set in the time between their discovery of the room and meeting with security. Lights glittered and flashed in the dusk. People flocked down the Strip to the casinos. Life went on as usual.

Del walked over to her, watching her shoulders, knowing the strength that was in them, seeing the fragility. "Look, I don't always say the right thing. You'd think I would. I work with words for a living. Sometimes, though, when I'm angry or scared, it comes out wrong. And I'm scared for you right now and angry that someone's doing this to you. So I screwed up and I'm sorry."

Gwen raised her head and turned to look at him.

"The thing is, I don't think I'm wrong," he continued. "I think you're taking some risks with an unknown quantity. I think you think you can carry it off, and it worries me that something might happen to you." He jammed his hands into his pockets. "I don't think Jerry tossed your room. This is bigger than him. You've got to bring in the cops."

Gwen was silent for a long time. Finally she spoke. "I told you my grandfather's in the process of retiring. I didn't tell you everything. You figured out my grandfather owns the stamp store, the one Jerry stole from. Jerry didn't just take stamps from the store inventory, though. He stole the best of the stamps that my grandfather is depending on for his retirement."

"Your grandfather doesn't know?"

Gwen shook her head, walking over to sink down on the bed. "If I'd told him, he'd come back home the next day and he's in less of a position to get them back than I am."

"Insurance?"

She shook her head and laid back, staring at the ceiling. "He was planning to start selling them over the next two years. Four and a half million out the door and into Jerry's pocket."

It was still hard to accept that little chips of paper could be worth so much. A testament to human acquisitiveness, Del supposed, or to obsession. He sank down on the bed beside her and gathered her against him, kissing her hair and saying nothing.

"There's more to it than just the money, though. It would still leave him with a million or so in holdings, but he's an investment philatelist."

"Meaning?"

"He advises people on investment stamps. And because of the way his contracts with them are written, word getting out about the stamp theft could take everything that's left." She turned to face him. "I can't bail on this, even if someone's trying to intimidate me. Even if they're watching me. I don't care who they are, I've got to find a way to get those stamps back from Jerry without word getting out."

Del brushed a hand over her hair and pressed a gentle kiss on her lips. "You will. We'll do it together."

But long after her eyes had closed, he lay staring at the ceiling.

18

DEL STOOD AT HIS WINDOW, looking out at the Strip, wishing he could do anything but make the call he was about to make. Then again, unpleasant things were best done quickly, he thought and punched the numbers on his cell phone.

"Jessup."

"Greg, it's Del Redmond here."

"How's that story going, Redmond?"

"That's why I'm calling." He was calling because it was, quite simply, the right thing to do. "The story's evaporated."

"Evaporated?"

"It's not as big a story as I anticipated."

"Four and a half million in rare stamps isn't a story? What, did they show up? Did the owners miss seeing them the first time around?" The sarcasm was ripe in Jessup's voice.

"No," Del said evenly. "The more I investigated, the more it became clear that it's not a straightforward, clean story."

"Those are usually the best kind."

"Not this one. It's not going to come together and it's not going to be timely." That was always the card to play with a newshound. Late was as good as never as far as a good editor was concerned.

"Doesn't help us much, does it?"

"Would you rather I turned in twenty column inches of useless crap?" Del countered.

Jessup gave a bark of laughter. "Balls, Redmond. I like

that in a reporter. All these kids that I'm interviewing are afraid to stand up for themselves. Don't want to take a chance on irritating me."

"I've already got a job, Jessup. I was thinking I'd like a chance to work news for you, but I might be revising that opinion."

Jessup snorted. "I might be revising my opinion, too. That story would have helped you, you know that?"

"Only if it were solid. If I'd sent you twenty column inches that stank to high heaven, I don't think it would have done a whole hell of a lot for my case."

"I suppose not."

"And by the way, you can tell your little terrier Kellar to back off."

"Kellar?"

"Yeah. Calls himself your stringer? He hunted me down the other day."

"Oh, right. I thought he might be able to help you with some local contacts."

"Well, be sure to tell him the story's been spiked. I don't want him nosing around anymore."

"Uh-huh." There was a short silence. "You seem awfully anxious to have this story killed, Redmond."

"That's because it's the right thing to do." Del's fingers clenched the phone just a bit tighter.

"Well, I suppose I have to trust the instincts of my reporters."

"I'm not your reporter," Del reminded him.

"Well, you're still in the pool, anyway. I'm interviewing through the end of next week. You come up with anything I can use out there, send it along. If not, well, we'll be in touch."

THERE WAS SOMETHING ABSOLUTELY intoxicating about winning, Gwen thought as she grinned into the mirror over the sink in the ladies' room halfway through the day's play. Every two hours the tournament ran, they got fifteen minutes to stand up, move around and take a break. She dried her hands and looked over to where Roxy was slicking on a new layer of lipstick.

"You doing all right?" Gwen asked.

"Sweetie, I am doing fabulously. They're all like soft little bunnies and I'm the saber-toothed tiger."

"Now there's an image."

"I caught the guy in the number seven seat at my table staring at my knockers."

"Nice," Gwen said with a grimace.

"Hell, I don't care. If he's busy looking at my chest, he's not thinking about poker."

"On the other hand, it's going to be harder to pick out a bluff if the vein beating on the side of his head is throbbing for another reason."

"Nope, the vein that's throbbing because of that is a whole lot lower." She winked. "So, where are you at?"

"In a really weird spot. I feel like I can see what they've got and I know which way to push them. The cards just keep falling my way."

"Sounds like you're in the zone."

"I hope so." Gwen walked toward the door.

"So, are we going to go out and celebrate after?" Roxy followed her out into the lobby area where drinks and snacks were laid out. "What about going over to the vodka bar at Mandalay Bay?"

"Forget that. I'm having a party for all the winners up at my suite." It was Jerry coming up behind them to hang his arms over their shoulders.

Roxy made a face and did a little sidestep to get out from under him. "Watch out," she suggested, "or you might be missing a hand for the last go-round."

Gwen moved aside.

"Oh, come on, guys, it's going to be party time."

"We have to make the cut first," Gwen reminded him.

He snorted. "We all know it's just a matter of time."

"For someone," Roxy said.

"Hey, you gonna come or not?"

"We all win, sure, we'll stop by for a drink," Gwen said. "Won't we, Roxy?"

Roxy looked at her as if she'd lost her mind but gave a grudging nod. "Sure, for starters." The bell rang to summon them back to the tables. "Right now, though, we'd better go in and finish the job."

FORGET ABOUT LIQUOR—THE PURE, hard rush of making the cut beat it all. The field had been narrowed. Only a total of thirty-six players had survived round two, each of whom would walk away with at least eighteen thousand dollars. Those who stayed in longer, well, the sky was the limit— or as much of it as you could buy with two million.

Roxy came up and hooked an arm over her shoulders. "We're in the money," she singsonged. "Let's go get your main squeeze and a man for me and celebrate." She whooped and gave a little shimmy.

"The party, remember?"

Roxy made a face. "And we have to do that why?"

"You don't have to do it, but I do."

"He's an idiot," she said with a frown. "He was at my table the last part of the night and I had to put up with his poker-brat routine. What do you want to hang around with him for?"

"Hang around with who?" Del came up behind them.

"Jerry's having a party," Gwen explained. "I figured we could stop by and have a drink."

"Oh, if Jerry's buying, I think the least we can do is stop

by," he said. "But first I need to do some congratulating. To you." He leaned over to give Roxy a hug. "And to you." He gathered Gwen against him and pressed his mouth on hers, hard.

"And to you," Gwen said back to him. The heat from the brief contact surprised her. The promise made her want. Jerry's party didn't matter, she thought dizzily. The only thing that mattered was getting Del alone. Now.

"Hey, how do I get me some of that," Jerry said behind them.

Del shot him a frown. "I think the supply is all out, buddy. You're going to have to settle for a poker groupie."

"Don't listen to him." Gwen forced flirtatiousness into her voice. "Congratulations. We'll see you upstairs at the party," she told him, making herself lean in to peck him on the cheek before turning back to Del and Roxy.

"So," Del said, "party first, then I need to take you two poker superstars out to celebrate a little."

"Man after my own heart," Roxy said, ruffling his hair affectionately. "You don't happen to have a brother, do you?"

"Yep, but he's married with three kids."

"Rats. You'll tell me if anything changes?"

"You'll be the first," he promised.

THE PARTY MIGHT HAVE BEEN IN Jerry's suite, but it had spilled out into the concierge bar and lounge area. Guests milled about, only a fraction of whom he probably knew, Gwen was betting. Behind the bar a hotel staffer mixed drinks. Appetizers tempted the hungry from tables covered in snowy-white linen.

"Quite the host, our Jerry is," Del murmured in her ear.

"Just as long as he's not planning to pay for it in cash," she responded. "You might want to skip the me-Tarzan-you-Jane routine, by the way," she added in a low voice.

"As long as Jerry thinks he has a chance, he might tell me something."

"He'll tell you more if he's trying to impress you into dumping me and taking up with him."

She slanted a look at him. "Which would be the only reason you did it, of course."

"Of course," he said blandly. "And now I'll wander over and talk with Roxy, leaving you wide open for Jerry."

"You are devious." She gave him an admiring look.

"That's why you love me." He walked off, leaving her staring after him.

Just a joke, Gwen decided, blinking away her shock. Definitely nothing she should take seriously. It wasn't as though she could possibly be foolish enough to let herself have feelings for Del, anyway. It was just a fling while they were working together. What happened in Vegas stayed in Vegas, she reminded herself.

"Hey, you made it!" Jerry came up to her. "How you doing, babe? Ready to mow 'em down in the next round?"

"Careful. You might just wind up at my table."

"Hey, the other night showed us who was hot."

She tilted her head. "You mean the night I took you to the cleaners?"

He frowned, the memory coming clearer. "Yeah, but I'm on a roll now. I'm hot and the cards are loving me."

"We're all hot."

"I've got a license to print money," he told her.

A weedy-looking blonde with a deep tan and the carved lines of a longtime smoker walked up to them carrying a highball glass of what looked like whiskey. "Well, if it isn't the hotshot kid himself," she said and took a swallow of her drink. "I guess you're the host of this little do."

"Hey," Jerry crowed and gave her a sloppy kiss. "Rennie, I want you to meet Nina. Nina, this is Adrienne—or Rennie, as we call her."

Every atom of Gwen's being went on alert. It was Rennie—the Rennie listed in the matchbook, the Rennie who'd begun the whole chase.

The Rennie who might know something about where the stamps were.

Staying relaxed took work, but Gwen managed to put out her hand. "Nice to meet you. So, what do you think of our boy making it into the money round?"

"Oh, Jerry's always done well for himself," Rennie said in a not-entirely-pleasant tone. "I should know it. I've watched him for a long time."

"Rennie and I go way back," Jerry put in. "We met up in Reno. Used to joke about starting a radio show. 'And now,'" he announced, "'it's Jerry and Rennie from Reno.'"

"The way I remember it, it was Rennie and Jerry from Reno." She took another gulp of her drink. "It's that memory of yours, Jerry, always gets you in trouble."

There was definitely something simmering here, Gwen thought. If she could coax it to the boil, who knew what might bubble up? "Jerry, sweetie, can you go get us drinks?" Gwen asked, channeling a bit of Nina, a bit of Roxy.

"Drinks?"

She nodded. "A martini for me and what, whiskey?" She looked at Rennie inquiringly.

"Jack Daniel's," Rennie supplied and took a last swallow of what was in her glass.

"Okay, a martini and a Jack Daniel's." He went off a bit unwillingly, but he went, allowing her to concentrate on Rennie. "So, nice party, huh? Has to be costing a bundle. Of course, I'm just a guest, so I guess I shouldn't worry about it." *Poke the sore spot, see what happens*, Gwen thought.

"He always was a dipshit when it came to money." Rennie looked after Jerry with a scowl.

"So, you from here in Vegas or still living in Reno?"

"I'm a dealer here at the hotel. He wouldn't even have known about the tournament if it weren't for me."

And another puzzle piece clicked into place. "Wow. He's lucky he's got a friend like you. I just found out by accident. So, what did you guys do up in Reno?"

"Who, me?" Rennie took another look at Jerry. "I was dealing blackjack and passing odd jobs to the hotshot kid. 'Course, it don't look like he needs the work anymore," she added, turning to survey the concierge area. "Fancy place, his own bartender—looks like he's got all the money he needs." She bit off the words and stood staring moodily until Jerry returned.

"Here we go, a martini for you and a J.D. for you. Let's toast to the big payoff at the final table," he said, holding up his glass.

"Let's toast to payoffs, period," Rennie returned in a hard voice. "And promises. Remember promises, Jerry? You ain't too good on them." The bourbon was hitting her bloodstream; it showed in her eyes and the increased volume of her voice.

Jerry's eyes narrowed. "Maybe you ought to quiet down," he suggested.

"Don't tell me what I oughta do." Her voice rose.

"We're gonna talk about this in private," he hissed and half led, half pulled her into the hallway that led to the bedroom.

Del drifted over to Gwen. "That looked interesting."

"That was Rennie," she said.

"So maybe we need to go lean against the wall over there and canoodle a bit?"

"You read my mind."

The bedroom door closed, but Gwen and Del were able to get close enough to hear faint voices behind it.

"What's your problem?" Jerry demanded.

"What's my problem? You gotta ask? You owe me money, you asshole. You're here having a great old time with big bucks from a job that *I* threw your way. Meanwhile I'm spending eight hours a day on my feet dealing cards, waiting on that big lump of cash I was supposed to get from you. 'It'll pay off big, Rennie,'" she mocked savagely. "'Take a couple months off.' Pissed off? Damned right I'm pissed off."

"You'll get your money." Her response must have been a rude look because Jerry's voice roughened. "I'm working the deal as fast as I can."

"Keep talking, you're breaking my heart here. You look like you're workin' real hard, playin' poker, sucking down liquor, acting like the big man."

"There's been a holdup."

"Always is with you."

"Look, you brought me the guy. If he's a screwup, then it's partly your fault. If that means you got to sweat a little more, well, it ain't gonna keep me up at night."

"Asshole," she spat.

"Yeah? Right back atcha. He's the one who ain't paying. Until he coughs up the cash, I don't get it, which means you don't get it. Unnerstand?"

"Tell me you didn't make some idiot move like giving him the goods already."

"The stuff's in a safe place. It's cool. Everything's cool, or it would be if you'd stop being such a psycho bitch."

"I'll back off for now, but I'm warning you, I'd better see something soon."

"Saturday night is gonna be the handover, babe. I'll get you the dough, you can put in your notice. Maybe we'll take a nice trip or something."

"I'll show you a nice trip if you're feeding me a line."

"Hey, Ren, would I do that?"

"You always did have a habit of asking stupid questions," she returned.

GWEN LAY ON THE SHEETS, waiting for her breath to return to normal.

"Are you trying to give me heart failure so I'll forfeit my seat at the table?" Del croaked.

She grinned. "I just wanted to help you release your post-tournament tension."

"You helped me release my tension, all right."

"Mmm." She moved so that her head lay across his belly. "So, based on that conversation we overheard, it sounds like Jerry's planning the handoff on Saturday, which means we've got to get our act in gear."

"Yep."

"So, I think I've figured out a way to do it."

"How?"

"Well, it depends on Jerry making the final table. If he does, then we'll know without a doubt where he is during the last night of play."

"Of course, you might be there also."

"I suppose, but just because I start the game doesn't mean I'll be the last one standing."

"What's that supposed to mean?"

"Everybody but the champ has to lose sometime. If I'm the first one out, I'll be free to roam while Jerry's stuck there."

"Too chancy."

"Not at all," she argued, rolling over to prop her arms on his chest. "They'll be showing the play on the closed-circuit television system throughout the hotel. All I need to do is put it on and I can monitor Jerry the whole time. I know where they are, Del," she reminded him. "It won't take long."

"And what do you think he's going to do when he finds them gone?"

"What can he do? They were stolen to begin with."

"What about fingerprints, assuming he does go to the cops?"

She dismissed it. "We were just in his suite. My fingerprints are going to be all over the place anyway."

"You made sure of it, didn't you?"

She grinned at him. "Nina's no dummy."

"It still feels risky to me. What if someone catches you up there?"

"It'll work out fine. You can put money on it."

"That's what I'm worried about."

19

DEL LEANED AGAINST ONE OF the marble pillars of one of the casino bars—the Sun King Court—and watched Gwen being interviewed for the tournament video. It was one of the fifteen-minute segments the filmmakers were doing with all the front-runners. He'd done his only the day before. Somehow, though, Gwen's segment had stretched to nearly an hour. Not that he blamed them. She made a fetching subject and it wasn't just him being biased.

Behind him, on the stage in the bar, the singer of the house band warbled a version of Madonna's "Holiday." That was what this whole week felt like, a holiday from the real world.

He pulled out his cell phone to check his voice mail while he waited. It might feel as if he was on vacation, but there was still work to think about.

He punched in the number and then navigated his way through the voice-mail menus, punching the key to play his first message. "Hey, Redmond—" the voice jumped out of the phone "—it's Kellar." A casino waitress hustled past, her tray of drinks held high. "Jessup put me full-time on that stamp story you dropped. I need to get a list of your sources and where you left things, so give me a call or shoot me an e-mail, okay?"

Del jabbed at the key that deleted the message and stood, quietly steaming. Maybe Jessup hadn't been ready to let the story go so easily and had asked Kellar to follow up. More likely it was Kellar getting industrious, Del figured, hoping that a little sniffing around would net him a story and a clip. *Dream on, buddy.* No journalist who wanted to remain competitive coughed up his sources. Anyway, it wasn't as if he owed Jessup anything. The thing to do was sit tight and let Kellar cool his heels. With nothing to go on, the kid couldn't possibly get an angle on the story.

Del hoped.

Someone bumped him on the hip and he turned to see Gwen. "Hey, you," she said, giving him a quick kiss. "Sorry that took so long. Did I miss anything important?"

"Not a thing," he told her and hoped like hell he was right.

"WELCOME TO THE THIRD ROUND of the Tournament of Champions." The MC's voice came across the PA system as the players and audience milled around the tournament room. The mood had become even more focused, even more intense as the tournament had progressed. The good news was that everybody was in the money. The bad news was that the sooner a player went out, the less of a payoff they got. By the end of play that day, the field would be winnowed from thirty-six to the final table of nine.

And someone at that final table would walk away with a cool two million.

On the surface, players behaved just about the same, only more so. The loquacious ones coffeehoused just as much as they always had, perhaps out of nerves or as a calculated attempt to distract their cohorts. Punks like Jerry grated ever more on the nerves.

And the cool, focused players like Del just kept coming. The power balances had changed at the tables. The chip leaders, some of them sitting on several hundred thousand dollars' worth of chips, bet relentlessly, raising and reraising, trying to break their poorer competition.

Much to her own surprise, Gwen had worked her way up to over two hundred thousand dollars in chips by the time she was reseated at a shorthanded table with Jerry.

A chance for a little revenge.

She didn't want to knock him out of the tournament. She needed him there where she could keep an eye on him. The more of his chips she could steal away, though, the higher up the ladder she would move and the more of her grandfather's property she could buy back.

And she began to seriously play.

THE NIGHT AIR WAS COOL AS Gwen pushed through the doors that led out of the casino and onto the long, covered arcade that looked down on the front entrance. The hint of coolness in the air helped ease the stress headache that beat in her temples. After ten hours at the tables, the players had winnowed their numbers from thirty-six to thirteen, and the pressure rose every time someone dropped out.

Four more and they'd be down to the final table. Four more and she'd be guaranteed enough money to buy back all of the low-value stamps that Jerry had sold and then some. She'd taken a few chips from Jerry, but she'd left him with enough to survive and he'd built back from there. If luck were with him, he'd get to the final table.

If luck were with them both.

The message light on her cell phone flashed a peremptory red. *A minute,* Gwen thought, leaning down to rest her forehead briefly against the cold marble of the railing. She'd give herself just one precious moment before she hit redial.

When she did, Joss answered. "Hello?"

"What's going on?"

"It's Grampa. You need to call him."

"Come on, Joss, it's eleven o'clock at night."

"So? It's the middle of the morning there and he just called again. I'm out of excuses and he's starting to get suspicious. You've got to call him."

Gwen squeezed her eyes shut. "I can't now, Joss. We're down to the final thirteen. I've got to go back inside in, like, ten minutes."

"I told him you've been really busy. Just five minutes?" she wheedled. "He just needs to hear your voice."

The headache felt as though someone was merrily thumping Gwen's brain with a meat tenderizer. "All right."

Gwen repeated her grandfather's phone number as Joss read it out to her, repeated it again before she said goodbye, then recited the number out loud as she punched the keys. The clicking in the electronic circuits and the ring sounded farther away somehow. *Half a world away,* she thought suddenly. Half a world and a dozen time zones.

"Good morning."

It might have been coming from half a world away, but when she heard her grandfather's voice, it was as though he were right beside her. "Grampa. It's Gwen."

"Gwennie!" The pleasure in his voice warmed her, easing her headache. "I was about ready to come looking for you. What have you been up to? All Joss can ever tell me is that you're off somewhere busy."

"Oh, just working hard," she said vaguely. "I only have a few minutes to talk but I wanted to say hi. How's Australia?"

"Tasmania today," he corrected her. "And we leave for Papua New Guinea day after tomorrow."

His voice sounded richer, she thought, more thrummingly full of bass, as though a tightness none of them had been aware of had eased. "You sound happy, Grampa."

"We're having the time of our lives. Your grandmother learned how to use a boomerang a couple of days ago."

"A boomerang?" The image of her quiet, buttoned-down grandmother hucking around a boomerang made her laugh.

"Almost took my head off with it, but she had fun. Oh, we've been having a blast. I don't know why we didn't do this before."

"You were married to your business?" she speculated.

"No longer," he assured her. "That's someone else's job now. Speaking of the business, how'd that new kid you hired work out?"

The headache returned with a vengeance. "Oh, all right," Gwen said briefly, hating the fact that she wasn't being straight with him. But how could she tell him and chase away all the joy and pleasure she heard?

"How'd the Chicago estate sale go?"

"Great. Made a couple of surprise finds and already unloaded some of the issues."

"Nice work. But I know you haven't told me everything." For an instant her heart stopped. "What do you mean?"

"About the business."

"Have you heard something is wrong?" How could he have found out, she wondered wildly.

"No, of course not. I'm sure it's all fine and dandy with you at the helm. But that's what I'm talking about. I know you've been unhappy about closing the store down," he told her. "You haven't said anything about it, but you didn't have to—I know."

Gwen breathed a silent sigh of relief. "I'll miss it," she told him, "but I'll find something else I like. Maybe go to work for Stewart."

"It's not the same as running your own shop, though, is it?"

Her throat tightened.

"There's something I want to toss out to you, just food for thought. Your grandmother and I have been talking."

"In between throwing boomerangs?"

"In between," he agreed. "We've talked it over and the business is yours if you want it."

Gwen's jaw dropped. "You mean you want me to run the store?"

"No, we want to turn the whole business over to you, lock, stock and barrel. If you want it."

It was as though the world had been dropped in her lap. "Grampa. I—I don't know what to say."

"Don't answer right away," he returned. "Think about it and we can talk next month once we're all home. Oh, we can't give it to you outright, there are the other kids to consider. But if you'd like it, we'll find a way to make it happen."

"Like it?" Gwen spluttered, "I'd love it."

"Well, take some time and think it over. Owning your own business is a big job, remember."

"It's exactly the right job," she told him. The door opened behind her.

"Gwen." She heard Del's voice. "They're calling us back to the tables."

"Be right there," she told him. She'd get the stamps back, she thought with renewed purpose. She'd take care of her grandparents and she'd start into business right.

"You have to run?" her grandfather asked.

"I have to get back to the game," she said without thinking. "You're wonderful, Grampa. Give Grandma a big hug for me."

"Oh, yeah, I guess it is Thursday night back there," he

said, clearly thinking she was at the weekly home game. "You going to come out ahead tonight?"

"I'm going to come out ahead on everything," she promised him.

A ROUND OF APPLAUSE BEGAN IN the bleachers and spread throughout the room. Gwen looked up, blinking. That was it, she realized, stunned. A player at the other table had just gone out and now they were nine. The long night was over. She caught Del's eye and suddenly the excitement surged through her. They'd made the cut. They were in the serious money.

Without thinking, she rose and ran the few steps over to his table. He grabbed her in a huge bear hug and swung her around. "We did it," she laughed. "We're in."

And then his mouth was on hers, all heat and promise, and the room and people around them faded away. Everything faded away except the immediacy of him, the taste of his mouth, the feel of his body.

"God, I want you," he murmured in her ear.

It was intoxicating. Being in the running to win two million dollars was nothing compared to the way he made her feel.

"Are you two going to come up for air long enough to accept congratulations?"

Gwen opened her eyes to see Roxy watching them.

"Sorry." She could feel the heat of a blush on her face.

"Don't worry about me. The news cameras are having fun, though." She pointed to the black circles of the lenses pointed their way.

"Settle up your chips, folks," the tournament manager reminded them, walking through the tables. They all straggled back to their seats to count up their chips and sign and staple the colorful clay disks in Ziploc bags.

The final day of play in the tournament would begin the next afternoon and run until only one of them was left.

"So, where should we go to celebrate?" Roxy asked, her arms around both of their shoulders. "The Ghost Bar over at the Palms?"

"I'd settle for dinner," Gwen said.

"Dinner was only a couple of hours ago."

"For those of us who could eat."

"Nerves, huh?" Roxy winked at her. "Okay, let's go over to the Hard Rock and hit Nobu. I adore the tuna on miso chips. Meet in the lobby in, say, five minutes?" She waved and peeled off to the ladies' room.

Gwen and Del headed down the escalator into the casino and headed toward the elevators.

"Hey, Redmond, made the final table," came a voice from behind him. "Congratulations."

Del turned to look at the source of the voice.

It was Kellar. "Hey, I been leaving messages for you, you know?"

"I'll talk with you later, Kellar," he said and continued toward the elevators.

"No." Kellar's voice became more insistent. "You're a hard guy to track down." He followed them into the marble-lined elevator lobby.

"Kellar, let it go," Del snapped, punching the call button. "Later, okay? This is not the place."

"That's what you said before and it's later now. I'm not going to hold you up, I just need a list of your sources on the stamp story." Behind them one of the elevators chimed.

"The stamp story?" Gwen asked.

"Yeah. For the paper." He gave her a pugnacious glance. "I'm taking over."

"Really."

Del felt Gwen's hand drop away from his as she turned

to stare at him. Without saying a word she turned and got on the elevator. Del followed.

Kellar blinked. "Hey, Redmond, you can't do that," he protested.

"Watch me."

The atmosphere was glacial as the door closed. Gwen didn't say anything, just punched the button for her floor. When the doors opened, she got out without a word or a backward glance. Del followed her.

She did turn then. "Get away from me."

"Gwen, don't."

"Don't what?"

"Shut me out. Let me tell you what's going on."

"Why?" She glared at him. "So you can pump me for more information for your article, you and your buddy?" She headed toward her room. "When you talked about changing your career, you never told me that my family was going to be the means to your end."

"I didn't mean it to happen like that."

"Oh, yeah? Exactly how did you mean it?" She slammed her passkey into the lock and shoved the door open.

"Look," he said, following her into the room. "I proposed that story before I knew about your grandfather, before I knew about much of anything except that stamps worth a lot of money were missing and someone had stolen them. I wasn't even sure that they weren't stolen property to start with."

She threw down her key and turned to face him. "I told you they were ours. I told you I had proof."

"And you'd told me your name was Nina. I barely knew you at the time."

"I thought maybe you'd believe me."

"You'd just told me you'd been jerking me around for days, when you'd been swearing the whole time that there was nothing going on. What was I supposed to believe? Everything I knew about you in the beginning I found out on the Internet. You didn't give me any information."

"Obviously you had enough to pitch a story, though, didn't you?"

"It was stupid, okay? I admit it. I did it without thinking during a phone interview with the city editor."

"A phone interview?"

"For a news job I thought I wanted."

Her gaze was filled with disgust. "Of course. That's what really matters, right? Whether you get the job, no matter who else pays. So you pitched the story."

"And I unpitched it."

"What's that supposed to mean?"

"Yesterday morning I told the editor that I wasn't going to do it, that there wasn't enough meat to it. Why do you think Kellar's sniffing around now? He's hungry and he wants to dig something up."

Her eyes blazed. "So it doesn't really matter that you've gotten off the story—thanks to your little discussion with them, it'll still be in the paper."

"It would have been in the paper anyway, the minute you turned Jerry over to the cops."

"What is this, a way to make yourself feel better? I keep telling you I want to keep the police out of it."

"You mean, as long as you got back the stamps, you were planning to let Jerry walk?"

"I don't know," she burst out. "I thought I'd get the stamps first and then I'd figure it out. Of course, that was before you blew the whole thing out of the water. Goddammit," she said furiously, rounding on him, "I *trusted* you."

"Did you, now," he said, equally angry. "When was that? When you were telling me you were Nina? When you wouldn't tell me why you didn't want to call the cops?

When you wouldn't show me proof of ownership or even tell me where the stamps came from? You wouldn't even tell me who they were stolen from. Just when did you start opening up to me?" His voice dripped with frustration. "You've been playing a game with me from the beginning, pretending to be someone you weren't, telling me whatever was convenient at the time. You've been showing me the flop but holding on to your pocket cards. Well, this isn't poker, Gwen, this is life. It's supposed to be real."

"I haven't been pretending to be someone else."

"Oh, no? You think I haven't noticed every time you've put on your game face, every time you were doing Nina for me?"

"Doing Nina for you? Nina's the one you wanted. Nina's the one you're hung up on."

"I'm the one who's hung up on Nina? Sorry, that would be you."

"What are you talking about?" she demanded, two spots of color burning high on her cheeks.

"You're the one who's in love with Nina because she lets you do the things Gwen doesn't have the nerve to do. You don't trust Gwen for the important stuff. I see little flashes of her come through when you're not acting, and she's pretty gutsy. I like her. A lot. But you don't let her out often. You keep her inside, give all the flashy stuff to Nina when Gwen's the one who really gets it done."

"Maybe Nina's not just some role I'm playing. Maybe Nina's a part of who I am."

"I don't know who you are, do you? I'm not into hidden pictures, Gwen. That was what happened with my ex-wife. I don't want that. I can't do that again. I don't want to always be wondering who you really are."

"Then I guess you don't want me," she said softly.

20

IT WAS THE NIGHT HOURS THAT were the hardest. Gwen tossed restlessly, searching for oblivion that never came. Instead the awful scene with Del played itself over and over in her head. Her dreams, when she dozed, were dark and chaotic, full of faceless threats chasing her down shadowy passages. And in that dawn moment when the veil of sleep thinned to consciousness, loss crouched there waiting for her.

There was no point in searching again for the sleep that would not come. Lying in bed only gave her more time to think. Instead she rose, beaten with exhaustion yet unbearably present. In the shower she turned up the heat as high as she could tolerate, standing under the pulsating spray. After she got out, she concentrated on the little things: drying her hair, rubbing lotion into her skin, applying her makeup. She wished she had Roxy's skill with makeup; then again, it was unlikely that any cosmetics would entirely disguise what she'd been through in the previous twenty-four hours.

Activity, she told herself, doggedly getting out her computer and working. Finally it was late enough that she could legitimately call Stewart. It took tracking him down by his cell phone, but eventually she reached him. "Stewart, Gwen." She wasted no time on pleasantries. She had none.

"Gwennie?" Concern sharpened his voice. "What's going on?"

"You said for me to call if I needed your help."

"You've got it. What's up?"

"Can you get out to Vegas by this afternoon?"

He answered without hesitation. "Of course."

"It's not strictly legal," she warned him. "In fact, I don't think it's legal at all."

"Does it have to do with getting Hugh's stamps back?"

"Yes."

"Then I don't think it matters."

"Two wrongs don't make a right." The reminder was as much to herself as to him.

"I don't really give a damn," he said pleasantly. "You need help, I'm there. It's seven o'clock right now? I'll see you at one."

"Good."

"What do you need me to do?"

"Watch my back."

LIKE THE SHOWER, THE POOL drew her with the lure of oblivion. The water sluiced over her in a mind-numbing rush. As though she were a machine, she scythed her arms through the water in a rhythmic stroke, pulling herself along, concentrating on the feel of the water in her hands, the slide of it against her body, the number of laps.

Concentrating on anything but Del.

How painfully ironic that she'd feared he cared only for Nina, when apparently just the opposite had been happening. Only when he'd walked out had she realized just how much she'd let him into her heart.

Only then had she realized she was in love with him.

She'd been so preoccupied with the stamps, the tournament, the chase, that Del had snuck up on her blind side. In a terrifyingly short time he'd become necessary to her. And he'd betrayed her. The things he'd said about how concerned he was, how frightened for her, how much she'd meant to him, had been so much talk. Maybe she meant something to him, but his career meant more, obviously. He'd backed off on the story? Maybe. And maybe not. She had only his word to go by and right now his word didn't mean very much.

But that wasn't what tore at her deep down. What tore at her was that he couldn't accept her for who she was, couldn't understand that she could be both Gwen and Nina, that she didn't have to be one or the other. He'd fallen for Nina, he'd wanted Nina, he'd seen Nina and yet he'd castigated her for being Nina. *You're the one who's in love with Nina.* It wasn't true. She wasn't turning into Nina. She'd realized, perhaps, that Nina was one part of her—a part she'd always denied. Did that make it wrong? And why, when Nina was the one who'd attracted him, was he now using Nina as his excuse to walk away from her?

She couldn't bear it, Gwen thought.

She had to.

Suddenly she noticed the legs of a person standing directly in her lane. To avoid running over them, Gwen stopped abruptly. Treading water, she popped her head above the surface and blinked.

It was Roxy. "Hey, enough already. You know you've been swimming for almost an hour and a half? You're going to kill yourself."

An hour and a half? Had it been that long? Now that she'd stopped, Gwen felt almost dizzy. "I was just…I was…" Her arms and legs suddenly leaden, she gave up, wading the last few steps to the side of the pool through chest-high water. It was all she could do to get out of the pool and collapse on her chaise.

"So, what's going on?" Roxy settled on the chaise next

to her. "You suddenly decide to start training for the Olympics? You were like maniac woman there."

"I was just thinking."

"That must have been some thinking," Roxy said flippantly. "What's on your mind, the final?"

"What?"

"*What,* she says. You know, the final? That pesky game that could win you a couple million dollars?"

Gwen shook her head wanly. "Aw, hell, Roxy, I don't care about the tournament," she said, folding her arms over her face. It seemed like the least important thing in her life just then. It seemed like a part of another life. And she'd have to see Del again at the final.

She'd have to face Del.

"You know," Roxy said conversationally, "if I didn't know better, I'd say this smelled like man trouble. Of course, you being smart enough to not get involved, it probably couldn't be that."

"I broke things off with Del last night," Gwen said in a small voice, staring very hard at the brilliant, cloudless blue of the sky overhead.

"Aw, hell, hon." There was a wealth of sympathy in the three words. "Was he an asshole? They usually are, you know. Kind of goes with the DNA. 'Course, he didn't really seem like the type," she added thoughtfully.

An asshole? No, Gwen couldn't say that. He'd betrayed her, though by his lights what he was doing was right. The problem was that he didn't want her. It didn't make him an asshole. It just made everything impossible.

"Why don't you tell me about it? You'll feel better."

She wanted to, more than anything she wanted to just spill it out. And yet, hadn't she had a very clear object lesson what happened when she let information go? "I can't."

Gwen could feel Roxy staring at her. "What do you mean, you can't?"

"It's complicated. There's…something going on."

"Obviously."

"I'd tell you if I could. It's just that I told Del and now everything's a mess."

Roxy looked at her for a moment. "Yeah, sure," she said finally. "I understand." But Gwen swore she saw a spark of hurt in her eyes. "Well, if we can't do talking therapy, we'll have to do therapy of another kind."

"What do you mean?"

"Retail therapy," she said briskly. "Come on."

HER CHARGE CARDS—AND POSSIBLY her feet—would never be the same. Gwen walked into the lobby of the Versailles with her hands loaded with shopping bags. Shoes, makeup, resort wear, lingerie—they'd done it all. Somewhere in the mad shuffle of going from store to store, stopping for drinks and coffee, listening to Roxy's jokes, Gwen had actually found her mood lifting just a bit. She didn't need Del Redmond. She didn't need any man who could worm his way into her life that easily, who could abuse her trust, using what she'd told him in privacy to damage those close to her. She didn't need Del Redmond at all.

Except with every breath she took.

The man ahead of her walked along slowly, bent over slightly. She started to skirt her way around him and head to the elevators, then she caught sight of his face. "Stewart?"

"Gwennie?" He stared at her, incredulous.

"You're here." She wrapped her arms around him, bags and all. When he grunted, she stepped back. "Is something wrong?"

He winced. "I tripped on the trails while I was running this weekend and dinged up my ribs."

"Are you okay?"

"Sure. It's nothing serious, just a few bruises. Takes a little while to get over. I'm just not as young as I used to be, you know."

It was true, she saw. The two years that he'd been gone from San Francisco had added a lot more gray to his hair and a network of lines to his face. A subtle tension hung around him, or maybe it was just the stiffness, she couldn't tell. "Jeez, be more careful when you're running. Being too healthy can kill you, you know."

"I'll keep that in mind." He studied her. "So, is this the new you?"

She shrugged. "It's the me for now."

"It suits you." He hesitated. "I wish I could say that you look a hundred percent great, but you're looking a little rough around the edges. This whole stamp thing getting to you?"

She shrugged. "I've had better weeks. Where's your stuff?"

"I checked in already. Figured I'd come on up. So what's the deal?"

"The good news is that I think I know where the stamps are. The problem is getting into Jerry's room when he's not around. He's up on the concierge level, so it's a little tricky."

"I'd say the problem is getting in, period."

"Not exactly." She held up the key.

"How'd you get your hands on that?"

"I have my ways. Now, the only place I can guarantee he'll be will be the final round of the tournament tonight."

"You want me to search while you're playing?"

She shook her head. "I'm going to bail out of the tournament as early as I can without making it obvious. I'll meet you up here. The passkey will get the elevator up to the concierge level and get us into the room."

"They won't notice anything?"

"I'm Jerry's buddy. I was just upstairs partying with him after the last round. They won't think a thing."

"Remind me never to get in your way," he said admiringly.

"Save it until we've got the stamps back. They're showing the tournament on the closed-circuit TV system, so we can keep an eye on him at all times, make sure he's at the table where he belongs."

"It could work."

She fought back nerves. "I'm pretty sure I know where the stamps are, but it's not easy to get to. I'll need your help."

"You've got it."

"Great." She took a long breath. "Well, play starts in half an hour. I'm just going to drop this stuff in my room and I'll be back down to meet you."

"I'll be waiting."

21

A WEEK BEFORE, GWEN HAD watched the tournament start with no expectation of success. Now she stood with Roxy in the players' lounge waiting to be introduced as a finalist. Waiting to find out whether she was going to walk away with a hundred and fifty thousand dollars or two million. She should have been thrilled.

She couldn't muster up a modicum of excitement.

Roxy gave her a narrow-eyed stare and took her by the arm. "Come on."

"What?"

"In here." She dragged Gwen into the ladies' lounge. "Where's your head?" she demanded. "You're sitting down with the barracudas in about five minutes and you've got to be focused."

"I am focused," Gwen protested feebly.

"No, you're not. You space out tonight, you're letting him win. No matter what happened between you—and I'm not asking about it—you've got to get past it and play this round."

Roxy was right, Gwen realized, but not in the way she thought. Gwen had to get it together in order to exit the tournament without raising suspicion and get into Jerry's room to find the stamps. The previous Saturday she had tried and failed. This time, she had to make it work. She had to get her mind off Del.

She bent over and took several deep breaths and then stood quickly upright. "Okay," she said. "Let's do it."

"You've got every reason to be confident," Roxy told her as they walked out the door. "You're in the final round, so you're in the money. No matter what happens, you're pulling down some serious bucks. And we're seated side by side, so we're coming in with big advantages."

"Which are?"

"Hooters. Show me a man who can think straight when staring one pair of breasts in the eye, let alone two." She grinned. "Not even professional gamblers are that good. The money gets serious for the top seven finishers, so all we need to do is jettison a couple of these jokers and we're in there."

"After which, of course, it's every woman for herself."

"Of course."

"Don't expect your secret weapons to dazzle me," Gwen warned her, feeling her fog of depression lift a bit.

"I knew you wouldn't be so easy," Roxy sighed. "Oops, they're starting."

The room had undergone another transformation. Gone was the bustle, the explosion of tables everywhere you looked. Now only a single spotlit green oval sat before the bleachers in the darkened room, a strip of white illumination circling its base. Blue drapes around the walls dotted with pin lights added drama. Behind the table, on the dealer's side, a large projection screen showed an image of the empty table, the green baize with the brown leather padded rim. It looked innocuous, but over the next few hours it would be the site of something extraordinary, a pile of two million in bricks of hundred-dollar bills.

Seat by seat, the MC began introducing the players. Before, the tournament had been something of a cattle call, populated by hordes of nameless, faceless competitors. As the field had narrowed, the reporters had clustered around the well-known players and the crowd had begun following favorites, cheering them on by name. Now the MC was working the room, hyping the crowd more with each introduction.

Gwen watched Del walk to his seat to the accompaniment of whoops from some of the women in the audience. In a way she ought to have thanked him. If she hadn't been so numb, Gwen would have been nervous. Instead her emotions felt so deadened, it was hard to worry about anything too much, except maybe getting into Jerry's room.

The only thing left that mattered.

"In seat number six, placing seventh in last year's World Series of Poker and the winner of last year's Tournament of Champions, Roxanne Steele."

"Oops, that's me." Roxy gave Gwen a quick hug and broke away to sashay through the gauntlet of flashbulbs, waving her arms, the shiny tournament bracelet on her wrist winking.

Gwen swallowed and took a breath. "In position seven, competing in her first tournament, San Franciscan Nina Chatham."

Gwen walked across to the table, staring at Del. It felt as if someone were sitting on her chest, making it hard to breathe. Del sat there, his sunglasses reflecting her form as she approached. In a way it paralleled their relationship, neither one of them able to get past the wall between them. Whether that wall was mirrored sunglasses or the persona of Nina or something else, it was there. Maybe she never had gotten any deeper than the surface with him. Maybe she never had gotten through to what was behind.

Tucking her skirt under, Gwen sat. *Look away,* she told herself, but she couldn't. Was it the distortion of the lenses or did her cheeks really look that drawn, did her eyes really look so smudged with exhaustion? How was it that Del seemed just the same when her entire life had changed in a day?

The pain suddenly sliced through her and Gwen took a ragged breath.

Someone grabbed her hand and squeezed. It was Roxy. "Look at me," she commanded.

Gwen tore her gaze from Del and turned to stare into Roxy's gray eyes.

"Don't lose it, lion," Roxy whispered. "Hold on. Remember, walking away with the most chips is the best revenge."

The dealer shuffled and the dance began.

DEL STARED AT THE TABLE, trying to concentrate on the play and failing miserably. He should have been focusing on the nearby faces, some of whom were new to him. He should have been following their choices, logging them mentally so that when a crucial hand arose, he'd know how to handle it.

Instead behind his sunglasses he watched Gwen. He could see that the night had been no easier on her than it had been on him, but it was scant comfort. He'd never meant to hurt her. What he'd wanted was trust, honesty. What he'd looked for was some assurance that his feelings were valid, that the person he'd realized he'd fallen in love with was real.

Instead she'd thrown up a wall before him, a wall between them. And maybe that was for the best. Maybe they didn't have a future together. If so, better to know it now.

"Your bet, sir?" Not only the dealer but the entire table was looking at him, Del realized. Quickly he assessed and saw that nearly everyone at the table had folded save him and Gwen. She'd just raised and sat staring at him, eyes defiant, challenging him to take her on.

He took a quick glance at his pocket cards. Ace and king of hearts. There was a determined set to her shoulders that told him she had something. Queens? Jacks? He raised. It was worth it to him to hold on and find out.

Gwen called to stay with him and the flop brought a jack of diamonds and a ten and a two of hearts. There were hearts everywhere, it seemed, he thought as he raised. So why did his own chest feel so hollow?

Gwen called and they both nodded to the dealer.

The turn brought a four of spades. *Call a spade a spade, Del, old boy, and admit that you're not going to walk away from this one without leaving a piece of yourself behind.* Whether he'd intended to or not, he'd screwed up by telling Jessup about the story. He'd broken Gwen's confidence. Even if they managed to get past that, the fundamental problem of who she was and who she was pretending to be remained. He'd fallen for a pretty face and deception once already in his life. He couldn't do it again.

Gwen curved her fingers around her stacks of chips. For a few seconds she didn't move, as though she were steeling her nerve. She stared at the table and then raised her head and stared directly at Del. She moistened her lips. "All in," she whispered.

All in was a challenge, it was a confrontation. So why did it feel like a reproach? The seconds ticked by. He could see the pulse beating in her neck; he couldn't tell if her reaction was fear or excitement. *Stop making it personal and start playing the game.*

He called her.

All in meant showing everything. Gwen turned up her hole cards to reveal a jack and a seven. He turned up his king ace. The silence was deafening. The lights felt hot. He stifled the impulse to take Gwen's hand. For an instant he had the ridiculous thought that whatever they had to face, they could face together. And he knew he was wrong, because they were facing it apart.

The dealer laid the river card on the baize facedown and set his fingertips on it. The seconds crawled by. Then he turned it over.

And a cheer erupted from his supporters in the stands. Jack of hearts. His heart was on the table, Del thought aridly. He'd won the pot, his flush beating Gwen's three of a kind. He should have been overjoyed.

He wasn't.

GWEN SWALLOWED. EVEN THOUGH her goal had been to knock herself out of the tournament to go search Jerry's room, it had taken so much to push all of her chips forward. Watching Del rake them in was easy. He'd taken her heart already. What was a few hundred thousand in chips? He'd won the hand just as he'd won whatever had passed between them. And now her part in the game was over, just as her part in his life.

The humming silence within her matched the silence around the table. She rose, gave Roxy a hug and walked away.

And at the edge of the crowd she saw Stewart.

JERRY'S ROOM LOOKED THE worse for wear when they walked in, with clothing strewn around and empty bottles set out. As soon as they closed the door, Gwen crossed to the television and turned it on to the poker game, muting the sound.

And, of course, the camera was focused on Del's face as he stared down at the table. Was it her imagination or was there regret in the set of his mouth? *Foolish,* she chided herself, seeing what she wanted to see. It wasn't there. He was perfectly happy with the way things had worked out between them. There was no point in thinking differently.

Just as there was no point repeating her search. She knew where the envelope was. The challenge was to get it. "Over here," she told Stewart and walked into the minibar area. The refrigerator was just as difficult to get to as it had been before. With his thicker hands, Stewart had less luck than she had had.

Her hand on the refrigerator, Gwen looked around vainly for something long and skinny to use to draw the envelope out with. Why hadn't she come prepared?

"Let's just pull it out of there," Stewart said, edging past her.

He managed to get his fingers on the top and bottom of the refrigerator to pull it out enough that Gwen could get her hand underneath. So close, so close. "Can you pull it out a little more?" she asked.

"Can't. The cord's too short."

She edged her hand in just a bit farther, gritting her teeth against the discomfort. *Almost there,* she thought, brushing it with her fingertips. Almost… "I've got it," she cried out jubilantly and slid the envelope out.

It was stiffened with cardboard, still warm from its contact with the refrigerator. Finally, at last, it was in her hands. Now all she had to do was look. It was like taking the first peek at her pocket cards. She pulled up the flap of the envelope. And disappointment filled her, dry and bitter like ashes in her mouth.

The envelope was empty.

Stewart read it all in her face. "Gone?"

She nodded numbly, trying to comprehend the enormity of the disaster. "Gone."

"He couldn't possibly have sold them."

"It doesn't matter. They're not here."

"We need to search the rest of the place." There was a note of desperation in his voice.

"I've looked everywhere else."

"But that was almost a week ago, right? He could have moved them." Stewart went to the bedroom.

Gwen started to follow and froze. "Stewart." She gestured to the television. It was panning over the whole final table. And Jerry was nowhere to be seen.

Stewart cursed. "How long's he been out?"

"I don't know," she snapped. "I wasn't watching. Come on, get the refrigerator back in place, quick. We can go down the stairs to the next floor, take the elevator from there."

"All right. I—"

Before he could finish, there was a click at the door. It opened to reveal Jerry.

"What the—" He stepped through the door. "What the hell are you doing in my room?" he demanded, taking two swift steps inside.

Gwen opened her mouth, trying wildly to think of an explanation that would work. "It's not how it looks. I—"

"You've been a bad boy, Jerry."

The words came from behind her. Gwen whipped around to see Stewart staring ahead of her, staring at Jerry.

And in Stewart's hand, a gun.

22

DEL SAT AT THE TABLE, splitting a stack of chips with one hand and riffling them together as if they were playing cards. Outside he appeared calm. Inside his thoughts were buzzing.

Both Gwen and Jerry were out, within maybe twenty minutes of one another. Both of them had been high in the chip count. Both of them had gone out on a limb with only so-so cards—Gwen on a jack seven, Jerry on a jack two.

He didn't like it. He didn't like it a bit.

Her plan had been to bail out of the tournament and use the time to finish her search of Jerry's room. If she'd gone through with it, she'd be in Jerry's room right now. Del tensed. As soon as Jerry had cashed out, he'd left the table. For where? Maybe the bar, maybe a strip club.

Or maybe his room.

She'd told him it wasn't his problem. She'd told him she didn't want him involved. He should just sit here then and let her deal with it, right?

Bullshit.

Del looked around trying to spot someone from security. He needed to dig up Ahmanson and he needed him now. The last thing he needed to do was sit here flipping chips in a card game.

"Your bet, sir," the dealer said.

Just do it, Del told himself. So he'd played his way to

number six. He was an amateur. He'd probably be out legitimately any hand anyway. It wouldn't hurt. Not much.

He pushed his chips forward. "All in."

"STEWART, WHAT IN GOD'S NAME are you doing?"

"Please, Gwen, no more interference," Stewart replied in a strained voice.

She stepped toward him. "But, Stewart…"

Stewart moved the gun slightly in her direction, freezing her. "I mean it, Gwen. Please."

Jerry's face clouded. "Gwen? I thought your name was Nina," he said.

"Come now, Jerry," Stewart said mockingly. "Surely you ought to have recognized Gwen Chastain, even if she does look a little different these days. Gwen's been very helpful in all this. She was the one who tracked you down. Stealing the Ben Franklins was an idiotic, greedy thing to do."

Jerry glowered at them both.

"What's this all about?" Gwen demanded.

"Later. Mr. Messner and I have business to discuss."

"You got no business with me unless you got money," Jerry snarled.

"Well, yes, it's true—money has been a problem. That's why I brought this." Stewart tilted the gun slightly. "Changes the negotiating strategy, don't you think?"

"Oh, come on, Stewie. You been watching gangster movies lately, learning how to act like you've got balls?"

Stewart almost smiled. "I don't need balls. I have a gun."

"You don't scare me with that. You don't have what it takes to pull the trigger. Besides, you shoot me, you're going to bring a crowd of people running in here."

"Well, I guess that will be my problem, won't it? Since you'll be dead."

"You wouldn't," Jerry repeated, though suddenly a little more subdued.

"Not if I don't have to." Stewart turned to Gwen. "Gwen, search him. Pay close attention to his pockets. Shoes and socks off, Messner. Pretend you're at the airport."

Gwen obeyed him automatically, her mind trying to process the situation. Stewart and Jerry knew each other. Stewart was holding a gun. Her mind couldn't accept the obvious conclusion that the man her grandfather had trusted for over twenty years had betrayed him, betrayed them all. There had to be an explanation, she told herself. It was like having a suited king queen in her pocket. The flop and the turn and the river ought to come and convert them to a straight, into something that made sense.

Only the turn was already here, standing in front of her. And she had nothing.

She ran her fingers through Jerry's pockets, pulling out keys, a lighter, a pack of cigarettes, his cell phone—hating to touch him and wanting to get through it as quickly as possible. She put the collection on the coffee table.

"Smart enough not to have the stamps on you, not smart enough to protect yourself, huh, Jerry?" Stewart coughed and winced, holding his side.

"You're the one's going to need protection, Oakes," Jerry replied, suddenly more confident. "That ain't a cold you've got, is it? You've had visitors. What, your Swedish buddy getting impatient? Or are you running behind on the vig again?"

"Oh, Stewart," Gwen said as understanding began to dawn. "You said you had stopped."

"Yeah, old Stewie's gotten his nuts in a vise, haven't you, Stewie?" Jerry taunted. "Mr. High Roller here can't play poker for shit and he doesn't know when to say enough. So you can't kill me, can you? You can't afford not to have those stamps." The cockiness was back in full force. "So why don't we just cut the crap and talk about when I'm going to see my money."

Stewart looked at the pile of objects on the coffee table.

"Keep going, Gwen," he said quietly. "The jacket."

Jerry stiffened.

As soon as Gwen patted his breast pocket, she knew. The envelope felt stiff and just thick enough. She slid it out and stepped away from Jerry. Hardly daring to breathe, she opened up the flap—

And stared at the upside down airplanes of the inverted Jennys, rising and falling across the block. And in front, shimmering in glassine, was the rich blue of the two-penny Post Office Mauritius, the white profile of the monarch looking imperious and just a bit amused.

After all that had passed, here they were in her hands. She began to flip through to check the contents of the envelope. The Ben Franklins and the Columbians were gone, she knew that. She frowned.

"The red-orange Post Office Mauritius won't be there," Stewart told her matter-of-factly, "and whatever this idiot fenced from the store inventory. But the rest should be there."

"What do you mean, the red-orange Mauritius will be gone?"

"He means I gave it to him before I realized he was trying to stiff me and he's sent it off to his friend," Jerry put in.

"Not now, Jerry."

"Why not?" Jerry glared at Stewart. "You gonna shoot me?" He turned back to Gwen. "Old Stewie here got himself in a hole in Vegas, the kind of hole that takes a loan to get out of. I see it happen to losers like him all the time. You get a little bit of money and it costs a whole lot—and it costs more all the time. And once they own you, you stay owned. Unless they sell you. Is that what happened with your Swedish friend?"

Stewart's face looked gray and sweaty, tight with strain. "That was a legitimate business deal."

"Legitimate, my ass. These guys are connected and they sell information. Anyone got a paper on Stewie Oakes? And they flick the right lever and you dance."

"It would all have worked out if Hugh had sold," Stewart said, looking at Gwen. "Everything would have been fine. The commission I was going to make on the sale was enough. It would have taken care of…my problems." His jaw tensed. "But no, he's just so damned stubborn."

"He wasn't ready to sell yet, Stewart. And he wants to go to auction."

"Poor Stewie, no deal," Jerry said sardonically. "Too bad you already spent the finder's fee on keeping your knees intact." Stewart looked sharply at him. "Come on, don't be surprised—I know people in this town, I check jobs out before I take 'em. I'd be careful if you're thinking about taking your Swedish friend for a ride, though. I got a feeling he might take care of you good if you try. He sounds like the kind of guy who'll make sure you don't even notice your knees anymore. And it'll serve you right, chiseling me out of my cut," he finished bitterly.

"So you blew your commission on a gambling debt so you didn't have it to refund when Grampa wouldn't sell," Gwen said, putting the pieces together. "And then you went to Jerry."

"If Hugh had been insured, no one would have gotten hurt." Stewart's voice was barely audible. "I never meant it to work out this way. You have to believe me."

"We're all crying for you, Stew," Jerry sneered.

Stewart glared at Jerry. His eyes hardened. "Yes, well, since I have the stamps and you don't have the money, I guess some crying is in order." He turned his eyes to Gwen. "Gwen, bring me the envelope."

"Don't do it," Jerry snapped.

Stewart's voice was flat and cold. "Gwen…"

It all happened so quickly. She took a step toward Stewart, then Jerry's hand gripped her arm like a tourniquet as he spun her around. "Don't you give 'em to that rat bastard!" he yelled.

And then his voice was drowned out by the loudest sound Gwen had ever heard.

When she recovered her senses, Jerry was lying on the floor, his shoulder a mass of raw red.

Gwen stared at Stewart in horror. His eyes blinked rapidly.

"Oh, my god," he said faintly. "Oh, my god."

It was as though time had stopped. She couldn't blink, couldn't stop seeing Jerry, the torn flesh, the blood. She could hear him groaning softly. Then she looked back at Stewart, the man who had been her bridge to civilization, the man who had betrayed her grandfather.

The man who had just shot a person.

"He's still alive," she said, her voice sounding very far away to her own ears. "We've got to get him to a hospital."

Stewart looked down at Jerry, then back to her. "I still need the stamps," he said in a quiet, breathless voice.

"Stewart, he's going to die if we don't get him to a doctor!"

"You don't understand," Stewart continued. "It's so much money, more money than I could ever hope to pay."

"Stewart…"

"No," he said, the strength returning to his voice. "Bring me the stamps."

Gwen's heart was beating like a trip-hammer. Her gaze shifted wildly around the room—to the door beyond Stewart that might as well have been a million miles away, to the bar she'd hidden behind a few nights before.

The bar that couldn't protect her now.

On the television behind the coffee table the game went on. How inconsequential it seemed now. When she'd been sitting at the table, everything had been so simple, she thought, watching the dealer lay down the flop on the green baize. Watch the cards, watch Jerry. Get the stamps back. Now, in minutes, everything had all changed.

"Gwen, bring me the envelope," Stewart repeated.

The dealer laid down the turn. The camera panned up to show the players at the table, to reveal that their number had been reduced yet again.

Del was gone.

Hope vaulted through her.

"Gwen." There was a warning in Stewart's voice.

"I can't do that, Stewart." If she could stall for time, maybe she'd have a chance. "I can't do that to my grandfather. You know he loves you like a son? He wanted to pass on his business to you."

"No, he didn't." Stewart's faced screwed up in disgust. "I left because it was clear he was going to pass it on to you. All the years I spent working with him and suddenly I didn't count. Blood is thicker than water."

"Then you know why I can't give you these stamps—even though you were almost like family." Gwen did her best to force a smile onto her face. "You know how much it meant to me for you to teach me all those things about life in America, to help me to become a normal person here?"

Stewart's face softened. "Gwennie, don't…"

"It's true," she continued as soothingly as she could. "In many ways I owe my happiness to you."

"But you don't understand," Stewart said, almost pleading. "I have to have those stamps."

"I can't give them to you."

"Then I'll have to take them." Beads of sweat sprang out on his forehead. "I'm sorry, Gwen. You have no idea how sorry. I tried to scare you away. But you're like a pit bull, you just wouldn't give up."

"The guy who jumped me, the room search—you were behind that?"

"I hoped it would push you away, but you just stuck with it. And now I don't have a choice."

"Of course you do."

"No, I don't." Stewart raised the gun and pointed it squarely at Gwen's chest. "Now give me those stamps."

And for the second time a loud sound boomed through the room.

"Security!" someone shouted and pounded on the door again. Stewart's attention flickered.

And Gwen saw her moment.

It happened in a fraction of a second that seemed to last forever. Her leap toward him, the feel of his arm as she thrust up the gun, the shot that shattered the window.

And the form of Del leaping through the opened door.

Suddenly they were all on the floor as the gun went skittering across the carpet, coming to rest under the bed. Stewart scrambled after it on all fours and Gwen grasped desperately at his arm while Del jumped on him, slamming his fist into the back of Stewart's head. Then there was another body on top of them and she was trapped in a maelstrom of flailing arms and legs. Gwen rolled away to see Stewart fighting wildly with Del and the security man Ahmanson. She crawled quickly to the bed.

With a strength born of panic, Stewart broke loose and swung at Del, catching his jaw. His arms surged toward Del's neck and gripped.

"Stop right there." Gwen's voice shook a bit, but the hand that held the gun on him was steady. "Give it up, Stewart, it's over."

"AND THEN DEL AND AHMANSON came in," Gwen finished, looking at the young police officer who was taking her statement. Stewart had already been cuffed and hauled off; Jerry was in an ambulance on the way to the hospital. Del was giving a statement elsewhere. In the end she'd told them about the stamps, partly because the envelope was there in the middle of the room and partly because she hadn't a clue how to go about tracking down the one-penny Post Office Mauritius. This time she really did need professional help.

"We're booking him down at the station, but you're going to need to come down to the security area in the casino to press charges, ma'am," a young officer with eyes far too old for his face told her.

Gwen nodded. "Just give me a couple minutes and I'll be there," she promised. She was exhausted enough to fall over. Instead she walked out into the concierge area by the elevators.

And saw Del waiting for her on a couch.

She crossed to him and sat. "How are you doing?" he asked.

She nodded. "Fine. They're going to charge Stewart with attempted murder, assault with a deadly weapon and anything else they can think of. I'm sure Jerry will be eager to hang it all on Stewart, but I doubt he'll be looking forward to leaving the hospital himself."

"Do they know where the other stamp is?"

"They mentioned some Swedish guy—a collector, I think. Stewart's clammed up about it. From what they said before you came, it sounds like Stewart owed money to some leg breakers and just about the time they were getting serious about hurting him, the collector came asking if he could get my grandfather to sell the Post Office Mauritius pair."

"Those stamps are hard to find, I take it?"

"Almost impossible. All but two or three are in museums. Stewart figured it was a slam dunk because my grandfather was retiring, so he got ahead of himself and used the down payment to pay off the leg breakers. Then my grandfather said no."

"Oops."

"Exactly. Stewart knew Rennie from when he used to go to Reno and when he saw her in Vegas one weekend, he figured she might help him out. Enter Jerry." She shrugged. "You know the rest."

"All but who the collector is."

"I've got some guesses, but I want to wait and see if Stewart says anything." But why were they talking about what didn't matter now? What she needed to say was how she'd felt when she'd known he was coming, when she'd seen him hurtle through the door and she'd felt not only relief but a rush of recognition, connection, rightness.

He stared ahead a moment, a muscle jumping in his jaw. "You don't know what it did to me to come through that door and see him with the gun," he said at last.

"There aren't any words to thank you for today. You saved my life." And it made her tremble a bit to know the words were true. "If you hadn't been there, I don't know what would have happened."

"When I watched Jerry walk away from the table, it scared the hell out of me. All I could think was that you might be up in the room and he might hurt you."

"And you walked away from the tournament. God, Del, two million dollars."

He brushed it off as he might an annoying fly. "Gwen,

you could have been hurt, killed. Who cares about the tournament? You were all that mattered," he said softly. "You still are."

She swallowed. "Last night—"

"Last night we both said a lot of things. But not the really important stuff."

"I love you, Del. I know this isn't the time or place to say it, but I do and you should know that."

He stared at her. "God, Gwen, I don't—"

The elevator doors opened to arguing. Pete Kellar walked into the lobby, arguing with an officer. "Hey, I got a press pass. I'm coming through to meet with a colleague." He walked up to Del. "Hey, Redmond. Brother, you look like shit. The guy caught you with one, huh?"

Del's eyes iced over. "What are you doing here, Kellar?"

"Hey, gotta get the story. I heard it on the police band. I figure with an exclusive interview with you, this is going to be killer." He shoved his pocket recorder in front of Gwen. "So, you part of this? You the one with the stamps or you just helping him out?"

"Kellar." Something flinty and cold and absolutely dangerous looked out of Del's eyes. "You've got exactly one second to put that thing away before I put your nose through the back of your skull."

Kellar backpedaled. "Hey, you got no call to talk like that. I'm just doing my job. I've only got a coupla hours to get the story done."

Del stared at him.

"Hey, this could be front page in the Vegas paper, maybe even make the *Globe* or get picked up on the AP." He gave Del a look of disdain. "Come on, buddy, you're a reporter. You can't stand in the way of a story, particularly not one like this."

Del stared at him, then nodded slowly. "Okay. Five minutes, then we talk."

"Yeah? Cool." Kellar bounced a little on his toes. "Okay, I'll just wait for you out here." He gave a little wave and left.

IT WAS LIKE CLIFF DIVING HE'D done in high school from the bluffs of La Jolla—knowing what he had to do, scared as hell of what it meant, but still making himself take that step. And then flying through space, hoping to god that he'd do it right.

Gwen stared at him, her face paper-white, her eyes enormous. "What are you thinking?" she whispered.

Watching her, he felt as though he'd been gut-punched himself. "I have to work with him, Gwen."

"What, because of some fraternal secret-handshake thing? The Loyal Order of Reporters? I tell you I love you and you want to violate me in the papers with that guy?" Her words dripped with loathing.

"It's not like that," he told her steadily.

"Then what's it like?"

"Gwen, I have to do this story." He took her hands in his. "I don't have a choice. *We* don't."

She yanked them away. "Funny, that's exactly what Stewart said when he was holding a gun on me."

That one got to him. "Gwen, this story is going to happen no matter what. If I work with Kellar, I can spin it in the way that hurts you least. If I'm not a part of it, he's going to dig deep, because he's young, he's ambitious and he wants to move onto the main paper."

"And, of course, you don't have any ambitions at all, right? Nothing that a story like this would help?" Gwen rose and walked blindly toward the elevators.

"Gwen, wait."

"I don't need to hear any more, Del. You want to do this, fine, but don't sit there trying to justify it and make it all right, because it's not."

"Just listen to me."

"No!" She spun to face him, eyes burning with fury and betrayal. "I won't. You said just trust me before and I did and then I found out that you sold me out the first time. And then, dummy me, I fall for your line again. 'Gwen, you're all that matters,'" she mocked. "How *dare* you?"

He looked at her helplessly. She wasn't playing a role this time. This wasn't Nina doing the dirty work. This was Gwen in full righteous fury and there was no way to reach her. "Gwen, think about this for a second," he said softly. "I don't want this to be the end."

For a moment something utterly vulnerable looked out of her eyes and then was gone, supplanted by anger. "Just stay the hell away from me, Redmond. Stay the hell away."

23

GWEN SAT AT HER DESK IN THE familiar confines of her office and lifted up a bright vermillion stamp with a pair of tongs. She didn't inspect it, though. Mostly she stared into space.

She'd been doing that a lot since she'd come back from Las Vegas. Ever since Kellar's story had appeared in the metro section of the *Globe*. If it hadn't been as detailed as she'd feared, it still reported the basics of the theft.

It was missing a lot of the details of the case that would have gotten the media excited.

And it was missing Del's byline.

It had been picked up by the AP wire and, she'd heard, the *Los Angeles Times*. Then again, Stewart's fall was the talk of the stamp world. She'd fielded phone calls for a while, but not as many as she'd anticipated, and her grandfather hadn't found out. Without the sensational splash, the run she'd feared hadn't materialized. So far, so good.

If waking every morning feeling as if she'd had her heart cut out could be called good.

If she focused on the details, things were infinitely better than they'd been before she went to Vegas. All but one of the issues were back in their appropriate slots, the burgundy albums safely tucked away in a bank vault. Insurance now protected the store inventory. No more would they be vulnerable to theft. She was back in familiar surroundings, back in her own clothes, back in her old life.

So why couldn't she relax and be comfortable with plain old Gwen again?

So why couldn't she forget?

The phone rang. It was the San Francisco police inspector assigned to her case. "I just wanted to let you know, we're going to have to drop the investigation into the Swede."

"But he's still got one of the stamps."

"We think that, but we don't know it. If he does, it goes under international jurisdiction."

"But he's got something worth more than a million dollars," she said a little desperately.

"Or someone does. This whole Swedish thing may be an invention, something Oakes cooked up to tell Messner. Maybe he just wanted them to sell himself."

"He wouldn't have done that to my grandfather."

A world of disillusionment went into his sigh. "You'd be surprised what people will do for money."

Maybe he was right. Gwen wanted to think that Stewart had been desperate and frightened and grasping at the only out he could find. She didn't want to think the theft was calculated purely for his gain.

Just as she hadn't wanted to think that Del had calculatedly given her up for a news story. And how gullible did that make her, since she had proof of both of their treachery?

"What does Stewart say?"

"He says he never met or saw the guy, just dealt with an intermediary, and he had no fixed contact information for him. We've got no trail. We couldn't follow it even if we had the jurisdiction."

"So you don't do anything?"

"On the missing stamp, no. Let Interpol look into it. Maybe they'll take it on. On Oakes, you bet. Las Vegas has got him cold on the assault and we've got him on the conspiracy charges—Messner's so ticked at being double-crossed and shot that he hasn't stopped talking yet. Oakes will definitely do time."

"How about Jerry?"

"There, I'm not so sure. His shoulder will heal. He's got a deal with the D.A., probably to plead to a lesser charge, especially since nearly all of the property has been recovered."

"Except for the million dollars," she said, discouraged.

"Except that," he agreed. "I understand your frustration, but it's more important to put away the guys who wave guns around than the small-timers like Messner. You can always file a civil suit against them both to try to recover damages. See if you can get some of Messner's tournament winnings."

Yeah, right. Good luck. She didn't even want to think about lawyers and lawsuits just yet. "So it's in our laps."

"For a lawsuit, yes." His voice hardened. "Don't even think about trying to pull your detective stunt again to get the other one, though. You got lucky this time, but you could have wound up with a bullet in your brain."

If it hadn't been for Del, she probably would have. Did she regret taking the chances—with Jerry, with Stewart? With Del? *No,* she thought. It was the living with it that was the hard part. "You're right, Inspector," she sighed. "I appreciate everything you've done. Thanks for filling me in."

Some things were easily cleaned up, she thought as she hung up the phone.

And some things weren't.

She was doing better these days. She managed routinely to go as much as thirty seconds at a time without thinking about Del. It would get longer as time went by, and maybe someday she'd get over this hollow feeling.

Maybe someday she'd get over him.

It was just the contrast, she told herself, all that excitement, then going back to her quiet life. She wasn't comfortable anymore as just Gwen, but she wasn't Nina, either. She didn't know who she was. She hung Nina's clothes in her closet and found herself sprinkling the garments into her normal wardrobe. Joss did a double take the first time but didn't say anything.

It was the glamour, the adrenaline rush. Del was just part of what she associated with it all, that was why she couldn't stop thinking about him. It had only been two weeks, after all. Sooner or later she'd forget.

In the meantime it helped to be busy.

Joss walked into the room. "I've closed everything up."

Gwen nodded, concentrating on her stamp.

"That means it's the end of the day," Joss told her. "You know, as in quitting time? When normal people go home and have dinner and relax?"

"I'm going to stay and finish some things up. You go along."

Instead Joss plunked down into a chair. "Earth to Gwen. Working yourself to death isn't going to make it go away."

"What do you mean?" Gwen asked with forced casualness.

"You've been at it until nine or ten at night since you got back from Vegas. It's not like this is brain surgery. There isn't that much work to do here." She looked at Gwen sympathetically. "But then, it's not about work, is it?"

Gwen blinked. "I miss him, Joss. I shouldn't. I know it's stupid and I know he screwed me over, but I can't get him out of my head." Her eyes filled and she blinked furiously.

"It's okay to be upset."

"No, it's not." She wiped her eyes. "I figured being back here would help. You know, same old, same old." Settle back into her familiar routines, pretend that whirlwind of Vegas had happened to someone else.

She'd been wrong.

She missed it. She missed the tournament. She missed Roxy, who she'd never even congratulated on her second tournament win.

And she missed Del most of all.

"I keep thinking I'm going to run into him somewhere. It makes me afraid to go out." And it made her wonder, every street she walked down, every restaurant and store she entered, whether she'd see him, whether he'd been there. He haunted her everywhere she went.

He was going to for a long time.

DEL WALKED INTO THE UNION Square station of the Muni Metro, working his way around the rush-hour crowd. He walked up to the newsstand, scanning the magazines. There was a time he'd have read the *Globe* during his commute, but no more. All the paper was for him now was a reminder of all that had gone wrong.

He hadn't worked on the story after all, pleading involvement. Talking to Jessup hadn't gotten the story spiked, but it had pushed it to a small item on an inside page. He'd done what he could.

He didn't know when or if Gwen would understand. And he couldn't really blame her. Circumstances didn't matter. If he hadn't brought the original story idea to Jessup, none of this would have been put in motion. The gunshot might have wound up as a small item in the Las Vegas paper, if even that.

No matter how you stacked it up, he was at fault.

In the end he'd turned down the news job that Jessup had offered him. The cost, quite simply, had been too high. But it was more than that. Maybe he wasn't cut out for hard news. He liked investigating, but he couldn't maintain quite the remove from his subjects, he didn't think.

Certainly he hadn't when it had come to Gwen.

Regret twisted viciously in his gut. To have lost her was impossible, but to have lost her over a job that he now knew he didn't want was worse.

He now stared at the bright colors of the magazine covers. *Vanity Fair, Esquire, Harper's*—those magazines carried the kinds of stories that interested him. News but with depth. He wanted to get to know his subjects, not to be precluded from identifying with them. He wanted his insights to be a part of the story. He picked up *Vanity Fair* and flipped to an article on a lynching in the 1960s South. Then he stopped.

If these were the kinds of stories he wanted to do, why not pursue the magazines? It was all here before him, he realized, a chance to pursue the deeper, edgier stories that interested him with the depth he craved. He could keep writing for the newspaper and develop the magazine writing as a side career.

He handed the magazine to the cashier. Time to go home and start making some phone calls. It wouldn't be easy, he knew that, but with his track record he was confident he could get his foot in the door. Once he had a clip with one magazine, he could nudge his way into others. It wouldn't be easy, but it would be his, it would be something he'd made happen on his own.

Now if only he could make things right with Gwen as easily.

SUNDAYS WERE ABOUT ROUTINE, blessed routine. A long, lazy brunch at her little local café on Russian Hill that put tables outside when the weather was nice. The Sunday crossword with her orange juice. There was some small comfort in sameness, even if leisure time had become something to avoid. She'd stick grimly to her tradition and trust that eventually the pleasure would return.

"Pass me the comics, would you?" Joss asked, a piece of toast in her hand.

The morning sun was surprisingly warm on Gwen's shoulders—at least, by San Francisco standards. It was nothing compared to the baking heat of Las Vegas, though. She blocked the thought almost as soon as she had it. Las Vegas meant the tournament, and the tournament meant Del.

Gwen picked through the paper for the funnies, avoiding the sports page as she had ever since she returned from Vegas. She was having a reasonably good morning. The last thing she needed to do was see Del's picture above his column. These were the little tricks she'd found to help her get through the day. Avoid Las Vegas, avoid the *Globe,* but she was damned if she was going to give up the Sunday paper.

Joss took the comics from her with a sigh. "I missed this so much in Africa, the funnies every week."

"Me, too."

"Mom says it was the crossword puzzle for her."

Gwen fished out the *Globe* magazine that carried the puzzle. "That's my favorite part."

"See, you're more like her than you thought. You're more like me than you thought, too."

Gwen looked at Joss in surprise. "How do you figure?"

"Looks like a little of your alter ego rubbed off on you when you were out in Vegas. You're different since you came back."

"I am not," Gwen protested, but she knew it was true.

"I always wondered if you were really as quiet as you've always acted. About time you let that side of you out."

But what had been the cost, Gwen wondered as she flipped through the magazine, looking for the crossword.

And found instead a photo that dragged her back to the

final table at the tournament. It was a picture during play, a picture of all of them—Jerry sulking in his best poker-brat style, Roxy peeking at her hole cards, Gwen tossing forward a stack of chips. And Del.

And Del.

All In, read the headline. Life, Love and Tournament Play in Vegas. The author was Del Redmond.

His jaw was set, his face sober. His hair poked up in spiky disorder. And the silver lenses of his sunglasses reflected Gwen's face.

"She said her name was Nina," the article began. Palms damp, Gwen read on. When she reached the end, she blinked. The article had not, as she'd feared, been about the stamps. It hadn't even identified her, only mentioned Nina.

In the end poker is a little like life and a lot like love. You never know what's in the pocket cards of the person you're facing. Not unless you go all in. And when you do that, you hope to god you haven't totally misjudged the situation and lost everything. Because it can happen. I'm here to tell you it can happen. But sometimes, sometimes, you get it just right and the big risk gets you the big win.

The ones that haunt you, though, are the big losses. Those are the hands you play over and over in your head in the wee, wee hours when everything around you is still. Those are the hands you'd do anything in the world to have a chance to play again.

She said her name was Nina. I never got a chance to tell her I was sorry.

Gwen laid the magazine down on the table. "My god," she said faintly. "I've got to find him."

"SPORTS SECTION," ANSWERED A clipped man's voice.

"I'm looking for Del Redmond," Gwen said.

"He doesn't work on Sundays."

"Do you happen to know where I might find him? This is a friend of his from the tournament."

"Who from the tournament?" the guy asked suspiciously.

"Nina."

"Well." The voice was freighted with speculation. "I wish I could give you his number, but I can't."

"Could you call him and give him mine?"

The guy thought a moment. "Tell you what. He's doing his weekend radio show today. You could go down to the studio, maybe catch him afterward."

It was all she needed. Just a chance and a chance now. She couldn't wait.

GWEN SAT IN THE LOBBY OF THE radio station, watching the receptionist file her nails and listening to the current host trading badinage with a caller. Del's show was long over. Now she just waited patiently and tried not to scream.

The studio door opened and Del came out, laughing with another guy. There was that grin that had first stolen her heart, that devilment in his eyes. For a minute her heart just swelled. Then he caught sight of her and stopped. For a moment all he did was look, hope flickering over his face. He turned to his companion. "Hey, I'll see you later, man." They shook and he walked toward Gwen.

She rose. "Hello," she said stiffly. Now that she was here, all the words had dried up in her throat. When she'd been reading the article, she'd known what came next. Now she hadn't a clue.

"Hey." There was an awkward pause. "Big fan of sports radio?"

"I knew you were here. I saw the article in the Sunday magazine," she blurted. "I had to talk with you."

He nodded at that. "Talk works." As though remembering they had an audience, he looked around. "How 'bout we get out of here, then grab a cup of coffee?"

Outside on the street she felt as if she could breathe again.

Del sighed and thrust his hands in his pockets. "So, Kellar's article wasn't bad enough, you wanted to know why I wrote another one?"

"No, that's not it," she replied. "It was a nice article."

He looked at her, eyes direct. "I screwed up, Gwen, plain and simple. I know apologies don't mean much, but I wish there was some way to let you truly understand how sorry I am about the way things worked out."

"I'm sorry about the way I acted, too. I'm sorry about how all of it came out."

"I didn't work with Kellar on the story."

She nodded. "I saw."

"I tried to get them not to do it, but the best I could manage was convincing the editor it wasn't worth the full treatment."

"It wasn't as bad as I thought it might be. I think I have you to thank for that."

"It wasn't enough, but it was all I could do."

"It was more than I deserved." She paused. "Did you get the job?"

"I told Jessup I didn't want it."

"What?"

He shrugged. "I'm looking for magazine work. I think that's going to be a better fit for me."

She couldn't stop the smile from coming. "After reading your article, I bet you'll do a great job."

"Look." He stared into her eyes. "I meant what I said about the mistakes that keep me up at night. I fell in love with you in Las Vegas, Gwen." She caught her breath, but he pushed on. "I screwed it up and it's all I've been able to think about. I should never have said all those things to you about Nina. You're perfect just the way you are and I have missed you so much."

She moistened her lips. "I changed in Las Vegas."

"Maybe we both did." He reached out and brushed his fingers along her jaw. "I'm just sorry. And I'm sorry about the news story. It was a bad hand. I should have just gone out rather than play it the way I did."

"Well—" she gave an awkward laugh "—that game's over."

"Maybe we should open another," he said, watching her closely. "Start with a fresh deck, deal out a new hand."

"Okay, let's do that." Gwen stepped in and put her arms around his neck. "I'm all in."

His eyes came alive. "You mean it?"

"Weren't you the one who said that going all in was the only way to win big?"

"Only if you can get someone to match you."

"And are you going to?"

He pulled her to him and fused his mouth to hers. Then he raised his head and laughed. "You bet."

* * * * *

SEALED WITH
A KISS

BY
KRISTIN HARDY

To Ewa and Anna,
tack så mycket for all the help
and to Stephen kärlek

Dear Reader,

The stories I write are often influenced by my surroundings. When I found out I was going to go to Stockholm last autumn, I immediately began working on a way to bring that experience to my characters. I had great fun prowling Stockholm, searching out locations. Who knew they had a postal museum? And what a surprise to find in their collection a pair of post office Mauritius stamps, the very stamps featured in *Her High-Stakes Playboy*.

I hope you'll drop me a line at Kristin@ kristinhardy.com and tell me how you liked reading a Blaze® novel with an international location. Sign up for my newsletter at www. kristinhardy.com for contests, recipes and updates on my recent and upcoming releases.

Have fun,

Kristin Hardy

Prologue

San Francisco, July 2005

"WHAT DO YOU THINK of this one, Brandon, sweetie?" The woman looked at her towheaded young son, who sat like a spoiled prince in his tall chair. "It's got an airplane."

Maybe seven or eight, he thumped down his Game Boy and poked bad-temperedly at the stamps she showed him.

"Please don't touch them with your fingers," Joss Chastain said sharply. "They're easily damaged."

"Oh, Brandon doesn't mean anything by it, do you, sweetie?"

Brandon scowled. "I wanna play my Game Boy."

"In a minute, sweetie. This is something special you can do with Grandpop."

It gave Joss a twinge. She'd never collected stamps with her grandfather. Instead, while he'd been on vacation recently, she'd let a collection of the most valuable of his many rare stamps be stolen.

Giving her head a brisk shake, she laid a stamp collector's kit on the counter. "This has all the basics he'll need for collecting: an album, tongs, a perforation gauge, a magnifying glass and some nice starter stamps."

"Oh, this is perfect. He's got to join a club at school," she explained to Joss. "We thought stamp collecting would be good for him."

Meanwhile, Brandon's sister sat quietly on a chair nearer Joss. She was maybe three or four, quiet and big-eyed in a way that reminded Joss of her own sister. Joss smiled to herself and used sleight of hand to make the pen she held disappear.

The little girl's eyes widened. Her mother and brother bent over the merchandise, oblivious.

Joss winked at her. Enjoying herself, Joss made the pen reappear, then seemingly put it up her nose. She held her nose and blew, and brought the pen out of her ear and held it up.

The girl giggled.

"Don't bother the nice lady, now, Sarah," the mother said and the girl subsided obediently. Joss guessed she was often the quiet one in the background while darling Brandon got what he wanted.

Finally, the woman made her selection and Joss rang it all up. "That will be forty-three sixty-five," she said, making a mental bet that the purchase went in the back of the closet for good as soon as Brandon got home.

The woman handed her three twenties and Joss made change. "Here you are, that's ten, fifteen, sixteen ten and…hmmm, I seem to have lost the quarter somewhere. Do you see it on the ground?" Joss leaned over the counter and looked on the burgundy carpet. Sarah looked down, shaking her head.

"Nope," Joss said, "it's not here and it's not on the counter." She leaned toward Sarah. "I know, maybe it's here." Joss reached out and pulled a quarter from behind the ear of the little girl, who giggled delightedly. "Yep, that's it," Joss said, dropping it in the palm of the astonished Sarah.

She was still alternately staring at the quarter and looking at Joss over her shoulder as they walked out the door.

When the phone rang a moment later, Joss picked it up, still smiling. "Chastain Philatelic Investments."

"It's me," said a leaden voice.

The pleasure over entertaining children vanished in a sharp wave of concern as she recognized her sister's voice. "Gwen. My God, what's happened? You sound like hell." Gwen, who had spent the last three weeks in Las Vegas, as she tracked down the thief who'd stolen the rare stamps valued at four and a half million, and which represented their grandfather's retirement.

"It's done." Gwen let out an audible breath.

"You've found them? What happened? Did Jerry have them hidden in his room where you thought?" Jerry was the slick little hustler they'd hired to help Joss at the store while Gwen had traveled to some stamp auctions. It still made Joss burn in impotent anger to remember the way he'd conned her and broken into the safe to steal the stamps while her back had been turned.

"Brace yourself. Jerry wasn't working on his own. He was hired by Stewart."

"Stewart Oakes?" Joss repeated in shock. "How can that be? He worked for Grampa. He was Grampa's friend."

"He's not anyone's friend," Gwen said flatly. "Joss, he shot Jerry. I saw him do it. He was going to shoot me, too."

Joss groped for the chair behind her and sat. She swallowed. "Let me get this straight. Stewart pulled a gun on you?" On her little sister? She was going to hurt him, Joss vowed grimly. She was going to find him and wring his neck. He'd been like a big brother. No wonder Gwen sounded so shattered. "What was he thinking?" Joss demanded.

"I don't think he *was* thinking at that point. They said he owed money to some leg breakers and thought he'd pay them off with the commission fee he got from a collector who wanted some of Grampa's stamps. Only Grampa said no sale, and Stewart had already spent the money."

"He couldn't explain and pay the guy back over time?"

"I don't know. He won't say who the collector is but he sounds scared spitless."

Joss shook her head. "God, Gwennie, I just can't believe…I'm so sorry you had to go through this." She dragged a hand through her hair. "And I'm just sitting here being a lump. You could have been killed."

"I wasn't, though."

"As long as you're safe, that's what's important. And you got the stamps back."

"I didn't get them all. Stewart already sent one of the stamps to the collector."

"Not the Blue Mauritius?" Joss whispered, her hand tightening on the phone. The Blue Mauritius, their grandfather's prize. It was one of the most valuable stamps in the world, worth some one million dollars at auction.

"I got the Blue Mauritius back okay."

Joss closed her eyes in trepidation. "I hear a really big 'but' coming."

"The stamp that's missing is its companion, the one-penny Mauritius." Gwen hesitated. "If anything, it's worth even more."

1

San Francisco, two weeks later

"HEY, GWEN, I'm going to have wild sex on a jetliner today." Joss announced. She was sprawled on one of the chairs in the back office of the store, coffee in one hand and the newspaper in the other.

Gwen, blond and poised behind her desk, merely raised an eyebrow as she sat on hold. "And here I didn't even know you were going on a trip."

"It says so, right here," Joss said, pointing to her horoscope. "'Love and romance are in the air. Travel likely. Big dreams will come true if you leap for the stars.' And yours says, let's see, oh, yeah, 'Hunky, adoring sportswriter will sweep you out for dinner and wild sex in his marina condo afterward.'"

"You don't say." Gwen's tone was dry. "Horoscopes have gotten a lot more interesting, lately."

"So has your life," Joss observed, pointing to the photo of Gwen's new boyfriend smiling out at them from the sports page of the newspaper.

Gwen grinned, then snapped to attention as someone apparently came on the line. She cleared her throat. "Yes, this is Gwen Chastain of Chastain Philatelic Investments. I'm calling to check on the progress of the investigation of my grandfather's stamps."

Joss listened for a few minutes, then abandoned the effort. Better to wait until all was said and done and Gwen could fill her in. In the meantime, she took a sip of coffee and stared at the print on the paper.

Big dreams will come true if you leap for the stars.

Or maybe not. After seven years of leaping for the stars in pursuit of a career in music, she'd finally fallen to earth with a resounding thud. Four bands, four breakups, a résumé dotted with gigs at bars and small clubs around the Pacific Northwest. Along with doing street theatre magic shows, it had paid the bills, but not much more than that. At twenty-six, she wasn't a single step closer than she'd been as a nineteen-year-old with big dreams. She had nothing, no career, no money, not even a car. Maybe it was time to admit that she wasn't going to find the lucky confluence of circumstances that was going to let her perform for a living.

At twenty-six, maybe it was time to look for something else.

All things considered, she was probably fortunate that the most recent band implosion had taken place in San Francisco, home of her sister and her grandparents. After all, it had been a place to stay and a place to work while her grandparents went on their three-month tour of the South Pacific. For a few weeks, she'd pitched in without complaint, trying for once to fight off the inevitable restlessness and get on her feet.

And then everything had gone to hell in a handbasket.

"Dammit!"

Joss jumped at the sound of Gwen slamming down the receiver in the cradle. "You've gotten louder since you came back from Vegas, that's for sure. What's up?"

"Interpol," Gwen said, investing the word with an immense amount of disgust. "They're dropping the investigation of the one-penny Mauritius." Her voice vibrated with frustration. "A million dollar stamp, one of the rarest in the world, and they're just giving up."

"How can they drop the case? I thought you knew who had the stamp."

"I have a theory, even a name, but apparently that's not enough."

"They're investigators, aren't they?" Joss set down her coffee. "Can't they figure it out?"

Gwen pushed back from the desk in annoyance. "They can't find any leads. They say there's nothing to follow up on."

"I suppose Jerry could have just cooked up the story to make Stewart look bad," Joss speculated.

Gwen shook her head. "It doesn't make sense to me, not the way they were talking that night in the hotel room. I mean, Jerry says he stole the stamps for Stewart because the collector wanted them. It makes sense that Stewart might have slipped and said too much to him. They were buddies."

"Is that why they're testifying against one another?" Joss asked wryly.

"I think Jerry took it kind of personally that Stewart shot him."

"Sensitive. So Interpol doesn't believe that Jerry's Swedish collector is the same guy who tried to buy the two Mauritius stamps from Grampa?"

Gwen shrugged. "I don't know if they don't necessarily believe it, but they can't find anything to substantiate it." She rose and stalked over to rip a photograph of the smiling Stewart off a bulletin board and toss it in the trash can. "The stamps Stewart had stolen from Grampa's collection were for Karl Silverhielm, I'd bet money on it," she said, crossing back to her seat. "He's got a reputation for being obsessive and he's been after the Post Office Mauritius pair for the past five years."

It mystified Joss that anyone could be that hung up on little squares of colored paper. "What's the big deal about the Mauritius, anyway?"

"There are two of them—the one-penny and the two-penny. You know the two-penny stamp, it's the indigo one."

"The Blue Mauritius."

Gwen nodded. "The one-penny is a kind of red-or-ange."

"The Orange Mauritius?" Joss guessed.

"No one calls it that. They just say the one-penny Mauritius."

"Does anything about stamp collecting make sense? I mean, how can a measly stamp be worth over a million dollars? Why does anyone care?"

Gwen smiled. "They're over a hundred and sixty years old, for one thing, and they've got a story. It was all a big mistake, see? That's where the most valuable stamps usually come from."

"Like the upside down airplanes?"

"Sort of, only whole sheets of the Inverted Jennies are out there. Only a handful of Post Office Mauritius stamps exist."

"So what's the big deal? What was the error?"

"They were made by an island printer when the local post office ran out of stamps. The postmaster told him to print 'Post Paid' on them but he screwed up and put 'Post Office' on them, instead."

"The wrong words? That's what a million dollars of fuss is all about?" Joss shook her head in amazement. "You collector types."

"Silverhielm wants a Post Office Mauritius pair, badly."

"So why didn't Grampa sell? He's ready to retire, why not take the money?"

"I don't think he liked Silverhielm," Gwen said slowly. "There's something a little off about him and I think Grampa sensed it. Besides, his offer was only a million for each."

"I thought that was what they were worth."

"Separately. Together, they've gone at auction for as much as three million."

It paralyzed Joss to think about that kind of money. It paralyzed her that she'd been the one responsible for losing at least part of it. "Did Grampa have any idea they'd be worth that much?"

"He got them from his grandfather and they probably weren't cheap when he got them. Like investing in gold bars. Expensive, but worth it."

"Except that it's not so easy to stick gold bars in your pocket and walk away with them the way Jerry did with the stamps." Joss stared moodily into her coffee cup. "It kills me to think about telling Grampa about this."

"It's not as bad as it was," Gwen said softly. "We got most of them back."

"You got most of them back, and you almost got shot doing it." Joss picked a quarter up off the desk and began rolling it in her fingers. "So why is Interpol dropping the case? Didn't they look into Silverhielm?"

Gwen nodded. "They say they've done some investigation but their hands are tied at this point. They can't just walk in and search his house or his safe-deposit boxes."

"I suppose not, but have they interviewed Stewart?"

"He doesn't know anything."

"Or won't say." He was a thug and a liar. As far as Joss was concerned, there was no reason he might not be a coward. Still… "Why don't you try talking to him?" she asked suddenly. "He might tell you."

"I'm not sure I could do it," Gwen said, resting her chin against her hands. "It's too hard, knowing what he did and seeing him again. He was practically family."

Fresh anger coursed through Joss. Stewart had worked at the store when Gwen had been a gawky fourteen-year-old, looking up to him. She'd trusted him. They'd all trusted him and gotten only betrayal for their troubles.

Gwen shook her head. "Anyway, even if he confirmed that it was Silverhielm, what am I going to do, fly to Stockholm and camp out on the guy's front porch?"

"Stockholm?" Joss blinked and sat up. "Wait a minute, isn't the International Stamp Expo in Stockholm next week?"

"Yes, but I've got too much going on here. I can't go."

"No, but I could," Joss said, her eyes flashing. "Remember? *Travel is likely.*"

"Don't be ridiculous."

"Why is that ridiculous? You did it." A chance, she thought, a chance to make things right.

"I went to Las Vegas. This is Stockholm. You don't even speak the language," Gwen said in exasperation.

"I'll find someone who does. Hell, I'll hire a translator. Look, Gwen, all of this was my fault."

"It was both of our faults."

Joss shook her head. "If I hadn't left Jerry in the store with access to the safe, he'd never have had the chance to steal everything."

"He would have gotten to them sooner or later," Gwen countered. "I should never have hired him."

"Which you did because of me. I'm going." In an instant, it had gone from a passing thought to something Joss wanted passionately. Needed passionately.

"There are other ways."

"How?" Joss jumped to her feet and began pacing.

"You've done all the work here. I've just sat around doing nothing." And it had rankled her, every minute. "I want my chance to make it right. You already had yours."

"And I almost got a bullet in my brain, remember?" Gwen said hotly. "It's too risky. Silverhielm isn't just some rich guy. He had Stewart hurt, Joss. He scared him to death. It's not a job for us. It's a job for the police."

"The police aren't doing anything," Joss flared. "Do you want to just write off a million dollars of Grampa's retirement? I don't. I can't, Gwen. I couldn't live with it."

"You may not live if you try to get it back."

"So I'll get some help."

"Like who?"

"I don't know," she snapped. "I'll call my friend Tom, the promoter at Avalon."

"A music promoter's going to be able to go with you to Stockholm and get stolen property back from a criminal?"

"Why not? A sportswriter helped you. Look, Tom knows this town inside and out. He might be able to point me to someone who could help." Joss sank back down in her chair and looked at Gwen pleadingly. "I want to do this, Gwen. I need to."

Gwen sighed. "Well, we've still got most of my poker winnings as a war chest. We've got the money to do it, but only if you find someone who can really help you," she warned. "Not the music promoter. Someone who'll know what to do when you hit Stockholm."

"Okay." Joss reached out for her coffee and took a sip. "Can he be cute?"

"Wait a minute. You didn't cook all this up just so you could have sex on an airplane, did you?" Gwen asked skeptically.

Joss laughed. "Who, me?"

2

JOHN BAXTER leaned back in his chair and stared at the check in his hands. Smack in the upper end of the five figure range. Not bad for three months' work, he thought in satisfaction. For the first time since he'd started his executive security business two years before, he'd banished the wolf from his door. Not just banished it, kicked its ass from here till Sunday.

It was about time for a vacation.

The corner of his mouth curved a bit at the thought. It was an uncompromising mouth, some might have said hard, as they might have called the planes of his face hard with the high cheekbones, straight nose and taut jaw. Lines of care had been etched into his forehead and bracketed his mouth, but those who looked closely enough would see lines of humor as well.

Always, it was a face that was impossible to read. He'd cultivated the look in the seven years he'd spent working for the FBI and then Interpol. Even now, two years later, his eyes could still flatten into cop eyes that gave away nothing.

He hadn't left because he couldn't handle the work, he'd left because he'd been sick to death of politics and the endless levels of supervision and interference. Then again, he'd always done his best work alone.

He tore the check along the perforation and endorsed

it, laying it on top of the deposit slip he'd filled out so he could hit the bank on the way home. His office was spare, the mahogany desk clear of nearly everything but a blotter, the check and the phone that now burbled at him.

He picked up the receiver. "Baxter."

"Bax, Simon Fleming."

"Hey, Si." Simon Fleming, his contact at Mayfield, Cross and Associates. The young attorney was quick, a little cocky and hellaciously good at one-on-one basketball, as Bax regularly found out the hard way. Bax was under retainer to do occasional investigations for the law firm and they, in turn, sometimes steered clients his way. Like the client who'd written the hefty check Bax was currently admiring. "I didn't think you lawyers worked this late."

"Are you kidding? I'm trying to make partner. This is lunchtime."

Bax grinned and leaned back in his chair. "So what's up?"

"I'm sending someone over to see you. She's a friend of one of our clients, needs some work done."

"She?"

"Damsel in distress. Isn't that what you P.I. types live for?"

"I'm not a P.I., I'm an executive security specialist."

"So that's why your rates are so high."

"My rates are high because I'm good." Bax scrubbed at his wavy brown hair, kept cropped short for convenience. "So what's her problem?"

"Like I would know? I'm just trying to help out a client. It's your job to make me look good."

Bax grinned. "Is that covered by the retainer?"

"Making me look good? You know it, buddy."

"Then I want a bigger retainer." A light flashed on the

phone. Bax frowned. "Wait a minute, she's not coming over here now, is she?"

"Dunno. Depends on how desperate she is. I talked with her a little while ago."

"Hell, Si, it's the end of the day. I'm surprised the receptionist is even still out there to page me."

"Maybe you'd better go check it out."

"Whatever she wants, it's going to have to wait," he warned Simon. "I just finished the last job you threw my way. I'm taking a couple of weeks off." His first vacation in over three years, a trip to Copenhagen to see his cousins, maybe, or a jaunt to Prague.

"It's no big deal. A slick guy like you can probably figure it out while you're still booking your flight." He cleared his throat. "You make my client happy, you'll make me happy."

Bax snorted. "Next time we go back to contract, I'm upping my rate."

"Whatever you say, buddy, whatever you say."

Bax hung up the phone and stepped out into the hallway that led to the reception area of the communal office suites. So maybe having space here cost a couple hundred more in rent than a one-room office somewhere, but it gave him access to a receptionist, mail room and a slick conference room. More important, it gave his business an established air that reassured the kinds of clients he sought. Just because he worked without a staff didn't mean he had to look like a one-man show.

As long as he *was* a one-man show.

"MR. BAXTER will be with you in just a moment," the blond receptionist told Joss, punching the button on her console with one red-lacquered nail before she pulled off the telephone headset and prepared to go home.

Joss turned to the deep, pewter-colored couches that lined the walls. A receptionist? Who'd ever heard of a private eye with a receptionist? Then again, who'd ever heard of a private eye having a lobby with ice-blue carpet so thick you could snag a heel in it? And five-foot-tall ficus plants? Weren't P.I.s supposed to work out of tiny offices with venetian blinds and half-glassed doors, in tired old buildings on the wrong side of town?

Tom's lawyer was going to have a lot of explaining to do. She should have known better than to trust his referral. Simon Fleming had told her his investigator might be able to help her out. He'd neglected to tell her the guy was going to be some corporate clown.

An expensive corporate clown.

Scowling, Joss stalked over to the wall of windows that overlooked Montgomery Street, now pooled with shadow in the late afternoon. She didn't like the idea of telling her problems to some pretentious twit who'd look down on her. She knew the type—if you didn't have a brokerage account and an MBA, they wouldn't take you seriously. She could just imagine the kind of private eye who'd have an office here. He'd probably be short, for starters, pasty and soft. And balding, with a comb-over that didn't hide anything.

"Are you here for Executive Security Consulting?"

Joss jumped and whirled.

He didn't look soft at all, was her first thought. He'd come up behind her so quietly on the plush carpet that she hadn't heard a thing. Then again, he looked like he always moved silently. There was something about him that reminded her of a panther, dark, sleek and dangerous.

Then he smiled and the impression evaporated. He looked, if not entirely friendly, at least approachable.

"I'm John Baxter."

Tall, she thought, tall enough that she had to raise her chin to meet his eyes as he came closer. Not lanky, though. Self-possessed and lean, solid without being bulky. He looked like the kind of guy who could snatch flies out of midair or explode into violence if the need arose. Confident, capable and eat-him-with-a-spoon sexy.

She squared her shoulders and held out her hand. "Joss Chastain."

BAX WASN'T sure what he'd expected, but it wasn't her. She looked like nothing so much as a gypsy in her long flowered skirt and cropped T-shirt, her dark hair sweeping loose and wild down her back. It had red highlights, he noticed, then frowned at himself.

"Simon Fleming sent me over." Her hand was softer than he'd expected, and stronger. When she tugged it away from him, he realized he'd been holding it for far too long.

"I know. He called me. Come on back to my office."

He led the way down the winding hallway with its crown molding and subdued lighting.

"Pretty fancy digs for a private eye," she commented.

"I'm not a private eye. I'm a security consultant."

"Which means?"

"I check out security setups and do some investigative work—legal, industrial espionage, that sort of thing. My kind of clients expect to see this kind of office."

"Are you saying that I'm not your kind of client?"

Prickly, he thought. Nerves, maybe. Sometimes people got that way before they had to spill their story. Or maybe she was just feisty. She had that look. "I usually deal with corporate personnel. They're more comfortable with this sort of look."

"But you're not a cop?"

He opened his office door. "No. Strictly private sector."

"Exactly. Private eye." She walked past him, leaving a whisper of scent in her wake that had every one of his hormones sitting up and panting.

Now he was the one feeling prickly. Bax crossed to his desk. Taking his time, he studied her. She had the kind of bone structure that you saw in old Italian paintings, the mysterious arch above the eyes, the haunting hollows in the cheeks. Something in the set of her shoulders told him that she was very used to having her way. Her mouth was wide, the upper lip just a bit more full than the lower. When he'd first seen her, it had given her the look of a mistreated child, but now it made him think of stolen kisses in the darkness. He wondered suddenly what she looked like when she laughed.

"Let me know when you're finished," she told him, shifting to get more comfortable in his client chair, draping an elbow over the back. The trouble was, she didn't look like any client he'd ever had before and she was playing hell with his concentration.

Bax leaned his elbows on the desk and tried to ignore the taut belly exposed by her T-shirt. "So why are you so dead set on getting a private detective?"

"I need someone who's good at finding things. Are you?"

"When I decide to be. What do you need to find?"

She studied him in her turn. Finally, she nodded to herself, apparently deciding he passed muster. "A stamp."

"I've got a whole roll of them here in my drawer."

"Cute. This particular stamp is worth a bundle. It was stolen from my grandfather and I want to get it back."

"Why isn't he the one here?"

"He's on an extended vacation with my grandmother. My sister and I have been taking care of his business and the theft happened on our watch." She pushed the tumble of dark hair back over her shoulder. "I want to get the stamp back before he comes home."

Just for a second, that anxious kid expression came back. The urge to wipe it away flickered through him. "Do you know who stole it or where it is?"

"I have an idea. A colleague of my grandfather's, Stewart Oakes, was approached by a Swedish collector who wanted my grandfather's prize pair, the Blue Mauritius and the one-penny red-orange Mauritius."

"I've heard of the Blue Mauritius," Bax said slowly. One of the most valuable stamps in the world, as he recalled. "It's extremely rare, isn't it?"

"And worth a bundle. About three million for the two of them together."

Bax whistled. "I can see why you want them back."

"It. We got back the Blue Mauritius. It's only the one-penny Mauritius that's still missing."

"What happened?"

"The Swede made an offer, my grandfather said no. So Stewart hired a thief to get a job in the store and steal the stamps."

"Some colleague."

"Ex-colleague." Anger tightened her voice. "My sister was able to get most of the stamps back, and Stewart and Jerry—the thief," Joss elaborated, "are in jail."

"Sounds like something for the cops." The twinge of regret he felt surprised him. "It should be pretty easy to track since you know who the collector is."

"Well, that's just it. Stewart claims he doesn't know, just that maybe the guy is Swedish. He only met a go-between. As far as the police are concerned, the trail has dried up." Again, that look of desperation flickered across her face.

Bax shook himself irritably. No matter how vulnerable—and touchable—she looked, she was not for him. "You still have to leave it to someone like Interpol."

"They've given up on it. My sister is pretty sure she knows the identity of the collector, but Interpol said they'd investigated him and can't find any evidence to substantiate a theft or to allow them to search. They're on to more important things, I guess," she finished bitterly.

"Or maybe you don't have the right collector," Bax commented. Joss fixed him with a look that would freeze water. Definitely feisty. Amused, he leaned back in his chair. "All right, so, what do you want me to do?"

"Investigate, if you think you're up to it." She gave him an appraising look. "Simon said you'd worked in Europe and spoke a bunch of languages. I want to go over to Stockholm and check out the collector, see what we can find out. There's a stamp expo over there next week and we can—"

"Whoa." He held both hands up. "Hold on there just a minute. One, I haven't agreed to take on your case yet. Two, if you hire me, you have to let me do the job. There is no 'we.' I work alone."

"Well, maybe you're going to have to change the way you work. I can be a good partner." The corner of her mouth curved and for a fraction of a second he found himself putting a whole different translation on that phrase. "Besides, Simon said you'd help me."

"Simon's wrong." And he was way out of line sitting here getting hot for a possible client.

"He says you have a contract with him."

Simon had been saying entirely too much, Bax thought with annoyance, shaking himself loose. "But it doesn't guarantee referrals. All it says is that I'll talk to you." He pushed his chair back a little, preparatory to getting up. "It's an interesting case but I just finished a big job and

I've got some time off coming. And even if I did decide to take you on as a favor to Simon, I don't let clients work as assistants. It's not a game." The hurt kid look was back on her face, he noticed with discomfort.

His comments didn't dent her determination, though. "You want time off, come to Stockholm. Once we get the stamp back, you can jet off to anywhere you like. Who knows, we might have fun."

Then she smiled and the punch of sexuality blasted through him. Her smile was generous, radiant and filled with naughty promises. He found himself almost ready to say yes without thinking, just for the chance to see what came next. Still… "This isn't audience participation. If there's a crime, there's danger. I can't babysit and investigate at the same time. I can't have you involved."

"You have to," she blurted, then took a breath. "Look, you need me for your cover."

"What cover?"

"I've got it all figured out. We go over there together, as lovers. I'm Jerry's girlfriend—or ex-girlfriend, actually, only I've still got the Blue Mauritius that he's stolen and I'm trying to fence it." She rose and began to pace around the office intently, creating a picture with her hands as she walked. "I dangle it in front of the collector and tell him that for a small fee, he can have his property." Like her face when she smiled, her body in motion was a fascination that made it impossible for him to look away.

"*His* property?"

"You know that's how those people think."

He nodded as he folded his arms across his chest. "Oh, of course. And what happens after that?"

Her hands dropped. "I haven't figured that part out yet. But I'm working on it," she added hastily as he shook his head.

"No way."

"It'll work," Joss insisted. She leaned a hip on the corner of his desk, entirely too close for his comfort. "It'll at least let us confirm that he has the one-penny Mauritius and get a dialog going. You know how these criminal types work, Simon said you used to do undercover work. We can play like we're a couple, get a room together, all that." She gave him that smile of temptation again, like Eve holding out the apple. "Jerry's a hustler, through and through. I figure the type of girlfriend he'd pick would glom onto whatever guy could help her. Jerry's in the slammer? She'll find someone else useful."

He didn't want to want her. It had no place here. He groped for reason as her scent spread around him in an invisible net. "So why do I feel like *I'm* getting glommed onto as someone useful?"

"Of course you are. I'm trying to hire you, although you're making it difficult. What's it going to take with you?" Impatience filled her words. "I have to get that stamp back and I need your help to do it. Why not go over there and play pretend?" She leaned forward until she was just inches from his face. "Or do I have to make it for real? Would you do it then?"

It would take so little to close the distance between them. "Maybe." He regretted the response the minute it was out of his mouth. What the hell was he thinking?

He wasn't thinking, that was the problem.

A smile slid slowly across Joss's face. "Really?" she said, stretching the word out like it was hot taffy. "If I said I'd be your lover, no strings, the entire time we were in Stockholm, you'd do it?"

The situation was rapidly slipping out of his control. "Look," he backpedaled, "It's not that simple."

Something predatory entered her eyes. "Sure it is."

Before he could react, she'd risen to step in front of him, pushing his shoulders back against the chair.

"What are you doing?"

"A feasibility study," she told him and placed one knee on either side of his thighs, straddling him. Her eyes were deep and dark enough to dive into. Her scent wound around his thoughts. He watched without moving as she leaned in.

And when her mouth touched his, all he could feel was a hot, slicing arousal.

He had no business doing this, Bax told himself even as he closed his eyes. She was a client, or a potential client, they were in his office, at his desk and oh hell, he thought and gave himself up to it.

He'd kissed women before, even thought he'd loved one once, but he'd never felt anything like this. She was all he could touch. She was all he could feel even though she tempted him only with her lips on his, with the warmth of her thighs bracketing his own.

Her mouth was warm and mobile, her lips parted and ready to go deeper. With one impetuous move, she dragged him into want, into need. He wasn't used to needing anyone, but even as he struggled against it, she beckoned to him with her mouth, her hands and her body.

And he followed willingly.

SHE'D NEVER been able to resist a dare, Joss thought hazily as she let the taste of him flow over her. She'd planned to kiss him until his head spun, until the little head began to overrule the big head and he gave in and agreed. Maybe she'd been a little curious, too. After all, if she could give them what they both wanted physically and get him to Stockholm at the same time, what was the harm in that? She'd expected kissing him to be good and sexy.

She'd never in a million years expected the taste of him to rock her back. She'd never expected the feel of his hard shoulders under her fingers to set up a drumming demand in her head for the rest of him, naked. She'd never expected desire to take control. All too quickly, the kiss stopped being about persuasion. It existed for itself, for the tempting brush of his tongue, the soft slide of his mouth, the touch of his hands sliding up her back.

More. She wanted more. She wanted to toss aside caution and dive into this heady sensation, dive into him. And somewhere in there, she might lose control. Trembling, she pulled back.

"Well." She resisted the urge to press her fingers to her lips.

Bax stared at her as she walked back to the client chair. "What kind of a game are you playing?" he asked hoarsely.

"Just making sure we had chemistry." She sat because her knees wouldn't hold her. "So, do we have a deal?"

BAD IDEA, he told himself as his system refused to level. She was trying to play him and he was walking right into it. And yet, looked at a certain way, it made sense. Why not? Why not take the case? Solve her problem, make a little money and get a free trip to Stockholm and a warm and willing woman in his bed in the bargain. "Maybe," he found himself saying. "I'll think about it."

She ran her tongue over her lower lip. "You'll think about it?"

What could it hurt, he thought. "All right."

"Great. And you'll let me be part of the investigation?"

Not on his life. "Only if you can demonstrate to me that you know what you're doing," he hedged.

Joss rose and leaned over the desk to brush her lips against his. "Oh, I know what I'm doing, all right, Bax. Just wait and see."

3

"YOU'RE KIDDING." Gwen stared at Joss across the table at Rose Pistola that night, while the waiters bustled back and forth behind them. "You've promised to go to Stockholm and sleep with some guy you don't know from Adam?"

Gwen didn't sound nearly as horrified as she once would have, Joss reflected. Vegas had certainly changed her. "It's no worse than a one-night stand, which you've had recently yourself. Besides, I sort of know him from Adam. He comes with references anyway."

"How about blood tests? This is pretty out there even for you, Joss."

Joss forked up a bite of salad. "Why? The guy is sexy as hell. Why shouldn't I have a fling with him? You and Del just did out in Vegas."

"That was different."

"How? You might be serious about each other now, but it wasn't that way at the beginning. Look, we'll get the job done and have a good time while we're at it. Besides, you know the saying—if you've got 'em by the 'nads, their hearts and minds will follow."

"Ah. So, you're going to sexually enslave him and have your way with him, is that the plan?"

Joss considered. "It has its advantages." She leaned forward and the humor vanished. "The guy's good, Gwen, and we need someone good for this job."

Gwen looked at her, lips twitching. "Just don't bonk his brains out so much that he can't do any detecting."

"I sincerely doubt that'll happen, although you never know." Joss thought of the hard swell of his shoulders under her fingers. "If he was that good with his tongue when he was kissing, who knows what else he'll be good at."

Now Gwen did grin. "You're so bad."

"Oh, come on. Tell me the thought hasn't gone through your head when you've first kissed a guy."

"So, what's he like?" Gwen asked, ignoring her.

Joss considered. "Confident," she said finally. "Maybe a little bit of a control freak. Hot, though, really hot. He's serious but he's got this wonderful, strong face and you just know if he'd let loose, he'd be…" She thought of the way he'd looked after they kissed. "I got to him at the end, I could see it in his eyes."

"Watch out that you're not the one who becomes enslaved." Gwen pulled some bread out of the basket on the table.

"He's a guy. They're pretty easy to manage," Joss said carelessly, giving the busboy such a brilliant smile he accidentally overfilled her glass, slopping water on the tablecloth. "I'm not worried about it."

"So you fly to Stockholm together and then what? I mean, you can't just wander around asking everyone you meet questions."

"You said you knew this Silverhielm guy has the stamps."

"I said I *thought* he had the stamps. Not the same thing as knowing."

"Well, I hope you're pretty certain, because I've got a plan for getting in good with Silverhielm. It means taking a risk, though."

"How do you mean?"

Joss hesitated. "I need to take the Blue Mauritius."

"You're out of your mind." Gwen's reply was immediate. "That stamp is in the bank vault where it belongs, and that is where it's going to stay."

"We've got to have it to smoke out Silverhielm," Joss argued and outlined the plan, leaving out the fact that Bax had had doubts.

"It's too risky," Gwen almost wailed. "Do you know what it would do to the value of that stamp if it got so much as creased? Let alone wet or torn. It wouldn't even be worth the price of a replica. We can't take that chance."

"We have to," Joss told her. "It's the only angle I can think of. Don't you want the one-penny Mauritius back?" she coaxed.

Gwen pressed her face into her hands. "I can't believe I'm even considering this. You swear you'll be incredibly careful with it?" she demanded, raising her head.

"I swear."

"And you'll put it in a bank vault over there until you need it?"

"Don't worry about it, Gwen."

"Oh, like that makes me feel better. You need to take this seriously, Joss."

"I *do* take it seriously. Haven't I been different since I came back this time? Haven't I?" she demanded.

Gwen nodded grudgingly. "You've done a good job at the store. Frankly, I expected you to be gone a long time ago."

"I've changed, Gwen, I really have. Letting Jerry steal the stamps was a screwup by the old me. I need to make it better. Anyway, we've got Bax on the case, remember? He knows what he's doing."

"And what is he doing so far to earn his exorbitant fee?"

Joss shrugged. "He doesn't go on the clock until we leave, and that's got to wait for me to get my passport. Right now, he's looking into Silverhielm's background. I figure I'll see what I can find out, too."

"How are you going to do that?"

"Get a briefing from you, for starters. I need everything you know about the stamps Silverhielm has, who he deals with, where he lives, anything. If you've got it electronically and can send it to Bax, so much the better."

"That's not going to help you find him, though," Gwen pointed out.

"I know." Joss paused. "I need to go see Stewart."

Gwen sat absolutely still for a long moment. "Why do you need to go see Stewart?" she asked finally. "I told you before, he says he doesn't know anything."

"I don't believe that. Maybe nothing obvious, but I bet he knows some little nugget that will help us."

"He's in Las Vegas. It'll mean driving or flying."

"I know."

"It's not free, Joss," Gwen said with an edge to her voice.

"I *know.* You said we could use your winnings from the poker tournament to pay for Stockholm and Bax. I found a ticket that's twenty-nine bucks each way. I'll fly down in the morning and back in the afternoon. You won't even have to pay for a hotel."

Gwen drummed her fingers restlessly on the table. "What makes you think he'll talk to you?" she demanded. "He'll barely remember you."

"That might make it easier. He's probably so stir-crazy in the slammer that he'll see anyone just for something different. Besides, he's already pleaded guilty. At this point, he's just negotiating with the Vegas and San Francisco D.A.s, so it's not like anything he tells me will make a difference. What's he got to lose?"

Gwen mulled it over as the waiter set her grilled trout in front of her. "I feel like I should be the one doing it, but I just can't." She swallowed. "Do you understand?"

Gwen had always been so self-sufficient that she sometimes seemed more the grown-up than Joss. Seeing her vulnerability now, Joss felt fury at Stewart Oakes anew. "Of course. Don't worry about it. I've got it handled." She stared at her sister. "I'm going to bring back the one-penny Mauritius, Gwen, I swear it."

"Well, you'd better be quick about it. Grandma and Grampa are due back in a month."

Joss grinned. "Hey, with me and Superhunk on the case, it's a done deal."

JOSS SAT in the visitation room at the Clark County jail, waiting for Stewart. Even though she was on the outside, there was a heaviness in the air that made her shiver a little as she sat in front of the Plexiglas window at her assigned booth. She was here voluntarily. She could leave at any time. What must it be like to be inside, to be without a choice?

Except that an inmate like Stewart Oakes had made his choice long since.

Around her, the faces of the other visitors largely mirrored her unease. The expressions were sober, mostly, and distracted. It wasn't a happy room. People came here because there was trouble. Only the children seemed blithely unaware of the tension in the air.

For a while, nothing happened. Then she heard the faint sound of a door opening and the prisoners began to file into the visiting area on the other side of the Plexiglas, under the watchful eyes of the guards.

She wasn't sure what to expect. She'd had no recent connection with Stewart as Gwen had had. Then again, knowing him hadn't protected Gwen from nearly being shot, so Joss wasn't sure it really mattered. He'd either show or he wouldn't, he'd talk or he wouldn't. Either way, she'd at least know she'd tried.

The man who sat down, wearing tired-looking orange coveralls, looked nothing like she remembered. Joss had seen a photo of Stewart pinned to the office bulletin board. In it, he'd been laughing, his arms around Gwen and their grandfather. Despite the streaks of gray at his temples, he'd looked young, lighthearted.

He didn't look lighthearted now. Jail had not been kind to him. Age sat heavy on his shoulders. Dark smudges underlay his eyes and his skin looked grainy, his expression defeated. Some of her anger morphed to pity. She picked up the phone on her side of the transparent barrier.

Stewart blinked at her and scowled, picking up his phone in turn. "What do you want?"

"I'm Gwen's sister Joss. I was hoping we could talk."

He studied her. "Is Gwen here?"

Joss shook her head. The disappointment that flickered over his face erased her pity and aroused her anger all over again. "Are you surprised? Stewart, you held a gun on her."

He closed his eyes for a moment and then shook his head. "I wrote her a letter. Did she get it?"

"I don't know." She wasn't going to give him an inch, not here. After the damage he'd wrought, a letter of apology was laughable. "You put her through the wringer. She's still getting over it." Joss watched him rub his temples. "It looks like you're doing the same."

He gave a humorless grimace that might have been a smile. "That's all right. I've got lots of time to work on it. But then, you're probably not here to talk about me." He frowned. "Exactly why are you here?"

Joss studied him. "Trying to undo some of the damage. I'm hoping you might be able to help."

Before she even finished the words, he was shaking his head. "No. No way. Not without a lawyer."

"Stewart, you're already pleading guilty. It's all over but the shouting."

"Yeah, well, that shouting you're talking about could mean the difference between doing a year or rotting in here for five to ten. Besides, like I already told the detectives and inspectors, I don't know anything."

"Maybe you know more than you think, something that could help us."

"You got no business coming here." His voice rose and he started to get up.

"I've got no business coming here?" Joss snapped like the crack of a whip. "You threatened to kill my sister, you stole millions from my grandfather, you betrayed us all and *I've* got no business coming here?" She clenched the phone receiver, fury making her dizzy. "I don't give a damn what kind of a sentence they hand down to you. That's not why I'm asking. I'm trying to undo the damage that you've done. I'm trying to get back the one-penny Mauritius and you're the only one who can help me."

"How do I know you're not taping this?" he demanded.

"How could I be?" She gestured at the phone. "Anyway, what would be the point? It wouldn't affect your case, except to help you. You think they're not going to look a little more kindly on you if my grandfather has back all his property? Come on, use your brain."

"My lawyer would kill me."

"Your lawyer's not here now and neither is the D.A. It's just you and me, Stewart," she said persuasively. "You can't erase what you did to Gwen but you can help make things better. Don't you want to? Don't you want to try to fix it?"

She waited in silence, hoping that she'd read him right.

Finally, Stewart sat back down and rubbed his eyes wearily. "You don't understand. I couldn't help if I wanted to. I dealt with an intermediary the whole time. I never even found out the client's name."

"Don't sit there and tell me you didn't at least have an idea. Gwen thinks it might be Karl Silverhielm."

Stewart's gaze skated off to one side. "I told you, I don't know. I only dealt with my contact."

"What did he look like?"

"It's all in the police report."

"Save me some work. What did he look like?" she repeated.

Stewart shrugged. "Light hair, tall, blue eyes. One of those Nordic faces."

"What was his name?"

Stewart snorted. "Do you think for a minute he gave me his real name? You can bet it was a fake."

"What was it?"

"Michael Houseman." When she rolled her eyes, he shrugged. "I told you, there's nothing I can give to help you."

"Was there anything else about him, anything that would let us identify him?" Joss persisted. "Think about how he moved."

"He didn't look like a thug. He was smooth, classy, even. And he moved like he was trained, like a boxer or something."

"Can you remember anything about him that couldn't be changed, his ears, maybe, or the shape of his fingers?"

"Nothing that stands out. His features were normal, nothing unusual about them. His hands were—" He stopped.

"What?"

"Well, it might not be important."

"Let me decide that. What?"

"His right hand. There was a scar on it, between the thumb and the forefinger. I noticed it when we were shaking hands."

"What was it shaped like?"

"A jagged line, like a knife had slipped or something."

"Nice company you keep," she said dryly.

He bristled. "Look, you wanted me to help, I'm helping."

"I'm sorry. You're right. Look, you've given me something that might be useful."

"And my lawyer would knock me in the head if he knew I was talking to you."

"You did the right thing, if it helps."

He gave a brooding stare. "Little enough of that lately."

"Stewart." Joss hesitated. "This'll mean something to Gwen."

"Tell her…" The tone signaling the end of the visiting period rang. He waited until it was silent. "I'd give anything to have done things differently," he said finally. "Tell her that, would you?"

4

BAX SAT in his chair with his feet up on his desk, rubbing the back of his neck. He'd spent too much time on the phone that day, trying to clear up business so he could leave for Stockholm. And wondering if he were nuts. Now, as the afternoon bled away, he was trying to decide whether to write up his notes or just call it a night. He hadn't slept well the night before, waking in the darkness from dreams of unfulfilled cravings and dangerous pursuit.

And Joss Chastain.

The bargain they'd struck the previous day had been absurd, he knew that. He'd given her his word that he'd take on the case and he'd hold to it, but there'd be no charades of being lovers, no charades of being partners. His better judgment might have been overruled at the time but it had reappeared and he needed to do the responsible thing.

With a thump, Bax dropped his feet to the floor just as Joss swept through the door, all color and light in a pleated royal blue miniskirt and a stretchy blue and silver striped shirt that wound around her body.

"I've found something," she announced.

She was something, something he'd fought all day not to dwell on. Now, with her standing in his office practically vibrating with energy, their agreement seemed just a way to make a formality of the chemistry that flowed between them. The wide ebullience of her grin tempted him to taste. The curve of her waist begged him to touch. In a whirlwind second, she filled the room with her presence and completely destroyed his concentration.

And it pissed him off. "Now what?"

"I just got back from Las Vegas and I've got a clue."

"Let me guess. You figured out that we'll all be better off if you leave me alone to do my job?"

"Not that kind of clue." She gave him a withering stare and sat in his client chair, taking her time getting comfortable. The getting comfortable involved lots of shifting and stretching that made him only more aware of her body. "Now, if you're nice, I'll share with you. If not, I'll just keep quiet and let you tell me what you found out today."

Irritating, he thought. "Let's get something straight—"

"As your client, I've got a right to a report on anything you've found out," she reminded him serenely.

What she didn't have was a right to blow in here smelling of summer and seduction and completely fracturing his ability to think. "As my client, you pay me to do the investigating. That means if anyone was going to Vegas, it should have been me."

She didn't rise to his tone. Instead, she gave him a smile that made his pulse bump. "Some things need a woman's touch. Anyway, in two days we'll be flying all the way to Stockholm. Vegas is small change, by comparison."

"You still should have told me before you went. I've already got the police report." He held up a thick bundle of paper and slapped it back down on his empty desktop. "You wasted your time."

"Not at all. I went to the Las Vegas jail to visit Stewart Oakes."

"Who told you to take a flying leap, I hope." Bax frowned. "His case is still in progress. You shouldn't be talking to him."

"His case is a formality at this point. He's copping a plea on both sets of charges. Talking to me won't change that. Besides, I can be persuasive when I want to be."

Didn't he know it, Bax thought, tearing his gaze away from her mouth. "All right, Nancy Drew, what did he tell you?"

Amusement crossed her face. She obviously knew where he'd been looking. "Well, I tried to get him to say something about the Swedish collector, but he played dumb."

"Now there's a surprise."

"Not dumb enough. I mentioned Silverhielm's name and his eyes shifted. Even if he doesn't know for sure it was Silverhielm, he believes it is."

"You flew to Vegas for that?"

Joss bristled. Good, he thought. Keep her at a distance. Don't let her get close with that gypsy hair and those eyes that promised everything. "No. I've got information about the intermediary."

"Right. Houseman or whatever his name was."

"Stewart said the guy looked Nordic, moved like an athlete."

Bax gave a dismissive shrug. "That's all in the police report."

"And just exactly how did you get your hands on the police report, anyway?"

"A friend or two in the right places." And his good fortune that San Francisco had jurisdiction over the larceny portion of the case.

"Did the report also mention the scar on his hand? Ooooh, I guess it didn't," Joss singsonged with enjoyment and walked over to lean against the edge of his desk, facing him.

Bax looked at her. "There's a perfectly good chair over there." And he'd be much more comfortable with her at a distance.

"I'd rather talk face-to-face." Mischief lurked in her eyes.

"You're on my desk."

"Good." She leaned on one hand. "Something ought to be. There's something slightly disturbed about a person having such a clean desk."

"I like things uncluttered." Which meant not sleeping with clients, he reminded himself, but he couldn't stop staring at the long, lean lines of her body.

"Sometimes clutter is a lot more fun," she purred and touched the tip of her tongue to her upper lip.

Bax cleared his throat. "What about the scar?"

"Well, obviously it's an identifier. If we find Silverhielm, we look at his soldiers and try to find the guy with the mark."

"It's a long shot."

"It's something concrete. Anyway, what did you come up with today, Phillip Marlowe?"

"My Interpol contact didn't know a whole lot but he promised to ask around. He was able to pass on a few interesting tidbits, though."

"Such as?"

"Our boy has his fingers in a lot of pies. Officially, he does import/export. Jewelry, mostly. He seems to consider himself a connoisseur of the finer things. Lives on a private island in the archipelago to the east of Stockholm."

"Nice. Has he been in trouble with the law?"

"Nothing that showed up on any of the systems my contact could access. He's rumored to be responsible for several ugly murders. Word on the street is that he's not to be crossed."

Joss nodded thoughtfully. "Interesting."

"Interesting? How about disturbing?"

"Are you scared?"

"No, but you should be. If Silverhielm is involved, you have no business coming to Stockholm with me."

"But how else are we going to be lovers?" Joss sank down to lie across his empty desk, propping her head on one hand. "Why Bax, a person would think that you've forgotten all about our agreement."

He swallowed, his mouth suddenly dry. "I've changed my mind."

"But how can that be?" She slid her hand over her hip. "Oh, I know, I forgot about your retainer."

IF HE THOUGHT he was backing out of their deal, he was dreaming, pure and simple. She was going to Stockholm with him and she was going to be part of getting the one-penny Mauritius back. And if it took sex to make him putty in her hands, well, then sex it would be.

Small sacrifice for the cause.

Joss moistened her lips. "Something about an office has always given me the urge to misbehave," she murmured, trailing her fingers down her neck, into the deep vee of skin exposed by her blouse and over the soft swells of her breasts until she saw Bax's eyes darken.

Fluidly, she rose and crossed to the door. "Perhaps I'll just lock this." She flicked the bolt with a metallic *snick,* then turned to face him. "Well, now that we're not likely to be disturbed, how much of a down payment do you require?" she asked. "Enough to need one of these?" She rummaged in her purse to pull out a condom.

Without asking, she walked over to Bax's side of the

desk and sat across his lap. Then she laughed, a low, husky sound of delight as she felt the unmistakable shape of a hard-on beneath her.

"That's enough, Joss," he ground out.

"Oh no, Bax, surely your services don't come so cheaply." She slid her hands around to the back of his neck and into the springy waves of his hair. "And if you'd wanted it to be over, you'd have stopped me long before."

Joss leaned in to nibble his neck, tasting the taut skin, roving to the hard line of his jaw and cheek. His chest rose and fell unevenly, as though he'd been running. His hands sat still and loose at his sides. With the tip of her tongue, she traced the line of his mouth, absorbing his flavor, teasing him.

"Poor Bax. You try so hard to be good." She pressed her forehead against his. "But you want this as much as I do. Why don't you just admit it?" Her lips were a hairbreadth from his, her breath blending with his. "Why don't you just give in?"

And in that instant his control snapped and he claimed her mouth with his own.

The kiss was hard and deep and heedless. Her head fell back, inviting him to devour. She might have done the tempting but it was he who laid claim to her. He didn't ask permission, he just took. Hard and proprietary, his hands roved over her back, along her side and hip, then up under her blouse to curve over her breast. He touched her as though she were already known, already owned and he could amuse himself at will.

Joss gasped at his touch and pressed against him. "Mmm, more," she whispered. She felt his mouth curve against hers, then felt the trail of his fingertips up the inside of her calf, the inside of her thigh. She shivered as the light touch traveled up under her skirt and higher still, searching for that place at the apex of her thighs, that place where she was already slick and hot and craving his touch.

And then his fingers dipped in under the satin barrier and Joss jolted against him, moaning into his mouth.

Outside, in the hallway, voices sounded, footsteps thudded as people walked home for the night. Within the room there was only the two of them, touch and taste, sound and scent.

Bax's fingers slid against her, teasing, tormenting her with each stroke. When they slipped inside her, his tongue dipped into her mouth and a coil of tension began to build, tightening with each stroke. "Oh my God," she whispered.

And she heard the low rumble of his chuckle. "I'm not nearly done," he murmured, then gathered himself and rose, still holding her. Taking a step, he laid her back on the desk.

She felt the wood, smooth and cool beneath her shoulder blades. When he reached up and stripped the satiny fabric of her thong down her thighs, it was another kind of cool and another surge of excitement. Both were overshadowed by the warm stroke of his hands up her calves, over her knees as he knelt before her, dragging her thighs over his shoulders. Joss caught a breath of anticipation. He folded back her skirt, blowing on the sensitive folds of skin. And then the heat of his mouth was on her.

He didn't waste time teasing her and she didn't want it. His mouth was relentless, driving her, taking her up until all she could do was feel. She wanted it hard and urgent, she wanted the orgasm that curled in her, still half-formed. As he brought her close, though, he slowed down to leave her balanced on the edge, half gasping with pleasure, half delirious with want. And a fraction before the point of inevitability, he stopped and stood.

"No!" Joss cried out.

"Oh yes," he said softly. She heard the clink of his belt, the growl of his zipper, the crackle of plastic and his slow exhale as he sheathed himself.

The tip of his cock brushed against her, making her jolt. She stared at him, at his face drawn in taut lines of concentration as he positioned himself. And then he pistoned his hips to slide into her, fast and deep, and she gave a strangled cry.

Hard and urgent. She wrapped her legs around his waist. It was what she'd craved, this rush of sensation. His hands were unwrapping her blouse, pulling up her bra to find her bare breasts. The feel of his cock possessed her, the fullness, the slick rub against her tender inner flesh as each move teased her clitoris, tormented, inching her closer and closer to orgasm.

Bax caught at her ankles, straightening her legs, pulling them apart to watch as he buried his cock deep in her tight, warm wetness. Stroke after stroke, he got thicker and harder, thicker and harder as the orgasm gathered. He gritted his teeth, holding on, promising himself one more stroke, and one more until she began to shudder and shake and cry out as orgasm burst through her. And when it was done, he let himself follow.

"I DON'T KNOW about you, but I'm thinking we'll be able to do a pretty believable job of pretending we're lovers," Joss said lazily as she pulled her clothing back on.

With her hair loose and wild and that light of satisfaction in her eyes, she looked more enticing than ever. If there had been a bed in the room, Bax would have been giving serious thought to tumbling her back into it.

"Too bad you don't have a couch in here," Joss commented, as though she'd overheard his thoughts. "Just think about Sweden." She leaned over for a quick kiss, and topped it off with a bawdy wink.

Bax tucked in his shirt. "I don't like the idea of you going over there," he said. "Silverhielm and his guys are too dangerous. Do you really understand what you're getting into?"

"It's not your decision. I'm going over there, whether you want me to or not," she told him. "Now, if you want to be involved and work with me, that's great, but I'm doing it no matter what."

The desperate kid look was back again and it tugged at him. Mentally, he cursed. He didn't get the sense she was doing it for show. She was telling him the truth as she saw it. Stubborn, contrary, unpredictable and somehow very good at getting over on his blind side.

He'd be better off stopping right now, but there was something about her that he couldn't walk away from. If it meant going to Stockholm with her to keep her safe, he'd do it, he realized.

And if it meant giving in to both of their desires against his better judgment, he'd do that, too.

5

AT FIRST GLANCE, Stockholm seemed to be as much water as land, vivid bands of blue weaving their way among the confusion of islands that formed the city. Whereas most metropolitan areas boasted a single river winding through, in Stockholm water charmed the visitor at every turn, from broad passes to narrow inlets between the steep rock, or tree-lined edges of the islands. Bridges vaulted from shore to shore and boats and ferries sailed in between, seeming more a part of the city than the streets and cars.

As the taxi brought Bax and Joss into the heart of Stockholm, the modern utilitarian structures that had dominated the landscape at the fringes gave way to the aged, graceful buildings of the old city. They sat shoulder to shoulder on the waterfronts, their ornate and gabled facades tinted ocher and blush, tan and pale yellow. The old city was a pastel fantasy, reflected in the rippling waters of lake and sea.

"It's lovely," Joss murmured. "So much blue and so many trees. I had no idea."

"You should see it farther east, in the archipelago," Bax said. "It's something else, just islands and water. That's where our friend lives, on his own private island."

"His own private fortress, more like." Joss stared out the windows of the cab, eagerly taking in the sights of the city. "So you've been to Stockholm before, I take it?"

"Passed through a few times."

"Often enough to know anyone useful?"

He gave her a pitying look. "Isn't that why you hired me? As a matter of fact, I've already arranged a meeting."

"I apologize for underestimating you," Joss said, looking over to see him relaxed on the seat in his travel clothes. She should have known he'd be organized. There was nothing for getting to know another person like taking a long and complicated international flight together. Bax always had ticket and passport in hand, chose the right line, knew where their seats were. That wasn't too much of a surprise to her. What had been a surprise was how quickly the hours together had gone, lightened up by his flashing humor and odd bits of knowledge.

She'd expected the trip to be illuminating on the subject of John Baxter. She hadn't expected it to be fun.

The taxi swung around a U-turn and pulled to a stop in front of a rococo fantasy of a hotel. "The Royal Viking," the cab driver announced. Windows topped with stylized lintels marched across the high, sheer front of the hotel. On the first floor, elaborate carvings decorated the rosy stone facade. Flags flew from the green copper roof, snapping in the breeze. Behind them, script letters spelled out Royal Viking against the sky.

At the foot of the hotel lay the waterfront, lined with the white tour boats and ferries.

The building had the same sort of presence as an aging prima ballerina, stylish and graceful, but mellowed. There were small signs, perhaps, of the passage of time, but the bones and muscles remained disciplined.

"The Royal Viking, huh? You've got expensive taste," Bax commented as they got out.

"I figure if we want to get our friend's attention, we've got to walk the walk, as well as talk the talk," Joss said with a little smile, watching the blue-uniformed bellhop bring a wheeled luggage rack out to collect their bags. "If I've inherited some of Jerry's stolen swag, I should already be living well off the more easily fenced items, right? Besides, if they think I'm not too smart, they're likely to drop their guard."

"To their peril."

She smiled at him. "Exactly. By the way, the room's under your name," she said over her shoulder and walked through the doors into the hotel.

"What?" Bax stopped her, brows lowering.

"Well, we don't want our friend to somehow find out that a Chastain is staying here, do we?" She didn't see the point in mentioning the fact that she didn't have a credit card to her name. That was the old, feckless Joss. The new Joss was getting her act in gear. Bax didn't look convinced, though. She tried again. "Look, if we're lovers, we'd be registered under your name, wouldn't we? It makes sense. Breathe," she patted his cheek. "We'll pay you back at the end."

"I'll make sure of it. Any more surprises?"

"Only of the most enjoyable kind," she murmured and continued through the doors.

Like the city outside, the lobby was a fantasy of gold and blue. Marble pillars with gold-leafed crowns soared to fifteen-foot ceilings ringed with crenellated moldings. Crystal chandeliers glimmered overhead. Underfoot, her-ringbone-patterned hardwood floors gleamed at the edges of royal blue carpet woven with twisting gold vines.

"Good evening," said the smiling woman behind the polished mahogany counter.

"Hej," Bax said, using the Swedish word for hello. He then astounded Joss by producing a stream of what sounded like Swedish. Once or twice, he searched for a word or the desk clerk frowned, but mostly they chattered

along like magpies. Finally, he signed the registration card and received the key.

"Was that what I thought it was?" Joss asked as the bell-hop collected their luggage and they headed toward the elevator. "Are you fluent in Swedish?"

"Not exactly. I'm fluent in Danish. I can get by in Swedish. Not all the words are the same, but the two are close enough that we can generally understand one another. I'm sure nearly everyone here speaks English—but I wanted to get the rust off."

"Didn't sound like there was any rust on it to begin with," Joss said, thinking of the lilting conversation she'd listened to.

Bax shrugged and punched the call button for the elevator. "My mother was Danish. I lived in Copenhagen until I was about six."

"No kidding. Was your father Danish, too?"

Bax shook his head. "American. He was a marine, an embassy guard. We lived all over Europe until I was about sixteen."

"Wow. You must be one cultured guy."

"I have my moments." The elevator appeared.

"So do you wish you lived over here?"

He shrugged and opened the door to let her walk into the car ahead of him. "I'm not sure I know. I don't exactly feel like an American, but I don't really feel like a European anymore. I'm somewhere in the middle."

"I know what you mean," Joss said as they got into the tiny car. "I grew up in Africa." An experience she wouldn't have traded for anything, but one that had left her homeless in a way, and always searching for more.

"Really?" He looked at her with interest. "How did that happen?"

"My parents are doctors," she explained. "We lived all

over. Zimbabwe, Botswana, Tanzania, mostly out in the bush."

"What was it like?"

"It was amazing, the animals and the landscape and the people. I loved it. There was always something new. I was free there, you know? No rules." And it had been so hard to get used to life in the real world.

"Ah. Now it all makes sense." The car stopped on their floor and they got out.

Joss gave Bax a quick smile as they stopped at the door to the room. "Are you saying that I'm not good with rules?"

"I'm saying that you like to make your own."

He stood there in his jeans and denim shirt, his jaw darkened with stubble from the long flight, looking just about good enough to eat. Joss took a step toward him and flowed into his arms. "Let me tell you about my rules," she began.

"Good afternoon," someone said cheerfully from behind them. They turned to see the bellhop walking toward them with their suitcases on the shiny brass birdcage luggage cart. "Welcome to the Royal Viking Hotel."

Joss gave Bax a rueful grin as the bellhop opened up their door.

It was like walking into a room in some eighteenth-century palace. Glossy white paneling with gilt moldings spread across the walls. White and gold swags of fabric framed the wide windows that overlooked the waterfront. Rich aquamarine damask covered the reproduction antique chairs—surely they were reproductions, she thought feverishly—as well as the coverlet of the half-tester bed. And what a bed, high and wide and piled with pillows, just made for all manner of aristocratic decadence.

She looked over at Bax and their eyes met. And desire throbbed through her.

The bellhop came through the door with their last bag and set it down. "Let me just get your suitcases," he began reaching for the luggage rack.

Bax took it from him and set it aside. "I don't think that will be necessary," he said smoothly.

"Well, then, I can show you—"

"Nope, won't be necessary," Bax told him, turning him around and ushering him toward the door. "In fact, I think we're all set." Bax slipped a twenty-five kroner tip in his hand and closed the door in front of his startled face.

"Now." Bax walked back toward Joss and tumbled her onto the bed with him. "What was that you were saying about rules?"

WHEN JOSS opened her eyes the following morning, it took her a moment to remember where she was. The big bed was empty but for her, the room silent. Yawning, she found her way to the bathroom, with its aqua and white tile walls and gleaming chrome. By the time she'd brushed her teeth and washed her face, she was feeling almost human.

Wrapping herself in one of the hotel's thick terry robes, she wandered over to the window to look out over the water. Beyond, in a pastel fantasy, lay the island of Gamla Stan, the oldest part of Stockholm. It beckoned to her from across the water. Forget about the room, however gorgeous it was. She wanted to be out there, exploring.

In time with her thoughts, there was a rattling at the door and Bax came in.

"Good morning."

"Good morning." She jammed her hands deep in the pockets of her robe. "I thought maybe you'd headed out for the day."

For a moment, he looked taken aback. "I was down-stairs having coffee. I didn't want to wake you. Sorry, I should have left a note."

It was awkward, she thought. They'd become lovers without warning. Now, they were essentially living to-gether as intimate strangers. She knew how to make Bax shudder with arousal but couldn't name his favorite color. They still hadn't found their rhythm with one another, they didn't know what to expect.

At least not out of bed.

"Well, I'm up and around now," she told him, sitting down on the bed. "Hey, is anything important going on today? The guide book mentioned a postal museum on Gamla Stan. I thought it might have some useful informa-tion for us. You know, stamps and stuff."

"Sure." He walked restlessly over to the windows to peer out. "By the way, I saw something in the paper about a stamp auction later on this week. The preauction view-ing and reception are tomorrow night."

"So?"

"So Silverhielm will very likely be there. It might be a good opportunity to make his acquaintance."

"Wouldn't that be convenient?" Joss said, watching Bax. He was tense enough that he was making her tense. Too many more days like this and they'd be crawling the walls. It was definitely time to do something about it.

She reached for the sash of her robe. "Well, if we're going to be meeting Silverhielm, we should probably get prepared."

"I think I told you, we're going to get a briefing."

"I mean you and I should get prepared," she said, slid-ing her robe off her shoulders.

"Get prepared how?" Bax turned away from the win-dow to look at her.

Joss gave him a wicked smile. "If you'll just come into the shower with me, I'd be happy to explain."

THE NARROW cobblestone streets of Gamla Stan wound between the high gabled buildings, the air still echoing with the past. Tourists and Stockholmers sat at the sidewalk cafés drinking coffee in the warm afternoon. The whole scene held the feeling of a gentler age.

Inside the postal museum, history permeated the air. All around them were displays with stamps from other eras, other places. They walked past the prize holdings of the stamp world. At least, that was Joss's assumption. Given that all the signs and labels were in Swedish, and her current vocabulary consisted of "hello," "goodbye," "please" and "thank you," it was hard to be sure.

Context was everything, Joss thought with a sigh. Otherwise, the stamps were just colored squares of paper. "I don't suppose you could translate for me, could you?" she asked Bax.

He gave her a calculating look. "I suppose, but it'll cost you."

Joss frowned. "Wait a minute, I thought you were supposed to be my devoted lover. Wasn't that what we were just talking about?"

"Well, I'm not sure that includes translation services beyond *la langue d'amour.*" He stuck his tongue in his cheek.

Joss raised her eyebrows. *"La langue d'amour?"*

"I was raised in Europe," he said blandly.

"I see." This was a new Bax. She'd never seen him be playful before. It was something she could get used to. "Well, if I could talk you into translating, I'd be happy to discuss some sort of compensation for your efforts."

"What do you have in mind?" He looked at her speculatively.

"Perhaps we could take it out in trade."

"I can work with that. Let's see," he squinted at the label. "Well, what you're looking at here is a stamp on a letter."

Joss crossed her arms and leaned against the doorway to the display case. "You don't say."

"It's true. If you want to hear more, I'll need a deposit."

It took her away, the taste of his mouth, the feel of his arms around her. It didn't matter that they'd just spent a couple of hours making love. She wanted more, and more wouldn't be enough.

Sounds echoed into the exhibits area from the next room, the voices of children in a school tour. Hurriedly, they broke apart.

"I trust you found that sufficient?" Joss pressed her lips together.

Bax grinned. "Well, we do have a minimum deposit, but I suppose under the circumstances I can waive it."

"You're so kind."

They worked their way slowly through the museum, past rare stamps and printing presses, past relics of ages gone by. In the next room, Bax drifted past her to look at a perforating machine with its pointy-toothed wheels. Just inside the doorway sat a small safe on a pedestal, its thick, black door swung wide. Inside, on even tinier pedestals stood a pair of stamps.

Joss took a look and blinked.

One blue, one reddish orange. A white profile of a queen wearing a circlet around upswept hair showed on each; the words Post Office ran along the left-hand margin in white block letters and Mauritius on the right. The indigo stamp was twin to the one they'd installed in a bank vault earlier that day.

"Bax," Joss said softly.

He was on the other side of the room.

"Bax," she said again.

"What?" He walked over to stand at her side.

She pointed to the safe. "It's them. The Post Office Mauritius pair."

He studied them. "The queen doesn't look the same on the orange one. Her hair's different. They look more like sisters than the same person. Look, the one on the Blue Mauritius almost looks like she's smiling."

"So, what are the chances that we'd stumble across them here?" Joss commented.

"Not necessarily that surprising, when you think about it. Maybe seeing them here is what whetted Silverhielm's appetite to have his own."

"Maybe." She continued to stare at the little squares of color, still vivid after all these years. So small, so fragile to have caused such grief. "I thought it would be a different color. More yellow, from what Gwen described."

"Didn't you ever see your grandfather's copy?"

She shook her head. "It was always in the vault. The only reason I've seen the Blue Mauritius is because we brought it here."

The two stamps sat on their little pedestals under the lights, the plump-jowled images of the monarch looking serenely off to the left.

"Hard to believe that people are willing to pay so much money for something like this, isn't it?" Bax said.

"Oh, I don't know. It's a bit like owning a piece of history, isn't it? A little bit of immortality. I think that's what my grandfather finds so magical about them." She stroked her finger down the glass protecting the contents of the safe.

"We'll get it back," Bax whispered. "One way or another, we'll get it back." He kissed her forehead.

First playful, now nice. Joss blinked back the sudden stinging in her eyes and blew out a breath. "Well, I think we've seen everything we need to here. You want to stop and get something to drink somewhere? Maybe that café we passed?"

He tangled his fingers in hers. "I've got a better idea."

SLUSSEN, just across from Gamla Stan on the island of Södermalm, was a whirlwind of motion. Cars and buses converged on the transportation hub from a dozen directions. Ferries lined the waterfront, poised for journeys to the archipelago and beyond. After the charm of old town, Slussen seemed garishly modern, but even here there was the beauty of the water, the green of trees, the aged loveliness of historic buildings.

Joss and Bax sat in the broad public square in front of the Swedish state museum, watching pigeons search for crumbs among the cracks of the cobblestone-striped concrete. To their right, the bluffs of Södermalm rose sheer and high. On their left, bridges vaulted to Gamla Stan. Directly ahead of them, propped up at the far end by a fragile-looking tracery of iron, a slender finger of blue projected out from the building that climbed up the face of the bluff.

"What is that?" Joss asked.

"Gondolen. It's a restaurant bar, very fashionable. The strutwork at the far end is the Katarinahissen, an elevator that takes you up to the public walkway on top. It's a pretty amazing view." Propped up on one side by the office building and across the street by the Katarinahissen, the restaurant hovered high in the air over one of the streets that fed into Slussen.

"It's almost cocktail hour," Joss said. "Why don't we go on up and have a drink and you can show me?"

"In a bit. We're here for a reason. Our friend Silverhielm has his city offices in the building attached to the restaurant." Bax glanced at his watch. "I'm told he comes out between four and five every afternoon." He rose and held out a hand to her. "Would you like a closer look at the Katarinahissen?"

Joss grinned. "Lead the way."

Crossing the various streams of traffic between the square and the Katarinahissen took longer than she expected, but eventually they stood by the doors to the elevator, across from the office building. Bax led her a few steps along the sidewalk, staring out at the water. Without warning, he swept her into his arms, his mouth hard on hers.

It should have been different. They knew one another's bodies now, they'd kissed plenty of times. It should have been pedestrian. It shouldn't have sent her blood fizzing through her veins.

It shouldn't have left her stunned with wanting.

"There, coming out of the doors," Bax murmured against her lips and lifted her off her feet to spin her a little, as though he were a lover overcome with the moment. "Take a good look so you'll know him later."

Face pressed into his neck, Joss opened her eyes and looked across the street.

There was no doubt which one was Silverhielm. Bodyguards flanked him but he walked as though he were alone, head raised arrogantly as he approached the gleaming black sedan that sat idling at the curb. He wore an impeccably tailored suit, slate-blue with a chalk stripe. His hair was thick, wavy and entirely gray; his eyes were pale. About him, there hovered an indefinable air of implacability and menace.

It was a well-choreographed scene, like the footage

she'd seen of presidents and prime ministers walking to vehicles. In seconds, he was safely ensconced in the car and his entourage was inside.

The sound of the car door slamming behind him echoed across the street. Joss shivered as the car drove away. "So that's him."

Bax nodded and released her.

It shouldn't have shaken her. There was no good reason why it did. Joss walked away from the lift building to lean on the railing and look across the water to Gamla Stan. "He looked…ruthless."

"He hasn't gotten to where he is by being kind. So are you ready to step back from this and let me take care of things?"

"No." She turned to him, shoulders squared. "I know who we're up against now, which is going to make me that much better against him."

"Stubborn," Bax commented, bouncing his loosely curled fist lightly off her chin.

"Determined," she countered.

"Not to mention sexy as hell. I seem to remember something about a payment due, by the way."

"Payment?" she echoed innocently.

"If I don't get it, I'm going to have to send you to collections," he warned.

Joss smiled. "Well, then, I guess I'd better pay up."

6

THE CHERUBS SMILED at her, golden-haired and rosy-cheeked, their bellies coquettishly round. Hanging on the wall over her head, their lively faces stared out, not at Joss, but at the sailing ship behind her, the enormous relic of a bygone age, the ornately carved king's folly that hadn't even made it out of the harbor before capsizing centuries before.

It was hard to say what was more extraordinary, Joss thought, the fact that for over two centuries people had forgotten where the *Vasa* warship lay, just a few hundred yards from the bustling waterfront, or the fact that the ship had been rediscovered and brought up to the surface nearly intact.

When she'd capsized, the sailors on the *Vasa* must have prayed to God for salvation. Now, the vessel was ensconced in a temple of its own, a soaring building of soft light designed to protect and display the ripe and luscious lines of a sailing ship that barely sailed.

"It's incredible," Joss murmured turning to stare at the stern rising high above them as she and Bax stood on one of the observation floors of the multilevel museum. "How can anything be this big?" As they walked toward the front of the ship, the height of the ship's side dropped in a slow, graceful curve until they were looking down at the deck by the time they'd reached the midway point. "How could anything be so beautiful and yet so useless?"

"Makes you wonder if there wasn't some sort of collective memory behind the drive to Swedish functionalism."

"The *Vasa* begat Ikea?"

"It's a theory."

"As amazing as it is, though, I feel guilty playing tourist. Shouldn't we be doing something to get the one-penny Mauritius back?"

"We're not playing tourist. We're going to meet my contact here, see what he can tell us about Silverhielm."

"Mysterious meetings in public museums. And you told me being a detective wasn't glamorous."

"Most of it's not," he said frankly. "It's a lot of legwork, most of which winds up being pointless. But eventually if you get enough information, you'll find something you can use, just like we will with Silverhielm. We'll get to him and take the stamps." He considered. "Unless he keeps his goodies in a vault somewhere, in which case we're out of luck."

"He won't keep them in a vault," Joss said positively.

"How do you know that?"

"You could see it in the way he moves. Stamps aren't just a business for him. There are too many other ironclad ways to make money." She followed the mizzenmast of the *Vasa* with her eyes as it rose overhead. "There's something about the stamps that he wants and needs, and that means having them handy. Besides, with all his goons around, he's got to feel smug, like no one can get to him. That's how we'll take him down, his pride."

"She's right, you know," said a lightly accented voice. Next to them stood a stocky, round-faced man with an incongruously tip-tilted nose. More than anything, he looked like a middle-aged elf.

A smile broke out on Bax's face, though he merely looked at the gun ports of the ship. "Rolf."

"Bax."

"Rolf Johansson, meet Joss Chastain."

Following Bax's lead, Joss simply nodded. "It's a pleasure to meet you. Are you one of Bax's Interpol friends?"

"No, I'm with Stockholm's organized crime division. We met when Bax was working in Stockholm. Perhaps Interpol is where you learned this sort of rendezvous spot, Bax. Certainly, the Swedish police would not think of it."

Bax shrugged. "They should. Less likely that someone would follow you here than to a restaurant or bar."

Rolf considered. "Perhaps you have a point. So what brings you to Stockholm?"

"Work, of course."

"Ah. Our friend who lives in the archipelago."

"So you are watching him."

"Of course." Rolf leaned on the rail of the observation deck. "He is my favorite waste of time. What do you know about him?"

"Officially that he's an import/export man for jewelry." Rolf nodded.

"Organized crime?" Bax asked.

"Not in the classic way. In fact, he and the mob do not get on. Our friend is what you might call a freelancer, a very successful one. The mob disapproves."

"I can imagine. So how would you characterize him, a businessman pushing the edge of legal?"

"A criminal with a legal front," Rolf said flatly. "His jewelry business has been amazingly successful, from the very beginning."

"Isn't that interesting."

"Suspiciously so. We know he uses it to launder money but we can't prove anything."

"Where does he get the dirty money from?" Joss asked.

"Smuggling. Drugs, currency, rare goods, so the rumor

goes. And he's not shy about hurting anyone who gets in his way. We've had more than a few dead bodies attributed to his organization."

"Have you infiltrated?"

Rolf shook his head. "The one time we tried, the agent was killed in a convenient accident."

"Murder?"

"I honestly could not say. If he were not involved in Silverhielm's organization, I'd have no doubts it was just bad luck. Because he was…" Rolf shrugged.

"Can't you turn someone?"

"No one wants to talk." He smiled faintly. "It is not healthy. We occasionally get anonymous information. Always, we follow up but the leads come to nothing. Two years ago, we came close to putting him in jail and perhaps getting more. His wife of the time filed battery charges against him."

"Battery?"

"He beat her quite badly. She promised to testify to all she knew about his business."

"And?"

"What do you think? A few days passed, she had visitors, and she withdrew the charges. We could do nothing. She has since left Sweden. He sits out there on his island like the king of the archipelago and laughs at us and gets richer every day."

"Frustrating."

Rolf's eyes hardened. "He will make a mistake one day and when he does, we will be there."

"How would you like to have something to truly hang on him?"

Rolf casually walked a few steps past them toward the bow of the boat and leaned again on the rail, using small binoculars to examine the upper reaches of the mast. "Bax, my friend, nothing would make me happier. What's on your mind?"

"We have reason to suspect that he may have arranged to have a very valuable rare stamp stolen from Joss's family."

"That is work for Interpol."

"Interpol tried to run it down and came up with nothing."

Rolf put down his glasses. "He is very slippery, our friend. So you come to visit us, instead?"

"I figured I'd be more effective on site."

"We are watching him, Interpol has already pursued him. What makes you think that you can do what we can't?" Rolf's voice hardened a little.

"I'm not trying to run down mobsters, pedophiles and prostitution rings. I can afford to just focus on him. Besides, I'm not even trying to lock him down. I'm just trying to get back Joss's family's property."

For the first time, Rolf turned to look directly at him, eyes cool. "We don't think well of vigilantism in Sweden."

"Don't think of it as vigilantism," Bax returned. "Think of it as help."

"Help?"

"I'm having to poke around in Silverhielm's life to do this job. If I happen to come across evidence of a crime, I would pass that to the proper authorities."

The corner of Rolf's mouth twitched. "I am sure the proper authorities would be happy to pursue it. They are always glad of help."

"Help goes both directions, of course. Depending on what happens, I may need the help in a hurry."

"Perhaps now is a good time for us to trade mobile telephone numbers."

"It might be quicker than leaving a message on your voice mail," Bax allowed.

"You Americans," Rolf tsked, "always so impatient."

"We get that way when we face master criminals."

Rolf smiled briefly. "Don't we all."

THE SKY WAS still light as Bax and Joss walked across the cobbled expanse of Berzelii Park toward Strindberg's auction house. Trees hung over the broad stone benches and the reflecting pond glimmered. To the other side lay the sea that seemed to be at every turn in Stockholm, this time a narrow inlet that gleamed in the afternoon sun.

In such a beautiful city, it was easy to forget that their business was serious, indeed. He could imagine that Joss was just his lover, walking next to him in the slanting afternoon sunshine. She wore a splashy black and white patterned halter dress, her hair a loose mass of curls, big white hoop earrings dangling at her ears. Her spike heels were fire-engine red.

It had been a long time since a woman had captured his imagination so fully. Since Stephanie. Since his biggest mistake.

Bax stopped and drew Joss down to sit. "We need to talk," he said abruptly.

"Shouldn't we be getting inside?" she asked.

"Sure, but not together."

She frowned. "Why not? They'll find out we're a pair eventually. It's part of our cover."

"I want to get the lay of the land first. Information is power. If they know everything up front, we lose any advantage we have." And in a situation like this, they needed every advantage they could get.

"So how do you want to do it?"

Alone, was his first thought. Alone, he'd be efficient. Alone, he'd be free to do the most practical thing without worrying about her safety. Alone, he wouldn't have to worry about his own. "I'll go in first, just to check it out. I'll ring you on your cell phone when it's clear to come in." It was against his better judgment. Why in God's name had he agreed to this ridiculous situation?

Then he looked at the dapple of sun and shade on her bare shoulders and he knew why.

"So you'll stay back and I'll hook up with Silverhielm."

"Be casual. Don't tell him everything all at once. You've got time. Remember, you're the one who has something he wants, so ultimately you're in control."

"Have some faith, will you? I've stalked music promoters for years. I know how to meet someone accidentally on purpose. Don't worry, I'll find a way to start a conversation with him. Why do you think I wore this dress?" She glanced down at the swells of her cleavage.

To drive him nuts, Bax thought, remembering the feel of her naked body against his.

"I figure Jerry would be dating someone a little cheap, a little flashy," Joss continued, oblivious. "It fits with the profile."

"It fits a few other things, as well," he observed dryly.

Joss flashed him a quick grin. "Thank you. It'll get Silverhielm's attention, I think. And if it helps distract him a little while I'm talking with him, so much the better."

Bax couldn't say about Silverhielm, but seeing the way the dress molded itself around her body distracted him, and at a time he could ill afford it. "I'm sure it'll do the job."

"Thank you." She gave him an amused look, reminding him that not much got past her. "So once I get talking with him, how far do I go? Do I mention Jerry and the Blue Mauritius?"

"Play it by ear. Remember, we just want to catch his attention at this point. Keep him a little off balance. That gives us the advantage."

"Okay." Joss took a deep breath.

"You sure you're up to this?"

She blew the breath out. "Of course I am. So we meet at the hotel afterward?"

Bax nodded. Without thinking about it, he reached out to take her hand. "One important thing to remember. Don't trust Silverhielm and don't, under any circumstances, leave with him. No matter how good an opportunity it seems, we can't afford the risk."

"Even if he offers me a ride in his way cool limo?" Joss said, widening her eyes.

"Especially then."

"Relax." She gave a quick grin. "I get my adrenaline rushes other ways than hanging out with murderers."

Bax knew it wasn't smart, but he couldn't resist leaning in to kiss her, just for a moment. He wouldn't think about what a familiar pleasure the taste of her was becoming. For a few moments, he just let himself savor her mouth, warm and mobile against his. Finally, he straightened. She would be okay, he told himself. And so would he. "I'll beep your mobile when the coast is clear." He rose. "Be good."

Joss gave him a reckless smile of promise. "I'll be great."

7

STRINDBERG'S CATERED to the wealthy and it showed in every aspect of the auction house, from the tony address to the rich decor. The furnishings whispered of discreet luxury—thick carpets, softly lustrous silk wall coverings, fresh flowers everywhere. A sweeping marble staircase led to the second floor showroom, with a richly patterned Aubusson runner held in place at each step with brass rails. The carpet was worn slightly in the center from the footsteps of decades worth of Scandinavia's affluent collectors.

In the showroom on this particular evening, the sleekly designed mounting pedestals displayed a selection of rare stamps and coins from around the world. The Strindberg management had probably planned the event to coincide with the stamp expo, but it was the type of auction that dealers would fly in to attend—at least the kind of dealers who, like Gwen and her grandfather, bought issues for millionaire clients.

Joss wandered around the room, holding a martini and inspecting the lots to be auctioned off the following evening. A glance at the auction catalog showed her that there were no stamps of the caliber of the Post Office Mauritius set going on the block, but a number of them were valued in the mid- to high-hundreds of thousands of dollars. The auction would make a tidy profit for Strindberg's, no doubt, not to mention the owners of the objects.

She did another circuit of the room, glancing around casually for Bax. He stood near an alcove by some plants, holding himself in a way that rendered him innocuous and unmemorable, though he was neither. It made her feel better to see him there, to know that he was around if she needed him.

In the center of the room, a small knot of people chattered animatedly around a Lucite display case. In an art museum, it might contain a sculpture; here, it held the two most valuable lots in the auction.

And in front of it stood Karl Silverhielm.

Up close, his eyes were a pale gray, the same shade as his hair. He wore another elegant suit, this one the color of steel. His tie was a pattern of small, interlocking black and cobalt diamonds, tied in a Windsor knot. A matching blue display handkerchief showed in his breast pocket.

The force of his personality came across even more strongly at this distance than it had from across the street. This time, though, the sense of menace was banked back. He looked refined, courteous, even affable.

She mistrusted him immediately.

Unobtrusively, Joss made her way to the central display case as the couple talking with Silverhielm wandered away. She stared at the stamps, throwing all of her concentration into what she could see with her peripheral vision. He glanced over at her, looked away and then turned her way.

Score one for the dress.

"Can I answer any questions for you about these issues? I'm the current owner." His voice was deep and expansive, filled with confidence.

Joss favored him with a smile. "Josie Astin." She gave him the alias she'd agreed to with Bax.

"Karl Silverhielm." He spoke English with a faint hint

of an accent. When she held out her hand to shake, he raised it smoothly to his lips. "You don't look like the typical philatelist. To what do we owe the pleasure, Ms. Astin?"

"Oh, I've heard people invest millions of dollars in these stamps. I figured I'd come see some of them myself."

"And what do you think, now that you're here?"

She shrugged and took a drink of her martini. "They look just like anything you can buy in the post office, only older."

"Well, that's where the value comes in. When you own a stamp that's over a hundred years old, you buy a slice of history. That's power, in its own way."

"And you want to buy power?"

"I don't need to."

She opened up her catalog and looked up the stamps in it. "But these are yours. If stamps are power, then why are you selling them?" Across the room, Bax moved to another spot by the wall, seemingly staring at the exhibits though she knew he was watching her.

"A collection changes all the time. You update it, consolidate, the same way a smart man consolidates financial holdings."

Joss considered him. "Are you a smart man?"

"I'll let my deeds speak for themselves."

"And what do you do?"

"I broker goods. Import/export."

"What do you import?"

"Whatever sells." He looked over her shoulder. "Hello, Markus."

Joss hadn't seen the tall, blond man materialize at her elbow and she started just a little.

"I apologize if I startled you." His English was entirely without accent. He had the high cheekbones and the sharp jaw line of the classically Nordic face.

Silverhielm nodded at him. "Ms. Astin, meet my associate, Markus Holm."

Joss found herself staring into a pair of entirely emotionless blue eyes. He looked at her the same way he probably looked at the potted plant behind her, and she had a feeling he'd cut her down with no more emotion.

Unnerved, Joss glanced down at the hand that clasped hers.

And saw a thin, uneven white line running between the thumb and forefinger.

A stir of excitement went through her. If Markus was the intermediary that Stewart had dealt with, that meant that Silverhielm was her man. Joss blinked and gave Markus her most brilliant smile.

"So very nice to meet you."

"The pleasure is mine," he said and released her hand.

"So what do you do for Karl?"

"I assist him with his various projects." Markus smiled so faintly she couldn't be sure she'd seen it.

"He is indispensable to me," Silverhielm assured her. "Excuse me a moment." Markus leaned close to him to murmur something in his ear. Silverhielm shook his head. "Take care of it," he told him. "I'll let you know when I'm ready." Markus nodded and left and Silverhielm turned his attention back to Joss. "So where are you from, Ms. Astin? You do not look like the usual collector."

"I'm from Las Vegas." Was it her imagination, or did he come to attention when she said it? "My boyfriend—actually, my ex-boyfriend—has acquired a few stamps. I was in town and thought I'd come here and see if I could make any contacts that would help me unload them." She drifted toward the floor-to-ceiling windows that overlooked Berzelii Park and Silverhielm drifted with her.

"Alas, I am not in the market for stamps at present. In

fact, as we were just discussing, I am reducing the size of my collection."

"Really? Does that mean you've just made a nice acquisition?" She stopped to study another exhibit.

He gave her a bland look. "I buy and sell stamps all the time, Ms. Astin. A collection that does not change becomes stagnant and loses its luster."

"Perhaps you should get something new. I was just at the Postal Museum earlier today and saw the Post Office Mauritius pair. The most valuable stamps in the world, or so they say." She reached the windows.

"Many collectors prize the Post Office Mauritius set," he agreed, looking at her carefully.

"So I hear. I understand you've been in the market for a Post Office Mauritius pair for some time."

That got his attention. "And who do you understand this from?"

"I also understand that you've managed to accomplish half of that goal," she continued softly, ignoring his question.

Had she thought that he was affable? The stare that he aimed at her was nearly toxic in its intensity. This was a man who'd killed more than once, she reminded herself. The hairs on the back of her neck prickled up one by one.

"I do not understand you, Ms. Astin." Silverhielm's voice remained calm but now icy cold, the control almost more alarming than anger would have been. She looked for Bax in her peripheral vision.

Brazen it out, she told herself. "Transactions don't always go as anticipated, Karl," she said, gesturing carelessly with her nearly empty glass. "I should know. My ex-boyfriend, Jerry, is an…associate of Stewart Oakes." She finished off her martini and turned toward the bar.

He caught her wrist in an iron grip. "You will explain yourself."

She refused to wince. Instead, Joss aimed an icy look at Silverhielm. "You will let me loose and I will go get a drink," she enunciated. "After that, I may choose to continue this conversation or I may not." She saw Bax come to attention and shook her head infinitesimally at him.

"No." Silverhielm signaled Markus, who appeared at her elbow. "Another martini for Ms. Astin."

"Ketel One, with two olives," Joss told Markus. She trembled down inside but her hand remained steady as she pulled the skewered olive from the remains of her current glass.

"So, Ms. Astin." Silverhielm stared at her as Markus walked away. "Pray continue."

Joss looked right back at him, refusing to be intimidated. Then she turned to look out at the moonlit cobblestones of Berzelii Park. "I can make it very simple," she said calmly. "I have something you want. You have something I want. We ought to be able to come to an agreement."

"What do I have that you want, Ms. Astin?"

She raised her martini glass. "Money," she said and took the final swallow.

SILVERHIELM ESCORTED her down the marble stairs that led to the front door of the auction house, Markus trailing behind them.

"I am sorry that the other potential bidders interrupted our very interesting conversation, Ms. Astin," Silverhielm said. "There is a very fine bar nearby. We can go for a drink and talk further."

"I must be getting back to my hotel." She slipped the strap of her small black evening bag over her wrist.

Silverhielm suppressed a flare of irritation. He was a man used to being obeyed. "Where are you staying?" he persisted. "Perhaps I could offer you a ride home." He opened the door and gestured for her to pass through.

"That won't be necessary. I can get a cab, thanks."

"Oh no, I insist." He waved and his gleaming black car pulled smoothly up to the curb.

"Thank you, but no." She turned to shake hands. "I will be in Stockholm for several more days. I am sure we'll have an opportunity to talk." She smiled and turned to head across the square toward the lights of the boulevard and a taxi.

A wave of fury washed through Silverhielm. People did not treat him this way. People did as he told them. He watched her go and Markus stepped up beside him. "A lone woman playing a dangerous game," Silverhielm said softly. "She has the Blue Mauritius, she hints."

Markus looked at Silverhielm impassively. "Is she here to deliver?"

"For a fee." The gleaming black car idled gently in front of them. "I refuse to pay twice for something I should already possess." His voice hardened, the polished sophisticate erased by the ruthless thug. "You will take care of it."

8

BAX STOOD INSIDE the doorway to Strindberg's and watched Silverhielm's soldier close the door to the sleek black limo, shutting Silverhielm inside. Then the car pulled away, leaving the blond man at the curb. For a moment, he just stared after Joss. Then he tucked his hands into his pockets and set off through the gloaming, across Berzelii Park.

After Joss.

Bax stepped swiftly out the door. She'd stood her ground with Silverhielm and refused to get in the car, he reminded himself as he followed them, suppressing a little twist of concern. If she was taking a risk now by crossing the park alone in the evening, at least there were people around. Anyway, it was only until she'd reached the broad boulevard where she could get a taxi to the hotel.

He quickened his pace a bit to get closer to Silverhielm's man. Once she got into a cab, her tail would be stymied, unless he wanted to try a "follow that cab" routine. Bax had a pretty good feeling that the guy was a little too smart for that one.

And then he cursed. It looked like Joss was going to save the guy the trouble. She didn't even bother to stop on the corner but just made the turn down the street that led toward Gamla Stan and the Royal Viking.

It was why he didn't like working with a partner, Bax

thought in irritation. When he worked alone, he didn't have to worry about someone deviating from plan, he didn't have to worry about them taking foolish chances and putting the whole operation at risk. Even on a busy street, especially on a busy street, a professional would have no problem pulling someone like Joss aside and threatening her until she told him what was really going on. She didn't have the skills to fight off a professional thug or to withstand an interrogation, even a short one.

And Bax couldn't stand the risk.

He worked his way closer to Silverhielm's man. It wasn't easy to follow someone solo, but Bax was operating at an advantage this particular night. The Swede appeared convinced that Joss was alone and wasn't worried about being shadowed himself. He seemed to be focused entirely on her.

Bax was good enough at reading lips and body language to be pretty confident that Joss had brought up the stamps to Silverhielm, who hadn't been happy about it. It was a good guess that Silverhielm had put his guy onto her when they chatted outside of Strindberg's.

The question was what were his orders? Was he following her to see where she went, following her to get her alone somewhere and scare information out of her, following her with an intent to do harm? Bax had been trained over his years on the job to suppress any emotion while he concentrated on the task at hand. Somehow, it was more difficult this time around. He couldn't quite get rid of his concern for Joss.

He cursed again. It was what he got for working with an amateur.

Instinct warned him to drop back further on the tail so that the Swede wouldn't make him, but he didn't dare. He couldn't take a chance of being too far away to react if Silverhielm's man made a move.

Joss crossed the boulevard and the Swede followed as the light turned yellow. Bax broke into a slow jog but the light had already gone red and a steady stream of cross traffic was whizzing by when he hit the corner. A bus stopped in front of him to let off passengers.

Bax moved impatiently through the bus riders, skirting the front bumper of the bus when the light changed and sprinting across the crosswalk.

Joss and the Swede were nowhere in sight.

His pulse began hammering in alarm. The boulevard he was on led straight to the waterfront and the street of the Royal Viking. It was the quickest way to get there. There was nowhere else they'd logically be. Unless the Swede had pulled Joss aside and was now interrogating her.

Or worse.

Keep the feelings out of it, Bax reminded himself. When you felt too much, you started acting on emotion and not reason. There was no place for the Swede to pull Joss aside on the brightly lit main boulevard. He slowed his steps and looked around before leaving the corner. Half a block away, he saw the opening to a narrower street that paralleled the boulevard to the waterfront.

Bingo.

He knew the street, a narrow lane of exclusive shops that would be thinly populated at this time of night. He jogged over to it, wishing that he had a weapon on him besides his hands, his feet and his wits. Holding his breath, he stepped around the corner.

And saw Joss a block and a half away, ambling slowly past the storefronts, glancing at the window displays. Well away from her, the Swede hung in the shadows of a doorway on the other side of the street for several seconds before following.

Bax let out a breath he hadn't been conscious of holding. When Joss made the turn onto the waterfront, Bax watched the Swede stay back and follow her in his turn. Finally, Bax himself reached the end of the street to observe Silverhielm's man watch Joss walk into the hotel.

She was safe. For a split second, it was all he could think.

The Swede wandered over to the waterfront to stand by the ferries, looking back at the hotel facade. He lit a cigarette and stood for a few more minutes, watching. Finally, he walked briskly away.

Bax strode hurriedly from his shadowed corner to the hotel, his concern morphing into irritation, an irritation that intensified moment by moment as he made his way up to the room.

"It's him." Joss jumped off the couch to meet him as he walked through the door.

Bax glowered at her. "Which 'him,'? The one you talked with at the reception or the one who just followed you home?"

"Oh, did he follow me?" she asked happily, ignoring him. "I was hoping he would but I couldn't quite see him in the shop windows."

"What?"

"Well how else are they going to know where to find me?" she asked reasonably. "I didn't just skip the cab for the heck of it, you know."

"Are you out of your mind?" he demanded.

"To walk half a mile in these shoes? I'd have to be," she told him as she sank down on the couch and pulled off her stilettos with an expression of bliss.

"Joss, it's not a goddamn game," he snapped.

Her effervescence evaporated, making him feel like a bully. He was only trying to get her to understand the risks she was taking, he told himself, fighting off the guilt.

"Bax, I didn't just do it to be foolish. I did it because I thought it was important. He's Silverhielm's guy and Silverhielm's our man."

"You think."

She raised her chin. "I know. I saw the scar on the hand of the blond guy. His name is—"

"Markus Holm," Bax said flatly.

Joss blinked. "Yes. How did you know?"

"I know him. We ran into each other during an undercover assignment I did for Interpol in Amsterdam."

"He's Interpol?" she asked incredulously.

"No, he's a genuinely bad guy. I was Interpol, posing as the shooter for a Dutch heavy while I looked into Markus's boss."

"Silverhielm?"

"Someone else. Markus is an equal opportunity employee," he said sardonically. "If the fee's right, so is the job."

Joss gave a little shiver. "He kind of gave me the creeps."

"He should." Bax stalked over to the minibar to pull out a scotch. "He's dangerous. Stable, which is more than you can say for a lot of people in that line of work, but capable of doing just about anything if he considers it the most expedient means to an end."

"I could see it in his eyes. It was like he didn't even register me as a human being."

"He's very smart and very, very good at what he does. It ups the stakes considerably." And if it was an advantage to have an enemy whose moves he knew well, Markus would have just as much of an advantage on him.

"So what's our play now?"

"Stop taking foolish chances, for one. Go slow, for another. Having Markus involved changes things. The longer we can go without him knowing I'm involved, the better."

"Did Markus know you were with Interpol?"

Bax shook his head. "I was pulled from the assignment long before they took action. As far as he knows I'm a Danish-American shooter named Johan Bruhn, just another freelancer like him. Brothers in arms." He smiled faintly.

Joss shivered a little. "You and he are worlds apart."

"Not so far as you'd think. I got to know him well during the time I was on assignment. He has a code of honor of a sort, it's just not the kind that you or I recognize."

She frowned. "You sound like you like him."

"I don't know that like is the right word, though he can be intelligent company. Respect, maybe. By our lights, he's totally amoral, but he seems to have a set of standards that he lives by. And I saved his life once."

Joss raised her eyebrows in disbelief. "Now this I have to hear."

"In a minute. First, I want to go get some ice." He took the bucket and a key and went out the door.

JOSS LAY BACK on the bed and stared at the ceiling, trying to imagine Bax working with Markus, saving his life. It seemed incomprehensible. Then again, she didn't know Bax very well. She had to remember that.

The phone rang. Joss reached out to grab it from the bedside table. "Hello?"

"Ms. Astin." Unaccented English. Markus.

She sat up, the hair on the back of her neck prickling. "Yes."

"It is Markus Holm."

Attitude, she reminded herself and took a deep breath. "Well, when I said I hoped to hear from you soon, I had no idea it would be this soon."

"Your discussion with Mr. Silverhielm generated many

questions. More questions than answers. Of course we need more information, much more information, before proceeding."

Hook, line and sinker, she thought. "What did you have in mind?"

"We should meet with you to continue the discussion. Tomorrow morning, perhaps?"

"I'd have to think about it." She looked at the door, waiting for Bax to return. How far did a person have to go in this hotel for ice, anyway?

"What is there to think about? It is just a discussion. Mr. Silverhielm wishes to know more about your proposal. If you are interested in progress, we must talk."

"I guess, but…"

"So a meeting is good, yes? It is a simple thing to do."

In concept, delaying was a good strategy, but somehow it wasn't working. "All right."

"Good. Look out your window."

She felt a little twinge of consternation. She wasn't surprised that he knew her hotel, but her room location? The hairs on the back of her neck prickled as she picked up the phone and carried it with her to the glass.

"There is a small park ahead of you, just off the water. It is called Karl XII's *torg,* in front of the Kungsträdgarden, the King's Garden."

Cobblestone walks separated tidy flowerbeds in the moonlight. "I see it."

"Meet me there tomorrow morning at seven."

"Why so early?"

"Mr. Silverhielm does not care for enigmas. He wishes more information as soon as possible."

The words sounded vaguely ominous. At first she was alarmed, and then it just got her back up. "Then perhaps he should show up for the meeting instead of you."

"Mr. Silverhielm will attend when it is time. For now, you and I can discuss what needs to be discussed. It is enough. Until tomorrow morning, Ms. Astin."

"Okay."

At first, she was merely irritated at being outmaneuvered. Quickly, though, excitement began to bubble up. It was progress, real progress. She wasn't sure where it would take them, but going forward beat standing still.

Behind her, the door opened and Bax walked in.

"How good am I," Joss crowed. "See, my little walk home paid off. I just got a phone call from your friend Markus."

Bax set down the ice and stared at her. "And what did my friend Markus have to say?"

"They want more information. I'm meeting him tomorrow morning." She began to speculate, thinking aloud. "We'll have to work out what I should say. Do you want to be there? I wonder if—"

"What are you, nuts?" Bax's brows drew together. "Meeting with Markus? Haven't you heard a word I've said?"

"Of course I have. He wanted an answer. They want more information. What was I supposed to do?"

"Stall." He bit the word off.

"I tried to. He wouldn't fall for it."

"You didn't push hard enough. He would have caved eventually. You've got what they want, or at least they think you might. They'd do whatever was necessary to find out more. And we'd tell them more, on *our* timeline." He paced across the room. "Joss, listen to me, you can't run around doing whatever you feel like whenever you feel like it. You hired me to do a job. Stand back and let me do it."

"I'm trying," she flared. "Look, I was supposed to drop the bait tonight. I did just what we'd agreed."

"And then turned around and went totally off plan."

"Off plan? We hadn't worked out a plan yet. I was winging it."

"You don't know enough to wing it."

"Thanks very much." She rose and paced across to him. "What would you have liked me to have done?"

"Make him wait. Give me some time to check with my contacts on what Markus has done lately." He dumped his scotch into a glass and added some ice.

"Stall, wait, that's all you want to do. I thought this was about getting the stamp back, not collecting a nice per diem in a cushy hotel."

"Trust me," he said through gritted teeth, "right now I'd be thrilled to have that stamp in my hand so that I could end this case before I wring your neck."

"Oh, nice, Baxter."

"You didn't hire me to be nice. Now, you are not going to that meeting tomorrow. We don't know enough yet. It's an unacceptable risk."

"It's an unacceptable risk not to show."

"Cancel."

"I don't know how to reach him."

"You didn't even get a number?" he asked incredulously.

"You think the bad guys give out their cell numbers?" she retorted.

"Okay, so you just don't show. Leave them wondering. They'll call."

"Will they? What if they think it's all a fabrication?"

"They can't afford to. Look, you're not going tomorrow and that is final."

Mutinously, she rose. "I'm going to take a bath," she muttered and walked into the bathroom. If he thought he was going to push her around and make all the decisions, Mr. John Baxter, P.I. was going to have another think coming.

9

MORNING SUNLIGHT slanted across the bathroom floor as Joss stepped out of the shower. She yawned, drying herself with a blissfully warm towel hot off the rack. Bax might have effortlessly transitioned to Stockholm time, but she hadn't found it so easy. Let him have his early morning ritual of going downstairs for coffee. She'd stay in bed until she was good and ready.

Except for this morning. This morning, she had a different plan.

She dressed quickly, throwing on a scarlet studio jacket over jeans to ward off the morning chill. Then she slipped out the door and looked for the emergency exit. It would bring her to a back stairwell, she figured. Once she'd exited the hotel unobtrusively, she could work her way around to the waterfront and from there to the park.

The fire stairway dumped her out on the lane that she'd come down the night before. Hurriedly, she backtracked toward the boulevard and cut across the back of the hotel before heading to the waterfront and on to Karl XII's *torg*.

Bax might be furious with her for sneaking out, but he had only himself to blame. He'd refused to discuss the matter further the night before, seeming to think that his veto was enough. Well, it wasn't. He was wrong, wanting to skip the meeting. They couldn't take a chance on losing contact with Silverhielm and they couldn't lose another day, not with her grandfather's stamp at risk. Markus was expecting to see her. She had to be there.

Karl XII's *torg* was a smallish formal garden right on the waterfront. Tree, shrub and flower, everything was exactly in its place. Decorative black metal railings edged the tidy beds of plantings. Painted wooden benches dotted the flagstone walks. In the little café next door, a ragged queue of Stockholmers lined up for coffee. The occasional cyclist whizzed down the bike lane on the opposite side, but at this hour on a weekday, the park itself was nearly empty.

Joss glanced around the park, looking for Markus. He materialized behind her shoulder.

"Good morning, Ms. Astin."

Silent as a cat, she thought, trying not to jump. In the warm morning sun, he looked icily Nordic as ever, with his pale hair and pitiless eyes. Bax's voice echoed in her head. *He's a genuinely bad guy.*

Well, maybe he was, but it was broad daylight in a public park and she refused to be intimidated. As far as he and Silverhielm were concerned, she had what they wanted. She had the upper hand, that was the important thing to remember.

"Good morning." Figuring that shaking hands was bad form, Joss moved, toward a bench.

"Perhaps we should walk, instead," Markus suggested.

"Certainly." They began to stroll slowly down one of the pathways toward the water where the white tour boats bobbed, waiting for their first customers.

"You made some surprising allegations to my employer, last night," he said without preamble.

"Not at all."

"Karl Silverhielm may have made inquiries about a Post Office Mauritius pair in the past, but so have many collectors in similarly fortunate positions. There is, after all, no crime in inquiries. Or in legitimate purchases, for that matter."

Joss admired a row of nodding pink blossoms. "True enough. It's theft that the authorities frown on."

"Certainly, if any transpired," he said blandly. "Mr. Silverhielm would of course find such activities reprehensible."

"Of course."

"But you accused him of such last night."

Joss shot him a quick look. "I find it interesting that that was his interpretation. I merely told him I'd heard from a reputable source that he'd obtained one half of a Post Office Mauritius pair, and attempted to gauge his interest in obtaining the other half. Hypothetically," she added.

"Of course. I believe the subject of money came up, as well."

"I'm a businesswoman, Mr. Holm."

"Call me Markus, please."

"It's a simple business proposition, Markus. I've found something of value that I have reason to think Mr. Silverhielm prizes highly. It seems reasonable to think that he would be willing to negotiate appropriate compensation for my trouble."

"My employer is a thrifty man," he told her. "He does not see why he should pay again for an object that should already be his."

"I wouldn't call it paying again," Joss said.

"What would you call it?"

"A delivery fee."

"Nonetheless, all fees and commissions have already been paid to Mr. Oakes. You are acting on behalf of Mr. Oakes and your boyfriend, I assume."

"Ex-boyfriend," she corrected him. "Actually, neither.

I'm acting on my own behalf. And Mr. Silverhielm's. I could just hand it over to the authorities. That's probably what I should do," she said thoughtfully and stopped to look at him. "Unless you have an alternate proposal."

"I believe I do, Ms. Astin," he said, unbuttoning his coat.

"Josie, please."

He smiled thinly. "Josie." He moved his arm a bit and his coat fell open enough for her to see the gleam of steel from the gun holster at his side. In a flash, it was in his hand and against her side. "Perhaps, we should go back into the hotel."

He caught at her wrist and pain shot up her arm. She tried to twist away, but it only hurt worse. Adrenaline vaulted through her. Stay calm, she reminded herself. He had nothing to gain by killing her and he wouldn't do it in public. It was all a game.

Joss took a breath through her nose, trying to ignore the pain. "If you're thinking that I'm foolish enough to have the Blue Mauritius in my room, you are going to be disappointed."

"I am sure once we chat in private, you will happily tell me where it is."

"It's a little early for threats, isn't it, Markus?" She stopped.

He twisted her wrist a bit and pressed the gun more firmly into her side. "It is not a threat, it is a promise. Now, you will begin walking."

"I don't think so," a voice said from behind then, followed by a metallic snick.

Both Joss and Markus froze. Slowly, they turned around.

And saw Bax standing there. He gave a not entirely pleasant grin. "Hello, Markus."

BAX DIDN'T LIKE surprises, not even a little. One minute, he'd been sitting in the front window of the Royal Viking's café area wondering how it was that European coffee tasted so amazing, the next he'd caught a glimpse of Joss's red jacket out of the corner of his eye. He'd watched as she slipped out of the side street and hurried along the waterfront, headed toward the park.

In an instant, he'd tossed down a few bills and headed out without a backward glance, even as he was over-whelmed with anger. For surely it was anger that crouched hard and cold in the pit of his stomach, not fear. How could she be so foolish as to put herself at risk yet again? After what he'd told her the night before, he couldn't believe that she'd been obtuse enough to barge out and meet Markus.

Then again, he thought grimly now as he took one hell of a chance and pulled a gun on Markus in the open to save Joss's stubborn neck, maybe he could.

Markus stared calmly back at him. "Ah, Johan, you know how much I hate surprises."

"It shouldn't be a surprise at all. I'm predictable. You threaten one of my people, I'll take steps."

"I didn't know she was one of yours," Markus said, slipping his gun back into the holster.

"Now you do," Bax told him curtly, easing off the hammer of his own gun and stowing it out of sight.

Markus looked him up and down. "You are no longer with van den Berg?"

"On to new things. You're no longer with Stuyvvens?"

Markus shrugged. "You know how it goes. A smart man follows the market."

"I do indeed." Bax stepped closer to Joss.

Markus studied the two of them together. "So you are working out of the U.S. now?"

"When the right opportunity comes up. Right now, it appears I'm working out of Stockholm."

"That makes us a pair yet again." Faint crinkles of humor appeared by Markus's eyes. "I have an employer who could use a man with your talents."

"I'm surprised at you, Markus, recruiting me in front of my current employer."

"I see your current position as temporary. My employer would have steady work for you."

Bax shrugged a little. "So let's resolve our current matter and after that we'll talk."

"So we will."

"Now, what were you discussing with my client before you tried to strong arm her into the hotel?"

Markus buttoned his jacket again. "That is an unfriendly way to put it."

"Pulling guns on people is an unfriendly business."

"She is asking my employer to pay again for a product he has already paid for."

"That's one way to think about it. Another is that it is a finder's fee for Josie, who did not turn in the stamp and has instead brought it to Silverhielm. He could easily pay her and still get his goods for a bargain price."

"But my employer is a proud man."

"Pride is a luxury."

"Ah, and Mr. Silverhielm is a man accustomed to luxury."

"Then he must also be accustomed to paying for it."

"Perhaps you are right."

And in that moment, Bax knew they would get what they sought. "So let us be clear what we're talking about. It'll save time."

"Ah, Johan. Always impatient. It is reassuring to know you haven't changed. So what's on your mind?"

"Some rules, first."

"Such as?"

"No more private meetings with my client. You want to talk with her, I'm present. Always." Even if he couldn't get it through Joss's thick skull, he might be able to get it through Markus's.

Markus inclined his head. "Of course. And?"

"A discussion with your boss, the four of us. We don't negotiate with you, we negotiate with him. No offense."

"None taken, but Mr. Silverhielm is a very busy man."

"I'm sure we can find a client who's not so busy." Bax began to turn away. "Excuse us—"

"Johan, please rein in that impatience for a moment."

"Yes."

"Allow me to consult with my employer."

Bax's teeth gleamed. "I thought you might."

"I will find out what will suit him."

"Soon, Markus."

"Always, with you. Very well, then. You will hear from us." He nodded sharply and walked away.

JOSS WATCHED Markus climb into the passenger seat of a polished gray sedan. In seconds, the car had disappeared into the flow of traffic into Gamla Stan and she was left trying to absorb the surreal—she'd just had a gun pulled on her in broad daylight. Trembling started in the long muscles of her thighs.

Bax turned to her with a face like thunder. "What the hell were you thinking?" he snapped. "You could have gotten yourself killed." Then his eyes narrowed and he took her arm.

She pulled away from him. "Don't grab me."

"Sit," he ordered, "now. You look like you're going to keel over."

She stood, face mutinous. "I'm fine."

"You almost weren't."

"He wouldn't have hurt me," she retorted with more confidence than she felt.

"He had a gun on you, Joss." He took a few steps away and swung back to her.

"He was trying to scare me."

"And you're a fool if he didn't succeed. He doesn't mess around."

"He wouldn't have done anything here in public," she insisted, clinging to it. "Too many people could have seen him."

Bax gave her an incredulous look. "You have no idea who you're dealing with. I once saw him shoot a man in a crowd of people and just walk away."

Her jaw dropped and she closed it with a snap. "I don't believe you." But in her gut, she knew it was true.

"Joss, accept it," Bax said wearily. "You're out of your league trying to deal with him. You don't know what he's capable of. I do."

"But you said you saved his life. How could you save the life of a killer?"

"Because it wasn't my place to say he should die."

"That sounds like a line from a bad TV show."

"It's anything but TV, which you have got to realize if you're going to go any further with this. And you have got to start listening to me or this little game is over," he said, coldly furious. "I thought we'd agreed that you weren't coming out here."

And now they were getting to the heart of it all. "We never agreed to anything. You just gave the orders and assumed I'd go along. Well, it doesn't work that way, Bax." She stood nose to nose with him, glaring. "This isn't about just you. I'm a part of this too, remember? We're a team."

"Then act like it. You can't just go off and do things on your own without telling me."

"And you can't just arbitrarily run the show and order me around," she retorted.

"You hired me because of what I know."

"I hired you to help, not to wade in and be John Wayne. I told you from the beginning I was going to work on this project, too." Her voice rose.

"This isn't a game, Joss. You're not some character in a novel."

"I know that, but I've got to be a part of this."

"Why?" he demanded in frustration.

"Because it was my fault," she burst out.

On the bridge leading to Gamla Stan, horns rang out. Bax stood staring at her.

Joss swallowed. "The one-penny Mauritius isn't just a valuable stamp, it's a big part of my grandfather's retirement. And it was my screwup that let it get stolen." She turned and sank down on the bench behind her, putting her face in her hands. Bax sat beside her.

"You had a lot of very driven people after those stamps. One way or another, they were going to get them."

"It doesn't matter. Reality was, I was the one who made it easy for them."

"And how, exactly, was that? Did you hand them over?"

"No."

"Did you insist the stamps be kept in the safe instead of a bank vault where they belonged?"

"No, but I just as good as handed Jerry the key. He'd come to work for us because I didn't want to work alone. He and I were the only ones in the store when he stole them. Gwen was out of town—she'd given me the key and combination to the safe. I locked them in the desk and went out for lunch." Joss turned to look out at the water. "That was all it took."

Let her deal with it, Bax told himself, but he found himself reaching out to rub his hand comfortingly over her back. "If he was a pro, he'd have found a way."

Joss turned back to him. "He didn't have to because I made it easy for him. That's why I've got to be a part of this."

Her face was pinched and pale with misery. It was the face of the hurt kid, again, looking back at him, and all he wanted to do was fix things. "We'll get it back," he said helplessly, knowing there couldn't be any other outcome.

"It has to be we, Bax. It can't be just you. Gwen already did more than her part. Now I have to do mine. I need to know that I was a part of it."

"You will be," he assured her with a sinking heart and folded her against him. "We'll do it together."

10

CLOUDS DRIFTED IN as they sat in the *torg,* watching the tour boats come and go from the dock.

"So how are you doing now?" Bax asked and kissed the top of her head. "You okay?"

"What, with the gun thing?" Joss stirred and grinned at him. "I'm tougher than you think, Bax. I've played some truly scary dives, slept on the street, even gotten mugged once. There's not a whole lot that gets to me."

At their feet, a pigeon trundled along, searching for crumbs on the pavement.

"So what's with the whole music thing? You mentioned it last night, too."

"My brilliant career, or at least that was the plan." It was increasingly embarrassing to talk about, increasingly discouraging to realize that she'd devoted seven years of her life to music with almost no success. How clueless did that make her?

And where did it leave her now?

"So what were you, a singer? A musician? Both?"

"A singer. Or maybe just wanted to be. I was going to be the next big thing, a huge star." She sat up and leaned forward, elbows on her knees. "It didn't quite work out that way."

"Band broke up?"

"Bands," she corrected. "I've played with one group or another all over the Pacific Northwest."

"How long?"

"Seven years." Her smile held no humor. "I'm a slow study sometimes." How she'd loved performing, the feeling when everything clicked, the band in a groove, the audience feeding into it. It had been because of those magical nights that she'd had such a hard time finally giving it up. "I just really loved doing it," she said wistfully.

"Then why quit?"

"Because sooner or later you've got to admit that it's not going to work, you know?"

"Couldn't you work a day job and still perform nights?"

She reached down to pick a small stone up off the cobbles, rolling it between her hands. "I suppose. The problem is the day job. I don't really know how to do anything."

"College?"

"A year. I dropped out of the drama program to go on the road with the first band. We were going to do a spring and summer tour of small clubs. I never went back. Used to do street theatre for food money."

"Street theatre?"

"Merlinda the Magnificent." She held up the stone between her thumb and forefinger and passed her other hand across it. "Voila!" The stone was gone.

"Nice."

"Oh, I was a big hit on the pedestrian mall circuit. I probably made more money at that than singing."

"So what comes next?"

It was the question that kept scaring the hell out of her. "TBD. The last band went kaput the week before I came back to San Francisco and went to work for my grandfather's store. It was supposed to be a temporary gig while I got my act together, only I managed to screw everything up."

"We're going to fix that."

"And then all I have to do is decide what to do with my life," she said wryly.

"Sooner or later, we all do."

Joss tossed her hair back and rose, catching his hand in hers. It wasn't in her nature to be gloomy for long. "This is not a crisis. I'll work it out. Sorry to bend your ear."

"You weren't bending my ear. It was educational."

"Educational?"

"Joss Chastain 101."

"You've been doing very well in the course so far." They began walking toward the waterfront.

"Thanks. I've been studying."

"That's good. There's a practicum coming up, you know." She leaned in for a quick, teasing kiss. "It might be very involved," she murmured against his lips. "Maybe we should go back to the room."

He ran his hands down her back. "Maybe we should." They turned toward the hotel. "Of course, now that I know you're hell-bent on doing risky things no matter my advice, I'm thinking that there's a better course to take."

"A better course than making love until we're both cross-eyed?"

He cleared his throat. "Different, anyway. How about Defense 101?"

She gave him an amused look. "You're going to teach me how to kick ass?"

"That might take a little more time than we've got. What I can do is teach you a few nasty tricks that might help you discourage the bad guys long enough to get away, though. Come on." He picked up the pace. "Let's get to the hotel."

"I like the sound of that," she said.

INSIDE THE Royal Viking, they walked across the elegant lobby and into the elevator. Bax didn't punch the number for their floor, though. He hit the button for the top floor.

"Wait a minute. I thought we were going to the room."

"There's not enough space there to do what I have in mind."

"There's enough space in our room to do what I have in mind." She pressed him against the elevator wall and traced his lips with the tip of her tongue. "In fact, there's enough space here." She felt the stir of his cock against her, and that quickly, all she could feel was need.

The chime sounded and the doors opened on the top floor. Joss hit the button for their floor. "Back down."

Bax put his hand in the door. "Let's do this first."

"Can't it wait?"

"Look, waiting for you to get yourself in trouble is already making me old before my time. Let me at least teach you a few things so I can let you out of my sight."

It gave her a little pulse of pleasure. "Why, Bax, you're worried about me."

"Don't let it go to your head," he muttered, a little flush creeping up the back of his neck as he walked down the hallway ahead of her.

Inside the emergency exit stairwell, they climbed upward the last few flights until they reached the top landing and the door that barred their way.

"You know," Joss said conversationally, "I can't read a lick of Swedish but there is an English translation there that says if you push that crash bar you're going to make an unholy amount of noise and have every security guard in the hotel down on us. Maybe we'd better go back to the room and try it there."

Bax gave her an amused look. "Who said anything

about a crash bar?" he asked as he pressed one palm against the door and pushed it open.

"Well," she said.

"It's one of those security tricks. Makes life easier on the maintenance guys and the warning signs scare off all the amateurs."

"Are you saying I'm an amateur?"

"You've got potential."

"I might surprise you. I might just decide to become an investigator. What would you say to that?"

"I'd be scared."

"Damned right."

The roof was broad and open, covered with some sort of grayish white pebbly tar paper. At intervals stood boxy heating and air-conditioning units and other structures too mysterious for her to identify. Near the edge of the roof, where the hip-high wall met the verdigris-covered facing that surrounded the outside roof, stood the Royal Viking sign. It towered over them in slanting cursive letters. By night, it was outlined in neon; by day, it was black sheet metal, with a line of metal rungs climbing up the slanting sides of the letters, just about where a stepladder would end.

"Their name in lights, huh?" Joss asked, slipping off her jacket and tossing it down at the foot of the *R.*

"Something like that," Bax said.

"Okay, sensei, tell me what to do."

The top she wore was white and stretchy and left absolutely nothing to the imagination. He watched her breasts rise and fall with each breath and shook his head. Business first, pleasure later, he reminded himself.

"I can't teach you martial arts in an afternoon. What I can do is teach you ways to hurt an attacker. You want to think about things like jabbing the eyes, chopping at the throat, hitting the nose with the heel of your hand. Sudden, surprising pain. It makes the eyes water and triggers an involuntary protection response. If someone's behind you, jab them with an elbow, stomp their foot with your heel."

"I stomped the mugger back in Portland," she said helpfully. "He let go of me real quick. I think I broke something in his foot. I don't know, I didn't stay around to find out."

"If you're dealing with someone trained, like Markus, this kind of stuff will only take you so far, but it's good to know."

"What about someone trained like Markus? How do I deal with what happened in the park today?"

"There's only so much you can do about a gun. He had you in a come-along hold, though, and we can talk about that."

"That was something else. Hurt like hell every time I tried to get loose."

"It's supposed to."

She grinned. "So how do you get out of it? I finally just stopped moving."

"That's the first part. You need to relax your arm, above all. A wristlock is designed to make you work against yourself. The more you do, the more you hurt. If you fight it, you can break your wrist." He wrapped his hand around her arm in a light wristlock, feeling the surprisingly fragile bones of her arm under his fingers. He liked her when she was spitting and fighting. He didn't like noticing her fragility. It unnerved him. "So if the bad guy has you in a wristlock, you want to rotate your arm like this and yank your hand against the thumb. The thumb is weaker than the rest of your hand, so you've got a chance to break the grip. Here, try it." At first, he had to shepherd her through the move, but surprisingly quickly she was able to break his grip with a quick motion.

"Looks like I've got it. Do I get a reward?"

"What do you want? I'm all out of chocolate treats."

"I'll settle for something noncaloric," she murmured, leaning in to press a kiss on him.

It was always new, the way she tasted, the way she felt, the way her avid mouth moved under his. He'd been with other women before, but somehow Joss stood out. Somehow, Joss erased all the others, as though there were only her, ever before and ever after.

"So how do you break this hold?" Joss whispered, licking his earlobe.

By keeping the end point in sight. Bax raised his head. "Let's move to the next topic. What if someone's trying to throttle you?"

"This isn't some deep-seated urge of yours, I hope."

"You're safe for now," he said dryly. "So come on, what do you do?"

"Apply pain," she said promptly. "Poke the attacker in the eye or stomp their foot."

"Good idea. The down side is that you might miss or the assailant might be out of range. Breaking loose before applying pain is better. Think, now. You want leverage. Move one of your feet back behind you. That's called Hidden Foot in martial arts. Look, let's do it. I'll put my hands around your neck." The slender column of her throat was soft beneath his fingers. Her pulse beat against his palms. The slanting letters behind them threw shadows over the gray tar paper of the roof. "Okay, now slide your left foot back. See how you pivot a little so your right shoulder comes toward me? If I'm a bad guy and I'm shaking you, I won't notice. Now here's the payoff. Take your right arm around and over my hands, scything, like you're trying to touch your left hip. Do it fast and all in one motion."

She whipped her arm up and over, knocking his hands down and away, taking him by surprise.

"It worked!" she said delightedly.

"It did. You're a fast learner."

"I'm a woman of many talents," she said, giving him a bold gaze.

"The thing to remember is to do it fast and hard."

"I always thought slow and hard was the ticket," she said with an entirely naughty look in her eyes. Her hands strayed to his belt buckle. "Shall I demonstrate?"

"You're a bad influence," he told her and pulled her to him for a long, deep kiss. When he felt her soften, he turned her in his arms to cradle her from behind, kissing her neck until her head fell back against him helplessly. "You should watch out," he murmured in her ear. "Kissing can be dangerous." He slid his arm up around her neck. "Now let's talk about choke holds."

Joss's hands flew up to his arm. "Dirty trick, Baxter."

"There's no one to make your opponents play fair," he reminded her. But she wasn't playing fair, either. Her hair was against his mouth, fragrant and sweet. He glanced down to see the tempting curves of her breasts. Desire tugged at him.

"Any time, sensei," Joss said and he shook it off.

"All right. I've got you in a choke hold." He wrapped his free arm across her taut body.

"It feels like a hold, all right." She slid her right arm down his side and over his butt. "Is this a kinky sex thing?"

"Pay attention," he said, as much to himself as to her. "You might need this some day."

"Kinky sex?" She slid her hand over his thigh and into his crotch. "Or maximum persuasion?" Quick as a snake, her hand surrounded his cock and balls. And she waited.

Bax stood absolutely still. "Careful."

"Mmm. So, what was that you were saying about playing fair?"

"It's bad form to emasculate your instructor," he said in a strained voice.

"Is that what's happening? It feels like something else," she murmured.

Indeed, under the heat of her hand, his cock was beginning to twitch and lengthen. She rubbed her fingers over the denim and the slight friction had him taking a breath. The second time she did it, he stiffened and tried not to think about her touch and what he could do with the woman in his arms. The third time she did it, he gave up.

Bax let his hands slide down over her body, feeling the lush curves of her breasts. It was ironic that he was teaching her self-defense. He was the one who needed defense, because when he got around her, his better sense went out the window and all he could do was want. Focus on the job, he thought, edging his fingertips under the hem of her tank. He managed pretty well most of the time, but when she was unzipping his jeans and sliding his cock into her mouth it just made him dizzy and work was the last thing on his mind. Instead, his world was wet heat and slippery friction that stood his hair on end as he looked down to see himself disappearing into her mouth, looked down to see her beautiful eyes, a glimpse of her breasts, the wonder of this gorgeous, sexy, amazing woman at his feet.

When he feared he was the one who was truly helpless.

He reached a hand out to brace himself on the slanting side of the *R* and touched her head, caressing her hair before stilling her motion. "Wait," he said hoarsely. "I want to be in you." He dragged out his wallet, fishing out the condom he'd tucked there even as Joss eeled out of her jeans and thong.

"A condom? Bax, you must have been a Boy Scout," she purred, taking it from him. She took him in her fist, stroking her hand over him from root to tip until he stiffened. "Well, you're hard enough to put it on, but maybe not slippery enough." Then she knelt on her jeans and slid him into her mouth, alternately licking him and rolling on the latex until he was sweating and grinding his teeth to keep from coming.

Then she stood and leaned back against the side of the *R*. "Now," she whispered, and wrapped one leg around his waist as he pressed against her.

Bax held his cock in one hand, his fingers sliding into her slick folds, rubbing her sweet juices down over himself. He traced the tip of his cock over her clitoris, running across it, down it, circling, over and over.

Joss moaned. Reaching up over her head, she touched the lowest of the steel rungs that climbed up the side of the letter. Her hand gripped the bar, pulling herself up so she could wrap her other leg around Bax's waist. "Put your cock in me. I want to feel it," she panted.

And in one swift push of his hips, he was inside her.

It was better than any buzz he'd ever had, the feel of having her wrapped around him, tight and hot and wet, so wet. Knowing how aroused she was, knowing that he had aroused her intensified the feel of every stroke. He looked down and watched his cock slide in and out of her. He could never get tired of this, seeing it, feeling it, hearing the cries she couldn't keep from making. When the sensory onslaught dragged him toward the edge, he resisted, changing his motion to prolong the experience. He pressed his finger against her mouth and slipped it between her lips, feeling her suck on him. Then he pulled it out and slipped it between her other lips, feeling her clitoris standing out in a hard, slick nub. He stroked it in time with the stroke of his cock, feeling her shudder, hearing her stifled moan.

And when she flushed and began the gulping, gasping cries that he knew heralded her orgasm, he abandoned control, surging against her hard and fast and deep until it launched him into climax with her.

THE TOUR BOAT dock was a stone's throw from the Royal Viking. Joss had watched the low, white, glassed-in boats navigate in and out of the little inlet by the hotel, alternately taking in and disgorging their crowds of passengers. Now, she and Bax stood in line at the kiosk to buy tickets of their own.

"First the museum, now a tour boat?" Joss asked. "This isn't just an excuse for sightseeing with you, is it?"

"Our friend is out in the archipelago, so we ought to get oriented. And you never know what you might learn on a tour like this. It's worth doing," Bax said, picking up the tickets that the counter clerk passed over. "We might learn something."

They wandered over to stand at the gate to the dock. The clouds that had blown in earlier had brought a light drizzle with them that had the happy effect of discouraging sightseers. Instead of the normal crowd, she and Bax stood among a small handful of tourists lined up waiting for the flat, white boat to arrive.

It chugged merrily toward them, churning up a froth of whitewater with its blunt bow. As the boat neared the dock, gradually slowing, a young deckhand appeared on the prow with a line. He gathered himself as the landing neared and leaped across several feet of open water to gain the dock and make the ropes fast.

Even though it was just a quick water tour of Stockholm, Joss couldn't suppress a little charge of excitement.

She ought to be above it, she told herself as they lined up to board. After all, she was in Stockholm for serious business. Hadn't that just been graphically demonstrated to her?

But it was the first time she'd been somewhere foreign, other than Africa, somewhere historic. Surely it was understandable for her to want to enjoy herself just a little bit, wasn't it? After all, they were going on the boat whether she liked it or not. Having fun would be the best use of time and money.

The little tour boat sat low in the water. A narrow central aisle threaded through the ranks of padded crosswise benches that bracketed narrow tables, like a series of restaurant booths. Headsets hanging on hooks on the tables played the tour narration in a dozen languages. Bax chose a seat up front and the boat was thinly populated enough that they had their entire booth to themselves.

Joss put on her headset and looked around. The whole top of the boat seemed to be made of Plexiglas. The windows rose from beside them and curved over to form the top of the boat, allowing them an unimpeded view on nearly all sides as the vessel backed out and began to chug away from Gamla Stan.

They headed east past the island Djurgården with its amusement park and open-air museum. The swells were larger here, sweeping in from the outer margins of the archipelago.

"If we keep going this direction, we'll find ourselves out by Silverholmen," Bax murmured to her.

"We'll have to go out there eventually, won't we?" she asked as the boat came around and headed for the pass between Gamla Stan and Södermalm, the SoHo of Stockholm.

"Probably. First, we've got to find a boat."

"Do you know how to pilot a boat?"

"It's been a little while, but yeah. I can navigate too, if I need to, but most boats come with GPS units these days. Takes away some of the guesswork."

The boat slowed as it went under a bridge and in between the high stone walls. Joss frowned and put on her headset.

"And now," announced the recorded narration, "we will proceed into the locks that will allow us to enter Lake Mälaren, at a different level than the Baltic."

The tour boat moved slowly into the lock, stopping and idling by the high stone walls. The pilot looked forward and back to check his position. The mate stepped lithely out of the forward hatch of the boat and up onto the transparent roof over their heads. Guide rope in hand, he vaulted onto the stone sidewall of the lock, walking nonchalantly along, directing the boat.

There was a careless efficiency to his movements that belied his skill as he guided the tour boat to the proper position and tied it down as the water level changed. Slowly, a hair-thin crack of daylight appeared at the center of the massive gates of the lock, widening as they parted, moving smoothly and ponderously backward. Finally, they had moved completely out of the way, leaving the path clear. The deckhand unwound the rope from its cleat to let the boat move forward, leaping lightly onto the foredeck at the last minute.

As they moved onto Lake Mälaren, the mate came back into the main cabin. He collapsed onto the seat opposite Joss and Bax and grinned. "All the work is done for a while." He was in his early twenties, with disordered spiky dark blond hair and a charcoal sweater that had probably seen better days.

"Hard work?" Joss asked.

"I'm outside all the time and on the water," he said with a shrug. "It is not so difficult a life."

"It's so beautiful, here." Joss gestured to the tree-covered slopes of Södermalm and the smaller island of Langholmen. "Stockholm is gorgeous."

"Ah, if you want to see true beauty, go out to the archipelago," he said. "No buildings, just islands and sea."

Joss felt Bax come to attention, though he looked as outwardly relaxed as ever. "How would you suggest we get there?"

"You would have to get a ferry in the Nybroplan or perhaps Slussen. It depends where you wish to go."

"The central archipelago, probably. A small island between Nämdö and Bullerö."

The mate tipped his head and looked at them consideringly. "Sightseeing?"

"Could be," Bax answered. "What if we wanted to pilot ourselves? Is it difficult to navigate the archipelago?"

"In places, of course. There are shallows or narrow passes between islands. Charts help. Do you have experience boating?"

"With launches and speedboats, not with sailboats."

"Motorboats are best, here."

"I will need help finding a place to rent one."

"Maybe I can help you out." The kid grinned and stuck out his hand. "I am Oskar. My friend and I have a boat. We do some deliveries to the archipelago. Perhaps we can do business."

"I'm Johan and this is Josie."

"A pleasure to meet you both." He put his hand out to shake.

Behind them, the pilot turned and barked something in Swedish. Oskar answered in the same and turned to them. "He tells me not to socialize with the passengers, that I am boring you, perhaps."

"Not at all. I think it's been a very interesting conversation, indeed," Bax said. "I'd like to continue it."

"As would I. Alas, we are approaching the lock to return to the Baltic. I must attend to my job."

"We all have to, sooner or later. Say I wanted to reach you about a boat. How would I contact you?"

Oskar considered. The pilot barked at him again and he took a quick glance behind him. "There is a restaurant called Pelikan on Södermalm. You can find me there most nights after work."

Bax nodded. "I might need information, also."

"I know much about the archipelago and many people. I can help you find out whatever you need." He touched his fingers to his forehead and was off and through the hatch.

Joss leaned in toward Bax as the tour boat lined up behind the other boats waiting at the lock. "Well, wasn't that convenient. 'Let's go on a boat tour and get oriented?'"

"Serendipity is a wonderful thing."

Joss gave him a narrow-eyed look. "Remember the whole talk about partners? If you were looking for specific information on this trip, you should have told me."

He digested it for a moment. "You're right," he said finally. "And I'm sorry. The thing is, I don't always have a goal, at least not one I'm conscious of. Sometimes I just do things on gut instinct, because they seem right. All I can say is I'll tell you what I can, when I can."

"I think that's good enough for me," Joss said. "And now, I suppose, we need to figure out where Pelikan is, right?"

Bax grinned. "You read my mind."

11

THE CEILING of the Stockholm convention center exhibit hall arched high overhead as Joss and Bax dodged the foot traffic in the aisles at the stamp expo. She'd known that philately was a popular hobby, but it had never occurred to her that thousands of people would flock to a stamp convention on a gorgeous summer Saturday in Stockholm, where warm weather was fleeting. It had also never occurred to her that so many stamp dealers existed in the world. Unlike her grandfather, who specialized in investment and did a small storefront trade, most of the exhibitors did the bulk of their business with casual hobbyists.

"What is the name of your sister's friend, again?" Bax asked her.

"Ray Halliday. Booth 1057," she read from her exhibit guide.

Bax scanned row signs hanging overhead and pointed. "Down there."

The booth for Halliday Philately was large and colorful, with a backdrop covered in blowups of famous stamps. Joss stopped to stare into a glass case displaying tongs and humidifiers for removing stamps from envelopes.

A spare-looking man in a white polo shirt approached them. "May I help you?"

"I'm looking for Ray Halliday," Joss told him.

He smoothed back his slightly frizzy red hair. "That's me."

Joss put out her hand. "I'm Joss Chastain, Gwen Chastain's sister. This is my friend Bax."

"Yes, of course." He shook hands with both of them. "Gwen e-mailed me you might be stopping by. Why isn't she here?"

"Too much going on," Joss said. "Someone had to mind the store."

"And you're the lucky devil who got stuck coming to Stockholm."

Joss grinned. "Someone had to suffer. Gwen said you might be able to help us with some information."

"Sure, whatever I can." What looked like a father and son stopped in the booth and Halliday glanced at Joss. "Give me a minute, will you?" He crossed to the pair and began chatting with them.

Bax glanced at him. "So how well does Gwen know this guy?"

"I gather she's been doing business with him for some time. She trusts him."

"She also trusted Oakes," Bax pointed out.

"So did my entire family. There's always the chance that someone's going to screw you over," Joss said. "Halliday sounds like a person who keeps his mouth shut and might be able to give us information that we need. It's worth taking a risk."

"If you say so."

Joss glanced over at Halliday. The discussion with the father and son had turned animated and he was pulling out stamp albums to show them. Finally, he broke loose and crossed back over to Bax and Joss. "Listen, I'd love to talk with you but I need to take care of these two first. You know how it goes."

"The customer comes first," Joss told him. "Don't worry about it."

"What about if we talk over dinner tonight, instead? Are you free?"

Joss looked at Bax and nodded. "Sure."

"Great. Say, seven-thirty at Fredsgatan 12? It's this great restaurant near the Royal Academy of Fine Arts. It'll be my treat."

"Too good an offer to turn down," Joss said. "We'll see you then."

THERE WAS SOMETHING fascinating about seeing a woman dress for the outside world, Bax thought as he watched Joss slide into a low-cut red and gold patterned dress. Seeing her go from bare skin and a towel to the silks and satins and little pots and bottles of mysterious girl stuff that smelled so good…he couldn't help but be intrigued.

She walked over to stand in front of him and turned around. "Can you zip me up?"

There was a familiarity to the gesture that floored him temporarily as he pulled up the zipper, watching the dress mold itself to her body. Unzipping a woman's dress was about sex. Zipping it was about…it was about intimacy, he realized in sudden discomfort. He'd been on that particular battleground before and the scars were still tender. Time to back away.

"All set," he said briskly and breathed a sigh of relief as she walked to the vanity area. Still, he couldn't keep from watching her apply her makeup and hold her jewelry against herself to choose exactly the right look. He didn't recognize the feeling as proprietary because he'd worked so hard to avoid any emotional connection to a woman—to anyone—for so long.

The phone rang. Bax looked at Joss, who nodded, and he picked up the receiver. "Hello."

"Ah, Johan. Keeping a close eye on your client, I see." It was Markus.

"Wouldn't you?"

"Your job appears to have extra benefits this time around...although it is unwise to overindulge."

"I'll keep that in mind. What do you want?"

"I have spoken with my employer and he has decided to meet with you."

"With the two of us, you mean."

"Yes, of course," Markus said impatiently.

"All right. Where?"

"Mr. Silverhielm's city office."

Bax snorted. "Neutral ground, Markus. You know how this works."

"One would think you do not trust us."

"One would be right," Bax agreed. "Neutral ground, a public place."

"Such as?"

Bax considered various candidates and rejected them. "How about Skansen?"

"You wish to be a tourist, now?"

"I think it would be a good location. In fact, the more I think about it, the more I like it." An outdoor museum that collected together historic buildings from all over Sweden, Skansen was public, open and on a Sunday afternoon would very likely have just enough people to prevent any funny business while affording some empty space to talk.

"Mr. Silverhielm will not find that satisfactory."

"If he wants the goods, he will. Tell him it's a chance to get back in touch with his culture."

Markus's only response was a snort. "A moment,

please." There was quiet murmuring in the background, then Markus returned. "Mr. Silverhielm says he will be indulgent. This time. Where in the park shall we meet?"

"How about at the temperance hall?"

"How very appropriate—9:00 p.m.?"

"Daylight."

"This is Stockholm in August, 9:00 p.m. is daylight."

"Broad daylight. Let's make it earlier, say seven."

"Private business needs to remain private, you know that."

"It'll be private enough, I guarantee." And every concession he pushed Markus into gave him that much more authority.

"All right, seven at Skansen. See that it is just the two of you."

"See that it is just the two of you."

"For a well-known figure like Mr. Silverhielm, bodyguards are an unfortunate necessity," Markus said smoothly.

"Not at the meeting," Bax persisted.

"It is a matter of safety."

"My point, exactly. He should be safe enough with you watching over him."

Markus chuckled. "You flatter me. Very well, no bodyguards, then. Do we have a meet?"

"We do."

"Until tomorrow."

"We'll see you then." Bax hung up the phone and turned to Joss, who stared at him.

"So?"

"A meeting at Skansen. Markus and Silverhielm. Now we just have to figure out what happens next."

Bax rubbed his knuckles along the edge of his jaw. He had a germ of an idea, but no real understanding of how to make it work. Somehow, they needed to tempt Silver-hielm into bringing out his one-penny Mauritius, and do it without risking the Blue Mauritius. "Maybe we'll get a fix on what happens next when we talk with Gwen's friend tonight. Speaking of which," he glanced at his watch, "we've got about half an hour to get there."

"Then I guess we don't have time to fool around, do we?"

She smelled of seduction and his body tightened. "Depends on how efficient we are."

She twined her arms around his neck. "Oh, I can be very efficient when I want to."

THE RESTAURANT was open and airy with slate-violet walls and minimalist decor. The food at Fredsgatan 12 was minimalist, too, Joss discovered. The menu dispensed with quaint notions of starter and entrée, serving up exquisitely flavorful and astoundingly expensive dishes of just a few bites each. "You'll want four or five dishes," their severely dressed server said breezily.

"Get whatever you like," Halliday said expansively as he chose a bottle of wine. "Dinner's on me."

"We can't do that," Joss objected, staring at the menu.

"Of course you can. It's a business expense. I've done some good business with Chastain's. Buying you dinner is the least I can do."

"I take it you had a successful day?" Joss asked after they'd ordered.

Halliday nodded. "Good traffic, actually."

"I wouldn't have thought it," Joss said. "The weather is so gorgeous now I expected people to stay outside enjoying it."

"Ah, but true collectors are a different breed. It's all about the acquisition. Nothing else matters nearly as much, not even a sunny Saturday in August."

Interested, Bax leaned forward. "Tell us more about the psychology of a collector."

"Psychology? Pathology, more like it, depending on who you're talking about."

"Oh come on, surely it's not that bad," Joss disagreed.

The waiter appeared with the wine. "It depends," Halliday said, nodding at the bottle the waiter displayed to him. "You get all kinds. There are the harmless ones, like the pair who were in my booth today. They're excited about it and they enjoy it. It's something a father and son can do together. They learn about history and geography and enjoy themselves, but it doesn't run them. You can see the place it holds in their lives, just like you can see it in the eyes of the other ones." He took a sip of the wine the waiter brought for him and nodded.

"What other ones?" Bax asked.

"You know, the obsessives. For them, it's not about the process. It's not about the learning, it's not about gradual growth of the collection. Their obsession is having, and having more than anyone else." Halliday watched the waiter fill their glasses. "You'll see them throw away all their money on stamps, go into debt, even, pay tens or hundreds of thousands for a stamp, just to have it."

"But Gwen has plenty of customers who pay those prices as an investment," Joss objected, then sampled her wine.

Halliday shook his head. "Different thing. I'm talking about the ones who have to have. For some of them, nothing is too much. I had a client a couple of years back who was fixated on the Inverted Jenny. You know, the U.S. airmail stamps where they printed the plane upside down? He couldn't get enough of them, had a standing order for me to buy one any time I found it available, no mater how inflated the cost and no matter how many he already had."

"Are collectors always experts?" Bax asked.

"Some, not always. Sometimes they're so busy obsessing over having that they never really learn all the details. At least, not the kinds of details known by those whose passion is in the collecting process."

"Interesting. So talk to me about forgeries," Bax said as the waiter set their first dishes before them. "Do you see a lot of them out there?"

"Oh, some. They're always out there for the people who aren't smart."

"Like the obsessives?"

"Hopefully the obsessives have a trustworthy dealer to take care of them. Besides, any moderately intelligent person buying a stamp these days expects to see certification on the property."

"Of course, certifications can be forged, also."

"They can, for the person who's sufficiently determined. You hear about it occasionally."

"Are most forgeries made from scratch?"

"Fewer than you'd think. Some of them are antiques, and collectable themselves, ironically. Most of what you see as forgeries is really doctored up versions of existing stamps. The change in value of a stamp in good condition versus one in fair condition is pretty steep. You get stamp doctors who can add back gum and things to make a stamp look mint."

"What about forgeries of rare stamps?" Bax asked, watching him intently.

"How rare?"

"Oh, say, a Blue Mauritius."

Halliday gave Bax a long look. "The whereabouts of all the existing Post Office Mauritius stamps are known. A person coming up with a forgery would be taking a big gamble."

"What if a person wanted to gamble?" Bax asked softly. "Could you get me a forgery?"

"You've got a lot of nerve asking me a question like that," Halliday began angrily.

"Ray," Joss put her fingertips on his arm, "you know what happened with my grandfather's stamps. Gwen and I have hired Bax to help us. Please." She moistened her lips. "We need your help."

Halliday slowly studied her, then moved his gaze to study Bax. "All right. Well, first, a convincing forgery would require a good plate. One way to do it would be to find a person who could produce a new plate from a photograph. They use lasers, I understand. They'd have to doctor it, color match the inks, get the right paper and gum. It's not an easy process."

"But doable?"

Halliday nodded slowly. "I suppose. Another way is to do a reprint from the original plate."

"I would have thought they would have long since been destroyed."

"You'd be surprised. The original plates for the Post Office Mauritius pair still exist but they're not in a museum. They're reputed to be in the hands of a private collector. Perhaps they are. And perhaps that collector might rent them out to an ambitious forger for the right price."

Halliday took a sip of his wine. "Of course, even with the original plates, you'd have the same problems of inks, paper and gum. It's not a simple thing to find what you seek."

"Could you help us?" Joss asked, fighting the urge to hold her breath.

Halliday stared at her. "Perhaps you'd better tell me what this is all about."

DUSK WAS DARKENING to evening as Bax and Joss walked back to the Royal Viking. "So, what did you think of Fredsgatan 12?" he asked her.

"The food was wonderful, but I feel like stopping somewhere to get dinner, now. Do you know I calculated that the two scallops in my fish dish cost about twelve dollars each?"

"Maybe lemon juice is more expensive here."

She stuck her tongue in her cheek. "That must be it. Anyway, it was nice of Ray to treat us. We owe him."

"We'll owe him even more if he can find that forgery."

The last shades of evening were falling away as they walked toward the waterfront. "So just exactly what are you cooking up with a forgery, assuming Halliday can get one?" Joss asked, giving Bax a speculative look.

He shrugged. "I'm not sure. We're currently playing a very dangerous game with our friend Silverhielm. If our talks move forward, at some point he's going to expect us to come across with a stamp. I don't mind bluffing with the real Blue Mauritius, but we'd damned well better cook up some way to keep it safe from him."

"But how is having either a real or a forged Blue Mauritius going to help us get the one-penny Mauritius?"

"I haven't figured that out, yet." He grinned. "Feel free to chime in if you think of something."

It was that certainty that an idea would crop up that she admired. "Hey, it was my idea that got us this far."

"And it was a good one," he told her, sliding an arm around her shoulders.

It felt immeasurably cozy. "Could we try playing 'you show me yours, I'll show you mine'?"

"Possibly, though it would take some doing to get them to fall for it. Silverhielm doesn't strike me as a risk taker. He likes to have the game rigged in his favor, I think."

"Well, what if we get him thinking that it is?"

Bax considered. "Could work. Now we have to figure out practical implementation."

"Maybe we'll learn something when we meet with them. Have your sources told you anything more about Markus or Silverhielm that might help?"

They crossed another of the ubiquitous public squares and headed to the waterfront. "Just that Markus is working for him as a trigger man. Markus can be a very effective scare to pull out of your pocket."

"But you and he are buds, right?" There was something between Markus and Bax that she didn't quite understand.

Bax shook his head. "Never make that mistake. Nothing comes ahead of the job for Markus. He'll take care of his client, first and foremost."

"But he talks like you're friends."

"It's hard to tell with Markus. Maybe I just amuse him."

"And he still has no idea you worked for Interpol."

"Not as far as I know."

It seemed extraordinary to her that Bax could have lived this separate life, a separate life that he still maintained. How much of the person she knew was real? "How did you wind up working for Interpol, anyway? That's rare, isn't it? I mean, you'd need to know a lot of languages and European customs and everything."

"I grew up in Europe, remember? I speak Danish, Dutch and German fluently and bits of a couple of others."

"So you just picked them up as you moved around?" Walking through the warm twilight, it seemed natural to talk.

"Kind of. I seem to be a natural linguist, but it helped being exposed to so many different languages when I was young. Speech patterns aren't set then, so it's easy to learn different ways to think about the same thing."

"But you speak English without an accent." Ahead lay the cream and blush baroque palace of the opera house with a statue of a king on horseback before it.

"My father and the people at the embassies taught me. Besides, we moved back to the U.S. when I was about sixteen. I worked hard at getting rid of my accent."

"How did your mom take leaving Europe?"

"She died around that time, so I don't have an answer to that." Something in the tone of his voice warned her not to pursue that line of questioning further. He dropped his arm and moved away.

"So then, what, you went into the military?"

"The FBI, eventually."

"What did your father think of that?"

"He didn't like it, but then he doesn't like much that I do." The rancor in his voice was startling. "We aren't exactly a typical father and son."

"Sometimes being different can be good," Joss said, thinking of her own family.

"When it comes to my dad, being apart is good," he said with finality.

People lived what they learned. Joss reached out to tangle her fingers in his. "Being together has its moments, too."

For an instant, his fingers were still, then they softened. "So I've seen."

12

THE LONG SUMMER afternoon stretched out as Joss and Bax entered the back gates of Skansen. They ignored the funicular and began to walk up the winding path that led from the meadow below to the top of the bluffs that held the outdoor museum.

"Why did you choose this as a meeting place?" Joss asked. "Aren't we taking a chance being in the middle of all of these buildings? Silverhielm could have some of his people in here."

"Almost certainly. Then again, we're only here to talk, not to make a handoff or do anything where force would benefit them. I think Silverhielm's going to want to have additional people in place just to feel like he's got his extra measure of control, but they're going to essentially be aboveboard. The temperance lodge is in the open. We should be okay there."

Ahead of them, as they reached the top, clustered the wooden buildings of a nineteenth-century family farm.

Back in the previous century, Skansen had been conceived as a way to preserve the history of Sweden with a collection of typical buildings from all regions of the country and all time periods. Now, it stretched across acres of the island of Djurgården, dirt lanes leading from one to another of the dozens of buildings. During the day, crowds attended the festivals, filtered through the outdoor market in the square. Park employees in authentic costumes demonstrated the techniques of bakers, printers, metalsmiths and so on. During the day, Skansen was bustling with activity.

Now, although the park was ostensibly open, the grounds were largely deserted. They found their way to the temperance lodge, a low, red building surrounded by a wooden fence.

"Did temperance ever take off in Sweden?" Joss asked as they came to a stop by the information sign.

A corner of Bax's mouth twitched. "You're talking about a country that has a museum of alcohol. I'm thinking not. Here we are." His voice changed. "There."

She turned to see Markus and Silverhielm walking toward them, flanked by two bodyguards.

"No bodyguards, Markus," Bax reminded him as they came close.

"They are here to enjoy the culture," Markus said with a faint smile.

"Let them enjoy it elsewhere."

Markus nodded at the two men, who hesitated a moment and walked down the path toward another area.

"Good evening, Ms. Astin." Silverhielm held out his hand to take hers and kiss it as before.

He'd dispensed with the formality of a suit, but only just. Instead, he wore a dark blue jacket—cashmere, perhaps?—over khakis, with a white shirt unbuttoned at the collar, sort of a King-Karl-watches-polo outfit.

Markus wore a jacket as well, for the same reason, she assumed, as Bax—to hide a gun.

Her stomach tightened.

"Good evening, Mr. Silverhielm."

"Please, let us dispense with formality," he said comfortably. "You shall call me Karl and I shall call you Josie. And this is your friend?" He looked at Bax.

"This is my associate, Johan Bruhn," she told him.

"Ah. Markus tells me many things about you, Mr. Bruhn."

"Johan," Bax said.

"I hear you are a man of no small talent. Perhaps we should discuss that at some point."

"Perhaps. For now, though, we are here to discuss Josie's business and your business with Stewart Oakes."

"Ah yes, this business. Come, Josie." They began to stroll down the pathway that led to the reproduction nineteenth-century village, Markus and Bax following. "Such an embarrassment that Stewart Oakes confessed to the theft of such valuable stamps, he and his associate. A person dealing with Mr. Oakes would, of course, assume that he'd obtained the goods he brokered by honest means."

"Unless," Joss said, "that were impossible, in which case a client would have to know he might take extreme measures to attain the prize."

Silverhielm shook his head sadly, folding his hands together at his back. "Truly reprehensible. The news accounts were not clear about which issues were taken and which were recovered. Perhaps they were more detailed in the U.S."

"The papers were not, but I have the luck to have had a...close relationship with Stewart's associate." She let satisfaction creep into her voice as she glanced at the white and periwinkle wildflowers lining the sides of the lane.

"Mr. Messner, correct? I understand both he and Mr. Oakes are in jail at present."

"True. The last time Jerry—Mr. Messner—was at my apartment, he happened to leave a valuable piece of property with me for safekeeping." They turned up a steep cobblestone street. "A valuable piece of property that I believe you have some interest in. After all, just because the law caught up with Stewart and Jerry doesn't mean that your transaction has to be a complete disappointment."

Afternoon shadows stretched across the lane. Silverhielm examined the now-dark windows of the metalsmith's store and turned to her.

"So bold of you to ask for additional money to deliver the property I already own, is it not, Josie?"

"Think of it as a delivery fee." She gave him a brilliant smile. "After all, I wasn't a part of the original negotiations, and yet I have gone to the trouble and expense of flying to Stockholm to reach out to you."

"And how did you come to know of me?"

She spread her hands. "Pillow talk, Karl. You understand."

"But you are no longer sharing a pillow with Mr. Messner, I see."

Joss gave him a cool look. "Mr. Messner left me high and dry. A woman has to find a man who can take care of her."

"So you now share your pillow with Mr. Bruhn."

"Now you're the one who's bold." They approached the deserted town square with its array of wooden picnic tables. "What matters is the service that I can potentially render to you. After all, Stewart was unable to complete your agreement. If I hadn't stepped in, you would not have the opportunity to obtain your commissioned property. Because I took the time to come here, you have the choice of whether to receive it or not, depending on what it is worth to you." Joss sank down on one of the wooden benches. Below and beyond them, the lights of the Gröna Lund amusement park spread out against the water.

Silverhielm sat at the table next to her. Markus and Bax lingered nearby. "So you might have one of the objects that Stewart promised me?"

"Well, yes, but obviously a certain amount of risk and cost have been associated with getting the property over here. If I were to hand it over to you, for example, instead of the authorities, I'd expect compensation."

"You must understand, I have already paid a substantial commission to Mr. Oakes for his efforts. I naturally expected a positive result from the investment."

"Things don't always go as planned, though, you know that." A wave of screams erupted from the Power Tower at Gröna Lund as a group of thrill-seekers went into extended freefall. "I understand that you have a long-standing interest in owning a Post Office Mauritius pair. Wouldn't you like to see that interest brought to fruition?"

Something hot and proprietary flickered in his eyes and she knew she'd guessed right. Not just a collector, not just an investor. An obsessive, one for whom owning the object of desire was everything.

"So you have it, then."

"The Blue Mauritius? Yes."

His gaze became bright with avarice and he let out a slow breath. "It would bring me a good deal of pleasure to have the Blue Mauritius."

"The proper deal would bring me a good deal of pleasure, too."

"I do not like to have terms dictated to me." The Silverhielm she'd glimpsed in Slussen emerged.

She suppressed the urge to shift away from him. "You can dictate all the terms you like," she said instead. "I'll just exercise my right to say yes or no."

"I see. What is to stop me from, for example, directing my associates down the lane to bring their weapons to bear on you to force a 'yes' answer?"

"If you were going to do that, you'd have done it already." Bax stepped up and sat next to Joss. "Stop wasting our time. We've got something you want, something you're willing to pay for. We want two hundred thousand for it, cold cash."

"Kroner?"

Bax just snorted. "Dollars. I'm sure you can get a favorable exchange rate."

"'We want,' you say?"

Bax looked at him calmly. "I have a commission coming."

"Of course. I shall consider this proposal."

"Nothing to consider," Bax told him. "It's a fifth of the market value of the stamp. You're getting a bargain. Either you pay us or Josie takes it to the authorities, it's as simple as that."

"To the authorities?"

"Or, perhaps, to another collector."

Silverhielm's nostrils flared. "The stamp is mine. I will have it."

"Easy enough. All you have to do is meet our terms."

The Swede gave him a black look. The two bodyguards appeared at the edge of the lane where it opened out into the square. "I will not answer this now."

"You want time to think about it, take it. I'm sure it's easy to find a Blue Mauritius at a discount rate. Shoot, you can just have your goons break into the postal museum and take theirs. You'll get it for free."

"Do not mock me," Silverhielm said coldly.

"Then don't mock us. We know you've got money. That's not an issue. The only issue is whether you're willing to pay us what we want. That figure wasn't a top line bargaining number we're working down from, by the way. That's our number, period."

"It is a fortunate liaison you've made, this 'we.'" Hostility crackled in Silverhielm's voice.

"Yes, isn't it?" Joss interrupted and rose. "I think Johan is right, the conversation is over. Contact us when you've decided to get serious."

THEY WALKED AWAY from the town square toward the nearby front entrance of Skansen. Joss ignored the tickle between her shoulder blades and tried not to imagine the red dot of a laser sight dancing around the area between them.

It was easier once they'd gone down the hill toward the noise and life of Gröna Lund. "Thank God that's over," Joss murmured. She wanted to be among the lights, she wanted to be among people. Anything but around the grinding tension of the meeting they'd just had.

"You did well," Bax told her, resting his hand lightly on the small of her back as they went through the exit gates. "You handled him just right."

"Except for the part where he started threatening bodily harm." She'd been calm when it was going on. It was only now that she trembled.

"You're not used to it, that's all." They turned down the road that led back toward the mainland. "It was a bluff. He was expecting you to back down. Guys like him, they like the cat and mouse game. They're not happy if they can't flex their muscles."

Her shoulders felt like they were up somewhere around her ears, tormented with iron pincers as they walked through the wash of lights from the front entrance of Gröna Lund. "We'd better get the goods from our buddy Ray or we're going to be in trouble."

"We'll figure something out."

Again, the confidence. Joss shrugged, trying to relax, but the tension only got worse. It wasn't enough to know it was over. She needed to believe it. She needed to let it go.

She needed to scream her head off.

"Hey, come on." Seizing Bax's hand, she pulled him across the street toward the ticket kiosks of Gröna Lund.

"What are we doing here?"

She dug kroner out of her pocket and handed it to the cashier. "I need to get rid of some stress."

"I'VE BEEN TO an amusement park maybe twice in my entire life," Bax said. They stood in the line, waiting their turn on the roller coaster billed as Sweden's scariest. "There's a big amusement park in Copenhagen called Tivoli. I went one time when we were visiting my cousins."

He sounded just a bit uneasy, Joss realized, amused. "I'll make sure nothing happens to you," she reassured, patting his hand as the line moved. Slowly, they inched forward. Because it was the end of the weekend, the queue was shorter, but not by much. It was summer, after all.

"I always loved amusement parks," Joss said. "It was the one thing I really missed in Africa."

"No amusement parks there?"

"Not where we lived. I'd always make my parents take me to Great America when we went back to San Francisco each year, though. I dragged my mother and Gwen on the rides whether they wanted to go or not."

"And you always wanted to go on the scariest, craziest, most death-defying roller coasters, and over and over again, right?"

Joss grinned. "Maybe you do know me after all."

They'd reached the head of the line and the attendant waved them forward. A little frisson of anticipation ran through Joss as they sat in the car and pulled down the safety restraints.

"How did I let you talk me into this?" Bax muttered as

the air brakes hissed and the car rolled slowly forward. "I haven't been on a ride like this since I was about ten."

"Really? Well, then you're due."

A wave of pure, giddy pleasure swept over her as the car shot off without warning and they whipped up the first climb. There was no time to think, only time to feel. Only time to live in the moment. As the car crested the hill and began to drop, she threw her hands up in the air and screamed her lungs out. G-forces pulled at her and she could feel the crazy grin stretching her face. It was wonderful to be scared silly, completely, harmlessly silly in a way that didn't include guns and threats. The pit of her stomach dropped out as the car whirled into a sideways turn up in the air at a dizzying height, with the ground far below and only the slender rails restraining them.

This time, she swore she heard a whoop from Bax over her own giddy scream, though she couldn't be sure.

Joss was still laughing when the car wheeled into the station, even as she pushed her hair back out of her eyes.

She looked over at Bax. His hair was in disarray, his collar was flipped up from the wind of the car's passage. For the first time since she'd known him, that tense, watchful look was gone from his face.

"Satisfied?" he asked, taking his hand off the safety bar and flexing his fingers.

Joss grinned at him. "Don't give me that. You had fun and you know it."

He gave a sudden laugh, looking younger than she'd ever seen him. "You're right. Let's go again."

13

BAX STOOD IN LINE at the café next to Karl XII's *torg* wearing shorts and a T-shirt, still damp from his five mile run. When he went too many days without working out, he started to feel sludgy and slow. Not healthy, for a man in his line of work.

He was still too hot to think about going back inside for coffee, though. And even if he were, he had a pretty good idea that the café at the Royal Viking would disapprove of his current state. So he'd stopped at the outdoor café, instead.

The server turned to him. *"Hej."*

"Hej," he replied, ordering coffee in Swedish.

"You've picked up the language quickly, but then you were always very good in Danish," said a voice behind him. Bax turned to see Markus.

"I'm very good in English, too. Do you want coffee?"

"Yes, thank you. I see you have been running."

"I've got nothing else to do while I'm waiting for you and Silverhielm to get your acts in gear. Besides, Stockholm is a beautiful city. I may as well see some of it while I'm here."

"But you saw it all when you were here before."

Bax paid for the drinks and handed Markus his cup. By unspoken accord, they walked out to the tables.

"Back then my tastes were less…refined, shall we say."

"And now your tastes run more to tour boats than strip clubs?"

It didn't surprise him that they'd been watching. "And did your man like the tour?"

"He did not join you. He would have enjoyed the strip club more." Markus stopped to doctor his coffee with cream.

"I'm sure."

"You never cared for them, though, did you?"

Bax shrugged. "Not my call. When that's where the boss wants to set up to do his business, you do it."

"But he is your boss no longer."

"No." Bax eyed him. "You've changed as well."

"Yes. I have, as you Americans say, traded up."

"A smart man."

"You are a smart man also, Johan and you puzzle me. Your current client is not exactly up to your usual standards."

They reached a table and pulled out chairs to sit. "Do you make a study of my clients?"

"You have a certain reputation among our community. Or had. You disappeared." Markus took a drink of his coffee.

"I went to Miami for business and wound up staying on." And he had an acquaintance who would back up that story, if necessary.

Markus gave him a steady look. "For a man with your talents, I am sure there is work everywhere you go."

"As there is for you."

"Yes, but I prefer the familiar. So how did you wind up with the woman?"

Bax gave him an amused look. "You certainly get right to it."

"Do you blame me? You were not, I assume, surprised to find me working for Silverhielm."

"Not a bit."

"No," Markus agreed. "I have worked for many like him in the past, several that you know of."

"Several I didn't understand how you could tolerate."

"The price was right. And you, I could see you winding up in Miami. Or in Las Vegas, wasn't that where you met her?"

"It was."

"There are a number of men in that city who would find your services useful and pay you handsomely. Yet you are with the woman. Why?"

Bax grinned. "You've seen her and you have to ask that?"

"I have seen many beautiful women but none who would stand between me and money."

"Who says she stands between me and money? I stand to make a nice profit once we pull off the exchange."

"A trifle and you know it," Markus said contemptuously. "You are too smart to let your appetites control your professional life. Why are you here?"

"A favor for a lady, a free trip back to Europe and a nice fat commission."

"I don't believe that."

Bax took a swallow of his coffee. "And a chance to set myself up for my next job."

Markus looked at him consideringly. "That, I am more likely to believe. How did you find out about the stamp?"

"I happened to be at the right place at the right time and overheard a few things."

"Including my employer's name?"

"Including that. Including a description of someone who sounded a lot like you. I thought it couldn't hurt to come over and check it out. At worst, it is a paid vacation. At best, a chance to do a little career networking."

"Ah, now we come closer to the truth."

Bax let the humor fall away. "You and your employer have indicated an interest in me."

"An interest in your talents, yes. Mr. Silverhielm would like to know if they are for hire."

"He doesn't know the first thing about me."

"But I do."

"And that is enough?"

"In such matters, yes."

And suddenly Bax felt as though he were back undercover, when the objectives were clear but day to day life was ambiguous.

"What would I have to do?"

Markus smiled faintly. "Provide your usual sort of services."

"Does he have something specific in mind?"

"It is difficult to say. Mr. Silverhielm has his fingers in many pies, you might say. He wishes to have you on his team. I think you will not find his terms ungenerous."

"How not ungenerous?"

"He prefers to tell you such things himself."

"When?" The dance, the constant dance frustrated Bax.

"Perhaps in a day or so."

"First, we exchange the stamp."

"Of course. But there is no reason we cannot move forward down both paths, is there?"

Now it began to make sense. "Don't think that by offering me a job you'll have an easier time getting the Blue Mauritius."

"Of course not." Markus snorted. "I know better."

"So Silverhielm's ready to name a time and a place?"

"Always impatient."

"My client is impatient," Bax corrected. "Where and when?"

"You set terms for the last meeting. It is our turn."

"So what do you choose?"

Markus watched the steam rise off his coffee and glanced up at Bax. "Our territory. Mr. Silverhielm's home."

"Out on the archipelago?"

Markus didn't show surprise, but then again he wouldn't. "You have done your homework."

"As you no doubt expected."

"Then I shouldn't need to give you directions or arrange for your transportation."

A challenge, perhaps. Or a test. "We'll find our way."

Markus rose, taking his coffee with him. "Mr. Silverhielm will expect you on Saturday evening at seven-thirty. We will make our exchange and perhaps talk a little business."

"I look forward to it."

JOSS WAS AT the bathroom mirror putting on lipstick when her cell phone rang. She walked out into the bedroom to grab the slim phone from the bedside table. "Hello?"

"Joss. Ray Halliday."

She counted to three. It didn't do to look too eager. "Ray, how are you?"

"Today's the last day of the expo. I'm doing great."

"Ready to go home?"

"You know it. Hey listen, can you get over here before ten?"

Joss blinked. "You mean to the convention center?"

"Yeah."

She checked her watch. "It's already nine. Bax is out and I'm not sure when he'll be back. Can we be a little later?"

"Not really. There's someone I want you to meet before the show starts. He might be able to help you out with…your problem."

She chewed the inside of her lip. This was an opportunity they couldn't afford to squander, whether Bax was there or not. "I don't know where Bax is, but I can come over now."

"Great. I'll see you then."

The last thing she wanted to do was run out while Bax was gone. This was just what they'd talked about. Bax would go ballistic if he came back and found her gone, Joss knew that. She dialed his cell phone number, only to hear the answering ring across the room, on his night table. Okay, so calling him was out. Now what was she supposed to do? Hang around, maybe miss the meeting with Ray? Or go to the meeting and fill Bax in later?

It was no contest. Reality was, she'd made the decision the minute Ray asked her to come out. The important thing was that she do what was necessary to get the stamps back. If it meant taking a risk, so be it. If it meant letting Bax down, she'd deal with his anger. It was what he got for forgetting his phone.

To salve her conscience, she scribbled a hasty note and left it on the bed. He wouldn't like it, but it was the best she could do. Shoving a handful of kroner and her transportation card in the back pocket of her jeans, she grabbed her key and cell phone and headed out the door.

It was still early enough that the ornate lobby was nearly empty. The people with morning plans were gone. Those checking out hadn't come down yet. In the front café, a trio of men in sober chalk-striped business suits held a breakfast meeting. A woman with a dog on a leash walked toward the elevator. On one of the gold padded benches by the door, a guy in jeans and a tweed jacket read the newspaper. And Bax was nowhere in sight.

Joss stood for a moment. She couldn't afford to wait for Bax to return, she thought desperately. In her shoes, he'd do the same thing. She checked her watch again. Be here in an hour, Ray had said.

It was time to go.

Outside, puffs of white clouds dotted the cerulean sky. In a perfect world, she'd have made the leisurely walk to the central train station, enjoying the clean streets and the morning cool of the air as she went. Today, she didn't have time. Instead, she headed directly for the Tunnelbana station a few blocks from the hotel. The subway would take her to Central Station and a fifteen-minute ride on the commuter rail would bring her to the convention center.

At least the morning rush hour was over. She wouldn't be fighting with a mob of commuters, not that all that many commuters probably lived in this exclusive tourist district. Indeed, she found herself alone as she clattered down the stairs to the station. Behind her, she heard the soft slap of footsteps. Okay, maybe the commute wasn't quite over, she thought as she walked onto the empty platform. Even in Sweden there were laggards.

The glare from overhead fluorescent lights reflected off the concrete of the platform. Joss blinked and frowned. Something was strange. The footsteps, she realized. They'd stopped without anyone ever appearing in the station. Perhaps the commuter had decided to go back home and to bed, she speculated. Then again, she hadn't heard the sound of someone climbing back up to the street.

The hairs on the back of her neck prickled.

It was ridiculous, of course. It was broad daylight, mid-morning. No one was going to bother her, not down here.

Still she breathed a little sigh of relief when she heard the distant rumble of the approaching train. Clean and open though it was, the empty station was a little too creepy for her. Any second, a train, other people, would be here. And maybe once she was on the train, she could stop wondering about those footsteps.

The rumbling intensified. It swelled to a roar, crescendoed, and a bullet of silver burst along the tracks. Shining and sleek, the cars slid smoothly to a stop, the doors snapping open.

Only a handful of people sat in the car nearest to her, newspapers open on their laps. Just working people on their way to the office. Just another normal day. For a moment, she felt incredibly foolish. She'd been dealing with the cloak-and-dagger world too much. Bax's constant alertness had rubbed off on her.

With an inner smile, Joss moved to board the train. Then the faint echo of a shout from outside the station had her looking reflexively toward the stairs that led to the street.

And she saw the tweed-jacketed guy from the hotel walking toward her.

BAX WAS WAITING to cross at the light, the Royal Viking just ahead when he caught the flash of scarlet far down the street, the scarlet of Joss's jacket below the dark cloud of her hair. She was walking quickly, head down. On the building before her he saw the encircled black *T*, the sign for the Tunnelbana.

Consternation surged through him. She knew better than to run out on her own. So what did that mean? Was it just an errand? Was it something too important to miss? Had Markus ignored him and gotten to her? For an instant, Bax stood indecisively. She was too far away for him to reasonably expect to catch up with her, yet he didn't want to let her go.

Then his gaze snagged on a man paralleling her course.

A man who kept pace with her from across the street, turning his head and shoving his hands in his pockets when she glanced up.

Doing his best to be inconspicuous.

Bax was walking before he realized it, breaking into a run when he saw Joss disappear into the entrance to the T-bana station. The man sped up now, crossing the street and moving swiftly after her. An errant breeze off the water caught at his jacket, molding it against him, outlining a bulky shape at his hip that had nothing to do with the human anatomy, a bulky shape that was deadly metal.

And Bax began to sprint.

IT PROBABLY didn't mean anything, Joss told herself as the train rumbled out of the station. After all, if the guy in the tweed jacket was staying at the hotel, it made sense that he'd go to the nearest T-bana stop. But why alone, and so suddenly after he'd been loitering in the lobby? What if it weren't just coincidence that he'd decided to put down his paper and go for a ride?

What if he was following her?

It was something she simply couldn't afford. And so, when she got out of the train, she purposely took her time walking down the platform. He stepped out ahead of her and she stopped to study one of the enormous street maps of the area that stood against the wall. It wouldn't hurt to stay behind and keep an eye on him. It was what Bax would do.

The walls of the tunnels were rough hewn, rising up to shadowed arches high overhead. All the lights in the world couldn't make the platform bright. For some reason, she thought of an old movie version of H.G. Wells's *Time Machine,* with its Morlocks and subterranean dangers.

Ahead of her, Tweed Jacket walked briskly to the end

of the platform and out of sight. She really was getting paranoid, Joss told herself. Clearly, he was just a tourist headed out for the day. Why shouldn't he be alone? She was worried about nothing. If Bax thought there was a risk of them being tailed, he surely would have said something.

Then again, he hadn't been expecting her to go out.

Joss made her way to the end of the platform. Tweed Jacket was off to whatever adventure he was having next and she was off to the convention center and the meeting with Ray. She turned into the first of the series of tunnels that would lead her through the levels of the Tunnelbana and eventually to the commuter rail station.

The Blue Line that she'd ridden in on was the deepest of the three lines that intersected at Central Station. She worked her way along moving walkways that carried her up gradual rises until she reached the long escalator that would bring her toward the higher platforms.

Here, the walls were plastered with ads for kitchen tools and department-store sales, interspersed with scenic tourist-board photographs of Götland. Joss looked across at the line of matching ads flanking the down escalator opposite her. Idly, she glanced back, down the steep slant of the moving stair.

And saw Tweed Jacket riding the escalator below her.

14

BAX BURST INTO the room at the Royal Viking. It was empty, as he'd expected. As the T-bana station had been empty when he'd raced down the stairs, lungs burning, only to find the train long gone. Over his head, an electronic sign in mocking red had told him to expect a train in four minutes. He hadn't bothered to wait. With no idea of where Joss was going, there was no point.

Instead, he'd run back to the hotel.

Now, he grabbed the note from the bureau, reading it with a curse. He crumpled it and threw it down, snatching up the cell phone. There was no answer to his call. Small surprise. Joss was probably too far underground to get a signal. If the phone wasn't ringing, she wasn't about to answer.

Or maybe she couldn't.

He refused to give in to the cold crush of fear that filled his gut and instead concentrated on what he could do. The note said she'd gone to the expo. Bax tore off his running clothes and reached for jeans.

THE ESCALATOR moved inexorably upward. Casually, Joss stared at the advertising signs across the way, watching Tweed Jacket with her peripheral vision, her heart pounding. The instant she'd turned to see him, he'd shifted as well, looking downward, making himself innocuous. He was there, behind her, where he had no business being. She'd walked off the platform behind him, she'd made sure of it, and now he was behind her again.

He had to be one of Silverhielm's men.

Run. All of her instincts screamed for her to flee as adrenaline flooded her system. It was the wrong thing to do, though. Losing control would only make her a target.

Instead, she made herself stand casually, looking as oblivious as she could manage. The longer she could go with him thinking she hadn't made him, the more options she would have. His feet made a dull, metallic thud on the escalator steps as he moved closer to her. She had to find a way to ditch him so that he'd stay ditched. The last thing she wanted to do was lead him to Ray.

She emerged onto the platform of the Green Line and found herself amid a crowd of people. Relief surged through her. People were protection, even if they were jostling and pushing to get to the train just coming to a stop in the station. The crowd could offer her camouflage, a chance to get away.

If she hurried.

Joss began to rush, pushing aggressively through the crowd, making him work to follow her. Making him abandon caution. If he were worried about losing her, he'd take chances, he'd make a mistake. She passed the end of the train, just steps from the escalator that would take her up to the level of the train station.

And spun to run back down the platform, dashing through the closing doors of the last subway car.

Tweed Jacket lunged after her, but it was too late. All he could do was stand on the platform and watch the train slide away.

IT WASN'T a big deal, Joss told herself as she walked into
the lobby of the convention center, trying to ignore the re-
sidual shakiness in her legs. She'd lost him and she was
safe, and that was all that mattered.

The expo hadn't quite opened yet so she pulled out her
cell phone. It was nearly ten o'clock. Time to find Ray.
She punched up his number and waited for him to answer.
"Ray? Hey, it's Joss. I'm out in the lobby." The missed call
tone of her phone beeped in her ear but she ignored it.

"Great." His voice crackled out of the phone. "Get a
seat at one of those round tables over by the windows and
I'll be right out."

"All right."

"Hey, are you okay? You don't sound so good."

"I'm fine." She was, now. It had taken her several stops
after she'd left Central Station on the green line before
she'd recovered enough to look at her transit system map
and figure out where the heck she was going. Making
sense of the tangle of colored lines with her rattled brain
took another couple of stops, leaving her barely enough
time to work out the sequence of transfers that would get
her to the commuter rail without going through Central
Station, where Tweed Jacket would doubtlessly be waiting for her.

Now, though, anger was replacing anxiety. Now, the
need for action drove her. She didn't feel shaky, she felt
energized and mad as hell. Edgy and tense, Joss found a
table and then paced restlessly beside it, staring out at the
greenery outside.

The missed call was from Bax, but she didn't get a response when she rang. Frowning, she switched it to mute
and shoved it into her jacket pocket.

"Glad you could make it."

She turned to see Ray behind her, standing next to a portly man in an expensive suit.

"Good to see you, Ray," she said, shaking hands with him.

"I've got a person here who might be able to help you with your problem."

Person. Not friend, not colleague. An odd way to put it. "All right." Joss put her hand out. "I'm—"

Ray shook his head. "No names," he said brusquely. "You guys talk and see if it gets you anywhere. I'm going into the exhibition."

The portly man took a seat at the table and looked at her calmly. His name badge was flipped backward so she could only see the name of the convention center and nothing else.

Joss sat down in a chair to face him. "So, are you exhibiting here?"

The man shrugged. "I am just walking the show, meeting with clients," he said with an accent that sounded vaguely Germanic.

"What do you do?"

"I specialize in reproductions of famous stamps."

"Forgeries?"

His eyes chilled. "No. Legitimate reproductions. I do not attempt to pass them off as true rarities. They are marked clearly on the back."

"Do you sell a lot of them?"

"There is a market for reproductions. They are for those who want the thrill of owning a stamp beyond their means."

"And what if I wanted a reproduction of a famous stamp that wasn't marked on the back?"

He drew himself up. "I could not, of course, help you. I am a legitimate businessman. I do not contribute to fraud."

"Of course, if the buyer buys one of your reproductions and pastes it onto an envelope, the mark wouldn't show," Joss said thoughtfully. "He could pass it off as authentic, if he wanted to."

He shrugged. "The world is a perilous place for the gullible. My job is to manufacture and broker properly marked reproductions. What happens to them after the sale is beyond my control."

All very neat and convenient, she thought. Ray's treatment of him suddenly made sense. "What if I wanted a version of a famous stamp that I could pass off as the real thing?"

"I am sorry? I do not understand."

"What if I wanted a pair of extremely good reproductions?" Joss kept her voice low, mindful of the exhibit attendees who were starting to circulate around the convention center lobby. "Something good enough to fool a knowledgeable amateur. They wouldn't have to pass an expert, but they'd have to be very, very good. Front and back."

"And what are the stamps of interest?"

"The Post Office Mauritius pair."

He nodded, digesting this. "It would be difficult," he said finally. "I myself cannot do such things. As I said, I am a legitimate businessman. I have heard of a man in Amsterdam who perhaps accepts these sorts of commissions, however."

"How do I reach him?"

The German gave her an oily smile. "I could, perhaps, make inquiries. How soon do you need these…reproductions?"

"Two days, perhaps three."

"Just a moment, madame." He rose and crossed the room, pulling out his cell phone to make a call. Minutes went by as Joss watched him.

If he could be trusted, and she wasn't at all sure he could be, he could help her get the forgeries. There was still the matter of cost, of course, not to mention timing. Late would be as bad as not at all. She wished passionately that Bax was there with her. He would know how to handle the German. Since he wasn't, though, she'd have to do her best.

The German walked back to the table and settled in his chair. "It is possible I have a way to contract this man in Amsterdam. Of course, such work as you require would take some investment. All the more so for such a rapid turnaround."

Which included his commission, no doubt. "Can I talk with him directly?"

"Of course, but he is a very cautious man. The nature of his business, you understand." He made a dismissive gesture with his hand. "You must travel to him, meet him at the spot of his choosing. And it must be you alone. Do not attempt to bring another with you."

"Impossible. I've got a partner."

"You must leave the partner behind. Or take the partner with you, but give up your hope for the stamps."

"It's a simple business deal."

"Madame, what you ask is not simple at all."

She could already imagine what Bax would say, but she didn't see that there was a choice. "All right, if that's the way he wants it."

"He insists, I'm afraid."

She tilted her head a bit and looked at him. "And what do you get out of all of this?"

"Merely the satisfaction of bringing two interested parties together."

"Merely?"

"Why, yes. Of course, it is a risk for me to give you this

name. It is a risk for me to be associated with this business at all. I am a—"

"Legitimate businessman," she finished for him.

"Indeed. However, if you wanted to make the arrangements proceed more smoothly, you might offer a token of your appreciation. After all, I still need to give you the name and location of the Amsterdam contact, and there are meetings to arrange…"

A shakedown, in other words. Joss's eyes narrowed. "What do you want?"

"I will leave that to you, but if your need is great, a thousand kroner would be a small price to pay. For my trouble, you see, and for international telephone calls."

"A legitimate businessman?" she asked sardonically.

"It is a risky thing I do for you."

"And I'm sure you've never sullied yourself with this sort of business in the past."

"Certainly not, madame."

Joss dug in her pocket. "I wasn't prepared for a shakedown. Would you take," she fumbled in her pocket, "five hundred?"

"I am not, despite what you think, a greedy man." The bills disappeared smoothly into his pocket. "And in exchange, the information. Go to Amsterdam on Wednesday morning."

"He can't come here?"

"He is a man with very special skills and connections. Such men are very rare. If you wish to do business with them, you must go to where they are."

"Amsterdam."

"The choice is yours, madame." He gave a shrug. "Perhaps your need is not so great."

She thought of Silverhielm and of the real Blue Mauritius, currently at risk. "What do I do?"

"It is very simple. When you reach the city, call this number." He handed her a small slip of paper. "When someone answers, ask to speak with Mr. Kant. They will instruct you where to go."

"How much money does he want?"

"I cannot say for sure. Perhaps two hundred times what you paid me."

More than twelve thousand dollars, she thought in shock. "For a forgery?"

"Madame, please." He looked around quickly to see if anyone was watching. "It is no small thing you seek. There is great risk involved."

Translation, they knew she needed it and they could gouge her. "How can he expect that much?"

"He expects nothing. You are the one who seeks something. If I were you, I would go prepared."

Joss nodded, thinking quickly. They'd have to fund this from Operation Recovery, as Gwen had called her poker tournament winnings. They had the money and Gwen, of all people, would appreciate anything that reduced risk to the Blue Mauritius. Still, it was hard to think of paying so much for something that had no intrinsic value.

Then again, if it let them get the one-penny Mauritius back, it would be worth it.

"All right. Are you going to let him know I'm coming?"

"He expects you."

"Can I count on your confidence?"

He shrugged. "Of course. After all, I do not know your name. Also, I do not wish to have my name associated with such questionable activities."

Although moral qualms certainly hadn't stopped him from pocketing the money earlier. She had no doubt he'd collect more. "Thank you for your help."

"I am happy to be of assistance, madame. I wish you a safe journey."

Show up safely with your money, more like.

He rose. "Good morning."

"Good morning." She stood to watch him go.

And looked up to see Bax staring at her from the entrance, face taut with some emotion she couldn't name.

15

ANGER. HE WAS SURE it was anger whipping through him as she walked out of the glass doors to meet him and he moved to hold her, just hold her. He pressed his face against the soft tumble of her hair, breathing in her scent, absorbing the reality of her against him, healthy and whole. Until that moment, he hadn't known just how certain he'd been that something had happened to her.

And just how much that would have hurt.

It hit him like the brutal, unforgiving shock of falling into a pool of very cold water. That wasn't the way it was supposed to go. She was a client, nothing more. He was too smart to get emotionally caught up in her and lose his focus.

So he loosened his hold on her and stepped away. "What were you thinking, going off like that?"

Joss blinked at him. "Ray called and wanted to see me. You were gone. I left you a note."

"I saw it. That doesn't answer my question. What was so important that you couldn't wait?" he demanded.

She walked past him into the semicircular entrance area with its cul-de-sac and line of taxis. "This isn't the place to talk," she hissed.

He stalked after her, staying several paces away to remove himself from the temptation of touching her again. To forget the metallic taste of fear that had filled his throat when he'd reached the empty T-bana station. "You took a damn fool risk," he ground out once they were on the shaded pathway that led to the commuter rail station up the hill.

"I took a calculated risk," she countered. "I wasn't meeting Markus again. I was meeting someone we knew and it had to happen now. And I tried to reach you. You didn't take your phone, you didn't say when you'd be back. Am I supposed to read your mind?" She stalked away from him and turned back in frustration. "Why don't you just admit that you're no better at this working to-gether thing than I am?"

And that quickly his anger ebbed away.

"Look." Joss took a deep breath. "I'm sorry I scared you. I knew you wouldn't like it but I thought you would understand."

"You had a tail. I saw him as you were walking down the street."

"You saw? How? Where were you?"

"Markus stopped me after my run. I was walking back from the *torg* when I saw you. I couldn't catch you before you walked into the station." And he remembered watch-ing helplessly as she disappeared into the station with the tail behind her.

"I thought I heard something as I was getting on the train but I wasn't sure. That was you? It made me turn, and then I saw the same guy who'd been in the hotel lobby."

Bax raked a hand through his hair. "It scared the hell out of me, getting to the station and finding it empty," he said unwillingly. "I didn't know what had happened to you."

"It kind of threw me for a loop, too," she confessed. "But I figured out a way to ditch him. Left him standing on a platform in Central Station," she said in a proud tone.

"No kidding?" Despite himself, he was impressed. "So you made it here without being followed?"

"I'm pretty sure. I saw that I missed your call while I was on the T-bana but I couldn't get an answer."

"It's okay," he told her, realizing that for the moment, anyway, it was. "So what did Ray have to say?"

Joss moved away to sit on a nearby bench. "Actually, he mostly wanted to introduce me to a friend. Or not a friend, but someone he knows. I don't think he thinks very highly of him, quite frankly."

"The one who was walking away when I came in?"

"Yes. He makes reproductions of famous stamps."

"Forgeries?"

"Reproductions marked on the back. Legal forgeries, I suppose, but they're not good enough for what we want. He knows someone, though."

"What's it going to cost us?"

"A lot," she said, and told him. "It's not so much that we can't afford it. I'll call Gwen and have her wire it."

"When's the handoff?"

Joss hesitated and his radar went up. "A couple of days. It's not exactly a handoff. We've got to go pick them up."

"Where?"

"Amsterdam."

He considered it. "You're looking at a one hour flight. It's not the end of the earth. We can do it the same day."

Joss looked down at the ground. "It's not that simple," she told him.

He had a bad feeling he wasn't going to like it, not a bit. "What's the catch?"

"I'm the one who's got to go get them."

"ABSOLUTELY NOT," Bax thundered.

Joss stared at him. A moment before, he'd seemed like

he was releasing the whole control thing. Now, he was back to telling her what she could and couldn't do. "I've got to go. We've don't have a choice."

"You're talking about walking into God knows where with a fistful of cash. You don't know these people, you've got nothing to trust but the word of a man Ray Halliday doesn't like very much. What if they try to rob you? What if it's all a scam? You don't have the experience and training to deal with it."

"I dealt with being tailed, didn't I?" she retorted. "And you taught me self-defense."

"I taught you a few emergency moves. Don't make the mistake of thinking you can deal with a professional. I don't want to see you get hurt," he said abruptly.

That was it, she realized. He was scared for her. It was just coming out as anger.

"Then tell me what to do. Get me as prepared as possible. If you stay here, or if you go out, even, Silverhielm's men will be busy watching you. It'll be easier for me to slip out alone than if we were together. You've got to let me do this," she pleaded. "If I don't, it'll screw everything up."

It took fighting every instinct he had for him to say yes, she could see that. The fact that he nodded, finally, meant that he put an enormous amount of trust in her.

Now all she had to do was pull it off.

PELIKAN WAS warm and dark, a hall lit with overhead clusters of luminous globes. It wasn't a restaurant so much as a beer hall, with heavy, square pillars that held up the twenty-foot ceiling. The walls above the walnut wainscoting were dark gold, some of them painted with jungle scenes, some merely darkened with a patina of age. Parquet tile covered the floor, making the room ring with a hubbub of sound.

Bax scanned the crowd, looking across the ranks of tables. "He's not here."

"What about the bar?"

On the other side of the wall lay Kristallen, the bar part of Pelikan. The two shared an entrance, but little else. Crowded Kristallen focused on electronic DJ music for the hip crowd. Cigarette smoke spiraled upward toward the ceiling. A shout of laughter erupted at the far corner and Bax looked over to see Oskar.

The young boat mate scrubbed at his hair as he leaned over to whisper to a pretty blond girl next to him. She turned in mock anger and punched him in the shoulder. He laughed again, and murmuring to her, he leaned in to steal a kiss. A flush stole over her cheeks.

Bax could tell the minute Oskar saw him, his gaze sharpening as he set down his beer mug. He said something to his friends and rose to walk down the bar toward them. The blond girl followed him with her eyes.

"*Hej.* So you have come to enjoy Pelikan. Welcome. Come have a drink with us."

Bax shook his head. "We were hoping to talk. Can we buy you a beer?"

"Of course." Oskar glanced down the crowded bar. "Let's go next door and get a table. It will be easier to hear."

They were able to get a table, that much was true. If anything, though, it was harder to hear in the echoing hall of the main room. Then again, Joss thought as the waitress led them to a table in the corner of the restaurant, that wasn't necessarily a bad thing. A blanket of sound made it difficult for anyone else to hear what they had to say.

It was a cozy spot. Bax immediately pulled a chair around so that they could sit, heads together. Expertly, he flipped a five hundred kroner bill onto the table in Oskar's direction. "We need to talk and we need to know it won't go further. Are we agreed?"

Oskar moved his hand away from the bill without touching it. "It is a question of what the talk is about. I don't break the law."

"This is not about breaking the law."

He relaxed fractionally. "What is it about?"

"Will it remain between us?"

Oskar gave Bax a long, searching look. Bax looked back at him impassively, seeking neither to convince or to intimidate. Finally, Oskar gave a slow nod. "It will."

"Good. We need a boat."

Oskar laughed. "All this secrecy over a boat?"

"There's more but we can start with that."

The waitress appeared and they ordered beer.

"We need a speedboat," Bax resumed, "one that can do sixty or seventy kilometers per hour."

"Such speed can be dangerous. Do you know anything about piloting such a boat?"

"I've got experience and I know how to navigate. I don't know the archipelago, though, so I'll need charts."

"Where are you going?"

"A private island."

"Ah, yes, I remember. Beyond Bullerö. Which one?"

"It's called Silverholmen."

For a moment, Oskar was perfectly still, then he leaned back and studied Bax. "So you want to go to Silverholmen. Are you invited?"

"We are, though I want to go out there a day or two before our invitation to check out the area."

"Karl Silverhielm is a formidable man."

"How do you know that it is Silverhielm's island?"

"I have heard stories. And are you a friend of his?"

"Would I be renting a boat to spy on a friend?" Bax asked softly.

"No."

The waitress appeared with their drinks. For a moment, they were occupied with the ceremony of beer mats and distributing mugs, but finally she was gone. Oskar gave Bax a frank look. "Are you sure you understand who you are dealing with?"

"I think so."

"He kills those who interfere with him."

Bax took a drink of his ale. "I'll take that chance."

"Are you willing to risk Josie, too?"

"I'm not his to risk," Joss spoke up. "It's my choice and I'm ready to do it."

"You don't understand what he's like. He is dangerous."

"You seem to know him awfully well," Joss observed, looking at the tense lines of Oskar's body.

Oskar stared at them. "You say I am not to talk of this conversation. What of you? What is your interest in Silverhielm?"

"He has something of ours, something we want to get back."

"And you're willing to cross him for it?"

"I'm eager to cross him," Joss said. "I want to get it back and I want it to hurt him."

Oskar shook his head. "You are both crazy, you know?" He circled his finger by his temple. "My advice to you is go home. Do not do this."

"That's not an option," Joss returned.

Oskar stared at them both moodily. "Let me tell you a story and see if you are still of this mind. I worked for Silverhielm, or rather I worked for a delivery company that brought goods to him. For a while."

"How was that?"

There was no humor in Oskar's smile. "It worked out as you would expect. Silverhielm was the barracuda and we were the herring. In the beginning, we delivered once a week, groceries, mostly. Some fuel for his generators. Then he offered to invest in the business, to help it grow, he said. A service for the archipelago. My boss was so eager, falling down to say yes." Oskar shook his head, an expression of pity mingled with contempt on his face. "You don't give a man like Silverhielm anything. My boss did not understand that. Not so smart, you understand? Or maybe too greedy."

Bax knew what happened to small, greedy players when they got involved with the Silverhielms of the world. "When was this?"

"About three years ago. At first, everything was just as Silverhielm said. My boss bought more boats, advertised to hire more pilots." He looked from Joss to Bax. "But you can guess, I am sure, what happened. Silverhielm sent over some people. Hire them, he said, and hire my dispatcher. Soon, we were making many more deliveries…and pick-ups."

"Smuggling." Joss said aloud. "They were smuggling."

"Congratulations. You are very fast. My boss did not believe for six months, until he saw one of the pilots hand off a package. He complained to Silverhielm, told him to stop or he would go to the police. They found him a week later in Lake Mälaren."

"Silverhielm?" Bax asked.

Oskar shrugged. "No proof. No proof of the smuggling, no proof of the murder. People saw him that night with a stranger in a bar. The bartender said he had only one drink but the police said that tests of the body showed he was very drunk. Maybe he stumbled into the water, police said." Oskar took a swallow of his beer. "Maybe not. Silverhielm bought the rest of the business."

"Didn't you tell them what you knew?"

"I had left the company by then. My statements were not enough to help, they said."

"Why did you leave?" Joss asked.

He gave them an opaque glance. "In the beginning, I made the deliveries to Silverholmen."

It was the foot in the door Bax had been hoping for. "Did you get into the house?"

"Not at first. His people came to the dock and took everything." Oskar moved his mug in small circles on the table, making little patterns on the scarred wood. "After a couple of months, though, they gave me a handcart and had me take the boxes up to the house."

"How much did you see?" This was what they needed, a layout of the house and the island. They needed to know what they were walking into.

"Mostly the kitchen, but sometimes I had to bring office supplies."

"Silverhielm has a home office?"

"With a desk the size of Gamla Stan. There is a fax, computer, copier, everything."

"A safe?" Joss asked.

"Probably, but I never saw it."

"Did you ever see him?"

"Oh yes. On the day I quit."

It was there in his voice. This wasn't the story he'd set out to tell them, but it had become the story they needed urgently to hear. "Why did you quit?" Bax asked.

For a moment, he was silent. A noisy group of students at the table behind them clanked glasses and shouted in a boisterous toast.

Oskar shifted. "I usually made my runs at the end of

the day, when the office was empty. One day I arrived earlier than usual. I put the groceries in the kitchen and started to deliver a box of printer paper to the office. There is a back passage there from the kitchen. I was by the door to the office when I heard loud voices. There is a peephole in the door and I looked."

He stared down into his beer, swirling the glass around. "Silverhielm was in the room along with some of his men. One very tall and blond. His eyes are flat, you understand? They were holding a man in a chair with his leg propped on another chair. And then Silverhielm said to the blond man 'Show him, Markus, why he should not have held back from me.' And Markus used a club to break his knee into small pieces."

Joss drew a breath in through her nose. Bax didn't move.

"That was the day I quit." Abruptly, Oskar looked up at them. "These are the men you are dealing with, do you understand? They are not to be trifled with."

"Neither am I," Bax said quietly, holding Oskar's gaze.

A second passed, then two. "I believe you," Oskar said finally. "So you are determined, it seems. How can I help you?"

"We need to know the layout of the house."

"Very well. Hand me a napkin." With a pen, Oskar began to sketch on the soft paper. "I can mark the charts to show you the way across the archipelago. You will require perhaps forty-five minutes to get there."

"And you can help me rent a boat?"

"I will supply you with my own. She is very fast." He pointed to the sketch with his pen. "The coastline of the island is curved, with a little inlet here. That is where the dock is, to one side of the house. A line of rocks stops the waves. What is the word?"

"A breakwater?"

"Yes. There are other rocks, maybe thirty meters out. Watch for the buoys. They mark the channel."

Bax nodded.

"The island is rock that rises steeply. From the dock, you must climb stairs to reach the level of the house."

"Can you see the house from the dock?"

"Only the roof. At the top of the stairs, a stone path leads to the house. It passes the main entrance here," he drew an *X* on the side nearest the dock, "and continues to a yard on the side away from the sea. The generator shed stands behind the main house. A door, here, goes to the kitchen."

"How far?"

"From the dock? A hundred and fifty meters, maybe more. Behind the house is grass down to where the rocks fall away to sea, you understand? And that side of the house, all windows."

"How about the inside?"

"I know only the kitchen and the office." He sketched them in. "The office faces the ocean. All windows on one side."

Bax nodded. "We'll need the boat on Friday during the day and Saturday evening, both. And can you mark charts for me to get out to the island?"

"Yes. Be careful. Silverhielm has a racing boat he uses to travel to the island. Do not think you can outrun him." Oskar tapped his fingers restlessly on the table. "I cannot take you out on Friday. I have work, you understand. In the daylight, you should be okay. The archipelago looks very different at night, though. I can pilot you Saturday, if you choose."

"Would you go back there?" Joss asked him.

"If it might ensure your safety, yes. They have no reason to be suspicious of me."

"Think about it. If you have not changed your mind Saturday, we would appreciate it," said Bax.

Oskar looked at them soberly. "Be careful. I do not want to see you dead, my friends."

16

JOSS THRUST a handful of kroner to the cab driver and got out, checking her watch as she walked into the SAS terminal. Her flight was in less than an hour, which was pushing it as far as the timing went. Then again, she was flying without luggage within the European Union and they'd bought her ticket online the night before. All she had to do was get a boarding pass and go to the gate.

Whoever was following her—and she assumed someone was—wouldn't know what flight she was on, couldn't tell without following her to the gate. To pass security, they'd need a ticket of their own. The line for purchasing new tickets was satisfyingly long, Joss noted as she walked to the check-in kiosk. Even if they were smart and bought the ticket by phone, she'd still be through the security gates before they could turn it all around.

All in all, a job well done, she congratulated herself as the kiosk printed out her boarding pass. She might be an amateur, but she was learning to ditch tails with the best of them. Now all she had to do was track down her forger.

"HELLO?"

Joss stood in the Amsterdam airport, watching a trio of KLM stewardesses walk briskly by with their wheeled bags. "Is Mr. Kant there?"

There was a short silence. "Where are you?" A man spoke in heavily accented English.

"The airport."

"Good. Make your way to a tavern named Polder. Be there at one. Sit at the bar. Someone will contact you."

She tried to guess his age, but it was impossible to tell from the clipped sentences. He was not old, not young. Just a man.

"Who should I look for?" she asked. "Is there a name?"

"Do not worry. We know you already."

"But I—"

He disconnected with a click.

The whole venture might have been risky but rather than being nervous, she was actually fairly calm. Better than calm. They were finally doing something besides watching and waiting. It was exhilarating, finally taking action. So what if it was risky walking into a meeting with total strangers, wearing a money belt stuffed with a small fortune? She could take care of herself. She had the self-defense moves that Bax had taught her and a squared-off steel rod about the size of a felt tip pen that could be used for a variety of interesting purposes. More than that, she had painfully earned street smarts that had gotten her out of more than one pickle in the past.

She was going to make it work, Joss vowed. No matter what.

BAX RAN. He ran across Gamla Stan, through Stortorget square, past the Nobel museum without noticing. He crossed the bridge to Slussen on Södermalm and fought off the memory of standing at the Katarinahissen with Joss their first day in Stockholm. She was in Amsterdam, out of his reach, out of his ability to protect.

To have gone with her would only have brought attention to them both, attention they couldn't afford. He hadn't liked it a bit, but he'd had to let her go. Now she was there and there was nothing he could do but wait for her to return.

And so he ran.

He'd always thought best when moving. Something about working his body pitilessly let him focus more completely on the task at hand. And the task currently at hand was getting the one-penny Mauritius back from Silverhielm.

Today, though, running didn't help. It just sent his thoughts moving in circles. They had entrée to Silverhielm's home, they had bait in the form of the Blue Mauritius. They had his trust, to a certain measure, or Markus wouldn't be recruiting Bax. The problem was getting the one-penny Mauritius out of the safe and into their hands. It would take the forgeries, inspiration and a fair amount of luck.

Inspiration, would come eventually. Luck, Bax could make. The forgeries were the big question, which brought him back to Joss.

She was resourceful, he reminded himself. The impromptu self-defense lesson he'd given her had taught him that. She knew enough dirty tricks that she had at least a fighting chance if anything funny started coming down. She'd promised to have her cell phone at hand. There was little more she could do to be prepared, nothing more that he could do save be with her, and this time he couldn't. He had to trust that she could manage the situation and come safely away with the goods.

This was what came of working with a partner, you were forced to trust them. The familiar thought came to him but oddly, he didn't feel much conviction in the sentiment. If he thought about it, what bothered him wasn't so much that he was trusting Joss to get the forgeries instead of doing it himself, or that he was working with a partner. What bothered him was that he didn't know if she was okay.

Which was natural, he told himself as he moved onto the ring road that encircled most of Södermalm. She was his client and, for now, his lover. Deeper involvement than that was out of the question, though. He wasn't built for anything serious, he'd learned that the hard way. Of course, he was concerned about Joss, and he'd be concerned until he'd closed the case and gotten paid.

But when that was done, so were they.

THE BAR wasn't pretty. It was neither quaint tourist bait nor worn and comfortable the way Pelikan had been. What it was was a dive, pure and simple. Cigarette smoke clouded the air. The floor felt sticky under her feet. The clientele consisted mostly of older lushes or hardened men with flat gazes, hunched at the bar or the handful of tables scattered at the front. When Joss walked in, they all turned to look.

Being stared at had never bothered her in the past. She'd always enjoyed being the center of attention. There was nothing that would be fun about being the center of attention for this group, though, unless fighting off the groping hands of men who smelled of cheap whiskey and stale cigarette smoke was someone's idea of a good time. It certainly wasn't hers. Scanning the room, she wondered which one was the forger, and tried to imagine handing over the money to any of them.

With a silent prayer that her real contact was yet to arrive, she slid onto a stool a few seats over from a guy the size of a small mountain who looked like he'd recently done time in a maximum security facility.

Anticipation—and nerves—fizzed through her. I can do it, she'd told Bax. Now she had to make good on that promise. She had to make the meeting come off, she had to come home with the forgeries in hand. She had to make it work.

The ex-con stared her way. He wore a dingy plaid shirt with the sleeves ripped off to show his thick biceps and blue tangle of jailhouse tattoos. More muscle than fat, but plenty of both. Joss gave him a dismissive glance. She didn't have time for him unless he was her contact, and in that case she was going to fly right back to Stockholm and tell Bax to come up with a Plan B, thank you very much.

"Can I get you something?" The bartender stopped in front of her. She had dyed raven hair, pale skin and lipstick so dark it looked almost black in the dim lighting.

Although Joss wanted a quick shot of tequila, it probably wasn't a good idea. "Just water for now, please. I'm waiting for someone." She scanned the bar again, studying the faces of the patrons, gauging whether their interest was purely male or held something more.

"Hey you, American?" asked the ex-con in a thick accent.

Joss looked away. There were times for a polite brush-off, but this was not one of them. The last thing she wanted was for some half-crocked criminal to be coming on to her when her contact came in.

Not that her forger wasn't a criminal, but she hoped he was a little more civilized than this.

"Hey, American," said the ex-con, shifting closer. "A drink?"

"No thanks," Joss muttered.

He pulled at his shirt to point to a set of Harley Davidson wings on his meaty chest. "Look, American."

Joss put her hands on the bar and opened her mouth to

reply when the bartender said something to him in Dutch that had him spitting out a curse and turning away.

"What did you say?" Joss asked.

"I told him you could date a convict in America if you wanted one."

Joss looked at her. "Thanks. I think."

"Don't mention it."

Joss checked her watch and drummed her fingers on the bar. The voice on the phone hadn't said when her contact would appear, only for her to wait. She glanced at her watch again.

"You said you're here to meet someone?"

Joss glanced up to see the bartender again and gave a shrug. "Yes, but I don't know what he looks like."

"He did not tell you it would be a man," she returned.

Joss blinked. "Excuse me?"

"Mr. Kant. The voice on the phone. He said only for you to come here and you would be contacted. I am the contact."

Joss stared. "I was expecting a guy," she said finally.

"Clearly. But as you can see, your options here are limited. Now, do you want to meet our friend or don't you?"

"Of course I do." There was a rushing sound in her ears.

Goth Girl smiled thinly. "Good. Go outside. There is a building on the opposite corner, a dark red. Buzz 2C and you will be let in. It is the third door on the second floor."

Joss rose to walk out when a hand clamped on her wrist. "Hey, American," snarled the ex-con. "Too fancy?"

The bartender spoke sharply to him in Dutch. He ignored her and tugged Joss toward him. He smelled sour and sweaty.

"Let go," Joss snapped, adrenaline flooding her system. Across the bar, men were looking up. No one was coming to her immediate rescue, though, she saw. No one wanted to tangle with this mountain of a man. She'd have to fend for herself. Taking a breath of mixed fear and fury, Joss flattened out her hand and chopped the ex-con across the Adam's apple, the way Bax had shown her. The edge of her stiffened hand bounced off the elastic feeling lump of his neck.

He gave a choked bellow and grabbed for his neck, releasing her.

"Hey," the bartender cried, but Joss ignored her. Instead, she bolted for the door, slamming out into the afternoon sun.

17

THERE HAD BEEN no reason to go through the whole bar routine, Joss thought as she stomped angrily across the street to the ruddy stucco building. They knew who she was, she'd been vouched for. It was a waste of time, and an irritating one at that.

She was in a working-class neighborhood of stark, utilitarian buildings that looked like they'd seen better days. The area held none of the charm and warmth of central Amsterdam. In the doorway of the red building, the directory showed no name next to unit 2C. Joss pushed the bell.

The door buzzed immediately and she pushed it open, her pulse speeding up just a bit. The entryway smelled musty in the warmth of the summer day. She climbed the stairs slowly, listening carefully, the self-defense rod out and in her hand. When she reached the right door, she knocked.

She'd expected someone different, was her first thought as the door opened inward. Someone who looked menacing. Someone who looked more criminal. Certainly she hadn't expected someone who looked like he could have been an eighth grade math teacher. She released the rod and brought her empty hand out of her pocket with an inner smile.

Slight and spare, he peered at her nearsightedly through thick glasses. He wore an ink-smudged blue canvas printers' apron over a white shirt. He didn't look like someone she'd need self-defense moves to overcome.

"I'm looking for Mr. Kant," she said.

"Ah yes. Come in, come in." He stepped back from the door.

It was clearly a working studio. There was a drafting board, shelves laden with inks and tools. On a solid wooden table sat a compact, old-fashioned printing press, and next to it a machine that looked very much like the perforator that she'd seen at the postal museum in Stockholm.

He smiled faintly at her inspection. "Sometimes the old tools are the best."

Joss turned to look at him. "Old tools to make new things?"

"Indeed. So you have come from Stockholm," he said. "What is it that you seek?"

Of course. Force her to declare herself so that if she were in law enforcement it would be entrapment. He was just doing what any smart criminal would. "I need a reproduction Post Office Mauritius pair. A very, very good pair. They should be able to pass inspection by an experienced amateur. They don't need to convince an authenticator."

He nodded, his dark hair gleaming under the lights. "You realize, of course, that these are the most famous stamps in all the world?"

"Yes."

"Then you understand that producing the type of reproduction you seek is not a simple thing. There is the ink, the paper, the gum. And there is the matter of the plate."

"I thought the original plate for the Post Office Mauritius pair still existed."

He raised his eyebrows. "I see you have done your

homework. The owner is not, however, prepared to participate in making reproductions, even for a very handsome sum."

And he'd probably offered that sum, from the sound of it. "So what do you do without a plate?"

"I do not need the original. I have the technology to make my own." He opened a door and flipped on the light. The room behind it was as high-tech as the workshop was old. A large blue metal box sat on a steel table, next to a computer. Waffled tubes ran to a humming box in the corner. Power cords snaked to a wall outlet. "This is a laser etching system. I scan a photograph of the stamp and the laser produces a new plate in copper. Very high quality. Very precise."

And undoubtedly expensive, Joss thought. "Impressive. So you can do the job, it sounds like."

"Oh, yes."

"How much do you want for it?"

He pressed his lips together as though he were considering a geometry problem. "It is risky, you understand."

"Your price?" she asked with an inward sigh.

"Fourteen thousand euros."

Fourteen thousand, she thought in shock. It was well over what the contact had told her, well over what she could afford. And well over what she had on her. "No way. That's too high."

"The Post Office Mauritius set is very valuable," he countered. "Of course such a fine reproduction should be of commensurate value. I seek merely a percentage of their price at auction."

"Your figure is higher than your broker suggested."

"My broker is not always privy to my production costs. Developing the correct ink colors for the Post Office Mauritius set, for example, has required visits to the Stockholm

Postmuseet. The papers are very specialized, and must be hand-treated to age them. Even the gums are specialized, and of course all of my printing equipment is rare and costly."

"But surely you have some of these materials in house."

"I have all of them, madame. I must recover the cost it required to amass them, though." He looked at her placidly.

The neighborhood was not particularly nice, nor was the building, Joss thought. He might make money on his various ventures, but he wasn't exactly prospering. It was worth taking a chance. "I'll pay you seven thousand," she told him.

"Ridiculous," he blustered. "This is precision work. My price is a fraction of the cost of the real stamp."

"I'm not getting the profit of the real stamp."

"You will be getting something. Thirteen thousand, then."

"Eight," she countered.

"It is impossible to do it for that price," he snapped.

"Then I'll go elsewhere." Joss turned to the door.

"There is no one else who does what I do." He raised his voice. "You are not just buying the stamps, you are buying my skill and experience."

"I'll take my chances." She laid her hand on the knob.

"All right. Twelve."

Joss stayed in place. "Nine." She held her breath.

"Eleven," he demanded. "Not one euro less."

She turned back to him, her face wiped clean of any expression of triumph. "Fine. How soon can you have them ready for me?"

"How soon do you need them?"

"Tomorrow? Thursday at the latest."

"That's impossible," he exploded. "Even Thursday is just two days from now."

"I have to have the stamps."

"This is an art," he protested. "It requires not just skill but time to produce a convincing reproduction."

"And you are a skilled and experienced man. If I don't have the forgeries by the day I need them, I may as well not have them at all, in which case I will not need your very expensive services."

He shook his head.

Joss studied him. "I would, of course, be prepared to add an expediting charge to your fee. Say, a thousand euros?"

He gave a grudging nod. "It is possible, I suppose."

"I thought it might be."

"I will need a deposit before I begin work. Three thousand now, the rest when you pick up the stamps."

"Of course," she said smoothly. "Tomorrow at the end of the day, then?"

"Tomorrow," he agreed.

JOSS HELD her cell phone to her ear and waited for the line to pick up as she walked down the avenue, headed back toward the city center.

Bax answered. "Hello?"

"It's me," she said.

Neither one of them considered the fact that Bax didn't have to think twice to recognize her voice.

"How'd it go?"

"Smooth as silk."

"No problems?"

"None," she said, conveniently leaving out the gorilla in the bar. "He came in high but I managed to bargain him down."

Bax laughed. "A smart shopper. So when are you going to get them?"

"Tomorrow at the end of the day, he says." She stopped on the corner and waited for the light.

"That will be cutting it close."

"He has to make a whole new plate. He was talking a week, I got it to two days."

"Not bad, Chastain," he said.

Pleasure warmed her. "I try."

"So it's what, two-thirty? What are you going to do in Amsterdam all by yourself for a day and a half?"

"I don't know. Wander, I suppose. It seems like a great city," she said, looking around. She'd come back into the city center, where the full charm of Amsterdam emerged. "I wish I had someone to play with."

"Do you want me to come over?"

It sounded perfectly splendid, but she was learning to be responsible these days. "We probably shouldn't spend the money."

"True. On the other hand, there's nothing to stop me paying my own way. I've done everything here I can at this point. I'm only going to be sitting around and Amsterdam is one of my favorite cities. I could be there in two or three hours."

"You mean it?" she began. "That would be a gas. We'd have to get a hotel, of course."

"Sure." There was tapping in the background.

"What are you doing?"

"I'm going online to get a ticket and a hotel. How would you like to stay on the Gentlemen's Canal?"

"I don't know, would you have to be a gentlemen when we're there?"

"I suspect there's some waffle room." He clicked keys some more. "Okay, we've got a room in the Huygens House, on the Herengracht." He spelled it for her.

"I was thinking somewhere cheap out by the airport. We're spending twelve thousand on the forgeries."

"This one's on me," he told her.

"Bax, you can't blow your money right and left like that."

"I'm not blowing it. Consider it a barter agreement. My flight gets in at 7:00 p.m., so I can probably be there by eight. I expect to find you in bed, naked, when I get there."

One corner of her mouth tugged up into a smile. "If you play your cards right." She sobered. "Of course, we do have one problem. What if you get followed?"

Bax's only response was a snort.

"Okay, forget that question."

"Good. I'll call you from the airport."

"I'll drag you to do tourist things," she warned him.

"I live for the Anne Frank House," he told her.

She disconnected with a foolish smile on her face. He was flying in to see her. He could have stayed in Stockholm but he wasn't. He was coming over to be with her.

BAX SAT in the back of the cab, watching the gabled buildings of Amsterdam pass by as they headed to the hotel. And to Joss. He'd seen her only that morning, so why was it that it felt like it had been days?

The decision to head to Amsterdam had been sheer impulse, an impulse that made him a little nervous now. One minute, they'd been talking about the case. The next, he'd been on a plane headed south over the Baltic.

Not because staying in Stockholm would have left him at loose ends, necessarily, he thought as the car stopped. He was perfectly happy prowling the city on his own. It was just that being with Joss would give him a chance to keep an eye on her, to be around in case of trouble. And being in Amsterdam would be no hardship—it was his favorite city in all of Europe. He wasn't getting in over his head with her. He was too smart for that. This was just a little bonus.

He got out of the cab, slinging his satchel over his shoulder, a little rush of expectation running through him. He bounded up the steps to the front door of the little hotel. He knew where he was going. Nodding at the proprietor, he didn't stop but climbed the steps to the second floor, looking for the room Joss had described to him over his mobile phone as he'd walked through the airport.

And then he was at the door and she was flowing into his arms, all silky, fragrant and soft against him. She wasn't a creature of his imagination anymore. She was here, safe in his arms. And for a moment he didn't let himself think about anything, she was all he wanted.

Dropping his satchel, Bax kicked the door closed with one foot and lifted her in his arms. "I thought I told you to be naked," he growled against her neck, then kissed the sweet rises of her breasts.

"Forgive me, master," she said, flipping open the towel she'd wrapped around herself to shield herself from prying eyes.

He knew the way desire for her could tear at him. Day after day, over and over he still got the slow thud of arousal in his blood every time he looked at her, driving him to bury himself in the tight heat of her body. At this moment, though, he wanted only to hold her, to feel her warm and close against him. Clothes were an impediment, a barrier that he dispensed with impatiently.

And then he buried his face in her neck and held on for all he was worth.

The need, when it came, was slow, gentle. It wasn't about the wild rush they usually encountered but a tenderness he hadn't known he had a capacity for. It was a coming together more than just a coming, and when he slid inside her and he heard her soft sigh, it was as though all the disconnected parts of his world made sense.

And as they rocked together, it was the gathering connection that bound them gently.

JOSS SAT on the bed, her legs folded, turning a euro coin over idly in her hands. Lovemaking, a romantic walk down the canals to dinner and now, a quiet evening. She felt lazy and satisfied as a tabby cat with a dish of cream.

All was right in her world. They were getting the forgeries, they had a meet planned with Silverhielm just three days away. Things were coming to a head. Soon, if all went well, they'd be getting the stamp and everything would be back in place. She could return to San Francisco, her grandfather could come home without facing ruin.

And Bax would fly off to Copenhagen.

A shiver of cold whisked through her and she blinked. Having him here, now, next to her felt so right. The hours before he'd arrived, she'd drifted around the streets and canals of Amsterdam. She'd taken in the sights, but it had all felt empty. It wasn't the same without someone to enjoy it with. It wasn't the same without Bax, his wry humor, his seemingly endless store of knowledge.

It wasn't the same without the feel of his hand in hers.

Knowing he was on his way had made it easier. In a week or two, she wouldn't have that. In a week or two, they'd go from essentially living together to leading separate lives.

It wasn't a surprise. That had been the plan from the beginning. She'd known she'd have to do it.

She couldn't imagine it.

Joss swallowed, shaking her head blindly. And the sudden knowledge snaked through her. This couldn't be. Surely she was smarter than that. She couldn't have been this foolish, she, who'd always skimmed blithely through relationships without so much as a bobble. She who'd always held the upper hand. She couldn't have been foolish enough to fall in love.

At first, the plan had been simple: sleep with him to get his cooperation. Indulging in her attraction was just a side benefit, and the fact that they'd been incredible together in bed had been a rather wonderful present.

Now, though, everything had changed. She'd lost control of the situation. She'd let her feelings get involved. How could she have let herself fall for Bax? Bax, of all people? Bax, the loner. Bax, who made it clear he was only in it for the job.

And yet, he'd seemed to slide easily into the togetherness they'd been forced into recently. Granted, their affair had started out as physical, but for all the moments of flash and fire, there were many more of sheer closeness.

She needed to say something, she thought, glancing over at him where he sat reading a book on Amsterdam. She needed to talk to him, see if there was a chance of continuing their relationship after the case was over. It was a simple enough question. Plenty of people did it. People dated all the time. Okay, they'd be coming at it sort of backward, but what was wrong with that? It wasn't like there was a rule book or anything. Whatever worked was the right thing to do.

Nervously, she began toying with the coin, rolling it between her fingers. "So, we've got the forgery and we'll be getting the stamp back soon, right?"

Bax looked over and watched her manipulate the coin. "Sure. All we have to do is figure out how to make the switch."

"What are your plans after that? After we get back to the States?" Don't be a wuss, she told herself. Tell him. "Because I'd really—"

"Do that again," he interrupted.

Joss blinked. "What?" She looked down at her hands.

"That's right," he muttered to himself. "You know sleight of hand."

"Yeah, so?"

"We might just have found our way."

"What do you mean?"

"The switch. You get Silverhielm to give you the stamps to look at and then you switch them for the forgeries."

"It would be risky."

"Not really. Besides, you're a pro." Energized, he sat bolt upright, the book set aside, forgotten. 'We can do this," he promised.

And Joss nodded and watched the moment slip away.

18

THE WIND WHIPPED through Joss's hair as the speedboat skimmed over the waves. Out here, on the Stockholm archipelago, the world was sky and water, rock and tree, both pristine and beautiful. Occasionally, they passed another pleasure boat or an inhabited island. Mostly, once they'd gotten out of Stockholm's inner harbor, they'd had the archipelago to themselves.

Joss adjusted her sunglasses. For more than half an hour, Bax had had the little speedboat going all out, setting it to autopilot while he squinted at charts and checked the landmarks that Oskar had written down for him. Occasionally, he muttered to himself but she couldn't hear a word of it over the roar of the engine. Since there was nothing she could do, she just leaned back and enjoyed.

The day before their meet with Silverhielm and it was unseasonably hot for Stockholm. Joss had started out wearing her jacket, but by the time they'd reached the dock to pick up the boat, the jacket was off and tied around her waist, leaving her in just a tank top and jeans. Even that had been sticky and uncomfortable.

Now, the wind blew the heat away. She felt the hot press of the sun on her shoulders and cheekbones, but the passage of air made it pleasant instead of oppressive. In the distance, the white shape of a ferry forged its way toward the horizon. Nearby, a gull skimmed low over the water.

Bax reached out to the controls. Abruptly, the boat slowed until it was going just fast enough for him to keep it aimed at the swells.

"Are we there yet?" Her hearing was so numbed by the sound of the engine that her voice sounded strange to her own ears.

"Near enough that we should slow down and make sure we know where we are." He checked the compass and the GPS unit and pointed to the low-lying islands to either side of them. "That should be Kymmendö and that over there is Mörtö, which puts us right about here." He pointed to the map. "Silverholmen is about another five or six miles. Call it half an hour."

"Thirty minutes to go five miles? I thought Oskar said this boat topped out at seventy-five miles an hour."

"Kilometers," Bax corrected, "kilometers per hour. That's about fifty miles an hour flat out. It doesn't matter, though. I want to go slow enough that we can stop as soon as we're in sight. This is our chance to get a nice, quiet look without them knowing we're out here."

Already, the heat was settling over her as though she were standing in front of an oven. "So what do you want to do besides roast for the next half hour?"

He handed her a bottle of water and picked up his binoculars. "Stay cool."

"HERE ARE YOUR keys to the room and to the minibar. Please enjoy your stay with us." Nils Andersson stood behind the polished mahogany counter of the Royal Viking hotel and handed the room folio to the American woman with her tightly permed hair. He liked working at the Royal Viking. It always impressed the women he met, especially when he lied and told them he was a manager.

Anna, the sunny clerk at his side greeted the guest in

front of her with a brilliant smile. Nils wished he could impress the lovely golden Anna with her tilted nose and her midnight-blue eyes, but she knew he was only a junior clerk. Besides, she looked down on him for the rules he broke. Like everyone didn't break a rule once in a while.

He was aimlessly skimming down the list of registered guests on the computer when a tall blond man caught his eye.

The man jerked his chin in a beckoning gesture. Andersson froze. He leaned to Anna. "Can you cover for me for a moment?"

"Nils, you just had a break. Mr. Hogberg will not like it," she protested, but he was already disappearing into the offices behind the counter. There were people more important than Mr. Hogberg. A moment later, he came out the side door that led into the lobby.

"Good morning, Nils," said Markus Holm.

"Are you trying to get me fired?" he snarled, walking toward the door to the luggage room with Markus following. "You have no business here. Go."

"I have business with you," Markus countered. "Mr. Silverhielm did you a favor. I would think you would want to return it."

"A favor?" he whispered. "They break me, these payments you extract."

"You have not been injured, have you? Your knees work well? Your hands? Your eyes?"

Andersson swallowed. "Yes," he faltered.

"I thought so. Few in the position you were in can say as much." Markus stepped closer to him, eyes cold. "You should be grateful."

"I am grateful," Andersson said huskily. "What do you want?"

"Please."

"What?"

"Please tell me what you want."

Andersson cleared his throat. "Please tell me what you want."

Markus smiled benevolently. "Only a small favor."

"What?"

"You have a guest in the hotel, Josie Astin. I need to get into her room and I need to get into the safe."

"I can't do that," he said emphatically. "It is not allowed. I would be found out. I would be fired."

"It won't be found out." Markus's voice was soft.

"You cannot guarantee it."

"Ah, but I can guarantee that if you do not assist me, information will be laid in front of your employers that *will* get you fired. I can guarantee that your life will get very uncomfortable, indeed."

Andersson gave Markus a look brimming with equal parts fear and resentment. "What if the guests walk in on us?"

"The guests just set off from the Nybroviken in a motorboat, headed for the archipelago. They will not return to the hotel for some minutes, probably hours. I only need a small amount of time."

Andersson stared at him, balancing one fear with another. Markus waited serenely.

"All right," the clerk said finally, his eyes shifting back and forth. "I'll do it."

BAX PICKED UP his camera phone and pointed it toward Silverholmen to take a photograph. The boat idled in the swells.

"What are you doing?"

"I'm sending this to Oskar to see if we're in the right spot." A few minutes went by and the phone rang. He heard Oskar's voice in his ear.

"Hello, my friend. Are you enjoying yourself?"

"Just doing a little sightseeing. I was wondering if we've hit that fishing spot you were talking about."

"Yes, it looks like you are there. Watch out for the shoals to the north. They're marked on the chart but you come up on them more quickly than you would think."

"All right." Bax picked up his binoculars with one hand and studied the waters ahead.

"Remember, some of the fish are very alert, so you should be cautious to avoid alarming them."

"I'll try. I have not seen the barracuda who lives around here."

"Stay away from the island. I'm told he swims near there."

"Don't worry, I have a very strong line," Bax said.

Oskar laughed. "It sounds as though you are well prepared. Good fishing, my friend."

"Thanks. I hope to hook him."

CHECKING THE HALL in both directions, Nils used a passkey on the door to the room. "Inside," he hissed, "quickly."

The room showed the disorder impossible to avoid with two people living in close proximity. A woman's jacket and trousers were draped over one of the chairs; books were piled haphazardly on the desk.

Markus looked at Andersson. "And now, I need to get into the safe."

Andersson slipped the master key from his pocket and handed it to Markus. "You know I will be fired if this is discovered," he muttered resentfully.

"Worse things can happen." Markus snapped on latex gloves. "I can demonstrate, if you like." He opened the armoire that held the safe and adroitly used the master key. With a click the door opened.

Humming, Markus began to poke through the safe, pulling out a woman's purse, some kroner, a packet of documents. No envelopes, he noticed with disappointment but no surprise. It was impossible to imagine Johan being sloppy enough to leave the Blue Mauritius in a hotel safe. Still, it was always worth checking.

He picked up the kroner and Andersson stepped up behind him. "You can't steal anything. The safe stores the time it was opened. I will be caught."

Markus stopped and turned to him. "Nils, it is time for you to go."

"I will not." Nils swallowed. "I have to stay here while you are in the room."

"Then go sit on the chair by the window." The tone was kind, the look was not. Andersson jumped to obey.

Shaking his head, Markus spilled the contents of the safe on the bed. "And who are you this month, Johan my friend?" He opened up the blue passport to see a photo of Bax. "John Baxter. Very good. And your companion?" Markus reached into the small handbag and pulled out the wallet and passport, appreciating for a moment the faint whiff of Joss's perfume. The wallet, he noticed, was small, with no credit cards or bank card such as most people usually carried. It did, however, include a driver's license. He looked at it and stilled. "How very interesting," he murmured.

"I cannot be gone from the desk for long," Andersson reminded him. "They will demote me to night shift. Haven't you found what you came for?"

Markus flipped open Joss's passport. "Much, much more," he said to himself. "All right, back to the front desk with you, Nils," he said briskly, putting the wallet back into Joss's purse. "I am done for now."

"Now? Will you be back?"

"Perhaps." Markus took his time returning the objects

to the safe, adjusting things carefully so that they looked as they had when he'd opened the safe. Johan, he knew, would notice.

"You must go," Andersson muttered, herding Markus back out into the hall like a nervous sheepdog.

"And so I will, Nils, and so I will."

SILVERHOLMEN WAS gorgeous, Joss thought, all rounded gray rock and green birches against the sapphire-blue of the sea. Small waves sent up occasional plumes of spume as they hit the shore. A few smaller islands dotted the sea around them, none even remotely large enough to be inhabited. Silverhielm had chosen his island getaway carefully. The nearest people would probably be ten miles away, maybe more. Out here, he'd have his privacy and then some.

Out here, he could do as he chose.

They'd come upon Silverholmen from the northwest and now circumnavigated it slowly. It was shaped a little like a lopsided lima bean, perhaps a mile and a half across at its widest. Birches and pine and heather covered much of it, at least what she could see. The house, Oskar had told them, was on the southern shore.

Slowly, Bax brought the boat around the island to come upon the house from the southeast, from the Baltic side rather than the Stockholm side from which boats normally approached.

Joss pushed her hair back out of her eyes and tried to ignore the heat. "Were Oskar's directions off or did you overshoot it intentionally?"

"It seemed like the best way to come up on them without being spotted. They may have guards watching the water with binoculars from the house, but they're not likely to monitor the northern exposure as carefully. And it doesn't hurt to have a feel for the whole island."

"In case everything goes south and we need to run that way?"

"If everything goes south and we're cut off from the boat, it won't matter whether we get loose on the back side of the island. We can't walk back to Stockholm. Eventually, they'll find us." He lowered his binoculars and looked at her. "Everything won't go south, though. This is just habit. The more prepared you are, the fewer surprises you have." The boat chugged along and slowly the trees thinned and the house came into view.

As they'd navigated the archipelago, she'd seen homes of glass and wood that looked to be made of air, homes built in traditional long-house styles that blended by virtue of their humbleness, homes that brought Swedish Modern to the age-old archipelago. In all this variety, though, she'd never seen a house like Silverhielm's.

It wasn't an island home, it was a transplanted manor house, suited to one who imagined himself lord and master of his world. Massive and baroque, it made no concession to its environment but dominated. The facade rose straight up, built of gray stone blocks, stolid and imposing. On the western exposure, they could see the ornate portico, designed as though for dukes and duchesses to roll up and alight from their coaches. Even the bottom floor, with all its windows overlooking the sea, was broken up with heavy columns and carvings.

Behind the house lay a stone terrace with steps down to the green lawn that rolled out to the shore. Stone lions sat in frozen vigilance on either side. It was the sort of manor house a member of the nobility might have built back in the eighteenth century. It said, Joss thought, a great deal about its owner.

"So do you think this was really the house he had in mind?" she asked.

"Of course. A man like Silverhielm always gets exactly what he wants."

"He must have an incredible view," she murmured.

Bax slowed the boat to an idle and threw an anchor overboard. "Always nice to have good scenery when you're ordering people kneecapped."

"Now, there's a thought I can do without."

"I'm glad you heard that story. You need to understand that Silverhielm is a genuinely ruthless man. It doesn't do to underestimate him."

Joss thought of the singlemindedness and disregard for anything but his own desires that it must have taken Silverhielm to build this sort of house out on a lonely island. Somehow the sight of the mansion, along with Oskar's story, made Silverhielm's character all too real. "It's too bad we couldn't just sneak on and swap out the forgeries without him knowing. He'd be happy because it's all about the owning, not the stamps themselves. We'd be happy because we got the stamps back."

"Why do you care about what he thinks?"

She didn't answer right away, but picked up the binoculars and scanned the island. "So what do you think he's going to do when he figures out we've scammed him?"

"That's a good question." Bax rose to pull one of the fishing rods they were using for cover out of its holder and opened up a container of chum. "I don't imagine he'll be happy."

"Will he come after us?" she asked, dreading the answer.

Bax drew his arm back and moved it forward in an arc, sending the baited hook sailing far out over the water. "He'll have to find us first."

"I don't think it'll be that much of a challenge for Markus to find us, do you?"

Bax finished adjusting the reel and turned to look at her. "So what are you saying?"

"Maybe we're better off finding a way to a standoff."

"We already have. The standoff we'll have is that we'll have the stamp mounts with Silverhielm's fingerprints on them, proof that he had them. Rolf, for one, would love an opportunity to send in a team with a search warrant. I think we can keep Silverhielm quite busy enough if we get the one-penny Mauritius back."

"If?"

He kissed her. "When."

"SO, HOW WAS YOUR visit to the Royal Viking?" Silverhielm leaned back in his expensive leather executive chair, staring out the windows of his Slussen office at the pastel buildings of Gamla Stan.

"Interesting," Markus said easily.

Silverhielm turned to face him. "Did you find the Blue Mauritius?"

"Of course not. The Blue Mauritius is most likely in a bank vault somewhere in Stockholm. Johan is well aware of the vulnerabilities of hotels and hotel safes."

"Did you find anything?"

"Indeed. Johan's current identity, for one."

"That is of little interest to me."

"He changes them at will," Markus agreed. "I did find out something far more useful, however. The identity of his lovely companion."

Silverhielm picked up a pencil and began tapping it against his desk blotter. "She is not Josie Astin?"

"No. The beautiful Ms. Astin has been lying to us. She is not the girlfriend of Stewart Oakes's thief. She is actually Joss Chastain, Hugh Chastain's granddaughter.

Silverhielm said nothing, but the pencil he held

snapped in two. "She is not here to sell the Blue Mauritius."

"Unlikely, but not impossible," Markus agreed. "Joss Chastain has no money, no permanent home, few records." He shrugged. "She may be here for profit. It is also possible that she is here to recover the one-penny Mauritius."

"Preposterous."

"It would explain why she has engaged the services of a man like Johan, however."

Silverhielm nodded. "We could have a family rebel, selling for her own profit. Why would she not tell us?"

"Afraid of suspicion, perhaps? It is more likely that she wishes to take the stamp back, as her sister did."

"Sentimental fools."

"Indeed."

Silverhielm put his elbows on the arms of his chair and steepled his fingers in front of him. "I do not care for being lied to. I will not be made a fool of. Or cheated." Anger vibrated in his voice as he glowered into space, his face ruddy. Minutes passed.

"Do you wish to cancel the meeting?" Markus asked.

Silverhielm exhaled and shifted his shoulders. He smiled slowly. "Not at all. It promises to be even more amusing than I'd anticipated. I will get the stamp, we will have some sport." His eyes turned cold and implacable. "And the very attractive Ms. Chastain will not leave Silverholmen alive."

19

THE SUN BEAT DOWN on them from its zenith. Joss sat on one of the bench seats along the side of the boat and trailed her fingers in the water. More than two hours had passed since they'd dropped anchor. Bax had merely kept his binoculars trained on the house. Despite her awareness of the importance of the surveillance, it was getting old. She was bored, tired, hot, restless and wholly impatient for something to happen.

"So you've monitored the guards and you've seen the layout. What are you looking for now?"

He shrugged. "I'm not sure. When I'm not sure, I watch and I wait. We know that they have a daytime patrolling schedule. I don't see Silverhielm's cigarette boat."

"The racing boat, you mean? Do you think he's in town?"

"Maybe. In that case, he'll either stay in his townhouse or come back out here. It might be nice to hang around and see what he does."

"That wouldn't be until five or so, right?" Joss checked her watch. "That's about four hours from now."

"About."

"And we've been here for two hours already."

"You were the one who wanted to come on the stake-out." He gave her a glance of amusement mixed with sympathy. "Welcome to the exciting life of a detective."

He was right, Joss admitted, but it didn't do anything to ease the oppressive heat. She was sticky and uncomfortable in her jeans, and the light breeze that had eased things that morning seemed to have died away. There wasn't even a shade over the cockpit of the boat. "So we're basically going to just sit here and wait."

"Yep."

Joss moved over to the captain's chair next to Bax and sighed, wishing she hadn't worn a black tank top. On the horizon, another ferry chugged its way north, bound, perhaps, for Finland.

She was so hot.

"Are there sharks out here?" Joss asked.

"You mean besides the ones on the island?"

"Besides them. Could I take a swim?"

"No. I don't want you in the water if we need to leave suddenly."

She fanned herself with one hand. "This is killing me."

"You look like you're dying. Here." Bax handed her another bottle of water. "We can stop when we get closer to Stockholm and you can swim all you like. Once we're done here."

"All right." She wouldn't act like a surly child, she told herself. If he could tolerate it, she could, too. "So how do you keep from getting bored on a stakeout?"

Bax shrugged and brought the binoculars back up to his eyes. "Oh, try to reconstruct *Goodfellas* in my head scene by scene. List the players on my all-time World Cup team." One corner of his mouth twitched. "Try to figure out the best sex I've ever had."

Joss snapped her head around to stare at him. "The best sex you've ever had?" she repeated dangerously.

His grin widened. "Uh-huh."

"If you're smart, your next comment will be that this

time that topic hasn't been particularly useful because you haven't had to think very much about it."

"Oh, this time around I've had an indisputable winner."

"Oh, really?"

"Yes, really." He leaned over and kissed her on the nose. "Of course, when we get back to the hotel, I might need to verify it." He raised his binoculars again and began watching the island.

The minutes ticked by and Joss picked at her sweat-dampened shirt. The heat of the sun baked her legs through the denim of her jeans. If only she'd worn shorts, she thought with a sigh. If only she'd thought to *pack* shorts. Sweden was north, for crying out loud. It wasn't supposed to hit the nineties all the way up here. It was like having a heat wave in Alaska.

On Silverholmen, the grass baked gently in the heat.

She had to do something.

Impatiently, Joss stood and unsnapped her jeans. Bax swung around to look at her. "What are you doing?"

"Don't let me distract you. I just want to cool down."

"I see."

"I forgot my bikini." She lowered the zipper and slid the denim off her hips. "I figured I'd improvise."

"You're stripping in broad daylight?"

"Who's going to see? The people on that ferry?" She pointed to the horizon. "I think they'll survive." She kicked off the jeans and stripped off her tank top, sighing in bliss as the faint breeze hit her sweat-damp skin.

"You'd better hope the Swedish coast guard doesn't show up and bust you for public exposure."

"I'll see them long before they get here." She reached back to unfasten the black lace of her bra and shrugged her shoulders to slip it off. "I'm just so hot. I thought if I took off a little clothing I'd be more comfortable." She slid her hands down to her hips, to the straps of her lacy thong, and paused. "You don't mind, do you?"

When he only stared, she hooked her fingers in the sides and began dragging the scrap of lace slowly down her hips, leaning over to pull it over her thighs, her knees and down to her ankles. "Oh, that's much better." She straightened to toss the thong on top of the pile of clothing she'd discarded. Sitting back in her captain's chair, she propped her feet up on the dashboard and poured water over herself.

Bax set his binoculars down slowly.

"Of course, there's always a risk of sunburn." Joss reached out for the bottle of sunscreen they'd brought.

His eyes followed her hand as she squeezed a line of sunscreen along first one leg, then the other. With a wicked smile, Joss slid her palm over the sleek lines of her thighs, stretching her legs up like a dancer. "I don't know why you don't at least take your shirt off." She nodded at the dark blue polo jersey he wore. "You must be baking."

Pouring out more sunscreen, she stroked her hand up and over the flat of her belly, spreading the cream over her waist, along the swell of her hips.

Utterly still, Bax just watched her.

Enjoying herself now, Joss slid her hands up higher, over the soft swells of her breasts. They filled her cupped hands, firm against her palm. To please herself, she caressed the skin, squeezing the nipples. "Aren't you hot?" she murmured.

In almost one motion Bax tossed down the binoculars and reached for her, pulling her against him and capturing her mouth with his. She chuckled deep in her throat in giddy delight. Once again, she'd made him lose the control he prized. Once again, she'd tempted him to give in to desire.

He dragged her to her feet with one arm, letting the other hand rove as he pleased, from her breasts to her ass to the slippery cleft between her legs. Arousal, pleasure flooded through her.

"You drive me nuts," he growled.

"That's why I do it," she whispered, her words filled with desire.

Bax stripped off his shirt, then leaned back against his captain's chair and reached for his belt.

"I can do that," Joss murmured, and brushed his hands aside. She unthreaded the strap from his buckle and found the button of his jeans beneath. "If you're not worried about the coast guard, that is." She pulled the zipper down and drew him out, already hard and pulsing. "After all, I don't know what they might think if they came across this." She brushed his silky soft cock over her cheek, licking the length of him like some erotic ice cream cone. "I could tell them that you're injured and I'm doing triage before applying first aid."

She swirled her tongue around his glans until she heard his rapid intake of breath. The first slick, faintly salty drop of precome emerged, and she spread it down the hard length of him with her fingertip. "Or I could tell them you've got a cramp and I'm applying warm compresses." She slid his cock swiftly into her mouth and he groaned.

It was incredibly arousing, seeing him, tasting him, feeling him, hearing him groan as she pleasured him and pleasured herself. There was no telling what would happen once they'd gotten the stamp back and the case was over. Bax might be true to his word and move on. She might never hear from him again. But she had him now. Now, of all moments, he was hers, hers to play, hers to pleasure. And if this had to be the end of it, this memory of sun and salt air and the gently rocking boat and the purity of pleasure would stay with her always.

She put a hand to her breast and caressed herself even as she felt him harden against her lips, knowing he was watching, knowing it would turn him on. When he dragged her to her feet, she went willingly, but she didn't move to the cushions of the bench seat that he urged her toward.

Instead, she pressed him into the captain's chair. As a breeze whisked over her, she straddled him and looked down at his hard cock, shuddering in the diamond formed by the overlap of her thighs and his. "Of course, if the coast guard does show up, maybe we're better off if we hide the evidence." And she rose to slide him inside herself, catching her breath at the feel of it.

Bax bent his head to her breasts, brushing his chin against first one nipple, then the other. The light scrape of his afternoon shadow against the hard nubbins of flesh made her murmur in pleasure. He reached a hand down between her thighs, rubbing his thumb against her clit until she cried out at the touch.

Joss clutched his shoulders and leaned into him, rising and falling, feeling him get harder and thicker, going deeper, so deep that it forced a cry from her at the intensity of each plunge.

And then his hands were on her hips, moving her up and down, setting the rhythm, setting the pace. The sound of the water, the rock of the boat, the slick rub of the base of his cock against her clit took her up, and up, the tension coiling up in the center of her. And then she broke, shuddering, leaning back from the waist to push herself hard against him for one final stroke that combined with her final contractions to bring him to a swift, hard orgasm in the sun.

"SO IS THIS what they taught you at Interpol, to have sex on a stakeout?" she asked him lazily, trailing her fingers over his chest.

They lay on the deck of the boat, cushions underneath them.

"Absolutely. It was part of the orientation class."

Joss made a husky sound of delight. "You must have had some instructors."

"They couldn't hold a candle to you." He stroked a hand down her back. "Actually, you may very well have ruined me for the future. I'm going to compare every single stakeout I'm on to this, and believe me, cold coffee and stale sandwiches in a car at night don't come anywhere close."

"So I win the award for best stakeout companion?"

"You win the award for best everything." He gave her a long, lingering kiss that carried much more than even he realized.

Joss stretched her arm above her to look at her watch. "Three o'clock. I suppose we should get dressed before Silverhielm comes home. If he comes home. Him and his goons."

"And Markus."

"Anyone who blows away someone's knees counts as a goon to me."

Bax frowned. "It's hard to say what he is, but he's not a goon."

"What is it with you two?" Mystified, Joss tapped her fingers on his chest. "I know you said before that you didn't like him, but you do. I can hear it in your voice."

"I don't even know that it's liking. It's more that I understand him."

"I don't see how. He's a bad guy, Bax. You were the one who told me that."

"There's a reason I understand Markus. There was a time when I wasn't a very good guy, either."

"I find that hard to believe."

"Believe it."

There was something hollow about his voice. Joss turned on her side to face him and propped herself up on one elbow. "When?"

"Right after my mother died, my dad and I were at each other's throats. I was sixteen and thought I knew it all. He wanted to run me like I was one of his buck privates."

"And you didn't like that at all."

"Now there's a surprise." He gave a wry smile. "He got put on the night shift, which was perfect for me. I got to running with a rough crowd, got in some trouble."

"What kind of trouble?"

"Little scrapes. I ignored the rules when they stood in my way."

"Like what?" She'd never been much for rules herself.

He moved his shoulders. "We ran wild, did some joy-riding, got our hands on some beer a few times. The more I did it, the more it made my father crazy and I liked that. The more I did it, the more I wanted to do."

"That doesn't sound like a kid headed to the FBI. What happened?"

"One night I took one too many chances and got caught with some kids who were breaking into a store. I was outside, across the street, but I got picked up too. They didn't charge me. I wound up sitting across from a youth counselor named Tom McDowell." He remembered the cramped office with its battered metal desk. Tom hadn't looked kindly and caring. Tom had looked like a hardass. Bax had given tough right back to him, but he'd been scared down deep, scared that he'd gone maybe too far. And Tom had seen.

He'd kicked away the cockiness that Bax had held around him like a shield, kicked away his pride in being a rebel. And as the weeks went on, he'd showed Bax that there were other things to have pride in, things that really mattered.

"The next step was getting arrested and winding up with a parole officer. But Tom didn't let me slide that far. He turned me around."

She traced her fingertip over the frown line in his forehead, erasing it. "He saw something of value in you."

"He was young and idealistic. I was lucky enough to be his project."

"His success story, it sounds like." She kissed him.

"I like to think so." When he'd confessed to Tom that he liked the idea of investigating, Tom hadn't laughed, he'd helped him look up the different ways to do it for a living. The day Bax graduated from the FBI academy, Tom had been there. They'd stayed in touch ever since. "He was the one who pointed me to the FBI after I'd gotten my head on straight. Luckily, I hadn't gotten in trouble bad enough to close any doors."

"And the FBI led to Interpol?"

"Eventually. The States never really felt like home to me. I always thought they would, but somehow…"

"I know what you mean."

"You do, don't you?"

"We're a lot alike, Bax."

In more ways than he'd expected. He nodded. "You get it. I thought Europe might be better for me, but I didn't quite fit in there, either. So I wound up back in San Francisco."

"And now you're trying Europe again. Isn't that why you took this job, to get back to Europe?"

"Partly."

"What was the other part?"

"I couldn't resist you."

This time, he kissed her hard and desire flared again. Roughly, he pulled her down to the deck of the boat. He wanted her underneath him, slick and strong, lean and taut.

Foreplay was irrelevant. The arousal of each fed off the other, their bodies straining together, the taste, the touch blending until the feel of her slickness against his fingers aroused him as much as the stroke of her palm against his hard cock. When she moaned, he felt the shudder of pleasure. When she quaked, it made him groan.

Then he rolled on top of her, lying between her legs, feeling them wrap around him like silken bonds. He slid his cock into her swiftly and they cried out together. He was into her up to the root, a part of her, connected as though they were one. And with every stroke, as he drove himself into her, he felt completed.

Part of a oneness he couldn't name.

He could say he was a loner, at this moment they were bonded in ways that went beyond physical. This time when he was inside her and they were moving together, pulling each other along toward climax, he didn't close his eyes and concentrate on his own pleasure. He cupped her head with his hands and stared into her eyes, watching her lips part as she gasped, watching her face come alive as he moved in her.

And as he saw her reach orgasm and begin to quake under him the crystal clear realization broke through him.

He was a man who'd lived through life-threatening situations. He was currently in a dangerous situation facing a dangerous man, without a clear idea how to make it work.

But he'd just realized the most dangerous thing of all.

He was in love with her.

20

JOSS RUBBED LOTION into her hands and listened to the sound of the television coming from the other room where Bax sat on the bed. He'd tuned in to a soccer game. Or football, she corrected herself. After all, she was in Europe.

"I hadn't realized you were a sports fan," she commented idly, leaning her head out of the bathroom.

"I'm not."

She watched him a moment. It was the first night since they'd been in Stockholm that they hadn't either been working or completely wrapped up in each other. Granted, they'd made an afternoon of it, but he'd definitely been acting a little strange since they'd been back. It made her edgy and unsettled, even more than her own feelings did.

She didn't want to be unsettled. She'd been unsettled for the past seven years. Enough, already. It was time for all of it to stop. It was time to build a life, a home, a career.

And she very much wanted Bax to be a part of it.

Nerves skittered in her belly. She'd never been vulnerable in a relationship before. She never wanted to hurt anyone, but you couldn't fake feelings. She wasn't faking the feelings now. If things ended, she would be the one getting hurt.

It gave her a queasy feeling in the pit of her stomach.

She had a choice, of course, you always had a choice. Do nothing, let him go, perhaps, and in time—maybe an aeon or two—the feelings would die away. Or maybe Bax would come to her and she wouldn't even have to say anything.

But doing nothing and waiting for things to happen was the coward's way. It had never been hers. She had to say something, pure and simple. She had to take her chance. And if she pancaked, at least she'd know she'd tried.

Joss stared at herself in the mirror. It would be okay, she told herself silently, remembering the way it had felt out on the archipelago, remembering the way it had felt in Amsterdam, where he'd come for her. It wasn't just her imagination. It was real. He cared for her, she knew he did.

She just needed to tell him how she felt.

Swallowing, she shook her hair back and walked out of the bathroom to sit on the bed in her silky robe. Unconsciously, she twisted her fingers together. "We had a good day today."

"I guess."

She cursed herself for making small talk instead of telling him what was on her mind. "We've been working pretty well together, haven't we?"

"Block the freaking ball," Bax barked at the goalie on television.

Joss stared at him. "Is everything okay?"

"Sure, fine," he said shortly, staring at the screen.

She nibbled on the inside of her lip and took a breath. "You know, I was thinking. This detecting stuff is kind of fun. I could get used to this."

"Oh, come on," he said disgustedly in response to a play, and then flicked a glance at her. "Don't get too excited. This isn't a real case. We're not investigating anything, we're just trying to figure out how to swindle Silverhielm out of something that's not his."

"Sure." She nodded. "Real investigating must keep you busy."

Bax just watched the soccer game tensely.

"Have you ever thought about getting someone to help you?" Her voice was elaborately casual. "You know, someone who could do the office stuff and maybe help you with some of the leg work? Someone you could train?"

Bax picked up the remote and punched at the button to mute the sound. "Joss, what's this all about?" he asked abruptly.

She blinked. "Well…"

"You've obviously got something to say. Say it."

Nervous, they were both nervous over tomorrow. This had to be said, though. She couldn't wait.

Now's your chance, she told herself silently. Do it. "I want to learn to become an investigator," she blurted. "I could work for you, doing whatever you needed me to. Maybe just secretarial stuff, or phone calls, street canvassing when you need to talk with a lot of sources. Whatever you want." With every word, she talked faster. "You know, learn how the business works from the ground up. Take away the dull stuff so you'll be more efficient."

For a long moment, he just watched her, some light of bewildered longing in his eyes. Everything would be okay, she wanted to tell him. She loved him. They could make it work. She moistened her lips and opened her mouth. "I—"

As though to ward off her words, he shook his head. "It's a nice offer, Joss, but no. Thanks."

"Wait a minute," she began.

"I've told you before, I work alone."

"You're not on the case alone now, though," she reminded him. "We've worked together just fine."

"Have we? We were on a stakeout today and I spent half

the afternoon focused on you instead of watching the island. That's not what I call working."

She stared at her hands and nodded her head as though to the beat of music only she could hear. Then she turned to him. "Okay, what's going on, Bax?"

"What do you mean, what's going on?"

"You've been acting strange ever since we got back. What got you so ticked off? So we fooled around on the job? Well, you were there, too," she reminded him, an edge to her voice. "And you didn't seem all that worried about it at the time. If you're going to get ticked, get ticked at yourself as well as me."

"It doesn't work. Having you around is screwing things up." He punched at the remote and turned the sound back up.

"So what was all that the other night about what a good job I was doing and how important I was? Or was that just a load of crap?"

His eyes skated off to the side. "Joss, you're the client. Of course I'm going to tell you you're doing a good job." A muscle at the side of his jaw worked. "Reality is, if I were working alone, I'd probably have the stamp back by now."

"Give me a break, Bax."

"What's that supposed to mean?"

"It means that it's taken two of us to pull this off, working together. Together, remember that? And it's been good, like it was this afternoon, until you got ticked off. Like it was in Amsterdam, and you came over there voluntarily, remember? That wasn't about work, it was about us."

"Amsterdam? Amsterdam was about taking care of you."

"Excuse me?" Her voice wavered.

"I wasn't going to leave you over there on your own. I came over to make sure you didn't get in trouble."

It sliced into her, wicked and unforgivable. "No. You came for me. You told me you did."

"You thought what you wanted to think."

"This isn't really about me coming to work for you, is it?" she asked, her voice a little wobbly. "This is about us, period."

"What 'us'? There is no us. That was a game we were playing, remember? A role to fool Silverhielm? It was never supposed to fool us, too. We're on the job and when it's done, we're done."

It was a cold, hard verbal slap and it silenced her momentarily. She'd always been the one who ended relationships, she'd always been the one who walked away without being hurt. Now, she was the one sitting here with her heart sliced open and he was just staring at the television.

At first it was just pain, harsh and undiluted.

And then the pain flamed back into anger. "There is no us? You are so full of it, Bax. Who do you think you're kidding with this, huh? You don't want anything going forward? You don't want us to see each other once this is over, fine, but don't sit there and try to pretend that nothing's happened here." Her voice rose in fury. "Even if you can't be honest with me, be honest with yourself."

"I am being honest."

"Oh yeah? What about this afternoon?" she demanded. "Not the sex, the other part. The part where we talked. The part where you told me things."

Now he did turn and look at her. "That was a mistake," he said bleakly. "I had no business telling you that stuff. I had no business spending the afternoon making love to you instead of paying attention to the case."

And because he had, he was trying to get as far from her as possible. It frustrated her, infuriated her and it hurt. Oh, it hurt. "What are you afraid of, getting close? You think because your father could never connect with you and your mom that you're hardwired to be that way, too? You think that because you grew up a loner that that's what you have to be your whole life?"

"You've got no idea what you're talking about," he said angrily. "You don't know what it's like to watch someone you love get hurt over and over again because they can't stop needing someone. My mom spent her whole life trying to open up to him and getting shut down every time. I saw what needing him did to her. I watched what it did to me."

"But that's them, that's not us. Let it go," Joss pleaded, reaching a hand to his face. "I care about you. I want to build something with you."

Bax jerked away and rose. "Sure. I've fallen for that one before, too. Her name was Stephanie." The first woman he'd ever loved, the first woman who'd ever loved him back. But time had told the lie of that. "She wanted to be there for me, too." He remembered staring into her beautiful face as she begged him to let her in. He'd done it, in incredulous wonder that everything could come together so easily, be the way it was supposed to be.

And he'd been so wrong.

Bax shook his head. "She wanted me to open up. And like a stupid schmuck, I did. And you know what? Surprise, suddenly I wasn't the man she'd fallen in love with. I wasn't the bulletproof tough guy. I was just a guy."

"You're the strongest man I've ever met."

He smiled humorlessly. "Not to her, not after that. She didn't really want to know me. No one ever really wants to know anybody. We're all happier with our fantasies."

"Bax," Joss whispered. "What did she do to you?"

"Oh, dropped that little bombshell before she walked off with a guy she met in a bar one night when we were out for a drink. A couple of weeks after I'd asked her to move in with me. Doesn't exactly make you want to get involved," he said, tossing the words at her shocked face.

She struggled to take it all in. "She was a witch. It wasn't about you, it was about her."

"It doesn't matter. Actually, she did me a favor. She taught me the most important lesson I ever learned—you can't depend on anyone but yourself."

"Just because one woman was an idiot doesn't mean every woman is." Impotent anger filled her words. "It doesn't mean that I am."

"And you telling me the same things she did doesn't mean that you aren't."

"Can't you trust me? Can't you try?"

He wanted to, part of him suddenly wanted to very badly. But he couldn't get there. It had been too hard, too long. "I believe you think you feel something for me, Joss, but it's not love. It's sex, it's excitement, it's danger. You want an answer to your life and you think I'm it."

"That's not true," she shook her head blindly. "I care for you Bax. I love you."

"You just think you do. You're not in love with me, you're in love with salvation."

"I don't need you to save me," she flared. "I just need you to be with me."

He hesitated. "Look, Joss, I can't be your fantasy man and I can't be your answer. We came into this knowing the score. Let's keep it that way."

"I'm not sixteen, Bax. I know what I feel."

"And I know what I know. It's over, Joss. We get the stamps back tomorrow and then we say goodbye."

"We won't have to," she spoke, almost inaudibly. "You've already said the only goodbye that matters."

21

THE DAY DAWNED gorgeous and clear with an exquisite
sunrise over the water by the Royal Viking. Joss stood at
the window and looked out toward Karl XII's *torg*. She
had no frame of reference for the misery she felt. She had
never experienced it before. She'd had breakups born of
anger and frustration, breakups fueled by incompatibility,
breakups driven by lack of desire. Always, though, she'd
felt a sense of relief after, a lightness at the idea of being
on her own again.

Now, all she felt was despair.

Bax had become a necessary part of her world. Only
two weeks had gone by since they'd first met and yet she
felt that he'd always been there, that his presence made
her days and nights complete in a way she hadn't realized
she'd needed.

And she had no idea what to do next.

They'd spent the night lying in the same bed. They
might have been inches apart, but the reality was millions
of times that distance. Eventually, Joss had dozed off into
dreams in which everything was right again. She'd woken
to find herself wrapped in Bax's arms, and for a moment
in the warmth and sleepy comfort, she'd forgotten that everything wasn't all right, that everything was as wrong as
it could be.

Her jolt into full wakefulness had woken Bax as well.

With the light of dawn just beginning to slip through the windows, he'd risen to pull on his running clothes and leave, without a word. Without a backward glance.

And in the empty room, she'd risen to stand by the window and watch him run away from the hotel, as he was running away from her.

BAX LISTENED TO the thud of his feet and waited for the run to do its work. In the aftermath of his breakup with Stephanie, he'd logged enough miles that he'd run the D.C. marathon and finished in the top one hundred. Whenever his thoughts would start chasing themselves in circles, he'd lace on his shoes and hit the streets or the trails, driving himself relentlessly. Running was Bax's escape, and that day should have been no different.

Except it was.

He turned the corner by the Opera House and found himself on Fredsgatan, just down from Fredsgatan 12. And suddenly he was hit by memories of walking there with Joss in the gathering evening, her fingers tangled with his.

Bax shook his head and sped up. *Block it out, block it out.* He didn't want to feel what he felt for Joss. There was no place in his life for letting another person in, for letting another person into his heart. For needing.

He knew what happened when you did that. He knew the danger.

His life was fine just as it was. So maybe it wasn't filled with people, but he knew what he could depend on. He knew who he could depend on—himself. When you started depending on other people, you put yourself at risk. Some people liked that. For his part, he could skip it.

He sped up, feeling the good burn in his quads and calves. Concentrate on the body, concentrate on the pain there. *Focus, focus, got to focus.*

Because if he stopped concentrating on physical pain he'd have to start registering the way it had felt to see the mute anguish on Joss's face the night before and that morning. And he'd have to start thinking about the loss he was going to feel when she was gone.

A SHOWER, clothes, coffee. The basics of life, the routine. If she clung to those, she'd get through this. She was strong enough, she knew it. She was tough enough.

And at the moment, there wasn't anything else to do but keep on, so Joss sat in the café at Karl XII's *torg* and held her coffee cup. She felt grainy and slow and out of sync with herself. More than ever before in her life she wanted to leave a place behind, but it simply wasn't possible just then. Not when the meeting with Silverhielm loomed. Once it was over, she could run to ground and lick her wounds, but for now, she had to stay with Bax to maintain their cover. No matter how excruciating it was.

"Hey."

She turned to see him behind her. He'd clearly just finished his run. His shirt was patchy with sweat, his unshaven chin, dark. He'd never looked better to her. But he wasn't hers, not anymore.

Bax set down his coffee and sat at the little table. He looked at Joss, but his eyes were hidden behind his sunglasses. It made him look even more remote and impassive than ever. "How are you?"

"Fabulous. I can't think when I've been better," Joss said, her voice brittle and hard. "Gee, this is fun. We ought to do this more often."

His jaw tightened briefly. "All right, dumb question. I'll just get right to it."

"Please do."

"We need to talk about what happens tonight."

"We finish the job. Isn't that what you've been waiting for?" Finish it and separate. So easy to say.

So difficult to do.

"Look, you've been waiting for this to be over, too. You can get back the one-penny Mauritius, close on what we came here to accomplish."

"Sure. So we've talked about the plan. What's your concern?" she asked, working to keep her voice as emotionless as his.

"You and me."

For an instant, hope bloomed. "Go on."

"Look, things are different now between us. You know it and I know it."

"And what do you want to do about that?" What had he come to talk with her about? What did he want from her, for them?

"Nothing," Bax said aloud. "It is what it is, but we can't go to Silverhielm's and let that show."

"Oh," Joss said tonelessly. He was talking about work. Of course. Foolish of her to expect anything else. "What do you want from me?"

"I want your assurance that when we go there tonight, we'll act like everything is normal, everything is like it was."

"Even though it's not." She searched his face for signs of regret, but his expression was so controlled she couldn't see anything at all.

"Exactly."

"So, why the big show? All couples have fights and break up. Why pretend?"

"Because tonight of all nights, we don't want them wondering about anything. Everything needs to go smoothly. I just wanted to be sure that you can carry it off."

It was like he was trying to pull a response from her,

trying to get her to plead with him one more time. "What, are you afraid I'm going to wail and weep and gnash my teeth?" Joss snapped, undone. "I can blow it off just as easily as you can, Bax. You're not as unforgettable as you think you are."

He stared at her for a moment and his mouth tightened. "I never thought I was," he said softly.

THE SINGLE red light flashed on the end of Silverholmen dock in the gathering dusk. Oskar slowed the little cruiser to a crawl and began to thread his way in through the breakwaters. He glanced at Bax.

"Just about there," he said.

Bax nodded. "You remember the drill."

"Yep," Oskar said cheerfully. "Stay alert and out of sight."

"The guards may come to talk with you."

"And I will tell them that you insist I stay with the boat."

"No matter what. Even if they tell you that I've sent word for you to come in. If anything changes, I'll come tell you personally. Otherwise, stay here. We may need to leave in a hurry."

"I have no desire to spend any more time with Silverhielm's men than I have to."

"Do you think they'll recognize you?"

Oskar shrugged. "It is possible, although almost a year has passed. Anyway, they have no reason to care if I am here. I did not leave under suspicious terms."

The long, wooden finger of the dock projected out from the steep gray rocks of the island. At the landward end, a short path made a sharp turn to the stairs that threaded up the side of the ten-foot bluff to reach the level of the back lawn and the house beyond. From where they sat on the boat, only the upper part of the house was visible.

Oskar piloted the boat up to the dock, stopping as close to the end as he could. On the other side bobbed Silverhielm's cigarette boat. And at the end of the dock, waiting for them in a charcoal shirt, jacket and trousers, was Markus.

"You made it, I see," he said.

Bax jumped to the dock to dog the bow line around a cleat, then moved to do the same with the stern line. "I wouldn't miss it." He brushed his hands off briefly and shook with Markus.

Meanwhile, Oskar shut down the engine and positioned a couple of fenders to protect the boat from contact with the dock.

Joss stepped up onto the side rail of the boat and reached out for Bax's hand. In deference to the occasion, she'd worn a little black silk jersey dress with a plunging neckline and long sleeves that ended in belled cuffs. The hem hit her at midthigh. Heels and dark hose added the finishing touches. It wasn't, perhaps, the best costume for walking down a dock at dusk, but it might distract Silverhielm at a crucial moment. Every bit of carelessness they could achieve was a benefit.

"Your pilot is welcome to come up to the house and stay with our men," Markus said, talking to Bax but looking at the boat. "Oskar, wasn't it?"

Oskar tilted his head in acknowledgement. "You have a good memory."

"So I do. How very clever of you, Johan, to find the one person in Stockholm who knows the route to Silverholmen well."

"I suspect there are others," Bax observed. "A man like Silverhielm is very popular."

"But private. It is not everyone who is invited to visit his home."

"Then we should consider it an honor."

"Indeed. Shall we all go up to the house?"

Bax glanced at Markus. "Oskar will stay here with the boat, thanks."

"That would not be Mr. Silverhielm's choice."

"I don't see why not. Oskar has delivered goods to Silverholmen in the past. He is trustworthy."

Markus considered and finally nodded. "You are right, of course. So, we will leave young Oskar here and hurry up to the house. Mr. Silverhielm has something very special planned."

FACETED CRYSTAL sparkled in the flickering light of dozens of candles. Decanters of doubtlessly expensive wine sat on an antique sideboard. The thick napkin on Joss's lap was of creamy white linen, as was the snowy tablecloth. The fork and knife she held had the heft of solid silver.

Stylishly ornate, the dining room suited the exterior of the house. Formal baroque carvings surrounded the high ceiling with its painting of Norse gods reclining on clouds. An elaborate chandelier formed of hundreds of crystal drops shimmered overhead. Paintings of hunting scenes adorned the wood-paneled walls. In one, a tusked boar bled, torn at by a pack of dogs.

It made Joss feel faintly sick.

"A toast." Silverhielm held up his glass. "To accomplishing long-held goals."

"To long-held goals," they echoed and crystal rang.

"The world is fraught with disappointment," he remarked, sitting. "What a happy occurrence, then, for a situation to occur in which everyone is satisfied."

"It's just a matter of having a common goal," Joss told him.

His eyes held some private amusement. "And so we do."

The butler began serving the dinner in silent ceremony. Course followed course, with wines to match the herring appetizer, the crab bisque, the stuffed lobster and the venison in port wine sauce.

It was surreal, Joss thought, watching Silverhielm slice off a piece of meat so rare that blood oozed out onto the white plate. How could he play the expansive host, catering to the comfort of his guests, when she knew the kind of acts he was capable of? What would he say if he knew why they were really there, she wondered, watching him chew the meat.

And what would he do?

"SO BUSINESS does not have to be all labor," Silverhielm remarked, taking a drink of his port. "There is always time for pleasure."

Dinner had given way to dessert, which had given way to brandy and cognac in the opulent living room with its deep, soft couches. A wall of French doors overlooked the water as the last rays of the setting sun gave way to the full moon. Markus sat in a chair against the wall, observing everything, saying nothing.

"Your house is exquisite," Joss told Silverhielm, doing her best to sound sincere. "As is your chef."

"He is very talented," Silverhielm acknowledged. "He is not my first chef, of course. The first chef, I found, used the kitchen budget to attempt to cheat me. I took it poorly, as you might imagine."

Joss swallowed. "Where is he now?"

"It is of no concern." Silverhielm swirled his brandy. "Will you have some more brandy?" he asked Joss.

"No thank you. I had too much at dinner. I'm wearing high heels. If I don't watch it, I won't be able to walk," she joked.

"Then slide them off. Come now, it is my house. I demand that you be comfortable." He stepped over and lifted one of her feet by the ankle, slipping her shoe off. "And the other?"

"I can get it," Joss said hastily, trying not to shudder at his touch.

"Now, some brandy for you." He picked up a snifter from the tray the butler had left and brought it over to her.

Joss took the balloon glass, cupping her hands around it. Without shoes, she felt a bit naked.

"And now," Silverhielm rose, "it is time to get to our private business, Ms. Astin."

"Josie," she corrected.

"Of course. So, if you will join me, Josie?" He put out his arm in a courtly fashion.

Bax stood as well. Silverhielm eyed him.

"Oh, I do not think that is necessary. This is a friendly meeting. Markus can keep you company here."

Bax looked at Joss. "All right with you?"

"We'll be fine," she told him. "Won't we, Karl?"

He led her into the hallway outside of the living room. "But of course."

MARKUS ROSE from his chair. "Come." He walked to the open door to one side of the room. "We can play billiards while we wait."

"Sure." Bax followed him into the dark green room with its carved mahogany table.

"Did you consider Mr. Silverhielm's offer any further?" Markus asked as he picked up a cue. "I think you will find his terms very generous. He rewards loyalty."

Bax began pulling balls from the leather net pockets of the table and setting them in the wooden triangle of the rack. "I have a job to finish here. When would Silverhielm want me to come on board?"

Markus chalked his stick and adjusted the position of the cue ball. He stroked the cue twice and slammed it against the cue ball so that it knocked the colored balls all over the table. "Perhaps now."

"PLEASE, SIT," Silverhielm said, relaxing back into his cordovan leather chair.

Joss sat looking past him to the deepening dusk and thought of the man who'd probably sat in this chair moments before getting his knee shattered. She suppressed a shudder.

"So, here we are at last," Silverhielm said.

"Here we are," she agreed.

"And you have the Blue Mauritius?" His eyes glinted with avarice.

"Of course." Her palms dampened just as she raised her purse into her lap.

"A momentous occasion, Ms. Astin. One I have waited for. I do not deal well with frustration, as you might imagine."

Was it her imagination or was there just a breath of malice in his voice? "Isn't it good that I came to see you, then?"

"Indeed." He opened a drawer and brought out a mat and a pair of stamp tongs. "I do not wish to wait any longer. The Blue Mauritius, please."

"The money," she countered, ignoring his clipped tone of command.

He smiled as though at some private joke. "You do not trust me? I thought we were friends."

"I still need to see the money."

"Very well." He pressed a button in his desk and a section of his bookcase popped ajar. "It is, perhaps, too dramatic, but for a man like myself, security must be of paramount concern. Always, there are those who attempt to cheat me."

Behind the bookcase was a panel that slid aside to reveal a wall safe. Like her grandfather, Silverhielm apparently believed in keeping his precious belongings close at hand.

Unlike her grandfather's, those belongings were guarded by killers.

He opened the safe and moments later returned with a banded stack of bills and a leather stamp album. "Two hundred thousand dollars U.S., as you requested. Would you like to count it?"

"That won't be necessary." She didn't really want his money. Taking it would be tantamount to stealing. All she wanted was her grandfather's property.

"Ah. You do trust me, then. I'm flattered." He opened the cover of the stamp album. "Well, then, I will show you the prizes of my collection. Of course, you are not a stamp collector so perhaps they will not please you as much as they would some."

"I appreciate rarities as much as the next person," Joss corrected him. "You have the other half of the Post Office Mauritius pair, right?"

"I suppose your ex-boyfriend would know that, would he not?" There was laughter in Silverhielm's eyes.

"I suppose he would."

"Here it is."

Joss let out a breath as he turned the page to display an orange stamp, the stamp that was a twin of the one she'd seen in the safe at the Postmuseet. "May I look at it?" she asked reaching for the album.

But Silverhielm raised a hand. "The Blue Mauritius, first, if you please."

Reaching into her purse, she pulled out the stiffened glassine envelope that held the Blue Mauritius.

"You have taken proper care of it?" he asked sharply.

"See for yourself." She slid out the transparent mount that held the stamp, then laid it on the mat in the center of the desk.

Silverhielm set aside his stamp album and reached out to move the mat directly in front of him. For a moment, he just looked at the stamp reverently. Using the tongs, he reached inside the mount to pull out the Blue Mauritius, his hands shaking just a bit. From a drawer, he produced a loupe and inspected the stamp at length. Finally, he let out a long breath. "It is genuine." He leaned near, brought his fingers almost into contact with the colored square of paper.

It made her sick to see it in his possession. Her only comfort was that it wouldn't be for long. "Of course it is genuine. And now you have them, side by side."

He blinked for a moment as though coming out of a trance. "Yes," he said briskly and reached for the album to pull out the one-penny Mauritius. Using stamp tongs, he reverently picked up the Blue Mauritius and slid it into the empty slot. "So long," he whispered. "So long I have waited for it to be mine."

Hands below the level of the desk, Joss reached into her purse and palmed the forgeries. "May I see them?" she asked, rising to lean over the desk.

Just then, a tone sounded. Silverhielm's eyes flickered over to his computer and in that instant Joss palmed the Post Office Mauritius pair and substituted the forgery.

"I can see why you're so fascinated by them," she commented. Silverhielm's gaze, she noticed, slid to her cleavage and she remained standing and leaning over his desk to look at what was now the forged Post Office Mauritius pair. Finally, she sat.

"So, I have the stamps and you have the money. I think

this calls for a toast," he said, raising his glass. "To the Blue Mauritius." He took a drink. "My dear Ms. Chastain."

"YOU KNOW where I stand on this." Bax squinted along his cue and popped the six ball in. "I have a client already. Until this job is done I can't switch."

"Perhaps the job will be finished more quickly than you had planned."

Bax flicked a glance at Markus and set up his next shot. "What's that supposed to mean?"

Markus smiled slightly and nodded his head forward a fraction. "I commend you on a most excellent charade. We initially had no idea of your client's true identity." Markus stepped up to the table as Bax straightened. "Fortunately, Mr. Silverhielm is a practical man who appreciates skill. Things may not go well for Ms. Chastain, but you may find yourself in a position to profit from your audacity."

Bax gave him a hard look. "What?"

"It means that you have a choice. Mr. Silverhielm, of course, has brought you here falsely—he has no intention of giving you or Ms. Chastain any money for the one-penny Mauritius. But then, you have come here falsely yourself. The fate of Ms. Chastain has already been settled. What happens to you has not."

Only through years of training was he able to keep from reacting. Joss was alone with Silverhielm, with a man capable of just about anything. And to get to her, Bax had to go through Markus, not to mention assorted other goons around the house. He needed to figure out a strategy but the fear for Joss kept rising up to choke him. Push it down, he told himself. Put all the emotions away and concentrate. "So what are you asking me to do? Beg for my life?"

"I know you won't. That's the kind of man you are."

Markus crossed to the other side of the table, keeping his distance, Bax noticed, keeping balanced. "Of course, the more important question is what kind of man is Mr. Silverhielm?"

"I'm sure you'll tell me."

"Indeed. He is a man who wants always to have his way. He is very vicious when he is crossed. Just as you and Ms. Chastain have crossed him. He would like to kill you. But I believe he would also appreciate someone like you on his side. And I can make that happen."

"In exchange for what?"

"A show of loyalty to your new employer, perhaps." Markus leaned his cue against the table. "Ms. Chastain's punishment is likely to be messy if not attended to with proper care. You have always been so neat." Markus reached into his coat toward the holster Bax was sure was there.

Their eyes locked.

"I believe it is your shot, Johan."

"WHAT DID YOU SAY?" Joss stared at Silverhielm.

"Did you really think we wouldn't find out who you are?"

Her heart began rabbiting in her chest. "I told you who I am."

"Come now." He thumped his glass down. "It is an embarrassment to both of us for you to try to maintain this falsehood. You are Joss Chastain, the granddaughter of Hugh Chastain."

"The rightful owner of that Post Office Mauritius pair you're so proud of," she snapped, unable to keep quiet.

"The Post Office Mauritius pair I won't be paying for now," he said smoothly, picking the stack of bills from the desk and slipping them into a drawer. "You were a fool to think you could fool me, Ms. Chastain, even with the help of Mr. Bruhn. It may interest you to know he's agreed to come to work for me, so you won't find any assistance from that quarter."

It was a trap, they'd been drawn into a trap on this remote island.

Or she had.

Joss moistened her lips. "He wouldn't betray me," she whispered, as much to herself as to Silverhielm.

"No? I think he would. But it is of no matter. You are on my private island, surrounded by my employees. I have the upper hand. Then again," he raised his eyebrows, "I always do. I don't like being cheated."

It stiffened her spine. She glared at him. "You stole those stamps from my grandfather."

"On the contrary. The thieves are already in jail." He smiled faintly. "Your fine American criminal justice system at work."

Her fingers tightened on the stem of her balloon glass. "You stole them."

"The Post Office Mauritius pair is mine," he snapped, goaded into anger.

"Then have them." She rose and flung the contents of the snifter over the album on the table.

Silverhielm roared and snatched at the stamps as Joss whirled and ran for the door.

It was as she'd gambled. He was more interested in saving his million dollar babies than in running after her.

She ran down the hall toward the living room, her stockinged feet slipping on the hardwood floors. Bursting into the living room, she stared at the empty couch. Gone? They couldn't be, he wouldn't have abandoned her. She looked around wildly.

And saw the light coming out of a door across the room, partially ajar.

She burst through the door to see Bax standing on the far side of a pool table. "Bax, we've got to go, *now*."

"Not so quickly, Ms. Chastain," said a soft voice from behind her.

She turned to see Markus Holm standing against the wall, his gun pointed directly between her eyes.

22

Bax froze, pool cue at his side, and stared at the two of them.

"Now is the time to choose your side, my friend," Markus said. "The girl can do nothing for you. Silverhielm can offer you money, a job. And, of course, since I am the only one in the room with a gun, I can offer you something more immediate. You have only to walk away."

Joss stood transfixed.

Bax shook his head. "I can't do that."

"That is a pity. I approve of honor, as you know. But I approve of intelligence more."

"It's more than honor, Markus."

Markus looked at him with curiosity. "More than honor." He moved the gun slightly in Bax's direction. "More than your life is worth?"

Bax returned his gaze. "Yes."

"Why?"

"Because I love her," he said calmly.

Joss snapped her head around to stare at him.

Markus shook his head in disgust. "When did you become a fool, Johan?"

"I'm not sure. Maybe the day I met her." His reply was to Markus but it was Joss he spoke to, even as he calculated ways and means to get the two of them out of there alive.

Markus studied him. "I could shoot her."

"I'd come for you."

"I could shoot you, too, of course. Probably first. Perhaps now."

"You think so?" Bax asked. "Is your memory really that short?"

Their eyes locked together and the seconds ticked by. "So," Markus said at last, "you wish my debt repaid."

Bax said nothing.

A slight smile played on Markus's lips. "It is perhaps not so great a price as you now think." He nodded to the French doors that let out from the living room to the terrace and the lawn beyond. "I will let you go and count to ten. You and the lovely Ms. Chastain will get a chance to escape with your lives and you and I will be even. Go." He jerked his head and lowered the gun. "One…"

And they went.

Markus replaced his gun in his holster and walked out into the living room. "Two," he said softly to himself as footsteps sounded from within the house.

"Stop them," Silverhielm roared from the hallway. "She has the real stamps." He burst into the living room and stopped, staring first at the open doors and then at Markus, who stood impassively before him. "Where are they?"

Markus nodded toward the lawn, toward the two running figures.

"What have you done, you fool?" Silverhielm demanded.

Markus looked at him serenely. "Nothing that will matter."

"Go after them. Warn the others."

"Don't worry," Markus said, reaching in his pocket for a walkie-talkie. "It is taken care of."

BAX RAN ACROSS the slick grass with Joss. Moonlight bathed the scene in a deceptively calm wash of silver. Beyond the grass, the sea was a presence of darkness broken by the distant haze of light that was Stockholm. If Markus were true to his word, they might have time to make it to the boat before the others pursued them. They might be able to make it to open water.

For now, they needed to reach the staircase that hugged the side of the low rock bluff. Once they were on it, they'd be protected from anyone running toward them, at least until their pursuers got close. He grabbed the hardwood banister and took the stairs two at a time, listening to Joss behind him. Then they hit the landing at the bottom, turning around an outcrop toward the dock.

Only to come to a scrambling halt.

Small lights on the railings silhouetted a guard at the landward end of the dock as he leaned against the railing, nodding his head a little, not looking up. The light offshore breeze brought them the scent of the smoke from his cigarette. Out at the other end of the dock, by Oskar and the boat, the red light flashed. Waves slapped quietly against the pilings.

Joss tapped Bax's arm. "He has a headset on," she whispered. Bax nodded, edging forward. The closer he could get without warning the guy, the better. He couldn't see a gun, but he knew there had to be one. A staticky buzz like that of a walkie-talkie broke the silence. Even as the guard slid off his headset to answer, Bax pounced.

The guard was bigger than he was, solidly built in a way that suggested more muscle than fat. Size wasn't everything, though. Bax was on him before he could raise his gun, chopping at the hand that held it. The revolver spun away.

"Run to the boat," Bax bellowed to Joss, then stepped in to catch the guard with a punch to the eye, pain exploding up his arm. The punch should have decked the guy but he only stepped back, shaking his head. Not a good sign, Bax thought, trying to step in before his opponent had gotten himself set. A fraction of a second later, Bax found himself bouncing dizzily off the dock railing, struggling to keep his feet while his ears rang.

The guy was definitely quicker than he'd anticipated. And so were the others, judging by the shouts he heard.

"Watch out," Joss screamed.

Bax looked to see the guard moving in again, sending a looping roundhouse toward Bax's temple. Ducking to get inside of it, Bax summoned up a fast uppercut and snapped the guard's jaw shut. The man stood for a moment, then his knees softened and he sagged toward the ground.

Bax vaulted over him and pounded down the dock to the boat.

"Oskar's gone," Joss shouted from inside the boat.

Cursing, Bax unfastened the bow and stern lines. He gave the front of the vessel a shove and jumped in.

"Did you hear me?" Joss cried. "Oskar is gone."

"He's not all that's missing," Bax said grimly. The keys, as he'd feared, had also been taken and they'd disconnected the GPS unit. Silverhielm's men had been thorough. Bax reached under the dash to fumble for the ignition wires. And the boat drifted slowly away from the dock, turning back toward Stockholm.

Figures appeared at the edge of the bluff and a bullet ricocheted past him with a whine.

"Get down," Bax shouted and ducked himself.

"Bax, we can't leave," Joss shouted. "What about Oskar?"

Bax ignored her and squinted to see the wires in the moonlight as he untwisted them. He couldn't think about Oskar, he couldn't think about feelings. Compartmentalize. The key to survival was focusing on action and admitting no distractions.

A spark jumped from one wire to the other and the engine chugged once. Pumping the gas, he touched the wires again and the engine caught with a roar. With a spin of the wheel, he headed the boat back toward Stockholm.

Joss caught at his arm. "What are you doing?" she demanded.

"We have to get out of here." He grabbed her, shoved the throttle forward and the boat leapt out of the water.

"We can't just leave him behind." Her voice rose in fury. "They could do anything to him."

Bax glanced back to see figures spilling over the edge of the bluff and clustering around the fallen figure at the head of the dock. Another shot whined past them. "There are people shooting at us, in case you hadn't noticed. We have to leave him." He stared at the water ahead, trying desperately to see his path. The moonlight threw a silver glaze over the water, making it easier to see land but harder to see hazards. He aimed the boat away from the islands and tried to remember landmarks from the previous day. "If we stay here, they'll take us, too and we'll be no good to him at all."

"We're no good to him if we just let them have him. What kind of a man are you?"

As cold and calculating as he could make himself be. "We can't help him right now, Joss. The only way we can help him is by getting back to Stockholm and Rolf."

"And if they hurt or kill him in the meantime?"

"That's a risk we have to take. Don't you finally understand who we're dealing with, here?" Bax glanced back as a roar started up behind them and he cursed. "Do you hear that engine? They're coming after us in that goddamn big cigarette boat. We'll be lucky to make it back in one piece, but we're guaranteed to die if we try to go back to Silverholmen alone." She opened her mouth to protest, but he rode right over her. "We don't have the tools, Joss, and you're not helping me by being hysterical."

Her mouth clamped shut and she glared at him. Good, he told himself, and tried not to care. If she was angry she'd be focused. "Fine," Joss snapped. "What do you want me to do?"

The conversation wasn't over yet, he knew that. At some point, there was going to be hell to pay. First, though, they had to survive. "Concentrate on getting back to the hotel in one piece and then we can figure out what to do. We've got a mile on them, maybe two, but they can out-run us and they've got guns. Here," he stepped back. "Take the wheel for a minute. Aim for that light over there." He pointed.

"I've got it," Joss said.

Bax reached up under the dash and searched for the gun he'd duct taped in place earlier that evening. "Okay." He brought it out. "It's not much fire power, but it's all we've got. You cock it by pulling back the action, like this. The safety is right here." He showed her. "If you want to help, when that boat pulls up to within eight or ten feet, try to take a shot. See if you can get them to keep their heads down." He took the wheel and adjusted their course. "Sit down and steady it on the gunwales. Remember to squeeze the trigger, don't pull."

"What about extra ammunition?"

"There's another clip." He handed it to her. "If we're not out of trouble by the time you've finished them both off, we're not going to be."

She nodded and took the gun from him.

And in that moment, compartmentalization be damned, he loved her.

JOSS STARED tensely back at the lights of the cigarette boat as it drew inexorably nearer. They'd moved through the line of barrier islands on the outer archipelago. Ahead of them, the inner islands formed a funnel of land that would bring them into the narrow, tree-lined pass that led to the Stockholm harbor. She felt their speed drop a little.

There was a whine and a corner of the little boat's windshield exploded into shards.

"Get down," Bax hollered. "They're within firing range."

Joss dived down on the deck of the boat and scrambled over to the gunwale, her anger and fear forgotten. Survival was all that mattered now. "They're a good half a mile away."

"So they've got a rifle." He slalomed the boat a bit to make them less of a target. "It's getting shallow and tricky in here. They're going to have to come down off the plane, soon, and that's going to bounce them around more. Make them less accurate, slower. But we're going to have to slow down, too." Another shot whined past them.

The entrance to the pass was tantalizingly near yet frustratingly distant. The gun felt heavy and useless in her hand. Turning, she searched for an answer in the darkness.

And felt a surge of hope. "Bax," she shouted, "the ferry." Coming up from their left, the white boat looked like a waterborne chandelier, the deck lights shining out over the water as it steamed majestically along toward the Stockholm inner harbor. "Could we use them as a shield in the pass?"

He stared at her a moment, then understanding broke.

It was a chance, she thought. If they could get ahead of the ferry before they went into the narrow waterway, the cigarette boat couldn't get to them, Silverhielm's men couldn't shoot them. If they could head off the ferry they might be safe.

Another shot whistled by them. Bax made a minor adjustment in their course and inched the throttle forward, his expression hard and focused as they rocketed through the dark waters. The ferry steamed along, closer and closer to intersecting their course. Would they get there in time, was the question. Behind them sounded the relentless engine of the cigarette boat.

Ahead of them lay the pass between the island of Nacka and the island of Ingarö. The ferry began its long, slow turn across in front of them, aiming at the pass.

And everything began to happen way too quickly.

One minute, they were behind the white ship. The next, Bax was whipping the boat around the ferry, skimming terrifyingly close to the rocky margins of the islands. The high, white side of the ferry towered over them mere feet away as they surged past it. The coastlines flowed in toward them.

Joss's hands tightened on the gunwale. If Bax miscalculated, they'd be wiped out like a bug on a truck windshield. And if he lost his nerve... Another shot from their pursuers whizzed past them, ricocheting off the white side of the ferry and clipping the edge of the speedboat's gunwale. Reminding them of what lay behind.

Foot by foot, they neared the ferry's bow. Time stretched out, the seconds crawling by. Then Bax shoved the throttle all the way up. The speedboat jumped forward and shot ahead of the ferry, slipping in front of the white painted prow with only a few feet or so to spare. The ferry's airhorn blared in protest.

Then they were in the narrow pass, the solid bulk of the ferry behind them and no room for the cigarette boat to get by. They'd made it. They were safe.

For now.

23

JOSS WAS a pacer from way back. Sitting still made her want to scream. When she was upset, she had to move. Stay away from the window, Bax had told her, so she moved from the bathroom to the bed and back, four steps, turn, four steps, turn. It kept her from going crazy.

It kept her from worrying about Oskar.

Across the room, Bax cursed. "Dammit, Rolf." He tossed Joss's cell phone on the bed. He'd been using it to stay off his own, which remained stubbornly silent. "Your big chance to nail Silverhielm and where are you?"

Four steps, turn, four steps, turn. "Forget about Rolf," she told him. "Call the police directly."

"I've been trying to. It's nearly midnight. The people I need to talk to aren't exactly at their desks."

"You swore to me that if we got back here we could find a way to help Oskar." She rounded on him, her voice tight with anguish. "We have to do it."

"They'll call, Joss. Trust me."

"Why should I trust you about anything? You left him there, just to save your own skin."

"Looks to me like your skin is in one piece, as well. They're not going to do anything to Oskar. At least not yet."

"How do you know?"

"Because Oskar is leverage. You don't hurt leverage, you use it."

The electronic burble of the phone broke into their conversation, silencing them momentarily. Joss stared at Bax. Stiffly, she walked over to pick up the receiver.

"Hello?"

"Ms. Chastain. Did you enjoy your trip back to Stockholm?" It was Silverhielm.

"Perhaps if someone hadn't been shooting at us."

"It added to the excitement, did it not? By the way, please pass my compliments to your associate for his maneuver with the ferry. I'm told it deeply frustrated our captain."

"You didn't call to discuss his piloting skills."

"Of course not. I called to discuss a meeting. After all, we have something of yours and you have something of ours. Your forgeries were good, but not good enough."

"We don't have anything of yours." An edge entered her voice. "The Post Office Mauritius set is stolen goods. They belong to my grandfather."

"An interesting assertion. Would you care to hear what your young friend Oskar thinks?" There was a muffled curse by the phone.

"What are you doing to him?" Joss demanded.

"Nothing permanent." Silverhielm's voice was smooth and lightly amused. "We can do worse, though. You know that."

"What do you want?"

"A swap. You bring the stamps, we will bring Oskar. If the stamps are authentic, we will release him to you."

"And what is to stop you from killing us as you tried to do on the way back to Stockholm?" she asked hotly.

"I want only the stamps."

"I don't believe you."

"Whether you do or don't is irrelevant, Ms. Chastain." An edge entered his voice. "We are wasting time and your friend does not have much of it."

"If you want the stamps, you will see to it that nothing further happens to Oskar," she said steadily. The blood pounded in her temples but she felt curiously calm.

"He will not be harmed, I assure you. What is your decision?"

"Let's do it now."

"Tonight, then."

"Where?" She motioned to Bax, who leaned close enough to hear.

"The Djurgården, behind the restaurant Ulla Winbladh."

Bax shook his head violently again and held out his hand for the receiver. "Silverhielm? You know who this is. I want someplace inside, neutral ground."

Joss put her ear near enough to the phone to hear Silverhielm's reply. "Neutral ground? But what is the Djurgården?"

"A good place to get shot. Inside, Silverhielm, where there's people."

"My Slussen office, then."

"Stop wasting my time," Bax said impatiently. "Neutral ground. You come in with Oskar, you and Markus alone. If I like the look of things, Joss comes in with the stamps. We trade, everyone goes home happy."

"Very well. Erik's Gondolen, in Slussen," Silverhielm said finally. "One hour."

Bax tensed as though to protest and Joss could almost see when he decided not to. "All right. We'll be there."

He hung up the phone.

"But that's the bar in the building where Silverhielm's office is. It can't possibly be neutral ground."

"It won't be."

"Then what are you thinking of, setting up a meet there?"

"I'll tell you."

GONDOLEN LOOKED like the sort of place Silverhielm would like. Stylish and sleek, it oozed sophistication, from the dark and light wood parquet floor to the wavering chrome bars of the railings that separated the bar area from the restaurant.

Bax had been there for more than half an hour, using the faint reflections of the windows to monitor the people moving in and out. The goons had been there before him, sitting uncomfortably at a table near the entrance of the bar. They tried, he'd give them that. But even in an upscale establishment like Gondolen, where sport coats were de rigueur and not merely worn to cover up guns, they stood out. It wasn't just the dress. They were too big, too bulky, too rough-looking.

Bax checked his watch. Almost showtime.

A moment or two later, Markus and Silverhielm walked in. They didn't look around but came directly for him. Bax took another swallow of his beer. "Right on time, gentlemen."

Silverhielm looked around. "Where is Chastain?"

"No Ms.? You're losing your manners."

"And you will lose your young friend if you are not careful." Silverhielm dropped his hands to rest on the back of the wood barstool. "Where is she? Where are my stamps?"

"The stamps, and Ms. Chastain, are in another location." Bax finished his drink and set the glass on the bar. "Where is Oskar?"

"Your young friend will appear when the stamps appear."

Bax rose. "He appears now. You, Markus, Oskar and I go together to the meeting place or I don't take you."

Silverhielm's face darkened. "I will not be threatened."

"Do you want the stamps?"

"Do you want to ensure that nobody dies?"

"I'm doing my best. Now are you coming?"

Markus spoke up. "It would be well to let him have his way this time."

The back of the chair creaked under Silverhielm's fingers as he glowered. Finally, slowly, he released his hold. "All right. We will take my car."

"We walk," Bax interrupted.

"What?"

"It's only half a mile. We'll walk." He gave a friendly smile. "Safer that way."

"And where are we going?"

"You'll find out when we get there."

JOSS SAT in Pelikan, at a table near the entrance, her back to the wall that separated the beerhall from Kristallen. She glanced at her watch. Midnight, the witching hour. She wished she were a witch, that she could make Silverhielm and his men into rabbits, or their guns into harmless water pistols.

Instead, she could only wait for them to arrive.

In her purse was the glassine envelope that held the Post Office Mauritius pair. Nothing had ever mattered to her less. Bax hadn't been able to reach Rolf Johansson for assistance, so their best chance of saving Oskar was for her to hand over both of the Post Office Mauritius stamps. It didn't matter. Next to a man's life, stamps and money meant nothing.

At this hour, both Kristallen and Pelikan were still busy with the usual young crowd, but things were beginning to wind down. The electronic music from Kristallen throbbed against the wall behind her shoulder blades. She heard a shout and looked over to see Bax walk in, followed by Silverhielm, Oskar and Markus.

Oskar's face looked pale and pinched. A dark thread on his neck looked like dried blood. From the stiff way Oskar held himself, Joss had a pretty good idea Markus had him in a come-along hold. Her heart went out to him.

Joss raised her hand. Silverhielm and Bax headed her way.

"Ah, Ms. Chastain, so we meet again." Silverhielm took a seat across from her. "We have brought your young friend. And you, have you brought my property?"

Joss's heart hammered against her ribs. "Perhaps." She looked over to where Oskar stood with Markus next to the door. "Bring Oskar over here so that I can be sure he's all right."

"Show me the stamps," Silverhielm countered.

Bax sat down beside her. "Oskar seems to be okay."

"What do you mean, okay?" Joss demanded. "He's bleeding."

"Do you wish me to make it worse, Ms. Chastain?" Silverhielm asked gently.

Just then, the pretty girl they had seen Oskar with during their earlier visit peeked around the barrier and cried out in mixed pleasure and concern. She ran across to Oskar, jostling Markus as she put her fingers to Oskar's neck. Others came around the barrier from Kristallen. In moments, Oskar was surrounded by a barrier formed of his friends.

"Who are those people?" Silverhielm demanded, half-rising from his seat. "What are they doing here?"

"I can't imagine," Bax drawled.

Silverhielm's eyes narrowed in fury and there was a sudden, metallic click. "No one betrays me," he growled.

Joss tensed.

"You are not the only person who can call for a change of locations, my friend," Silverhielm said, jerking his head at Markus, then nodding toward the door. "We are going outside."

"Hey, what are you doing," one of Oskar's friends cried.

Silverhielm looked over to the door and in that instant, Joss shoved the table at him. The heavy wood caught him in the chest as he was rising from his chair and sent him tipping over backward. There was a deafening explosion and Bax spun away.

Joss dived over on top of Silverhielm, adding her weight to that of the table, pinning him against the floor and his chair. As he struck out at her, she jerked her head back out of his way. Where was Bax? What had happened with the shot? Silverhielm landed a punch and pain exploded through her head.

Then she heard shouts and hands were on her, pulling her away.

"No," Joss screamed desperately as they lifted her up, kicking. "Let me go. You don't understand. He's a killer."

"We know," said an urgent voice and she turned to see Rolf, surrounded by a phalanx of officers.

And behind him she saw Bax lying on the floor, a red stain spreading across his side.

24

HOSPITALS LOOKED the same no matter where you went, Joss thought as she walked down the ward. Clean, cheerful walls, purposeful doctors and nurses, ranks of rooms, ranks of beds.

And always the underlying sense of crisis and disaster, because except for childbirth, no one would be in a hospital by choice.

She waved to the ICU nurses she'd grown to know well in the previous days and ducked into Bax's room. He was asleep, his face relaxed in the way it so rarely was when he was awake. His lashes formed little fans on his cheeks; she'd never realized before how long they were.

She couldn't bear to walk away from him.

She had to.

Bax stirred, his mouth tightening slightly in pain as he awoke. Then he opened his eyes. For a moment or two, he frowned in puzzlement that cleared when he saw Joss.

"Hey," she said softly. Without thinking about it, she sat in the chair she'd grown all too used to. "How are you feeling?"

"Like I've been kicked by a mule."

"You get kicked by mules a lot?"

He smiled crookedly at her. "No, but I've got a vivid imagination." He closed his eyes briefly. "I've definitely been having some weird dreams. How long have I been in here, two or three days?"

Joss swallowed. "Try a week."

IF HE THOUGHT about it, it would make him crazy, so Bax did his best not to. All right, so he'd lost a week, a week of days blurred into nights, waking in pain, sliding back down into the sweet oblivion of medication. A week of his life and he remembered nothing of it. Or almost nothing, he corrected himself. There was one thing there, always. A hand in his, soft, strong, determined. A hand that wouldn't let him go.

"You were here," he said.

"I might have checked in on you now and again." Joss looked back at him and he saw the lines of exhaustion carved into her face. And a dark smudge under one eye that was more than lack of sleep.

Bax frowned in concern at the bruise. "How did you get hurt?"

"Silverhielm caught me a pretty good one when I was trying to pin him down." Her smile was shaky. "I didn't want him to get loose. I didn't know what he'd do to you."

"What happened? I remember noise from Oskar's friends and the table going over and that's pretty much it."

Joss slid the chair to the side of the bed with the ease of long familiarity. "You didn't miss much. When I shoved the table at Silverhielm, his gun went off, which is how you got shot. It was a good wound, or so the doctors tell me. Went through your side without hitting anything important."

"Nice to know so much of me is irrelevant."

"It's a good thing," she agreed. "Anyway, I jumped on top of Silverhielm and the table to keep him down, which is how I got pasted. Dinged up a couple of his ribs, too, I'm told," she said, grinning unrepentantly.

"Where was Markus in all of this?"

She shrugged. "Anyone's guess. Oskar's friends were too busy pushing him away and he backed out the door."

"Markus, back away from a bunch of kids?"

"Maybe he felt sorry for them." She smiled faintly. "By the time Rolf and his team showed up, he was gone."

"And Silverhielm?"

"In jail under charges of kidnapping and assault, not to mention the Swedish equivalent of grand larceny. Rolf got his search warrant. Now that he's got access to Silverhielm's records, he's expecting to put him away on stronger charges for a good, long time."

"And the stamps?"

"Got them both. The police have to hold on to the one-penny Mauritius for a while until they prosecute Silverhielm. The Blue Mauritius is back in the vault for the time being."

Bax nodded, suddenly exhausted. He fought to keep his eyes open, to focus on her face. When his lids drifted closed, she was the last thing he saw and she followed him into his dreams.

When he awoke again, he was in another bed in another ward. But one thing was the same—Joss was there.

"Awake now?"

He stirred a little bit and for the first time felt the itch of healing on his side instead of the merciless whip of pain. "Now. When is it?"

"A day later than last time."

He glanced around. "The room looks different."

"You're in a medical ward, now. No more ICU. The doctor said you've bounced back amazingly well."

He smiled wryly. "That's me, star of the class." He studied her. She looked different too. She wore her red jacket; her battered leather satchel sat in a heap on the floor by the foot of the bed. Bax felt a quick spurt of alarm. "Are you going somewhere?"

She nodded. "You're on the mend. The doctors expect you to be up and around in a week or so." Her voice was falsely bright.

"So you're going back to San Francisco?"

She glanced away. "Time to get on with life, don't you think?"

There was a time he'd have been relieved. There was a time he'd have been happy at the prospect of being on his own again.

But that time was long past.

Joss STOOD by the bed where Bax stared up at her.

"Don't go," he said. "We've got things to talk about."

But if she didn't go now, she'd never be able to. "It's time, Bax."

"No. That night at Silverhielm's, when I saw Markus with his gun on you, I realized—"

"Don't," she said sharply. She wouldn't let herself listen, she couldn't. She knew what would happen later, after he'd gotten out of the hospital, after he'd recovered. "Until everything went to hell in a handbasket, you knew what you wanted. And when I'm no longer your bedside companion or your damsel in distress—"

"I was wrong, before."

She wanted to listen, she wanted to believe him, but she knew it was only temporary. "How can you be sure things are different?" she demanded. "How can I?"

"Trust me."

"I can't." Her eyes softened. "Right now, you're feeling like you want me to be a part of your life because you're hurt. I'm not going to take advantage of that. Take your time. Heal and get past this and then we'll see."

"I'm thinking just fine, Joss. I don't need to get out of this hospital bed to know how I feel about you."

"You need time, Bax, we both do. I've got to get my life straightened out, too. On my own. You told me once you couldn't be my salvation, remember? You were right." She smiled and tried to pretend her heart wasn't breaking.

"So that's it? You're saying goodbye?"

"I'm saying goodbye for now." She would not cry, not now, she told herself fiercely and rose. "Maybe one of these days..." Her voice caught. She leaned over and kissed him on the forehead, smoothing his hair back. "Be well, Bax."

And she made herself walk out.

"Has it landed, yet?"

Joss and Gwen stood in front of the monitor in the international arrivals hall at the San Francisco airport, checking the screen for their grandparents' flight from Sydney. Only days before, Joss had walked out of the gates from customs herself, coming home from Stockholm.

Having left everything that mattered behind.

Joss skimmed the list of world capitals until she spied their listing. And then stared helplessly at the listing for a flight from Stockholm just above it. For a moment she missed Bax so badly it was like a physical pain. If she'd been at home, she could have curled up into a ball of misery. Here, she was in public so she just stood woodenly and stared at the letters as though the sight of them would prop her up.

"Hey," Gwen said softly. "You okay?"

Joss gave a quick, empty smile. "Yeah, sure. Why wouldn't I be?"

Gwen slung an arm around Joss's shoulders and

squeezed. "I was just where you are not too long ago, remember? Don't try to hide from me."

"Ah, hell, Gwen, what am I supposed to do, keep being a basket-case every time I see anything that reminds me of him?"

"No. On the other hand, you've only been home a week. Cut yourself some slack. It's going to take longer than that, you know."

"I know," Joss agreed. It was going to take a lot longer than that.

It felt like it was going to take forever.

"Anyway, there are better things to think about," she said briskly, moving to the sliding glass doors that shuttered the hall from Customs. "Gramma and Grampa are home and we've got good news instead of bad. How great is that?"

"God, I've been dreading this moment for two and a half months, ever since Jerry stole the stamps," Gwen said. "I couldn't imagine telling Grampa about it. I can't believe we got them back."

"You can't? Since when have we set our minds to something and not done it?"

"The Chastain sisters, a force to be reckoned with?"

"Damned straight," Joss agreed. "Look, there they are!"

Their grandparents came through the doorway looking tanned and healthy and about a decade younger than when they'd left.

"Over here," Gwen said, waving to them and then running up to greet them with hugs.

"You girls are a sight for sore eyes," said Hugh Chastain, blue eyes twinkling.

"Oh, we've had the most fun, you can't imagine," said his wife, kissing Joss on the cheek. "We've got so much to tell you."

"So do we," Joss murmured. "So do we."

A NEW LIFE. She'd come back from Stockholm knowing what she wanted to do with her life. Now, she had a career to pursue. Now, she had a goal. And if hours and minutes of her new life dragged every time she thought about Bax, she had plenty to distract her. In fact, she'd packed her schedule with so many classes and practice sessions and study hours that she barely had a minute to herself.

How then, was it that she still found time to miss him?

Joss shook her head impatiently. It had been weeks. Weeks, and the hurt was still as fresh as it had been. She ought to be able to get past it. This was her new life. She shouldn't be spending most of it thinking about the old.

Gwen walked into the empty showroom. "Grampa's headed out for the night. Are you just about ready to shut down , here?"

Joss stirred. "Just about. Can you close out the register? I've got to get going, tonight. I've got an early Tae Kwon Do class."

"Are you sure you're not trying to do too much?"

"I'm fine," Joss replied quickly. "The more I take, the faster I'll get my P.I. license."

"Yeah, but it won't do you any good to have a license if you run yourself into the ground before you get your first client. Work doesn't make it go away, Joss."

"I know, but it beats Parcheesi."

Gwen rolled her eyes. "Get out of here. I'll take care of things." She glanced up at the chime of the front door. "Whoops, actually, let me check something in the back, first."

"Hurry, Gwen," Joss said over her shoulder as Gwen walked into the back. "I don't have much time."

"Do you have time to talk to me?" asked a familiar voice.

And she turned to see Bax.

For a moment, she simply stared. He stood at the counter leaning on a cane, which looked incongruously dapper with his T-shirt and jeans. He'd grown thinner, she noticed, so that the bones stood out strongly in his face.

"When did you get back?"

"About three weeks ago." He watched her closely.

"How are you feeling?"

He shrugged. "Everything seems to be working all right. I should be able to get rid of the cane, soon."

He'd want to set it aside as soon as humanly possible, she knew. He'd look at it as a challenge, a barrier to be surmounted. And he wouldn't give up until he had.

"So how have you been?" he asked now.

"Okay. I've started martial arts training and I'm taking a course in the penal code. I'm working here while I get my investigator's license."

He raised his eyebrows. "So you were serious about that."

"I told you I was," she said shortly.

"Yes, you did. I should have listened. I screwed up that night. I said a lot of things I shouldn't have." He looked down at his cane and twisted it slightly back and forth. "And I missed saying a lot more that I should have."

"You did what you needed to do."

"No, I didn't. Can we go somewhere and talk?"

"I have a class to get to."

"Where is it?"

"Up the street."

"Well, then, can I walk you there?

"You don't look like walking's the best thing for you. We can talk here for a little while, if you want." She opened the register drawer and got out the spare key for the door. "Just let me lock up."

If she took long enough with the security gates and the door, maybe she could figure out how she felt about him showing up here. She didn't want gratitude. She didn't want guilt. It was impossible to squelch hope, but it was equally impossible to forget what they'd been through.

What she was still going through every minute of every day.

"There are chairs," she told him, pulling one over for him before she walked behind the counter. Keep the distance, she thought. "So, what's on your mind?"

For a moment, he was silent, just looking at her like a man stranded in the desert looks at water. "I've been doing a lot of thinking. I spent weeks in that hospital bed after you left with nothing much to do but think. About you and me, about the baggage you keep and the baggage you throw away." He rubbed his thumb along the chrome edge of the display case. "I know I said some bad things to you that night in the hotel. It wasn't about you. It was about me trying to run away." He gave a humorless smile. "But you know how that goes. You can't run away from yourself. And you can't run away from truths." He took a breath. "I love you, Joss, and that's the truest thing I know."

"You don't," she countered, panicked because she wanted to believe him. Panicked because she didn't think her heart could survive being broken again. "You just think you do. You're confusing love with gratitude and protectiveness."

"I'm not getting anything confused. I'm really, really clear now. You've got a right to be upset with me. I blew it. Getting involved with you scared the hell out of me and my knee-jerk reaction was to bolt. But that's over with. I don't want to run from it now." He smiled slightly and raised his cane from the ground. "Even if I could."

"How can you be so sure?" she demanded. "You say it's all different, but how do I know that in a week or a month you're not going to turn around and tell me you don't want to be in a relationship, that you just want to be on your own?"

He frowned and glanced away. "The same way I know that you won't." He looked at her, then. "I'm willing to trust in us. I'm hoping you'll do the same."

"I already did that, thanks. I'm not in any hurry to go through it again." Especially when the pain was still going on.

"Look, I was wrong." He rose, pressing his hands on the edge of the counter. "I'll say it again, if you want. I was wrong. I got caught up in the past but I'm telling you, it's done. And I am going to keep telling you until you believe me. I don't care if it takes a while. I've got the time and I am not going anywhere. I'll come back here tomorrow, and the day after tomorrow and every day after that for as long as it takes." His gaze arrowed through her. "As long as it takes, Joss, and when you're through testing me, I'll still be here. Because I love you and that is not going to change."

There wasn't enough air in the room, she thought, stunned. Surely that was why her lungs wouldn't work. Surely that was why she couldn't speak, why her mind couldn't assimilate it all.

A second passed, then two, and finally Bax shrugged. "Well, you've got to get to your class." He winked at her with a mixture of humor and defiance. "I'll see you tomorrow." He started to turn away, then swung back toward her. "Of course, while I'm happy to come to the store every day we could actually do something civilized like dinner. I'd join your class but as you can see, I have issues. Anyway, I'll see you later."

"No!" Suddenly, she found her voice. "I mean yes. I mean...hell, I don't know. Oh God, Bax, do you mean it?"

His lips twitched. "I stand here and pour my heart out to you, with your sister no doubt listening, and you have to ask that?" He smiled. "Okay, for the record, I am crazy about you. I think about you every minute of every day. I want to spend the rest of my life with you, and a couple of lifetimes after that, if we can manage it. And I would be very happy, honored, even, to stand up in front of a room full of witnesses and say it all again."

And it was that easy, Joss thought dazedly as she came around the counter and he gathered her into his arms. His body was hard and warm and real against her, and it was then that the tears started. "I've missed you so much," she murmured, blinking.

He exhaled. "It made me nuts, staying away from you, but I figured I had to or you wouldn't believe me." He pressed a kiss into her hair. "And then I figured the hell with waiting. I'd find some other way to convince you."

"Have you figured that out, yet?"

"No, but I'm working on it." And then he kissed her.

2 FREE

BOOKS AND A SURPRISE GIFT!

We would like to take this opportunity to thank you for reading this Mills & Boon® book by offering you the chance to take TWO more specially selected titles from the Blaze® series absolutely FREE! We're also making this offer to introduce you to the benefits of the Mills & Boon® Book Club™—

★ FREE home delivery
★ free monthly Newsletter
★ Books available before they're in the shops

★ Free gifts and competitions
★ Exclusive Book Club offers

Accepting these FREE books and gift places you under no obligation to buy, you may cancel at any time, even after receiving your free shipment. Simply complete your details below and return the entire page to the address below. You don't even need a stamp!

YES! Please send me 2 free Blaze books and a surprise gift. I understand that unless you hear from me, I will receive 3 superb new titles every month, including a 2-in-1 title priced at £4.99 and two single titles priced at £3.15 each. Postage and packing free. I am under no obligation to purchase any books and may cancel my subscription at any time. The free books and gift will be mine to keep in any case.

K9ZED

Ms/Mrs/Miss/Mr ....Initials ....

Surname ....

BLOCK CAPITALS PLEASE

Address ....

....

....Postcode..

Send this whole page to:
UK: FREEPOST CN81, Croydon, CR9 3WZ